# THE LADY OF
# ASTORIA
# ABBEY

# THE LADY OF
# ASTORIA ABBEY

## A HISTORICAL ROMANCE

# ANITA STANSFIELD

Covenant Communications, Inc.

Published by Covenant Communications, Inc.
American Fork, Utah

Printed in the United States of America
First Printing: October 2018

22 21 20 19 18    10 9 8 7 6 5 4 3 2 1

ISBN: 978-1-52440-704-9

# CHAPTER ONE

## THE DOCTOR'S DAUGHTER

*Cornwall, England—1840*

"Elizabeth White," Bess heard her father call from the other room. A shudder passed over her shoulders and down her back as if her body were attempting to shake off the negative effect of hearing him use her name in that tone. If Jonas White had been in the same room, she would have made a conscious effort to conceal her physical reaction to his demeaning tone. He knew very well she preferred being called Bess. Everyone else she knew called her Bess; it's what her mother had called her, a clear differentiation between the two of them, since she too had borne the name Elizabeth. But ever since her mother's tragic and unexpected death eight years earlier, Bess's father had taken the demeaning tone he'd often used in speaking to his wife and had transferred it to his communication with his daughter. As an only child, Bess had stepped into her mother's role to the best of her ability—although it was continually evident her father would have far preferred his wife had been alive to do the duties Bess was now doing, and it always seemed to Bess that this was somehow her fault. No matter how well she cooked and cleaned and assisted her father in his role as the village doctor, her performance was never good enough to warrant any praise or appreciation.

But Bess loved her father despite his gruff nature and closed emotions, and she felt certain that most of his disagreeable behavior was due to the very fact that he *did* miss Bess's mother, and perhaps he even blamed himself. He considered himself a very good doctor—and he was—but he hadn't been able to save his own wife. Bess understood that the ills and ailments of the world were often beyond the control of any mortal, and sometimes death just happened despite the best medical care. Her father had taught her that, and she knew he believed it—at least he believed it regarding every situation except that of his own wife. He'd never been the same since Elizabeth's death, but all Bess could do was keep trying every day to do all that was required of her, hoping that one day he might notice she was no longer the twelve-year-old child who had lost her mother; she'd become a woman capable of keeping the household and her father's medical practice under control.

"Elizabeth?" her father called again, sounding more impatient since she hadn't responded the first time. "What in the name of all that is holy is keeping you? We'll be late!"

Bess shuddered again and hurried to finish her task, barely glancing over her shoulder as her father appeared in the doorway of what he called *the medical room.* Jonas White was a tall man, and he'd grown thinner in the years since he'd lost his wife. His hair had once been as dark as Bess's, but it had now turned mostly gray with only hints of dark strands scattered throughout. He was already wearing his coat and had his hat in his hand, which meant he was ready to walk out the door. He glanced impatiently toward his medical bag, which was open on the counter near Bess, who explained in her usual even tone, "I'm nearly done cleaning the instruments. Don't forget it was *you* who taught me that cleanliness was more important than punctuality." She heard him sigh loudly at the reminder, but he didn't comment, even though Bess thought that an apology might be in order. Bess dried her hands and carefully placed all the standard medical instruments into her father's bag before she said, "I just need to get my coat and freshen up quickly; I'll only be a minute or two." Again, she heard her father sigh, but what could he say? She couldn't leave the house with him for any given amount of time without being somewhat prepared and looking respectable.

A few minutes later, Bess followed her father out into a magically lovely autumn day. Bess was able to quickly let go of her aggravation as she focused on the perfect temperature in the air, which made her lightweight coat barely necessary. The leaves on the trees were splashed with magnificent color, and the sky was a brilliant blue with scattered fluffy clouds that seemed to be hung there for aesthetic purposes alone. Together they went to visit many patients, and Bess couldn't deny she found the work enjoyable. She'd learned a great deal from observing her father, and the knowledge had settled comfortably into her spirit as something vital and important to her own purpose. She liked to chat with the patients while she assisted her father in any way that was needed, whether it was stitching up an open wound, monitoring a

fever, assessing damage from a fall, or delivering a baby. Bess especially appreciated the way her father spoke to her more respectfully in front of other people
than he did when they were alone. She had pointed out this fact to him once,
only to hear him adamantly deny the truth of what she was suggesting.

Little by little over the years, Bess had learned to see the good in her
father and appreciate all she learned from him and the inner satisfaction she
found in caring for him and working by his side. She had also learned to
simply reject anything he said or did that might feel hurtful. She'd developed
a mental game of imagining herself surrounded by an impenetrable shield of
light, as if she were standing in the center of a bright sunbeam, and nothing
and no one could penetrate her barrier of protection. When hurtful words
came out of her father's mouth—however unintentional—Bess simply
imagined them bouncing off the light that surrounded her. The shudder that
often rippled through her only seemed to help shake off anything she refused
to take into her spirit. She recalled well her mother teaching her that no one
had the right to make her feel anything less than strong and empowered,
and it was up to her to choose what she would accept or reject throughout
the experiences of her life. Bess had clung to her mother's words in this
regard, as well as many other lessons she'd learned from this amazing woman
during the twelve years they'd shared together. Life had been much sweeter
when Elizabeth White had been alive, filled with so much more kindness
and serenity. But Bess knew there was no good to be found in wishing for life
to be something it wasn't; instead she simply resolved to make the most of
each day—despite the many challenges she faced in trying to keep up with
her father's expectations.

That evening, after a long day of caring for patients, Bess worked
quickly to prepare supper while her father sat with his feet up near the small
fire he'd built in the parlor. Bess couldn't help thinking—as she had at least
a thousand times—that if she was expected to work alongside her father
in addition to keeping his instruments clean and his bag well-stocked, she
shouldn't have to cook and clean as well. Since she also helped keep track of
their financial books, she knew there was more than enough money to hire
someone to cook and keep the house in order. Bess had suggested more than
once to her father that this would be a good idea, and it would give Bess
more time to learn facets of medicine that could be beneficial in helping her
become a better assistant to him. But Jonas had insisted that her mother had
been able to keep *everything* under control, and therefore Bess could surely
do the same.

Bess pushed her frustrating thoughts away and put supper on the table, ignoring her father's silent insinuations of how late they were eating. She bit her tongue to hold back her desire to tell him that after they were finished eating he would relax with a book and she would be cleaning the dishes. Instead, Bess listened while her father spoke grace over their meal, all the while imagining his difficult attitudes bouncing off the light that surrounded her. While she ate in silence, Bess wondered why it felt more challenging than usual to let go of his silent accusations. Perhaps it was because she just felt so tired, or perhaps she was growing increasingly weary of always having to be so mentally on guard with her father—this man with whom she spent practically every waking moment. She had no significant friendships because she had no time for any kind of socializing, except for an occasional event, which she would attend only because her father wanted her there with him. He had allowed her to be a part of the church choir, even though he always seemed frustrated with her need to attend occasional rehearsals. But his pride over having her sing with the group in church generally compensated for his being less than supportive. Through her attendance at church and choir rehearsals, Bess had made a few friends, or perhaps more accurately acquaintances with whom she felt comfortable on the rare opportunities they had to enjoy each other's company outside of choir rehearsals. There simply wasn't time to develop any deeper relationships.

When she had finally completed the necessary tasks of the day, Bess dragged her weary body into bed, trying not to think of how her father had gone to bed more than an hour ago. She silently prayed for patience and compassion, while another part of her mind wished for a life far different from this. But she felt somehow guilty to even think of praying for that. Her father needed her, and she needed to be grateful for all that was good in her life. Jonas White continually reminded her of that.

Bess slept deeply and felt reluctant to get out of bed when morning came. But she forced herself to hurry along, making herself presentable for the public, knowing that sometimes the doctor was needed at a moment's notice, and she would be expected to accompany him. Bess was in the kitchen cooking breakfast when she heard a knock at the front door. She dried her hands, intending to walk in that direction until she heard her father answer the door, allowing her to resume her efforts to put breakfast on the table.

"Thank you, my boy," Bess heard her father say before the door closed, and a moment later he appeared in the kitchen with a note in his hands. Bess paused to watch him read it, hoping that it wasn't a medical emergency that would prevent them from being able to eat the breakfast she'd put so much work into preparing. There were freshly baked scones they could take with them and eat while walking or driving the trap to their intended destination, but the boiled eggs and hot sausages were not so easy to carry about. She hated the very thought of how many meals she'd prepared, only to have them sit and turn cold when a cook or housekeeper could have properly cared for the food if Bess had needed to leave quickly with her father. The reality was that Bess felt more and more like she needed to be two people, and the burden of responsibilities was not being equally shared. But Jonas White was a respectable doctor, a good man, and she was his daughter, not his wife. She'd tried so many times to express her feelings, but he just wouldn't listen.

Standing there in that moment while she watched him read whatever had just been delivered, she felt no shield of light protecting her at all. It was as if her arms were just too weary to hold up any kind of protection, and she was left feeling dark and heavy while she waited to see how the note in her father's hands might impact their schedule for the day.

"Looks like we'll be taking the trap out today," he said, tucking the note into the inside pocket of his jacket. Bess knew that meant they would need the horse-drawn wheeled vehicle to go farther than the center of the village in which they lived. "Fortunately, we have no other specific appointments today," he said, taking a seat to wait for his breakfast—rather than offering any assistance. He went on to explain, "The note is from Lady Agatha Buxton."

"From the Abbey?" Bess asked, wishing she hadn't sounded quite so overtly enthused. She was well aware of the Buxton family, and Astoria Abbey had always held a certain fascination for her. Toning down her enthusiasm, she remarked, "We've not been there for at least a few years."

"No," Jonas drawled as Bess was finally able to sit down as well. "The note states that it's regarding her son. If you recall, he's never been healthy; he was born with some serious problems. But he's been in the care of a specialist the family found in London. So, I wonder why they might need *me.*"

*Us,* Bess corrected silently before her father spoke grace and they were able to eat their breakfast before setting out. While Jonas harnessed the horse to the trap, Bess was able to clean up the kitchen, glad to know that she didn't have to dread coming home to such a task.

There was very little conversation between Bess and her father as he drove the trap a good distance from town to the majestic Astoria Abbey. Bess often felt annoyed by the lack of conversation, because she enjoyed discussing her thoughts and feelings on many matters of the world, but Jonas was quite the opposite and preferred his solitude. Today Bess didn't mind the silence while she mentally recounted her prior visits to the Abbey. She'd been there several times with her father over the years—until this specialist from London had been hired to oversee the care of Lady Buxton's ailing son. The magnificent structure with its perfectly kept grounds had felt like a castle to Bess on her first visit there; given how young she must have been, her imagination had surely contributed to such a perception. But the magical idea had not diminished over the years, and Bess felt an excited anticipation to return there. She recalled clearly the enormity of the rooms, the lavish decor, and the paintings on the walls that she could have stared at for hours. She also recalled how kind the people there had been to her. All things combined, visiting Astoria Abbey today felt like the best thing that could have happened to Bess, and her mood felt lighter than it had in months.

As Jonas drove the trap around a wide curve in the road, with a cluster of forest on one side and a wide meadow on the other, Astoria Abbey came into view and Bess caught her breath. She'd never seen any other home so enormous or lofty, therefore she had no means of comparison; still, she felt certain that the Abbey surely had a unique beauty that was beyond compare. It had spire-like towers at each corner, and two at the front of the house that rose high above the portico that comprised the main entrance. The house was constructed of gray stone, but in no way looked dull or dark, perhaps because it was filled with so many windows of different shapes and sizes that altogether they created their own geometrical type of art. A grouping of three large, very old-looking trees were at each of the front two corners of the house, and Bess imagined they had been planted at the time the house had been built, which would make them practically ancient. She imagined what those trees had seen as they had kept their silent and beautiful vigil, and she felt a childlike urging to climb one of them and hide in the autumn-colored leaves where she could look down upon the comings and goings of the Abbey.

Bess was forced out of her daydreaming when the trap stopped in front of a door that was level with the driveway, some distance away from the magnificent portico with its massive marble steps and columns. She suspected that the portico was only used as an entrance for grand events and socials.

Bess stood beside her father while he knocked at a door that was none too small and not lacking in fine craftsmanship. A servant climbed onto the seat of the trap and drove it away so he could tend to the horse while they were attending to whatever reasons for which Lady Buxton had summoned them. The door opened and a nice-looking young man with a sweep of dark-brown hair near the color of her own smiled as he motioned them inside. Bess returned his smile, noting that he was likely not much older than herself, perhaps in his midtwenties at most.

"Please come with me," he said with a kindness that reminded Bess of her previous visits to this house. She managed to keep herself from craning her neck to view the arched ceiling and splendid chandelier in the enormous entry hall, but she couldn't refrain from recalling how she'd never come here without the servants providing tea and little elegant cakes and sandwiches. Despite having had a good breakfast, Bess couldn't help hoping that such would be the case with this visit. Just thinking of the possibility made her hungry.

"Please make yourselves comfortable," the young man said, motion-ing them through large, open double doors into a parlor that had a cozy atmosphere despite it being large enough to seat a dozen people or more. "I will let Lady Buxton know you have arrived."

"Thank you," Jonas said.

"Might I get you some refreshment?" the servant asked before leaving the room.

Bess wanted to say, *That would be lovely, thank you.* But her father quickly said, "No, thank you."

Once they were alone and seated at separate ends of the same long sofa, Jonas said, "I wonder why the lady of the house would be summoned, rather than our simply being taken to see the patient. This is certainly not the standard nature of a doctor's visit."

"No," Bess said, merely as a polite comment to indicate that she'd heard him and was acknowledging what he'd said. Since she often wished her father would afford her the same courtesy, she was determined to learn from his frustrating behavior and never mirror his difficult traits.

They sat in silence for another five or ten minutes before a lovely and refined woman entered the room. Her clothing was elegant but didn't appear restrictive or too lavish. Her silver hair was styled to perfection, and Bess realized it was likely the aging of this woman's hair that had made Bess slow to recognize her. She had met Lady Buxton more than once in the past, but her hair had been a blondish brown the last time Bess had seen her. Lady Buxton was probably five or ten years older than Jonas, although her face and figure had aged well. Bess followed her father's example by coming to her feet when the lady entered the room, but their hostess was quick to say, "Oh, please be seated. I want to thank you so much for coming."

Bess and her father sat back down, and Lady Buxton sat across from them, remaining at the edge of her seat and keeping her back very straight as she folded her hands in her lap. She made Bess want to do the same, so she would appear more ladylike, but she didn't want to do so now and appear too obvious in her motives.

Bess noticed that the young man they'd met earlier was closing the doors to the room, leaving her and her father alone with the mistress of the house.

"What might I do for you?" Jonas asked politely, and Bess wondered why she felt so agitated over the subtle inference that he was there alone, or that he alone would or could be of assistance. In fact, Bess wondered why such petty things were bothering her more and more. It was as if that shield of light around her was losing its glow, leaving her to feel somehow powerless against the facets of her life that were feeling less and less right.

Bess was distracted to see Lady Buxton look in her direction more than once as she spoke to the doctor about her son's condition, then she firmly settled her gaze on Bess—and she smiled. "I remember you, young lady. My, you've grown up so beautifully. And you're assisting your father now—in a more official capacity?"

"Yes, my lady," Bess said firmly but politely and respectfully; still she caught a tiny glare from her father. What was she to do? Speak like a mouse? Not speak at all?

Lady Buxton then began to speak openly of her son's medical condition, and the difficult state it had come to. Hugh Buxton had been born with a problematic heart. He'd always been somewhat fragile despite his personal determination to attempt to live life as normally as possible. The best doctors had declared he wouldn't live past an early childhood, but he was now an adult, and his mother spoke with fondness and pride of her son and the way his positive attitude and careful attention to his health had given them many good years together. She talked of how they had been living in their London home for quite some time so that Hugh would have access to the best possible medical care.

"However," she said, dabbing her eyes with a lacy handkerchief, "the most excellent doctors in London all concur that his condition is worsening at a steady rate, and he will not live much longer. Weeks . . . maybe months; it's impossible to tell. The reality is that his heart is weak, and it's affecting his ability to breathe—which is worse some days than others. He's extremely weak and most often unable to do very much if anything at all for himself. We've been told that the best we can do is keep him comfortable and allow him to have as much medicine as he requires to ease the pain. More than one doctor has told us that the concern for becoming addicted to any kind of opiates . . ." She looked to Jonas with a questioning expression. "Is that the right word?"

"Yes, my lady," he said and nodded to encourage her to go on.

The lady nodded in return and continued. "Apparently when someone is dying, there isn't a concern about addiction, but rather a focus on alleviating their pain as much as possible."

"I wholeheartedly concur with that," Bess's father said with compassion, and Lady Buxton nodded again, her bottom lip quivering until she bit it and remained silent long enough to regain her composure. Bess felt like crying as well; she didn't even know Hugh Buxton other than the possibility that she had come into brief contact with him during her father's medical visits in years past. But the evidence of how much this woman loved her son tugged at Bess's heart. How might it be to know that someone you loved so dearly was going to die? Bess quickly considered her own mother's death. She'd become ill and had died unexpectedly; they had anticipated a full recovery, which had made her death a complete shock. Bess had to believe that spending a lifetime wondering how much longer her son would live had surely taken a toll on Lady Buxton. She had likely grieved every day, dreading the loss of her son.

After taking a deep breath and straightening her back as if to shake off her grief, Lady Buxton went on, looking back and forth between Bess and her father, making a concerted effort to include Bess in the conversation. Bess had memories of liking this woman and feeling comfortable in her presence, even though their encounters had been very brief. But right now, she liked her even more. She didn't feel invisible or irrelevant in this lady's presence.

"I have called you here, Dr. White, because the specialists we've been seeing have all agreed that the end is coming for my son, even though we don't know how long he will yet live. It was Hugh's wish to cease our lengthy stay in London and come home to die here, where he's comfortable. He's always preferred this house over our London house. We have many servants here with whom he's grown up and he's comfortable in having them help care for him in most ways, but obviously we will need medical guidance and supervision regarding his care and his medication. I'm very glad to know that we have such a competent doctor here so close to home, and I'm hoping you will agree to oversee my son's care for as long as he needs it."

"Of course, my lady," Jonas said respectfully. "I will gladly do everything I can to help keep him comfortable, and I will make myself available to check on him as often as necessary. Perhaps every three or four days at first—depending on my assessment when I examine him—and more often as needed. As the end gets closer I will be on hand as much as you need me to be."

In that moment, Bess felt a familiar admiration for her father. Her personal relationship with him left much to be desired, but she could never deny that he was an excellent doctor. And he also had a natural kindness and respect that was always evident in his communications with his patients and their loved ones. Bess wished he could show more of these attitudes with her, but she pushed that wish aside and focused on his conversation with Lady Buxton, who breathed a deep sigh of relief and said, "I confess that is exactly what I'd hoped for. Of course, you have other patients, and there is no need for you to neglect anyone else while caring for my son. When you are needed elsewhere, you can leave instructions with those who will be available here to help care for him."

Jonas nodded. "We will take this one day at a time and manage everything in the best possible way to make this transition as smooth and pain-free as possible—for your son and for everyone who is affected by this difficult situation."

"You are very kind," Lady Buxton said.

Bess expected her to stand and invite them to go and speak with the patient so that her father could ask all the usual questions and do a typical examination. But Lady Buxton turned her eyes directly toward Bess and said, "I remember you well, Miss White, from your visits here in the past. I was very much hoping you would accompany your father today." Bess didn't even know what to say. Fortunately, Lady Buxton kept talking. "Even though we've spent very little time together, I consider myself an excellent judge of character, and I believe you are a kind and competent young woman, no doubt aided by all your father has taught you during your opportunities to assist him."

"She is indeed very competent," Jonas said, and Bess snapped her gaze toward him in surprise. She'd not heard a compliment come out of his mouth in years, which made her wonder if he really meant it, or if he was simply trying to be agreeable with this powerful woman.

While Bess was distracted by attempting to figure out her father's reasons for saying what he'd just said, Lady Buxton stood and said, "Let us go and speak with Hugh." Bess and her father also stood. "Clearly he needs to be involved in however we choose to manage the situation. He's quite adamant that he be told the truth about every facet of his condition and the options available to him—however difficult that information might be. I agree with him completely; therefore, we should include him in any further conversation."

"Of course," Jonas said, and they followed Lady Buxton out of the room, across the marble floor of the enormous entry hall, and up a staircase that was likely as wide as the home where Bess lived with her father. She realized that her memories of the grandness and elegance of Astoria Abbey had not been exaggerated over time. If anything, she had likely convinced herself that she'd overstated its size and beauty, and now she knew that such was not the case. Again, she had to exercise self-control and try not to crane her neck or miss a step due to her desire to admire every element of this artistic structure that was the home to a family and a great many servants.

They passed many beautiful paintings that were hung on the walls where a huge landing of the stairs created a corner as they turned directions and headed up another large staircase. Bess wanted to stop and look at each painting, but she had to satisfy herself with a few quick glances before she hurried to catch up with her father. She lost track of how many turns they made and how many hallways they traversed before Lady Buxton finally walked through an open doorway into a room that was filled with light due to the sun shining through enormous windows, spreading itself over the floral pattern in the carpet and the fine brocade sofas. Bess had expected that they would be taken to the bedroom of Hugh Buxton, which was standard when a doctor was called to check on a patient. But the young Mr. Buxton was sitting in a large, overstuffed chair covered in a dark red fabric, which contrasted nicely with the red and gold colors of everything else in the room. He had a blanket over his lap that flowed onto the floor, and her first glance at him revealed that his hair was blond and full of loose curls, and that he was dressed in a well-pressed shirt that was brilliantly white, as well as a brocade waistcoat that almost looked as if it had been made to complement the decor of the room. The fact that he was sitting up and dressed made him appear less ill than his mother had described, and when he turned to look toward them as they approached, Bess saw no sign of ill health in his face, except that he looked older than she knew him to be. He had wrinkles at the corners of his eyes and subtle lines in his brow, and were it not for his beard—which was a darker blond than the hair on his head—she felt certain she would be able to see lines of premature age around his mouth as well. He smiled the moment he saw his mother, and immediately looked younger; in fact, his eyes nearly glowed with the evidence of a genuinely tender relationship between mother and son. Bess felt momentarily envious, wishing she could share such a meaningful gaze with her father, rather than his seeming inability to see her at all.

Bess pushed away her self-pitying thoughts and focused instead on the favorable demeanor of this man she vaguely recalled meeting a few times in years past, although on those occasions she would have remained at a discreet distance while her father did his work, and she remembered that oftentimes she would wait in hallways or other rooms during examinations. She barely remembered Hugh Buxton, but she marveled now at how happy he seemed; he was dying, and he was happy. She was completely healthy, and she felt utterly miserable. Surely, she needed to gain some perspective in her life.

"Hello, dearest," Lady Buxton said, bending over to kiss her son on the forehead. "How are you feeling?"

"I'm fine, Mother," he said, smiling up at her. "I'm just the same as I was when you asked me not half an hour ago before you went downstairs." He turned to look at Bess and her father, and his smile widened—which Bess would not have thought possible.

"You remember Dr. White?" Lady Buxton said, motioning toward Jonas. "And his daughter?"

"Of course I do," Hugh said, holding out a hand toward Jonas, who stepped forward to share a handshake in greeting. "How good to see you again, Doctor. I assume my mother has told you my tale of woe."

"She has summarized the situation, yes," Jonas said. "And I have assured her as I wish to assure *you* that I am committed to giving you the best possible care in whatever lies ahead."

"Thank you," Hugh said, and Bess expected them to start talking about exactly what that care would entail. But Hugh Buxton looked past Jonas, gazing directly at Bess as he said, "You've grown up since we last saw each other. Bess, isn't it?"

"That's right," she said, taken aback to hear that he not only recalled her enough to compare her appearance now to that of their last meeting, but also that he even remembered her name. Realizing she needed to say something else, she cleared her throat and hurried to add, "Yes, it's been many years."

"And you're still assisting the good doctor, I see," Hugh said, adding a wink to his smile.

"I do my best," she said, wishing her father might say something to support her position, but he remained silent.

Instead, Jonas said to Hugh, "I'd like to speak with you about what other doctors have told you and do a quick examination."

"Of course," Hugh said, motioning the doctor toward a nearby sofa.

Bess was about to sit near her father as she generally did during such conversations, but Lady Buxton put a hand on Bess's arm and said in a light tone that seemed completely out of place, considering the impending death of her son, "Hugh is perfectly capable of telling you all you need to know, Doctor. I'm going to steal your daughter away while you men have your visit. We will be right across the hall if you need us."

"Thank you, Mother," Hugh said with another of his impressive smiles. Bess noted that her father said nothing, but she couldn't help but see the mild displeasure in his expression. It was as if he wanted her there with him, even if that meant her remaining completely silent and feeling invisible.

Bess ignored her father's silent insinuation and followed Lady Buxton out of the room. She closed the door, giving the men some privacy, and led the way through an open doorway across the hall into a sitting room very similar to the one they'd just left, although the color scheme was in differing shades of green, accented by touches of dark pink. Lady Buxton closed the door, once again implying the desire for privacy, and Bess wondered what on earth the lady of Astoria Abbey might want to talk to her about. Or perhaps she was simply being polite by not leaving her alone while they allowed the men to discuss Hugh's medical condition privately.

Bess sat down on a lovely and comfortable sofa, surprised to have Lady Buxton sit on the same sofa, where she turned to be able to face Bess as she smiled and said, "I remember you so well, my dear girl, and I confess that while I would have called upon your father to care for Hugh regardless, I was very much hoping that you would come with him and we would have the opportunity to speak."

"I feel honored that you would remember me, my lady," Bess said, "although I can't imagine what you might wish to speak to me about." As soon as the words were out of her mouth, Bess wondered if perhaps this woman simply wanted to share trivial conversation with another woman; perhaps she was lonely here in this big house with her only child dying. But Bess couldn't think of the words to express such a thought without the risk of sounding presumptuous.

"Are you happy, my dear?" Lady Buxton asked with genuine concern and sincere inquisitiveness showing in her expression.

"I beg your pardon?" Bess said, then hurried to soften her impulsive response. "I mean . . . I heard what you said; I suppose I don't know exactly what your purpose might be for asking, or how I should answer."

"You should answer honestly, my dear," Lady Buxton said.

Bess gave that a few moments of thought and wanted more than anything to just burst forth with all her pent-up frustrations. But she wasn't speaking to a close friend, or even a social peer. This was the lady of Astoria Abbey, and Bess needed to remain mindful of her place.

As if Lady Buxton sensed the reasons for her hesitation to speak, she added with sincere kindness in both her voice and her countenance, "I confess that I have my reasons for asking. I must tell you that I saw you last week in town, walking with your father, and my first thought was that you didn't look very happy. I asked around about you; I hope you don't consider that intrusive, because my inquiries were motivated by concern. And if you feel that I'm being too nosy, my dear, you must speak up and say so. Some people are more private than others, and I can't think of a single reason why you should feel that you are able to trust me enough to answer such personal questions."

"You've always been very kind to me," Bess admitted.

"I'm glad you feel that way, my dear," the lady said, making Bess realize she'd lost track of how many times this woman had referred to her as *my dear.* "Although some people are very good actors . . . good at pretending to be kind and concerned when they are really not. I can assure you that my concern is genuine, but it would take more time for us to get to know each other better before you could know for yourself if what I'm saying is true . . . or whether my words imply some ulterior motive."

"And what might that be?" Bess asked. "Your ulterior motive?"

"If you must know," Lady Buxton said with a smile, "I am both genuinely concerned for you *and* I do have an ulterior motive."

She paused long enough for Bess to say, "I cannot even begin to imagine what that might be."

"Well then, I will tell you." She drew in a long breath as if she were about to state something to which she had given careful consideration. "I want to borrow you, Miss White."

"Borrow me?" Bess echoed, having absolutely no idea what that could mean.

"I assume that your father relies a great deal on you."

"He does, yes," Bess admitted, hoping her expression hadn't given away how very displeased she was over the fact. Was that the visible unhappiness Lady Buxton had been talking about seeing previously?

"To assist him in his work, or to help at home in the absence of your mother?"

"Both," Bess said, trying to recall the last time she'd had a real conversation with another woman that went beyond the friendly chitchat she shared with patients and their loved ones, or some minor interaction with fellow churchgoers.

"Both?" Lady Buxton echoed, astonished. "Surely not! Whenever do you have time for yourself?"

"What might that entail exactly?" Bess asked, mildly sarcastic—immediately wondering whether this might be considered rude, but the lady laughed softly.

"Oh, my dear." Lady Buxton took her hand. "I've hardly been able to get you off my mind since I saw you in town, and I've begun to believe you might be the answer to many prayers, but perhaps I also might be able to answer some of yours. I suppose that's why I first asked if you're happy. A young woman such as yourself should be happy, doing work she enjoys, using these youthful years to experience the good things of life. *Are* you happy?"

At the repetition of this question, Bess unexpectedly—and uncontrollably—began to cry. Years of pent-up sorrow and grief, confusion and frustration, all came tumbling out. It occurred to her—not for the first time—that she'd not had the opportunity to fully mourn her mother's death. There simply hadn't been time. Bess had immediately taken over the care of the home, in addition to assisting her father, and she'd been expected to do it every bit as well as a grown and experienced woman had done. Embarrassment flooded over her as she grappled inside the hidden pocket of her skirt for her handkerchief. Before she'd found it,

Lady Buxton had wrapped a motherly arm around Bess's shoulders and was speaking words of a soothing nature, which Bess found impossible to understand through her own struggle to try and regain her composure.

"Forgive me," Bess finally said after wiping her cheeks with her hand-kerchief and then pressing it beneath her nose while she focused on steady-ing her ragged breath enough to behave like a lady.

"There's no need to apologize, my dear. At the risk of sounding pre-sumptuous, your reaction to my question has only made me believe more firmly that you may be the answer to my prayers—and perhaps I can be the answer to yours."

"What do you mean?" Bess asked this kind and remarkable woman while she wondered exactly what the answer to her own prayers might entail. In truth, she'd not quite dared utter her hopes—even to God. Putting them to words—or trying to form any kind of specific image in her mind of how her future might look if she were free from all that weighed on her—felt somehow disrespectful of her father, and far beyond any plausible expectation. How could this woman who barely knew of her existence be so insightful as to sense her unhappiness, and to declare that they might be able to answer one another's prayers?

Bess waited expectantly for an answer to her question while she watched Lady Buxton smile with a compassion in her eyes that tempted Bess to start crying again. "Once we realized that nothing more could be done to improve Hugh's health . . . that the end was inevitable . . . I began considering carefully how to make this final season of his life as comfortable—and enjoyable—as possible. I've come to feel very strongly, based on what I know of my son, that having the best medical care available is only a small portion of what he needs. There are two male servants who have been with our household for many years; Hugh is comfortable with them, and they've agreed to alternate shifts in being on hand to help him with whatever he might need. They grew up with Hugh and they are all friends; the division of their social status is barely recognizable at times when they laugh together and talk of their life's experiences."

Lady Buxton's eyes took on a faraway gaze, accompanied by a wan smile, as if the mental image of her son enjoying the company of his friends felt comforting to her. Then she suddenly looked directly at Bess and said, "As I see it, Hugh has only one missing element in his life that will help make these final months—or weeks—as comfortable as possible."

When the lady paused but kept her gaze fixed, Bess's heart began to pound, realizing that she was trying to get to the point where Bess could be the answer to her prayers. Bess couldn't begin to imagine what that might entail, but her impatience forced her to ask, "And what might that be, my lady?"

"You," Lady Buxton said, and Bess's heart beat even more quickly. "He needs a person with some degree of medical experience to be nearby and check on him at regular intervals, who might know whether he needs a doctor's attention. He needs companionship beyond that of his male servants who are often kept very busy in their work; they both have duties elsewhere in the house which we have minimized so they can help Hugh. Nevertheless, they do have responsibilities, which neither of them wants to completely turn over to anyone else. I believe Hugh needs someone who can read to him, given that he gets terribly bored and he's often too weak to even hold a book or keep his eyes open. He needs someone to talk to who is near his own age and might very well share many of his views—or if their views differ, he will have the opportunity for a good stimulating argument now and then."

The lady smiled, but there was sadness in her countenance. She knew her son was dying, and it was evident that her greatest focus in life was doing everything possible to make the remainder of his life the best it could possibly be. Despite the description she'd just given of what she believed Hugh needed, Bess was having difficulty imagining herself as the person who could fill these requirements. But Lady Buxton took Bess's hand and looked more firmly into her eyes, saying fervently, "My dear Miss White, I am offering you a job. I've thought this through very carefully, and while I don't know exactly what the situation is with you and your father, I believe I could guess at least a great majority of it. I suspect he relies on you far too much, and a pattern has developed that if not broken will eventually *break* you. A woman needs to find her own way, her own life. Correct me if I'm wrong, but I suspect that since your mother's death, you have stepped in to fill her role in caring for your home, *and* in assisting your father in his work. I know he's a good man, and he's an excellent doctor, but I dare say that in his own grief and loneliness he has lost sight of the fact that he is smothering you and being completely oblivious to your own needs. So," the lady appeared mildly nervous as she tightened her hold on Bess's hand, "I'm offering you a job. It's up to you whether you accept my offer, and you are free to negotiate its terms. I want you to be able to use your own mind and follow your own heart in making this decision. I want you to come and live here for the duration of what is left of my son's life. Your duties would include checking on him regularly to assess his medical state. I'm certain you have gained enough knowledge from working with your father all these years to be able to care for his daily medical needs. And I also want you to be a companion to him, as I have described." Lady Buxton took a deep breath. "Now, I know the biggest problem is that your father depends on you a great deal, but I suspect he could afford to hire help to cook and clean, and even to assist him in his professional duties. If he cannot afford to hire help, then I will provide him with the means to do so as a part of your salary. You will use the room just off this sitting room," she motioned with her hand toward a door, "and one of our maids near your own age will move to this room." She motioned in the opposite direction to another door connected to the sitting room. "Daphne will oversee taking care of *your* needs and being on hand to give you whatever assistance you desire. Her companionship for *you* will also maintain a necessary propriety. I'm not at all concerned about the need for a chaperone with you and my son, because I know your character and his; but for the sake of appearances within the household and the community, the presence of a female maid who is regularly on hand will alleviate any potential for ridiculous assumptions or gossip."

Bess felt a little unsettled over the very mention of such a thing, but she understood exactly what Lady Buxton meant, and it was clear that she had carefully considered every aspect of this situation.

"Now, the only thing I need is your decision, my dear," Lady Buxton said. "Should you choose to accept this position, we will assess together the path you choose for your life after Hugh has passed on. Clearly, this is a situation that must be taken one day at a time. I will respect your choice, but I cannot deny how much I'm hoping you will take this opportunity to break free from your father. I know he won't be happy about it; such a decision will take great courage, my dear, but I promise you that he will be a better man for letting you go at this time of your life—even if he doesn't see it that way right now. And once you break this pattern of your life, you will be able to choose where it might go from here. If you choose to go back and live in your father's home when this is all over, you will be able to do so with more confidence and the ability to declare your own boundaries in the situation."

Silence followed Lady Buxton's kind and generous offer while Bess tried to take in everything she'd said with all its implications and possibilities. To say she felt overwhelmed would be to grossly understate all that was swirling around in her mind. Was it possible that Lady Buxton's offer truly *was* the answer to Bess's prayers? Prayers that she hadn't even thought to utter—or hadn't dared? And if so, could she come up with enough courage to break free from the life in which her father had imprisoned her, and leap into a new experience full of unknown possibilities and challenges? She knew what she *wanted* to do, but she had to carefully consider whether she was brave enough to do it.

# CHAPTER TWO

## NURSEMAID AND NANNY

"YOU MUST BE TERRIBLY OVERWHELMED," Lady Buxton said, startling Bess back to the realization that she wasn't alone while her mind raced with battles of hope and dread.

"I am indeed," Bess admitted, then stated what she knew needed to be said. "I'm flattered and honored that you would consider me in this way to help care for your son, when it's evident how very important his care is to you. And I must confess that your perception of my situation is . . . well . . . very insightful." Bess grimaced slightly over the redundancy of her own statement. "I'm just not certain if . . ."

When Bess couldn't find the words to finish that sentence, Lady Buxton rescued her by once again proving to be very insightful. "I think it would be appropriate—and perhaps easier for you—if I speak to your father about my proposition. Perhaps he will be more reasonable while in his role as a doctor, than he would be hearing it from you."

"I would appreciate that very much," Bess said, more relieved than she could ever express. It occurred to Bess that this kind woman must have had some personal experience with a controlling and difficult man. Her perceptions were so accurate that they had to be based on hard-won experience. Bess wanted to ask her about that, but she doubted it would be appropriate—despite how kind and amiable the lady of the Abbey had been to her.

"Does that mean you *want* the position, Miss White?" Lady Buxton asked, her anticipation readily evident.

Bess swallowed carefully but felt hesitant for only a moment. If she pushed aside her fears over how her father would react—or how he would manage—her answer to the question was as easy as it was right. She couldn't recall ever feeling so right about anything in the whole of her narrow and limited life. "Very much," she said firmly, and Lady Buxton smiled.

"Come along," Lady Buxton said and stood up.

Bess stood and followed the lady out of the room and across the hall. The door to the sitting room where they'd left Hugh and her father was now open, as if to signal that their need for privacy was no longer necessary. The women entered the room where the men were chatting comfortably. Bess felt pride in her father when she saw him like this. He *was* a good man, a kind man. And a *very* good doctor. But somewhere in the midst of losing his wife, he'd stopped being a good father, and Bess felt as if her spirit truly would suffocate if she didn't get out from under his control of her life, and his constant need for her to take care of everything for him. Suddenly, ideas for carrying out this plan started sparking in her mind. She could see a possible course to hiring the people he would need to take over the duties she'd been performing. She found it remarkable that people they both knew well came to mind as possibilities. In that moment, she felt an unfamiliar confidence that this was meant to be, and it would all work out—no matter how angry her father might be over her decision to leave and take this position.

Jonas White stood when Lady Buxton and Bess entered the room; Hugh remained where he had been sitting previously, with a blanket still spread over his lap. He exchanged a smile with his mother before he smiled at Bess in a way that made her feel that she could be comfortable in helping care for this man. She couldn't think about the fact that he was dying. The very idea seemed so impossible, given his present appearance. But as his mother had said, they needed to take this one day at a time.

Bess sat down next to Hugh's mother on a sofa facing her father; she felt safe with the lady of the house next to her like she was a maternal sentinel committed to her cause. Bess's mind continued to swirl over the reality of what was happening, when she'd never even considered such a possibility prior to her conversation with Lady Buxton. She focused on trying to breathe evenly and not draw attention to herself in any way while she allowed this kind woman to take the lead in what needed to be said.

They listened while Jonas gave a report of his appraisal of Hugh's health—which strongly concurred with what the specialists in London had told them. Hugh's heart was weak and deteriorating, and nothing could be done to stop its inevitable failure. To hopefully extend his life as long as possible, he needed to put forth very little energy and be extremely careful, since the heart would have to pump harder with everything he did. Bess clearly understood all her father was saying, and she felt surprisingly confident in her ability to help care for Hugh in the way his mother was expecting. Bess noticed the faraway look in Hugh's eyes as his declining health was discussed and she wondered how it might feel to know that your life was coming to an end. She began to feel some measure of doubt in her own abilities to be able to handle the emotional aspects of the situation but reminded herself that she needed to exert some faith in her own wisdom and sensitivity, and to also remember that Hugh's mother would surely be available to discuss any challenge that might arise. And Bess already felt deeply connected and comfortable with this woman.

When Bess's father had concluded the oration of his medical opinions, he offered to come to the house every three days to examine Hugh and assess his condition. He made it clear that he would adjust the timing of his visits according to Hugh's needs, and he would make certain Hugh had all he needed to keep him comfortable.

"I must be blunt," the knowledgeable Dr. White said, looking firmly at Hugh, then at Hugh's mother, then at Hugh again. "As you get closer to the end, even your breathing will become painful as it becomes more difficult. There will come a point when you will need large doses of medication, which will mostly keep you asleep until the end comes. I know that sounds difficult to even think about, but I also know that you want me to be honest."

"Yes, I most certainly do," Hugh said.

"Of course we want absolute honesty," Lady Buxton added. "And we thank you for your candor, as well as your kindness. I feel greatly reassured knowing that he will be in the care of such a proficient physician."

Bess's father nodded slightly in humble response to the compliment, and again Bess felt admiration for him in his profession. She'd almost forgotten about what would inevitably happen next until Lady Buxton said, "There is another matter that I wish to propose to you, Doctor. Let me say that I'm aware that I am being somewhat presumptuous, but I've given it a great deal of thought, and I'm willing to help compensate you for the benefits in your life that I would be taking away from you—at least for a time. I've already spoken to your lovely daughter about it, and I hope you will agree with what I wish to propose."

"I don't understand," Jonas said, his brow furrowed in a way that Bess recognized as stern concern. He had to have noticed that Lady Buxton had said she would be taking something away from him, and that it had to do with Bess, but she felt certain he was entirely unprepared for what this powerful and respected woman was about to propose.

"I wish to hire your daughter," Lady Buxton stated with confidence, "to live here at the house for the duration of Hugh's life . . . to oversee his medical care between your visits—given the knowledge she has gained from you over the years about such things—and to be a companion to him in light of his physical limitations and inevitable boredom."

Bess's heart was pounding so hard she felt certain every person in the room could hear it. She noted that her father was doing well at hiding his astonishment, but she knew him well enough to know that he was stunned and perhaps even angry—although he would never betray such emotions in the presence of someone like Lady Buxton. Bess also noted that Hugh was completely surprised by his mother's proposal. Had they not discussed this possibility? What if he hated the idea? What if Hugh refused her help and all of this was for nothing? She felt a tiny measure of relief to see something in Hugh's expression that indicated he was *not* opposed to the idea; in fact, he wore the hint of a smile, and he glanced toward her with a warm expression in his eyes. She considered this evidence that he was indeed very bored and lonely, and any company or diversion would be welcome.

Hugh's mother continued speaking to Bess's father. "I can assure you that servants will always be nearby, and everything will be proper and appropriate. I trust that you will be able to acquire the help you need to compensate for your daughter's absence; and as I told Bess, if there is any difficulty on your behalf in that regard, I will gladly help compensate for her absence."

Bess was surprised by the way her father's pride dictated what came out of his mouth first and foremost in response to what had surely shocked him, but she couldn't help being pleased by the way his pride inadvertently strengthened her case. "I can assure you, my lady," he said with no hint of defensiveness or anger, even though Bess could see them brewing in his eyes, "that I have ample means to acquire any help necessary in my daughter's absence."

"I suspected as much," Lady Buxton said with kindness and respect. "I simply didn't want you to think that I would presume to remove your daughter from your care without consideration as to how that would impact your current situation."

Bess was amazed by her own ability to speak, and the words that came with confidence out of her mouth, a confidence that was surely inspired by Lady Buxton's commitment to giving her this opportunity. "I can help find someone to assist you, Father, both at home and with your work. I can make certain that everything is in order before I leave, and of course I would see you often, given your regular visits here."

Bess could see how her father wanted to argue with her or, rather, wanted to tell her exactly what he thought of such a preposterous idea and that he had no interest in her opinion or her ability to make the situation work. But he only said, "Clearly this is something we need to discuss privately before making a decision."

Bess's heart sank a little. What if her father simply refused? What was she to do? Run away from home like a naughty child? Once again Lady Buxton came to the rescue. "Allow me to propose this to you, Dr. White. In two days' time at noon, I will send Clive with a carriage to your residence; you met Clive earlier. Beyond being an invaluable companion to Hugh, he was recently promoted to the position of head butler in the household. He mostly delegates and oversees what's necessary so that he can take shifts in caring for Hugh, and he always does an excellent job at whatever we ask of him. He is most reliable and trustworthy and has been a good friend to Hugh for many years now. He will come to collect either Miss White and her belongings, or a letter from you that will explain in reasonable terms why this is not acceptable to you. Either way, I will expect to see you here in three days' time for your expected appointment to check on Hugh. If your daughter is not in my employ before then, I will very much look forward to discussing with you the reasons you do not find the situation acceptable."

Amazement overcame Bess as she considered how Lady Buxton had worded her proposal so carefully that her father would either need to write a letter to explain *in reasonable terms* why this offer was not acceptable, or he would have to explain it face-to-face. Bess doubted that her father could come up with *any* reason that might satisfy Lady Buxton, and he would be far too embarrassed to try and explain the way he relied far too heavily on his daughter and would prefer that she never leave his care for that very reason.

Lady Buxton stood as if to signal an end to the conversation. Bess and her father stood as well, and Bess was surprised by her father's silence. He merely nodded at Lady Buxton before she moved toward the door, saying to Bess, "I hope to see you in two days, my dear."

"Yes, I hope so too," Hugh said, and Bess noticed him smiling, but perhaps with some effort to not make his enthusiasm over the idea too obvious. In the brief moment when their eyes met, she felt a keen desire to be a part of his life, to be able to help him through the inevitable difficulties to come, and to perhaps become his friend. Deeper down in her consciousness she knew that assisting another human being in the process of dying would surely bring on personal struggles for herself, but it felt right, and she felt capable. If nothing else, she desperately needed to do something different with her life, and to put herself to the test in facing new challenges. Despite her certainty that an argument with her father was imminent, every piece of her heart and soul felt alive and eager to respond to Lady Buxton's invitation. It was as if she had collided with her fate somehow, and her spirit knew it. Perhaps this opportunity was indeed the answer to her unspoken prayers.

Bess barely listened as polite words of parting were exchanged between the others, then Clive magically appeared from the hallway, as if he had known the doctor and his daughter were ready to leave. He smiled and silently motioned for them to follow him. With Clive present, no words were exchanged between Bess and her father as they made their way from Hugh's room to the doors through which they'd entered the house. As Clive opened the door for them, Bess was surprised to hear him whisper near her ear, "I shall see you in two days, Miss White."

Bess turned to look at him in surprise and found a subdued smile and a sparkle in his eyes. He had clearly known about Lady Buxton's proposal; she had said Clive was very close to Hugh, and involved in his care, and yet even Hugh had seemed surprised by his mother's idea to hire her. Bess felt strangely comfortable with Clive in that moment and intrigued to know what he knew. She already felt involved in these people's lives, as if her spirit had settled comfortably into this situation, even though there were many details to be worked out—and the sure resistance from her father. But Bess felt surprisingly calm, even about that. It was as if something inside of her had been prepared for an inevitable separation from her father. As much as she loved him, she knew she could never keep doing all she was doing to make his life easy and comfortable without completely losing herself. And she also believed it was not beneficial to him or his happiness for her to make everything so easy for him.

Bess nodded slightly toward Clive and returned an equally subdued smile, not wanting her father to pick up on their secretive exchange, but her stomach fluttered at the thought of Clive coming to her door in two days to rescue her from a life that suddenly felt like bondage, as she allowed herself to really see it for what it was.

Bess's father helped her step into the waiting trap before he got in himself and took hold of the reins to begin their trek back home. After minutes of grueling silence through which Bess could practically see her father attempting to remain calm and find the right words, he finally said with a sharp edge to his voice, "You cannot possibly think it prudent or practical to accept Lady Buxton's offer, given our present circumstances."

Bess took a few moments and a couple of deep breaths before she responded with an even voice. "I deeply believe that Lady Buxton's offer will bring valuable opportunities into my life. I love you very much, Father, but I cannot continue to spend every waking moment taking care of our home and assisting you in your duties."

"Is that how you see what you do?" he asked, but not in a way that made Bess feel that he was interested in how she perceived her life; he sounded angrier that she wasn't finding satisfaction and fulfillment in devoting her entire life to his ease and comfort.

Again, Bess took the time to consider her words carefully, and she kept any hint of anger or frustration out of her voice, not wanting to provoke any kind of argument. "It is not simply how I *see* what I do, Father; it is a fact. I cook and clean; I keep all your instruments clean and your bag stocked and always ready to go. You have time nearly every day to read and relax. I work from the moment I wake up until the moment I am finally able to go to bed—which is always more than an hour after *you* go to bed. I'm tired, Father, not just physically tired, but tired of feeling unappreciated."

"Unappreciated?" he echoed, tossing an astonished angry glance toward her before he looked again to the road ahead.

"Yes, Father," Bess said, keeping her voice free of the anger and frustration that was mounting inside of her. "I am doing the work of two people—perhaps three—and yet you express no appreciation or—"

"Your mother did all that you do and never complained or—"

"I am your *daughter*," Bess said, unable to keep the sharpness out of her voice, "*not* your wife. Whatever your relationship with Mother entailed has little to do with me. I stepped into her place when she died, and I was still a *child*, and apparently, I fulfilled all her household duties, and those of assisting you in your medical practice so well that you have grown to simply expect it of me. And I cannot keep doing this. I cannot. I will end up a worn-out spinster with nothing to show for my life when you are gone. I need a change, and you need to learn to rely on someone else. You can afford to hire help, and I can make those arrangements."

Bess took a deep breath once she'd stated what she'd wanted to say for many months—perhaps longer. She felt her father silently fuming, and she wondered if his desperation to keep her in a position of servitude for his own comfort was so strong that he could not see the need to allow his daughter to step into her own life as a grown woman. She wanted to say *that* out loud as well but waited to see what his response might be. She sensed that he was trying to subdue his own anger, but minutes of silence made it clear that doing so was not easy. He was *very* angry. But Bess didn't feel afraid. She just wanted to have this conversation over with, so she could press forward with her preparations to leave the only home and life she'd ever known, to begin a new adventure. In that moment she didn't think about the inevitable difficulties of filling her position at Astoria Abbey; she simply had to get through the next two days. And the first step had to be making it clear to her father that there was nothing he could say or do to stop her from accepting Lady Buxton's offer. The decision was already firm inside of herself; she only had to make that clear to her father.

"If you've felt this way," Jonas finally said, his voice tight and strained as if it were taking his entire strength to keep from shouting, "why have you not said something?"

Bess let out an astonished gasp before she could even think of holding it back. Sounding as frustrated as she felt, she said firmly, "I *have* said something. I have spoken my feelings to you many times and you have either ignored me entirely or made trite comments that completely disregarded my feelings, that I should be grateful to have work to keep myself occupied, that I should be fulfilled with—"

"You *should* be grateful," he countered, making no effort to hold back his anger. "I have given you everything a young lady could ever want! I have taught you my profession when it is most often considered inappropriate for women to be educated in such things. I have treated you as an equal in our ability to learn medicine and—"

"I am grateful for all you have taught me, Father, and I will always use my knowledge to try and do good things in my life, but you have *never* treated me as an equal. I feel invisible when I assist you with patients. Beyond your introducing me to the people we encounter, you don't acknowledge me at all except to give me orders to do your bidding. At home you barely speak to me, even when I put well-prepared meals in front of you and keep everything in pristine order. It is time for me to make a life for myself." She took a deep breath and added firmly. "My leaving does not mean that I don't love you, Father. You are an excellent doctor and a good man, and I know that losing Mother was very difficult for you; but it was difficult for me too, and from my perspective, you have been completely oblivious to how you have expected me to do *everything* for you while you express no appreciation whatsoever. You tell me that I should be grateful, and yet I have no example to follow in that regard."

Bess could feel his anger rising but it felt so good to be saying all that needed to be said that she hardly cared. "I cannot believe," he said, "that you would just pack up and leave me to deal with everything on my own so that you can go and play nursemaid and nanny to a spoiled rich boy who is surrounded by servants already. It's preposterous!"

Bess's own anger grew upon hearing evidence that he was giving no acknowledgment to all the feelings she had just expressed; instead he was focusing only on the difficulties this would cause for *him*. She wondered if he would ever come to miss *her*, his daughter, or if he would only miss the convenience in having her be his cook, his housekeeper, and his assistant.

Knowing she would never be able to convince him of the validity of her feelings, or her powerful need to accept this miraculous opportunity, Bess simply said, "I will take care of getting you the help you need before I leave."

She said nothing more during the remainder of the drive home, and neither did he, but she could feel his anger brewing. Once they were at home, Jonas unharnessed the horse and cared for it while Bess went into the house where she found three messages that had been slid beneath the front door. The villagers knew that if the doctor was not at home they were to leave a message regarding any medical need and he would come as soon as possible. When Jonas came into the house she informed him of the messages as if nothing was out of the ordinary, and as soon as they'd had a quick lunch they were off to visit those in need of medical attention. They returned to the house late in the afternoon and Jonas immediately removed his shoes and sat in the parlor with his feet up and proceeded to read from a novel. Bess would have normally started preparing supper or doing some laundry, but instead she freshened up and announced to her father that she was going out.

"Out?" he echoed as if she'd announced that she had fallen into a life of sin.

"I have some errands to see to," was all she said before hurrying to the door. If he wanted more explanation than that he would have to relinquish his comfortable position, and she doubted he would be motivated to do so.

Bess went first to the home of Mrs. Hubbard, a widow who was a little older than her father but in excellent health and full of energy and kindness. Bess knew Mrs. Hubbard through their both being members of the church choir. They attended rehearsals one evening a week and sang in church before the congregation one Sunday a month. It was the only activity Bess participated in that didn't involve her father, but over time it had come to offer little if any reprieve, given how rushed she always felt to get to rehearsals, and knowing that she would return home to find her work still waiting for her. The one benefit of being a part of the choir was the camaraderie she'd found with the other members. And Mrs. Hubbard was among those who had been especially kind to her. She'd often said to Bess that a young lady such as herself shouldn't be so restricted in her life; Bess had appreciated knowing that someone had noticed the ridiculousness of her situation, but she'd felt trapped, having no opportunity to do anything else. But she had an opportunity now, and she knew she needed to speak with Mrs. Hubbard.

"Oh, hello, dearie!" the kind woman said as she pulled open her door to see Bess standing there. "What a wondrous surprise! However did you escape?" she asked and chuckled.

"I'm glad you asked," Bess said. "We need to talk."

The woman chuckled again. "Your timing is perfect. I was about to put on the kettle. Come to the kitchen and we'll have some tea."

"How lovely," Bess said, already feeling the soothing effect of her free-dom beginning to take hold.

Bess sat down in Mrs. Hubbard's tidy kitchen, recalling her few brief previous visits, wishing now that she'd been able to call more often and stay longer than a matter of minutes. If not for the busyness of her life, she believed that she and this woman could have spent a great deal of enjoyable time together and been much closer. It was one of many things that Bess felt robbed of in the life she was living.

As soon as the older woman had set a teakettle on the stove to heat, she sat across from Bess, clasped her hands on the table, and asked, "Now what might I do for you, young lady?"

"First let me ask you a question," Bess said, having carefully thought through how she might approach this. "How are you liking your job at the pub? I know they love your cooking there, and they couldn't ask for anyone more efficient, but I also know that—"

"You also know how very much I detest working there and would leave in a heartbeat if I had any better opportunity. It's not as if we haven't talked about it a dozen times or more."

"Exactly," Bess said, "which I now believe might be the hand of Providence showing itself on behalf of both our situations."

"I cannot begin to imagine what you might mean," Mrs. Hubbard said, her eyes narrowing curiously.

"I've been offered a position," Bess said, unable to hide the enthusiasm in her own voice, "at Astoria Abbey."

"No!" Mrs. Hubbard said with pleasant astonishment.

"Yes!" Bess said and laughed softly. "It feels right to take the job; you yourself have said I need a change. But of course, that means leaving my father and—"

"And he can't be too happy about that," Mrs. Hubbard said knowingly.

"No, he is not," Bess said, "but I assured him I would make arrangements for everything before I leave . . . which is where you come in."

As if Mrs. Hubbard had just remembered how this conversation might relate to her, she gasped and took on an expression that implied she almost dared not hope that Bess was going to actually give her an opportunity to get away from the job she'd disliked for a very long time. The older woman held her breath as Bess said, "How would you feel about being a cook and housekeeper for my father?" Mrs. Hubbard let out her breath on the wave of something that sounded like the combination of a sob and a laugh. Bess just kept talking. "The two of you have known each other for years, so I'm certain he'll not feel uncomfortable having you coming and going and taking care of the needs of his home. I know you're competent and tidy and a good cook, and that you can do everything I've been doing— perhaps better. The pay would be the same as you're making now, although from what you've told me, I believe the work will be much less strenuous. Whatever you cook for him you can eat yourself, so you don't have to prepare meals twice."

Mrs. Hubbard got tears in her eyes before she stood up long enough to step around the little table and hug Bess tightly, declaring that it was indeed the hand of Providence. "Like a dream come true," she said, sitting back down.

While they shared tea and two varieties of delicious homemade biscuits, Bess told her friend all about the situation at Astoria Abbey with Hugh Buxton, and how Lady Buxton herself had offered Bess the position. Mrs. Hubbard was proud of Bess for being determined to take the job despite her father's disapproval.

"He will get past this," the woman said. "I promise you he will. He's a good man; he's just grown far too dependent upon you. Trust me when I tell you that I will take very good care of him, and you'll not need to worry about a thing. Once he's realized that he doesn't need you for every little thing, perhaps he might come to see you once again as his daughter."

Bess felt the sting of tears over such an idea. "Do you really think so?"

"Oh, I do! Or at the very least we can hope for that," Mrs. Hubbard said.

They talked a long while about exactly what Mrs. Hubbard's duties would entail and what her schedule would be. With paper and pencil provided, Bess wrote down everything they discussed so that Mrs. Hubbard could refer to the list until she became accustomed to the doctor's schedule, needs, and habits.

By the time Bess left, she felt confident and reassured that all would be well. Even though it was past supper time, she had one more stop to make and hoped it would go equally well. When no one answered the door after she'd knocked repeatedly, she returned home to find her father not reading but staring at the wall of the parlor. He ignored her greeting, but she figured that was better than having him yell at her. Perhaps that would come later.

After freshening up, Bess put out a cold supper with fresh apples she'd washed and cut into sections, slices of the bread she'd picked up at the bakery a few days earlier, butter, jam, and some cold roast lamb left over from the previous day. She called her father to the table where he scraped his chair across the floor more noisily than usual and said, "Supper's late. Where have you been?"

"After grace, I'll tell you," she said and sat down. Listening to her father speak a blessing over their food, she silently added a prayer that he might be able to have the kindness toward her that he showed to everyone *but* her.

Jonas looked at the simple meal before them and made no effort to conceal his displeasure. It was far from the first time they'd eaten a similar meal, given how some days could become unexpectedly busy when there were many patients to see; but apparently the fact that *this* meal was less than ideal due to Bess having gone out for her own purposes was a problem. However, Bess ignored that. She simply told her father about having visited with Mrs. Hubbard, and how she'd hired her to be a cook and a housekeeper. He stopped eating and looked at her as if she'd thrown cold water in his face.

"You really mean to go through with this nonsense?" he asked, his tone expressing hurt and betrayal.

"My mind is made up," she said and hurried to tell him how Mrs. Hubbard intended to quit her job at the pub the following day, and she would be here early the following morning to begin fulfilling her duties. Bess reassured her father that even though it might take Mrs. Hubbard a little time to adjust to his preferences, she would keep everything in the household running much more smoothly than Bess had ever been able to do—especially when she'd always had to be out and about assisting her father with medical visits.

"And what of assisting me in my practice?" he asked, sounding even *more* hurt and betrayed. "Mrs. Hubbard won't be able to do *that.*"

"No, she will not," Bess said, resisting the urge to say that since her father had become accustomed to her doing the work of two people, it would take two people to replace her. "But I promised you that I would get everything taken care of, and I will. You'll have to manage without me tomorrow. I have some errands to see to, and I need to pack, but before I leave, everything will be under control."

Jonas threw his napkin to the table and stood abruptly, his supper only half eaten. He looked at her as if she'd just told him she was unmarried and with child, and she wondered how he could be *so* disappointed in her when she had done nothing but try to please him every day of her life. The obvious answer was that her decision to leave was displeasing him so deeply that he could not see how childishly he was behaving.

She wondered for a long moment if he would say anything at all while they just stared at each other, silently battling their wills. Jonas finally repeated—word for word—what he'd said earlier, as if it were his greatest defense. "I cannot believe that you would just pack up and leave me to deal with everything on my own so that you can go and play nursemaid and nanny to a spoiled rich boy who is surrounded by servants already. It's preposterous!"

"First of all," Bess said, surprised at her own calm strength, "he may be surrounded by servants, but none of them have the medical knowledge that I have. Secondly, he may be rich, but you have said yourself that Lady Buxton is a good woman and I hardly think she would raise spoiled children; therefore, your comment sounds very insulting to *her.* And given the fact that he has never lived a full life and is now dying, I would hardly call that being *spoiled.* Taking in the fact that he's dying, I would say he needs a nursemaid and nanny a great deal more than a strong, healthy man such as yourself who has come to depend so thoroughly upon his own daughter that he's forgotten who she is." Bess silently thanked Mrs. Hubbard for giving her that last comment. As the hurt in Jonas's expression deepened, Bess was also grateful for Mrs. Hubbard's belief that her father would get past this. She hoped and prayed that he would, but for now she simply had to do what was best for herself; she felt certain she would shrivel up and die if her life didn't change. Now that she'd been given this opportunity, she couldn't imagine any other path to follow.

Jonas left the room and went up the stairs. Bess just finished eating her supper and cleaned up the kitchen. With the pleasant absence of her father, she checked to make certain that everything was in readiness for Mrs. Hubbard to take over, and mentally reconsidered the list they had made together to make certain she'd not forgotten anything. Carefully recalling every facet of her usual daily routine, she made a few more notes for Mrs. Hubbard and took the paper upstairs with her so that her father wouldn't find it. Alone in her room, Bess began packing what she cared to take with her, which was very little. She knew the job was temporary, and at this point she couldn't predict if she would find employment elsewhere or return here. In the meantime, she would just leave many of her clothes and books. She was grateful to have inherited her mother's traveling trunk, since she herself had never traveled. Bess had stored some personal belongings in the trunk, but it had remained mostly empty. Now she added the finest of her clothing, the journals she'd written in—not wanting her father to find and read them—and a handful of her favorite books, wondering if they might be anything that might interest Hugh Buxton, given the fact that his mother had suggested she read to him. Bess felt certain there was an enormous library at Astoria Abbey, but she couldn't be certain they would have *these* books.

Bess became so caught up in her packing that she lost track of time and couldn't believe how late she'd stayed up. She went to bed, doubtful that she could sleep when her life had changed completely in one day, but she finally drifted off, certain she slept with a smile on her face.

The following morning Bess got up and dressed before her father was up and about—which was not unusual—but she quickly ate some bread and cheese and left the same for him on the table, along with a note—which *was* unusual. The day was cloudy with gusts of wind that were tugging the autumn leaves from the trees and blowing them through the air and across the road upon that she walked as she hurried to her destination. Knocking again on the door which had gone unanswered the previous evening, she wondered what she would do if *this* proposition didn't work out as well as things had gone with Mrs. Hubbard. But thoughts of this conversation had come to her mind even while Mrs. Buxton had still been speaking with her the previous day. Bess believed that she knew of the perfect assistant for her father, just as she'd already known who the perfect cook and housekeeper would be. But what if he was busy, or out of town, or didn't want the job? She couldn't deny that she felt less confident about this situation than she had been about hiring Mrs. Hubbard. Reminding herself of all she had to offer this fine young man, she took a deep breath and knocked once more, praying she wouldn't have to come back—again.

The door came open so abruptly that it startled her. Archie Wilson looked at her curiously through the round frames of his eyeglasses, and smiled, showing his crooked teeth and deep dimples. He was a little younger than Bess and lived with his widowed mother—both of whom also attended church with Bess and her father. Archie had straight brown hair that had a stiffness about it that prevented it from ever staying in place. He was unusually thin, extremely kind, and amazingly efficient—even Jonas White had said so. Quite by accident, Archie had ended up assisting the doctor on a day when Bess had been ill, and her father had gone to check on Archie's mother who had twisted her ankle rather viciously, having fallen on a patch of ice. According to the way Jonas had told the story to Bess, after Archie had efficiently helped the doctor by handing him everything he needed to properly bandage the ailing ankle, Jonas had asked if Archie might be available to attend him on the remainder of his visits that day since Bess was ill and the appointments would go more quickly with some help. Archie had been thrilled and had done an excellent job, and the pay he'd received for his efforts had been received with gracious surprise. Jonas had called on Archie two or three other times when Bess had been unable to accompany her father but had scoffed at Bess's suggestion that he hire Archie as a permanent assistant.

Now, Archie was employed assisting the local veterinarian, and he was fascinated by all things medical. But the animal doctor also ran a livery, and Archie had told Bess more than once during casual conversation after church that he did much more mucking out of stalls than assisting with any kind of medical procedures, which was his favorite part of the job.

Archie's smile inspired Bess's hope that this would go well, and she was glad to get out of the wind when he invited her in.

"Look who's here, Mother!" Archie said, leading the way to the kitchen where Mrs. Wilson was sitting at the table reading and sipping a cup of coffee.

"What a pleasant surprise this is," Mrs. Wilson said as she stood and kissed Bess on the cheek.

"I wonder if I could speak with both of you," Bess said.

"But of course," Mrs. Wilson said as she poured Bess a cup of coffee and put it in front of her before she sat down again, passing cream and sugar across the table.

Once they were all seated, Archie and his mother looked expectantly toward Bess, silently questioning the purpose of her visit. Bess got right to the point and said to Archie, "I've come to offer you a job."

Both Archie and his mother gasped before Bess hurried to explain the situation as quickly as possible, and she wasn't disappointed when they both responded with enthusiasm equal to that of Mrs. Hubbard. The hand of Providence was indeed helping Bess bring all of this together. It felt like it was meant to be, and she left the Wilson household happier than she'd been since her mother's death.

Before going home, Bess did some shopping for some personal things she might need, and she treated herself to lunch at a tea shoppe, which served the most delectable little sandwiches and cakes. She remembered coming here with her mother and was saddened to think that she'd not been here since. Impulsively, she purchased food to take home for both herself and her father for supper. She considered it a great blessing that her father made a comfortable living from his medical skills, and that if nothing else he'd paid her a minimal wage for her work, telling her that she should put the money away to be prepared for the future. She'd rarely if ever had time to spend money on anything but that which was absolutely necessary. But today, spending some of it made her feel more prepared for her upcoming endeavor, and it would give her the ease of not having to worry about preparing an evening meal. The reality that Mrs. Hubbard would be at the house early enough tomorrow to cook breakfast made Bess's stomach flutter with excitement. She looked forward to spending her days with an entirely different kind of responsibility, even though she understood her new occupation would come with its own brand of challenges.

Bess returned home to find her father absent. He was likely making a call on a patient, no doubt grumbling to himself about the burden of having to do so alone, even though Bess knew that most doctors did not necessarily even have assistants who went everywhere with them. But that's how Jonas White had done it ever since he'd been married, and according to him, he couldn't work as efficiently without someone to help him. Well, tomorrow he would have Archie to accompany him as he went about his work, and Bess believed that her father would adjust to this change in routine much more quickly than he believed.

Bess took advantage of having the house to herself to once again make certain everything was in order. She laundered some of her underclothing and hung it to dry and rechecked her packing to make certain she had everything she needed. She laid out the personal items she would use in the meantime on top of the other contents of the trunk, and she draped a conservative dark green dress over a chair in her room so that it would be ready for her to put on the following morning. She bathed and washed her hair, surprised that her father hadn't yet returned—but still willing to enjoy the absence of his anger, or perhaps worse, his silent pouting.

It was past supper time when Bess enjoyed the little sandwiches and cakes she'd purchased earlier, along with a soothing cup of chamomile tea that she knew would help her relax. Leaving the kitchen in perfect order, she put the bag from the tea shoppe, which contained her father's supper, in the middle of the table, along with a note. Then she went up to her room to get ready for bed early, intending to read until she became sleepy. She was nearly to the top of the stairs when she heard her father come in. Quietly she slipped into her room and closed the door without a sound, grateful to have avoided any interaction with him at all. Tomorrow morning Mrs. Hubbard would be here early, and Bess felt certain the presence of another person in the house would prevent any further arguing between herself and her father, and the carriage would arrive for her at noon.

Bess read until her eyes felt droopy, but after she'd doused the lamp and settled into bed, her mind swirled with all kinds of senseless worries. What if the carriage *didn't* come for her? What if Lady Buxton had changed her mind and instead sent a message stating they wouldn't need her after all? What if Hugh Buxton was far more difficult than she'd assessed from their brief inter-action and she quickly came to hate working there as much as she'd hated working with her father? The *what ifs* became so deafening inside her mind that Bess began to hum a song she'd sung with the church choir. The music began to suppress her thoughts, and with it, she finally fell asleep, waking to sunlight peeking through the curtains in her room, illuminating the particles of dust in the air. Glancing at the clock, she realized Mrs. Hubbard would be here in less than an hour and Archie would arrive an hour after that.

Bess hurried to put on the green dress she'd chosen for her first day as Hugh Buxton's *nursemaid and nanny,* as her father had dubbed the position. She twisted the full length of her brown hair before efficiently rolling and pinning it to the back of her head. With her bed made, her room tidy, and her trunk ready to go, Bess waited in her room with the door open just enough to be able to hear a knock at the front door downstairs. She didn't want to encounter her father until Mrs. Hubbard had arrived. Thankfully, she only had to wait a few minutes before the expected knock came and Bess rushed down the stairs, thrilled and excited beyond words to know that today she would escape the ridiculous confinement of her life and embark upon new adventures. Like a bird fleeing a gilded cage, she hurried to the door to welcome her replacement. The cage she'd lived in might have been lovely and secure, but it was a cage just the same.

# CHAPTER THREE

## THE PATIENT

WITHIN MINUTES, MRS. HUBBARD HAD made herself at home in the kitchen so easily that if Bess had felt any concerns about this transition, they completely vanished. Bess quickly gave the new housekeeper a tour of the kitchen and laundry where she would do most of her tasks, then Mrs. Hubbard got straight to work cooking breakfast, refusing any assistance from Bess. Bess took the opportunity to retrieve her underclothing, which was now dry—and which she'd forgotten about—and take it upstairs to tuck it down into one side of the contents of her trunk before she closed the trunk and latched it. After sliding it into the hall, she went back downstairs to find her father sitting at his usual place at the table, chatting comfortably with Mrs. Hubbard while she cooked.

"Oh, there you are," Mrs. Hubbard said with a smile toward Bess. "Have a seat, my dear. You must eat a good breakfast."

"Thank you," Bess said and took her chair. "Good morning, Father," she added, nodding toward him while she forced herself to ignore the obvious awkwardness between them.

"Good morning," Jonas responded just before Mrs. Hubbard set a plate in front of both Bess and her father, with sausages still sizzling next to the fried eggs. There were also scones on the table that she'd brought with her, and two flavors of jam along with fresh butter. Bess had already discussed with Mrs. Hubbard how she would be expected to purchase groceries and other household necessities, and the money would be provided. It seemed everything was going perfectly.

"You must join us," Bess said when she realized that Mrs. Hubbard didn't intend to sit down.

"Yes, you must," Jonas said, although Bess sensed he considered the situation awkward.

Mrs. Hubbard insisted that she'd already eaten her breakfast, but Bess wondered if she had picked up on the tension and would simply wait to eat until Bess and her father were finished.

Not a word was spoken at the breakfast table, which made Bess glad to hear a knock at the front door just as she put the last bite of sausage into her mouth. She dabbed her mouth with her napkin and stood, saying, "I'll get that."

Bess answered the door to see Archie there, smiling as if he'd just been given a prestigious honor. They exchanged greetings and she invited him into the parlor where he sat on the edge of a chair, holding his hat in his hands.

"Father," Bess said, going to the doorway of the kitchen. "Please come into the parlor as soon as you're finished. Archie Wilson is here. He's going to be your assistant. There are some things we need to discuss."

Jonas tossed his napkin abruptly to the table, as if that alone could express his displeasure. He silently followed Bess to the parlor, where he was nothing but smiles and kindness to Archie. They all sat down and discussed what would be expected of Archie, and Bess was pleased to note that—just as with Mrs. Hubbard—her father seemed comfortable and relaxed with Archie. She felt confident that the tiny hint of awkwardness would disappear quickly once they became accustomed to the new routine.

Jonas and Archie were still discussing how they would manage seeing to emergencies during odd hours when a message was brought to the door regarding a villager in need of medical attention. Since it wasn't an emergency, Bess took a few minutes to show Archie the medical room just off the kitchen while her father went upstairs to get ready to go out. The little tour didn't take long, since they had already discussed the necessary process of keeping all the instruments clean and the bag stocked, and Bess had written everything down for Archie so that he wouldn't miss any little detail. As an added precaution, she had already shown Mrs. Hubbard the little medical room, pointing out a few basics in case Archie had difficulty finding anything he might need. Before Jonas came back down the stairs, Archie was waiting at the door, holding the doctor's well-equipped bag, which Bess had shoved into his hands.

As Jonas was putting on his coat, Bess handed him his hat and said, "I'll see you tomorrow, Father, when you come to the Abbey."

He looked a little taken aback, as if he needed a few seconds to fully absorb her meaning. For a moment she caught the tiniest glimpse of sadness in his eyes, but it was quickly suffocated by the glint of anger. Oh, how she wished he would allow himself to admit to his sadness! It would have made all the difference! Oh, how she wished he would embrace her, since she was officially leaving home to embark out on her own! But he didn't. He just nodded, saying nothing of good wishes or farewells, and walked out the door, with Archie following behind him, looking as excited to be at his new job as Bess felt regarding the changes that would take place in her own life today.

With her father gone, Bess swallowed any temptation to cry over their unsavory separation. She would see him tomorrow, and surely with time his difficult feelings would dissolve.

Bess was glad to find Mrs. Hubbard now dishing up a plate of breakfast for herself. "So, you fibbed," Bess said to her. "You *didn't* eat earlier."

"I was just being polite," Mrs. Hubbard said. "I know well enough your father doesn't want to be sharing his meals with the housekeeper." She sat down, and Bess decided to sit with her and have another cup of tea. "Don't you worry a bit about me. I'll make certain he has what he needs and that everything is taken care of, and I'll have plenty of time to take care of me in between." Bess smiled, more appreciative than she could say for the reassurance. "And how are you, little missy? You must be excited to begin your new adventure."

"Quite nervous, in truth," Bess admitted, but it was a good kind of nervousness.

Mrs. Hubbard insisted she eat an early lunch and go to the Abbey with a full stomach. Bess agreed with the concept but didn't feel much appetite; still, she was grateful for Mrs. Hubbard's company as she waited for noon to come and the carriage to arrive. A loud knocking at the door occurred at three minutes before twelve and startled Bess, which made Mrs. Hubbard chuckle. Bess opened the door to see Clive smiling expectantly at her, as if he were almost as thrilled as she with this arrangement. She found it interesting that a man so young had been promoted to head butler, but rather than wondering what circumstances might have brought that about, she simply considered what his position meant regarding the level of trust and respect Lady Buxton obviously had for this man. The fact that she had sent him personally to retrieve her was touching.

"Do you have luggage, Miss White?" Clive asked as she glanced over his shoulder to see the magnificent carriage waiting in the street, and a driver seated atop it, reins in hand.

"Um . . ." She had to think. "A trunk at the top of the stairs." She motioned. "I hope it's not too heavy."

"I think I'll be able to manage," Clive said and hurried up the stairs, coming down only moments later with her trunk hoisted onto his shoulder, carrying it as if it weighed nothing.

Clive walked past Bess and out the door. Bess hurried to put on her coat and gloves before she hugged Mrs. Hubbard, who said with confidence, "You'll do wonderfully!"

"Thank you!" Bess said and hurried outside to where Clive was holding the carriage door open for her.

He bowed gallantly with a subtle smirk that made her smile before he took her hand and helped her step inside. He closed the door and she felt the carriage rock slightly as he stepped up onto the box seat to sit beside the driver. As the carriage rolled forward, Bess felt as if she'd slipped into a fairy tale, but she was glad to be able to stop worrying about whether Lady Buxton's offer had all been a dream. It was real; she was leaving home. And she could only pray that all would go well for herself as well as for everyone else who was impacted by this enormous change in her life.

During the brief carriage ride out of the village and over rolling country roads, Bess closed her eyes and breathed deeply, feeling a sensation of freedom. She prayed that she wasn't making a mistake in light all the facets of the situation that were unforeseeable. Reminding herself of this had felt right from the moment Lady Buxton had proposed it, Bess looked out the window of the carriage, now able to see Astoria Abbey in the distance. When she'd come here with her father two days earlier, she never would have imagined this turn of events. That fairy-tale feeling washed over her again, while at the same time she could almost literally hear her father's words in the back of her mind telling her that real life was difficult and often brutal, and she shouldn't fill her head with fanciful things. She'd always found his edict ironic, given that his favorite pastime was reading fiction, and he far preferred the stories with happy endings.

Bess became so caught up in her musings about what the future might bring that she was startled to feel the carriage come to a halt. Only a moment later Clive opened the door and held out a hand to help her step down. "My lady," he said with a hint of humorous drama that made Bess chuckle. She'd barely encountered Clive, but she liked him very much. Given that he was apparently close to Hugh, she wondered if they might have the opportunity to get to know each other better.

Clive opened the door to the house and motioned her inside as he said, "I'll have your trunk taken up to your room. Wait in the parlor to your left, and the lady will be with you shortly."

"Thank you, Clive," Bess said. He smiled and jogged away with an implication that he was either in a hurry or he had a great deal of energy he needed to expend. Maybe both.

Bess walked through the open doors into the same parlor where she and her father had been invited to wait on her previous visit. She sat down and took in the beauty of the room with more interest than she had before. The last time she'd been here, she'd never imagined that she might live in this magnificent home—if only temporarily. She made herself comfortable, certain she'd likely wait a long while; surely the lady of the house was not going to rush down the stairs the moment she was informed of Bess's arrival.

Bess was craning her neck to study a design of gold-leafing on the ceiling when she heard footsteps and looked up to see Lady Buxton enter through the open doorway. Bess erupted to her feet, saying, "Forgive me, my lady. I couldn't help noticing how beautiful the ceiling is; in fact, everything is beautiful."

"Yes," Lady Buxton said, looking up. "Funny you should point that out. I think we are often so preoccupied with what's going on around us that we don't take the time to look up."

Bess wanted to comment on something pleasantly metaphorical in the statement, but the lady added, "Come along, my dear, let me take you to your new room." They walked out of the room side by side. "I know you may be thinking that one of the servants certainly could have made certain you found your way, but I wanted to talk with you anyway. I'm so glad you came; I wondered if you might not."

"I must say I've surprised even myself, but it felt right and . . . I'm very glad to be here."

They started slowly up the grand staircase as if they were in no hurry whatsoever. "Did you have much difficulty in making arrangements for your father's needs?"

"None at all, actually," Bess admitted. "In fact, it worked out so nicely that it's either too good to be true, or it was certainly meant to be."

"I do hope the latter," Lady Buxton said with a smile. "It's been my prayer that everything would work out for you—ever since the idea came to me. I do believe when something is right it has a way of coming together, although not always." She added the last with a deeper thoughtfulness to her tone. "At times when a path is right, everything goes wrong, as if some evil force of the universe wants to keep us from succeeding."

Bess thought about that a moment, loving how comfortable she felt with this woman and how impressed she was with her wisdom and insight. "And how do you tell the difference?" Bess asked.

"By trusting your instincts, my dear," Lady Buxton said with a smile. "And I believe you are very good at that. At least it got you here today."

Bess was overcome by the beauty and elegance of her new room. It had every possible comfort and more, and the windows overlooked a magnificent view of a blanket of green lawn, which merged into the distant woods.

"As soon as you've settled in," Lady Buxton said, "we can go and speak to Hugh about your opinions on his care; I've already spoken with the housekeeper to establish a schedule for those who will be helping him—and you. But adjustments can certainly be made according to your needs."

"I can settle in later," Bess said with confidence. "There is no need for you to wait for me. I'd like to get started right away."

"Very well." Lady Buxton smiled, apparently liking Bess's enthusiasm.

They walked together across the hall to a different room from the sitting room where they had met with Hugh previously. Before Lady Buxton knocked, she said quietly to Bess, "We have established that knocking on the door will alert the male servants if they are assisting Hugh with anything personal—such as bathing and dressing—and they will call out to avoid having anyone enter; although, I believe they lock the doors during such times. If you hear no response you are free to enter uninvited. Hugh most often doesn't have the strength in his voice to call out loudly enough to be heard." Bess nodded to indicate that she understood before the lady said, "You'll become accustomed to the routine very quickly, I think." She then knocked at the door, not loudly enough to wake Hugh if he might be sleeping, but with a sound sufficient to alert any servants in the room, just as she had explained.

"Come in," Bess heard a man call, knowing it couldn't be Hugh because the voice was strong and boisterous.

Lady Buxton opened the door and Bess followed her into the room, which was clearly Hugh's bedroom. Having assisted her father with countless patients who were ailing, Bess was well accustomed to meeting people in their beds, generally looking their worst. She noted that the drapes had been opened wide and the room's large windows admitted a great deal of light.

"This is excellent," Bess whispered to Lady Buxton. "The sunlight is good for him."

"That's what I've always believed," the lady said, and Bess turned her attention to the manservant who was presently putting folded clothing items into a bureau drawer. "This is Lewis. He officially works as Hugh's valet; unofficially they are very good friends, and he will be around a great deal. I hope you won't find him too annoying."

Bess was surprised by that last comment until she realized Lady Buxton had been teasing. Lewis chuckled and nodded politely toward Bess. His build was robust, and he had very little left of the dark hair on his balding head. "Begging your pardon, my lady," Lewis said, tossing a glance toward the bed before he finished his task. "But it's your son here who is known to be severely annoying. I've learned my every bad trait from him."

"Of course you have," the lady said with mild sarcasm and a smile before she motioned toward Bess and added, "This is Elizabeth White. We've already discussed her reasons for being here so there's no need to repeat any of that."

"A pleasure, Miss White," Lewis said, nodding again.

"The pleasure is mine," she said, nodding in return. "But please . . . call me Bess. Everyone does."

"Very well," Lewis said, and Bess's attention turned to the central figure in the room, and the reason for this great magnitude of change in her life. The bed in which Hugh Buxton was propped up by many pillows against the headboard was a work of art, with intricate carvings in the wood, and high posts at each corner. But Hugh didn't look nearly as well as he had only two days ago. He had less color in his face and less sparkle in his eyes. Bess knew that getting right to work meant analyzing his needs and making certain he knew that she was here to see to his health and comfort.

"And how are you feeling today?" she asked, sitting on the edge of the bed without asking permission.

"I assume you want me to be honest," Hugh said with a hint of cynicism. Not only did he look worse, but his mood was far less favorable.

"You must be absolutely honest with me, Hugh," she said. "May I call you Hugh?"

"Calling me anything else would be ridiculous under the circumstances," he said with a subtle raspiness that indicated he was having some mild difficulty breathing.

"I agree," she said. "And I can't do what your mother wishes for me to do while I'm here if you are not completely honest with me. So, let me ask again: How are you feeling today, Hugh?"

"Utterly dreadful," he said. "I broke the rules yesterday and decided to go for a little walk. Apparently, I overdid it and today I'm paying the price."

He looked at her as if he might be expecting a scolding for having *broken the rules*. But Bess knew that one of the most important facets of gaining the trust of a patient was to try and understand how the situation must feel for them, rather than seeing it through the eyes of concerned loved ones, or even as the person being called on to help. She also knew that being kind but firm with a patient was mandatory; in fact, she marveled at how assertive she could be with a patient in contrast to the timidity she'd most often felt with her father.

Bess softened her voice in a way that she hoped Hugh might recognize as an expression of genuine concern when she said, "That must be incredibly frustrating for you, that you can't even go for a little walk without suffering greatly for it." He turned his head more toward her and his eyes showed more intrigue than cynicism. "I can't even imagine how difficult it must be for you to be unable to do the simplest things that everyone around you takes for granted."

"That is exactly right, Bess," he said before he looked at his mother and added firmly, "I believe she's the first person who has ever said such a thing to me. Perhaps you were right, and I was wrong." His eyes shifted to Bess. "Perhaps we *should* keep her."

Bess was a little taken aback by his boldness but had no trouble countering it. "Am I to assume then that you don't want me here?"

"I *didn't,*" Hugh said. "But I do now—if only to have one person around here who doesn't scold me for having the nerve to get out of bed to look out the window."

"We will work together to manage your symptoms and gauge what you are able to do," Bess said, "so that you can enjoy your life as much as possible, and at the same time stay with us as long as possible. Does that sound like a balance we could work to achieve?"

"Yes, I believe it does," Hugh said and smiled slightly, glancing for a moment toward Lewis as if they had some private form of silent communication.

Bess glanced over her shoulder to see Lewis leaning against the bureau with his arms folded over his chest, almost looking smug. She could only guess, but it seemed that Lewis had been highly in favor of having Bess involved in this delicate and difficult situation, but Hugh had been against it—until now. Bess glanced in the other direction to see that Lady Buxton was sitting in a nearby chair. She seemed pleased, but there was no denying the concern in her eyes. Her son was dying, a fact with which Bess needed to try and remain objective. Her father had taught her well that death and dying were a big part of the medical profession, and it was important to maintain a careful emotional distance, even though—as he'd often pointed out—that wasn't always easy when they lived in a community where they knew almost everyone. Bess had no prior personal association with Hugh Buxton, but seeing the concern on his mother's face and the harsh evidence of his failing health, she could already tell she would need to put a great deal of effort into not allowing herself to become emotionally involved.

Bess turned again to look at Hugh and said, "Tell me about your symptoms right now." She discreetly pressed her fingers to his wrist to monitor his pulse while they talked. He glanced for a moment to where she was touching him before he looked back at her face but said nothing. Knowing that people could often have difficulty describing the details of their ailments, she got more specific. "Are you having trouble breathing?"

"Yes," he said.

"Is it worse than what you would consider normal for you?"

"A little."

"Do you feel an awareness of your heart beating?"

"Not right now," he said, "but I often do, especially when I exert any effort . . . like getting dressed or eating, for example." The last held a hint of that cynical bite, but she couldn't blame him. He'd lived his entire life with great limitations, and the symptoms had only gotten steadily worse.

"Are you experiencing any pain right now?" she asked, removing her fingers from his wrist.

"A headache," he said. "Headaches are common; this is worse than usual."

"Does it hurt more at your temples, your forehead, or in the back at the base of the skull?" He looked surprised by the question and she added, "What?"

"No one has ever asked me about that so specifically," he said. "It's worse in the back . . . where you said; but there is some pain at my temples, as well." He let out a lengthy, ragged sigh that expressed his frustration while at the same time indicating that it was difficult for him to take a deep breath.

"I know there's medicine that can help with the pain, but it makes me sleepy and I'm sick to death of sleeping away what little I have left of my life, so I only take the medicine when it's *really* bad."

Bess thought about that for a moment and said, "I might be able to help with that; I know an alternative that might be worth trying. First, may I see your ankles?"

"Feel free," he said, and Bess took that to mean he was modestly dressed beneath the bedcovers. She moved them over just enough to see his lower legs, but she could tell he was wearing a long nightshirt that came below his knees. She could see that his bare ankles and feet were swollen even before she touched them to try and determine how much. "Does that hurt?" she asked.

"No," he said.

"That's a good sign," Bess said. "Have you ever had pain from the swelling?"

"A little sometimes, yes," Hugh responded.

"If that happens again tell me. I might be able to help with that . . . at least a little."

"How glorious," Hugh said, not at all cynical or sarcastic.

"Well," Bess declared, standing up, "I think the first thing we need to address is the headache. Let's see if we can get it to calm down so you can be more comfortable."

"You can do that without medicine?" Hugh asked.

"I can try," she said. "Not every method works for every person, but it's worth trying. The problem is . . ." She glanced around the room, at the bed with Hugh in it, and said, "Lewis, I need Hugh to be able to lie flat on his back, so that I can sit down and reach his neck and head. Do you think you could help him turn the other direction on the bed?"

"I can do that," Lewis declared.

"Are you all right with that, Hugh?" Bess asked, knowing she always needed to allow the patient to have a say in their own care.

"I'll try anything once," he said with a little smirk. "This is the most adventure I've had since . . ."

"You can't remember," Lewis said lightly. "Because your life is boring and we both know it."

"Oh, I *do* remember," Hugh said as Lewis helped him lie the other direction on the bed. "It was when we rented that boat to go down the Thames and you had to do all the rowing."

"That was over a year ago," Lewis declared.

"But it was a lovely adventure," Hugh said dreamily, as if he were relishing the memory.

Bess moved a chair next to the bed so that she was sitting right above Hugh's head. She noted that the bed was so huge his feet didn't even reach the other side.

"Now close your eyes and try to relax," she said, putting her hands beneath his neck. "I know it's difficult for you to breathe deeply, but I want you to focus on your breathing. Take a breath all the way in and let it all the way out as much as you can; just do that over and over and don't think about what I'm doing."

Bess felt a little self-conscious, considering that Lady Buxton and Lewis were watching her with overt curiosity, as if she might perform some magical feat. But she ignored them by closing her eyes so she could focus on weaving her fingers into Hugh's golden curls and gently massaging the tight muscles at the base of his skull. Initially she could feel him resisting, no doubt because the muscles were tender to the touch, and he'd likely never had anyone touch him this way before. "Try to relax," she said in a very soft voice. "Focus on your breathing." Bess felt him making the effort to relax, but she could hear the shallowness of his breaths going in and out. She just kept massaging gently, and with the passing of minutes she felt his head completely relax. Bess's hands continued their work while she did as she asked Hugh to do; she focused on his breathing. She knew that one of the most difficult and apparent symptoms of a failing heart was the difficulty in breathing. There were many other symptoms, but breathing was a constancy in human existence about which most people never had to think. However, for someone like Hugh, he likely had a keen and almost constant awareness of his need to breathe. As minutes passed and she continued to press her fingertips gently against the tight muscles that were surely contributing to his headache, Bess felt him relax even more, and she began to hear a change in his breathing. She could see his chest rising and falling more naturally and with less strain. A few minutes later, she realized he was sleeping.

"I'm going to move my hands now." She whispered, in order to be certain he was asleep. He made no response and she carefully slid her fingers away before she gently eased a pillow beneath his head, glad that doing so hadn't awakened him.

"He's asleep," Bess whispered, turning toward her onlookers.

"That's incredible!" Lewis said in a soft voice that wouldn't wake Hugh. "He's tired all the time but has such trouble going to sleep."

"Then he must be exhausted," Bess said, standing up. "We should let him rest."

Lewis declared he would stay in the room and plopped onto the sofa, picking up a book he'd left there. Lady Buxton put a blanket over Hugh, tucking him in as if he were a young child. Bess whispered to Lewis that she would be just across the hall if he needed her, then she left the room with Lady Buxton following.

"My dear," she said, putting a hand on Bess's arm as soon as she'd closed the bedroom door, "you were wonderful with him. I already feel so grateful to have you here."

Bess felt surprised but reminded herself to be gracious. "Thank you; you're very kind. And I too am grateful to be here. I promise you that I'll do everything I can to help keep him comfortable—just as we discussed."

The lady smiled and said, "I'll let you get settled in. You should find everything you need to freshen up and be comfortable. If Daphne isn't nearby now, she should be showing herself soon. Rely on her as much as you need. Are you hungry, my dear? Should I have something sent up from—"

"Thank you, but I ate before I came. I can wait."

"Very good. Tell Daphne to have tea sent up for you when it's sent up for Hugh and Lewis," Lady Buxton said.

"That will be excellent," Bess replied, and the Lady of Astoria Abbey walked away.

Bess returned to her new room and was glad to now be alone and have the time to just take in these new surroundings and try to acquaint herself with the idea that this was her home for the time being. After just standing in the center of the room to turn and look at the fine furnishings, the lovely drapes and bedcovers, which were coordinated in different shades of blue, Bess had to stand at one of the windows for many minutes and fully absorb the view. She wondered how her father's day was going, and if Mrs. Hubbard or Archie were having any regrets about their new employment. But Bess could do nothing about any of that beyond hoping that in time it would all settle in for all of them, and that perhaps one day her father would forgive her. She knew he was coming here tomorrow and dreaded facing him, but she felt even more sure about her decision now that she was here and believed that she truly *could* help Hugh be more comfortable.

She reflected on their short time together before he'd fallen asleep and felt a little surprised with herself, but also pleased with the way she'd been able to use her knowledge assertively and with kindness, as opposed to mostly being a silent spectator or an extra pair of hands. Her own confidence had already been bolstered by her brief time with Hugh, which eased her nervousness over being able to press forward and do whatever might be required of her.

Bess freshened up and took off her shoes, preferring to be without them when indoors. Stockinged feet were far more comfortable—or leaving them bare if the floors were not too cold. Given the length of her skirt, no one would ever know the difference, and it helped her feel more at home. She opened her trunk and began putting her personal things into the bureau drawers. She was putting her favorite books on top of one of the bedside tables when Daphne arrived and introduced herself. The maid was younger than Bess with a fresh face and slightly crooked teeth that did not diminish the genuine kindness of her smile. Her dark hair had tight curls that could not be hidden, even with the way she had her hair brushed back tightly into a neat bun at the back of her head.

"Let me help you," Daphne offered and took some folded nightgowns out of the trunk. "I'm certain you're capable of unpacking your own things," the maid said, "but it's up to me to see that all of your needs are met, so I should be knowing what you have and where it's put."

Bess felt comfortable enough with Daphne to readily admit, "You should know I've never had a maid. This is a new experience for me in every possible way. I know you have a job to do, but I don't want to be a burden to you or—"

"Come sit down," Daphne said, sitting on a little dark-blue sofa positioned against the wall opposite the bed. She patted the sofa next to herself, and Bess sat down. Daphne proved to be confident for such a young woman when she said, "Lady Buxton has explained to me in detail your reasons for being here, and I can speak on behalf of many who work here when I say that we are grateful she made the decision to employ someone such as yourself who can help with this difficult situation. Lady Buxton made it inescapably clear to me that I was to be on hand to assist you in any and every way. There are other maids who might be here in my place should I have any personal needs to see to, but it is my job to see that *you* are comfortable and have everything you need. Lady Buxton told me that you would not be accustomed to a maid and therefore it might take us some time to adjust, but we will surely do so. She wants you to focus your time and attention on helping her son. It's my job to launder your clothing, keep your living area tidy, and bring you whatever you need from the kitchen. I will be sleeping in the room just on the other side of your sitting room, and if you don't find me there, all you need to do is ring," she motioned toward the pull rope nearby, "and either myself or one of the other maids will come straightaway. I was asked to tell you that you are welcome to join other members of the staff in the kitchen for meals, or they can be brought to you, so you can eat privately, or perhaps with your charge if you would prefer. I'm guessing that each meal might be different, depending on what's taking place; therefore, we will make those decisions one meal at a time." Daphne took a deep breath as if she'd memorized this little speech, which she'd known Bess would likely need to hear. "Now," the maid added, "is there anything you need right now?"

"No, but thank you," Bess said and instinctively reached for Daphne's hand. She looked surprised but pleased. "I'll depend on you to advise me on what is or is not appropriate, which makes me feel much less nervous about being here."

"I'm glad to help in any way."

"Well then," Bess said, looking at the open trunk, "as you said, if you're going to be helping me, you should know where my things are kept, so let's start by getting them put away, and then I'll go check on my patient."

"Very good, miss," Daphne said, and they worked together to put Bess's clothes in the bureau while they chatted casually about the usual mealtimes in the house, and the other maids with whom Daphne worked.

When everything was in order, Daphne declared that she was going down to the kitchen to see that tea was sent up for Bess at the proper time—just as Lady Buxton had suggested. After Daphne left, Bess looked around her room again, feeling strangely at home—especially now that her things had been put away, which made the room feel like her own.

Bess went across the hall to Hugh's room where she'd left him sleeping. She knocked lightly as Lady Buxton had told her to do. Hearing no response, she opened the door and entered quietly to see that Lewis was dozing on the sofa, and Hugh was still asleep, although he'd rolled from his back onto his side—even though he was still lying sideways on the bed. She could hear him breathing and considered the sound of it reassuring, most especially since his breaths seemed less strained than earlier.

Bess quietly adjusted the position of the soft chair, which had been left near the bed. She had sat in it earlier while massaging Hugh's neck. Now she just wanted to sit where she could watch Hugh sleep. She made herself comfortable and began to read from the book she'd brought with her. But she found it difficult to focus on her reading when her mind kept reliving the whirlwind that had carried her through the last two days to bring her here.

When she kept having to force herself to not worry about her father or how he might be feeling toward her, she turned her attention to her reason for being here. In sleep, Hugh Buxton looked younger, somehow. She could already tell it would be difficult to keep herself from becoming emotionally involved with the situation; how could she not be affected by the fact that a man so young was going to die? For all she knew, her job could be over within a few weeks. Lady Buxton and her household would be left to grieve Hugh's death, and Bess might end up right back where she'd started—working night and day to keep her father pleased.

No, Bess thought with certainty. She wouldn't go back to that. Even if she ended up returning home, she would either care for the household or be his assistant. Not both. Her very brief exposure to Lady Buxton had strengthened her confidence a great deal regarding her own life and how she lived it. For the first time in a long while, the shield of light she tried to imagine around herself felt stronger and more resilient. She already felt as if something inside herself was healing from the wounds her father had inadvertently inflicted upon her.

Watching Hugh sleep, Bess considered how all of this must seem to him. He'd never lived a normal life, and soon it would come to an abrupt halt. Bess wondered how it might feel to know that death was imminent. She would cry if she thought about it too deeply, therefore she chose not to. Surely she could do her job and do it well without crossing emotional boundaries that would only make this more difficult.

Bess was startled by a sound in the room, then remembered that Lewis had been napping on the sofa. She turned to see him stand up and stretch. They traded a nod and a smile in acknowledgment before he whispered, "Will you be all right here if I leave for a short while?"

"Of course," she whispered back and tipped her head toward the bell pull. "I'll ring if I need anything."

He nodded again and left the room as it occurred to Bess that Daphne was likely right across the hall; it would surely be rare that Bess would be left completely alone in charge of Hugh's care. He'd been born into great privilege, which meant he would die with every possible comfort and no need unmet. Bess had seen much the opposite as she'd followed her father about on his medical visits. She wondered why the world was so divided by class and wealth, but she couldn't deny that Lady Buxton and her son had thus far proven to be very kind people.

Bess forced herself to focus on the book she was reading, realizing she could not spend the forthcoming weeks—or months—just watching Hugh while he rested. She had to establish good habits and proper balance from the beginning. After rereading the same paragraph three times, she finally managed to become engaged in what she was reading and move forward. Only a few minutes later she heard Hugh say, "Am I to find you sitting at my bedside for the duration of my life?"

Bess looked up from her book, noting how he stared at her with brilliant green eyes. The angle of the sun in the room showed their color more than she'd been able to see before. Responding to the mild teasing tone in his voice, she replied, "Do you not think I have other things to do with myself, sir?"

"I would hope," he said.

"How do you feel?" Bess asked, leaning forward to press her fingers lightly against his throat to check his pulse, which was a little faster than it should be, but she already knew it was normal for him. His heart needed to pump more quickly to try and compensate for its weakness.

"Surprised," he said; it certainly wasn't an answer she'd expected to hear.

"How so?"

"That I slept, that I feel somewhat rested. And especially that my head doesn't hurt. What kind of magic did you perform on me?"

"Hardly magic," Bess said and leaned back in her chair the same moment he adjusted his head on the pillow so that they were facing each other more directly. "It's just a matter of knowing that tight muscles at certain pressure points can cause pain."

"Did you learn that from your father?" he asked.

"Actually, no," she admitted. "I learned it from an elderly woman with whom I sang in the church choir. Her husband had suffered many years with terrible headaches that no doctor was able to remedy. She had taken it upon herself many years ago to seek out unconventional possibilities for alleviating her husband's pain, and she spent some time in London with a relative there while she received some training from a man who called himself an alternative healer. Her husband was never without headaches while he lived, but what she learned helped lower his pain levels a great deal and made it possible for him to function and lead a somewhat normal life. After she told me this story, I asked her if she would teach me. Truthfully, I had been suffering from some headaches myself. She told me I was carrying too many burdens, and all the tension from them had gathered in my neck. She taught me as she worked on me, and I too found great relief. I had hoped that my father would be more open to the idea of my being able to use what I'd learned to help his patients find relief from certain kinds of pain. He wasn't opposed to it, but he found it strange and only allowed me to use such methods a few times when nothing else was working. It doesn't always make a difference, but I'm *very* glad it helped you."

"I'm glad of it too," he said. "For that reason alone, I'm already glad you're here."

Bess glanced away, then reminded herself not to be timid *or* intimidated. She looked at him again and said, "If I may speak candidly, I'm relieved that you're glad. I feared you might be opposed to my assistance—since I knew that my being here was your mother's idea."

"My mother and I don't always see eye-to-eye, but generally she's very perceptive of my needs. I fear she's spoiled me terribly."

"I dare say," Bess said thoughtfully, "she's likely tried to make up for things in your life that you've not been able to do. Perhaps you deserve spoiling."

"Perhaps?" he repeated with a chuckle.

"I don't know you well enough yet to know whether or not your being spoiled has adversely affected your character."

He chuckled again, and she purposely widened her eyes to silently question his reasons. "I like your directness, Miss White," he said. "And I like the sound of your voice. It's soothing. May I admit that there are a couple of maids whose voices only somehow add to the pain in my head when I hear them in the room talking?"

"You may admit to anything you like," she said. "I will keep your confidence and I promise to always be honest and direct if you promise to do the same. But you must call me Bess. We will not be constrained by any kind of formality, since we will be seeing far too much of each other for that. As for my voice, I'm glad you like the sound of it because I certainly can't change it, and your mother said that one of my duties would be to read to you, that you enjoy reading but it's difficult for you. I doubt I could ever consider reading—whether silently or aloud—any kind of duty; rather it is a privilege. I love to read."

"Then we are off to a good start in many respects," Hugh said.

Bess sensed that he was less relaxed just before he added, "I need to get up and . . . well, is Lewis or Clive nearby or—"

"I'm right here," Lewis said, walking through the open doorway with a large tray containing everything required for a pleasant tea. Bess knew from what Hugh had said that he needed help with something personal. And even though Bess had been exposed to many personal things in her life, since it was simply a part of treating patients, she was glad that either Lewis or Clive would be on hand to help see to such things. Hugh couldn't have been resting for as long as he had without the need to relieve himself, and Bess felt no embarrassment or discomfort when Lewis set down the tea tray and then joked with Hugh about how his favorite aspect of their being friends was the privilege of helping him back and forth to the privy, the door to which was not far from Hugh's bed.

"Well, I'm glad you enjoy the privilege," Bess said to Lewis, already feeling like they were friends. They were united in the cause of caring for Hugh, and that had already given them much in common. But she felt comfortable with Lewis, and she could tell that Hugh did as well. "Because I certainly don't want to do it."

"Then we're all happy with the arrangement," Hugh said as Lewis helped Hugh sit up and get his feet to the floor. He then held to Hugh's arms to help him stand in a way that was obviously well-practiced. Lewis grabbed a dressing gown that had been hanging over the foot of the bed and helped Hugh put it on, even though the nightshirt he wore covered him from his neck to his knees. Once Hugh was on his feet he was able to walk slowly to the privy, but Lewis remained close by his side, which made Bess wonder how common it was for Hugh to have dizzy spells or feel faint.

While the men were absent, Bess set out the teacups on a lovely round table near one of the room's large windows. She sat down on one of the comfortable chairs surrounding the table and poured herself a cup of tea and added the perfect amount of milk and sugar before she held the cup in her hands to absorb its warmth until the tea cooled enough for her to be able to drink it. She took in the view out the window for only a moment before the men appeared and came to the table.

"Ah, a woman's touch," Lewis said when he saw the way Bess had arranged the teacups and the plates of little sandwiches and dainty cakes that had been sent up from the kitchen. Bess smiled at him and took a careful sip of her tea only to gauge that it was still too hot.

"Lewis," Hugh said as soon as he was seated, "my feet are cold. Could you—"

"Of course," Lewis said and quickly retrieved a pair of thick, soft stockings from a bureau drawer. He went down on one knee to help put them on Hugh's feet.

"Thank you," Hugh said, and Lewis was seated. To Bess, he said, "Given the situation, you should know how much I detest needing help with every silly, stupid thing."

"Oh, I think you secretly enjoy it," Lewis teased as Bess poured tea into the other cups.

"Yes, of course I do," Hugh said with a sarcasm that seemed humorous, but Bess sensed an undertone of bitterness. And she couldn't blame him. Changing the subject seemed like a good idea, or perhaps stating it more accurately, steering the subject in a different direction might elicit more humor.

"I, for one, am determined to enjoy this lovely tea that I did *not* have to make myself. It's a luxury for me to *not* have to do every silly, stupid thing. So, if the two of you will stop bickering, perhaps I could relish the experience."

Both men chuckled, which she believed was a good sign. It was evident that Hugh had no trouble admitting honestly to his feelings about his circumstances, and it was equally evident that he was most comfortable dealing with anything awkward or difficult by reverting to sarcasm or humor. Bess was more than all right with that. Her father had never appreciated Bess's sense of humor; he'd called it socially inappropriate and annoying. So, Bess had learned to hold back such comments when they came to her mind—at least when she was with her father. During her rare visits with friends she'd made at church, she had loved the way she could make them laugh over trivial and insignificant comments. Sitting there with a warm cup of tea cradled in her hands, Bess thought of what her patient had said about how he was feeling when he'd awakened. *Surprised.* That was how she felt now. She'd only been here a few hours and she already felt more comfortable and more like herself than she had since her mother's death.

Suddenly feeling hungry, she asked Lewis to pass the cucumber sandwiches. As she bit into her second one, she caught a subtle smile across the table from Hugh. The fact that he seemed comfortable with her presence also surprised her. She had expected it to take longer for them to establish a rapport. But here they sat sharing tea as if they'd done so a hundred times. She noted that he didn't have much appetite, but from what she knew, that was normal for his condition. Instead of expressing any concern for how little he ate, she joked about how glad she was that she could eat *his* portion of the cakes and sandwiches, which made both men laugh.

"Did they not feed you where you came from?" Hugh asked, smirking pleasantly at her as she sank her teeth into a little cake with sugar icing.

"I was properly fed," she declared with a smile after she had chewed and swallowed her cake. "Although I confess I was somewhat nervous about coming here, so I might not have eaten much prior to my leaving home."

"Now, why on earth would you be nervous?" Hugh asked, leaning back in his chair.

"Why?" Lewis countered with feigned astonishment. "Surely she's heard of your reputation. Who would want to work day and night for a grumpy and cantankerous bloke like you?"

Hugh chuckled and said to Lewis, "Have you ever considered that I might be grumpy and cantankerous because I've only had you and Clive to take care of me?" He smiled at Bess. "I dare say the scenery around here has improved immensely, not to mention the mood. You're far more annoying than Bess here, and you're not much to look at."

"Well, the same to you," Lewis said, pretending to be insulted. Bess laughed softly, which made it easier to cover her mild embarrassment over Hugh's overt compliments. She was simply glad that he felt comfortable with her—and she with him. She wanted to go seek out Lady Buxton right now and hug the woman for giving her this opportunity. Great difficulties lay ahead, but if there were moments such as this to balance them out, Bess felt certain she would very much enjoy caring for Hugh Buxton.

# CHAPTER FOUR

## A WOMAN'S TOUCH

THAT EVENING, WITH DAPHNE'S ENCOURAGEMENT, Bess made certain all was well with Hugh before she left him in Clive's care and went with Daphne down to the kitchen where she met many members of the household staff and shared supper with them. Soon after tea, Clive had come to take over the job of remaining near Hugh, and Lewis had left. Bess knew that she needed to be careful not to insert herself too much into Hugh's routine and to allow things to continue as usual before she had come to Astoria Abbey. Clive had teased her a little as he helped Hugh get comfortable in his bed with many pillows behind him, stacked and situated against the headboard just so. Bess liked both Clive and Lewis, which she considered a blessing given that she would have to work with them a great deal. But there was something endearing and intriguing about Clive that made her want to get to know him better. He frequently winked and smiled at her, as if he either enjoyed teasing her, or he wanted her to know that he enjoyed her company. Perhaps both. She looked forward to the opportunity to spend more time with him.

In the kitchen with Daphne, Bess very much enjoyed her meal and complimented the cook and her staff on their excellent culinary skills, which seemed to please them. Everyone was kind and respectful to her, and it was obvious they had all known about her reasons for being hired—and in fact it seemed they knew practically everything about her. She had clearly been gossiped about in the household—but not in any derogatory way; everyone was well acquainted with Hugh Buxton's tragic health condition and how deeply it had impacted his mother. It was easy for Bess to tell which of the servants were more personally involved with the situation and therefore more somber when discussing it; and there were others that worked in the huge household—or in its accompanying stables and gardens—who had probably never even met Hugh. Bess felt slightly awkward at the way some of the other servants treated her with a deference that was difficult to define. Thinking about it while she ate and mostly just listened to the conversations taking place, she realized that her personal association with Hugh Buxton had put her at a level that seemed among the highest of an unofficial hierarchy within the house. The very idea felt strange, but Bess focused on enjoying her meal and trying to keep track of people's names. She feared she wouldn't remember any of their names by tomorrow, but with time she would be able to become better acquainted with these people, which was something she looked forward to.

Bess was savoring her last bite of dessert when a maid who had eaten her supper on an earlier shift with another group of servants came to the kitchen to tell Bess that Lady Buxton wished to speak with her when she had finished eating.

"Oh, I'm finished," Bess said and came to her feet. She paused a moment to nod politely and say, "It was a pleasure meeting all of you. I hope you'll be patient with me as I try to learn your names and become acquainted with the routine of the household. You've all been very kind." Some nods and smiles and pleasant murmurs came in response before Bess looked directly at the cook and added, "It was a lovely meal. Thank you."

"A pleasure, miss," the cook said, and Bess wished she could remember her name. She thought for just a moment of Mrs. Hubbard feeding her father his supper. Jonas would eat alone, and after Mrs. Hubbard had cleaned up the kitchen she would leave for the night. Bess felt a twinge of missing her father—or perhaps more accurately it was her habitual feeling of being concerned over his every need. Within a second, however, she reminded herself that he would be fine, and she would see him tomorrow. She dreaded his coming, certain he would make it clear he was still upset with her. But that was something to think about tomorrow.

Bess followed the maid—whose name she did not know—up the back staircase and through a maze of hallways and other steps going up or down, here and there. The maid barely responded to a polite comment Bess made, seeming to indicate that she preferred not to talk; so Bess remained quiet while she became utterly lost and hoped she wouldn't have to find her way back to her rooms on her own.

"The lady is waiting for you," the maid said as they finally stopped at a door that had been left partially open.

"Thank you," Bess said, and the maid hurried away as if she had something very important to do.

Bess took a deep breath and knocked lightly at the door, even though it wasn't closed.

"Come in, my dear," she heard Lady Buxton call.

Bess entered to see that it was an elaborate sitting room with red velvet drapes that had been drawn closed against the darkness outside. Everything in the room was either red or white, including Lady Buxton who was wearing an elegant red dressing gown and whose silvery white hair had been brushed out and hung around her shoulders. Bess noted that her hair was thick and quite lovely for a woman her age. She wanted to compliment her but felt it might be inappropriate.

"You wanted to see me?" Bess asked.

"Yes, dear," the lady smiled. "Close the door and come sit down." She motioned to a chair very near the chaise where she was relaxed with her feet up.

Bess did as she was asked and couldn't keep herself from saying, "You look very tired, my lady. Are you feeling well?"

"Oh, I'm fine," she said with a tiny hint of laughter. "I confess that I haven't been sleeping well since we returned from London. Perhaps I had become accustomed to the noise of the city, or maybe it's simply the fact that our decision to come back was based upon accepting that nothing more can be done to extend Hugh's life." She sighed deeply and leaned her head back, smiling toward Bess, although her smile appeared somewhat forced. "But I have a feeling I'll sleep better tonight."

"Why is that?" Bess asked.

"Because *you* are here, my dear," the lady said with a more natural smile. "Lewis and Clive both do well at caring for Hugh and helping him in every way, but they do not have the skills to be able to assess his condition, nor the means to help him in that regard." Bess was surprised by the way the lady held out a hand toward Bess, who took it and felt the older woman squeeze gently as if they were dear friends. "May I be candid with you, my dear?"

"Of course," Bess said, deeply earnest.

"Your being here has already given me much more peace of mind and it has eased a great deal of my guilt." A subtle quivering in her voice accompanied the gathering of moisture in her eyes.

"Guilt?" Bess echoed gently. "I know that you love your son very much. Why should you feel any kind of guilt?"

"I *do* love him, of course. And I've tried to devote myself to moving heaven and earth on his behalf. But there is one thing that I know I should do more, and yet I have such a difficult time being able to even . . ." Her words faded as she hung her head, and Bess knew she was crying, however ladylike she was striving to be.

"Oh, my lady!" Bess said, scooting to the edge of her seat so that she could be a little closer while she squeezed Lady Buxton's hand more tightly. "I hope you know that you can trust me; I would never betray your confidence . . . *if* you need to talk about this. Losing a loved one is a complicated matter when it comes to the feelings we experience. I dare say you have held a great deal of grief throughout Hugh's entire life." As an afterthought she added, "He told me it was all right to call him by his given name. I hope it's not inappropriate to refer to him that way with you."

"No, of course not," the lady said, pressing a handkerchief beneath her nose as she lifted her head. "In fact, I would far prefer that you call *me* by my given name when it is just the two of us, or when we are only with Hugh. As we tread together into the valley of death, I detest the idea of any formality between us."

"Whatever you wish," Bess said.

"Please call me Agatha. I don't think a single person in the world calls me by my given name anymore. I would find it refreshing."

"Do you not have any friends?" Bess asked. "No one with whom you share a comfortable relationship?"

"Not anymore," Agatha said, and Bess sensed this woman's need to unburden herself. Bess knew well that loved ones of suffering patients often turned to those caring for the patient to share their grief and personal feelings. Holding someone's hand and listening to them cry and talk about their grief was something Bess had done more times than she could ever count. She had often wondered if that might have been one of the biggest reasons why her father had always wanted to have her accompany him, because it was an aspect of his profession that he preferred to avoid. Avoiding anything personal or emotional had become his creed ever since Bess's mother had died. Thankfully, Bess knew that Archie was kind and compassionate and he would do well with such things.

In that moment, Bess was grateful for her experience, but she'd never before tried to console someone of such a high social ranking. She reminded herself that social class and wealth were no protection when it came to life and death and the accompanying association with grief and sorrow.

"When Hugh's father was alive," Agatha went on, "we were very much united in doing all we could to give Hugh every opportunity to enjoy life as much as possible, and we were always vigilant about his medical care. We were able to talk privately about our fears and concerns."

"It sounds as if you had a very good marriage," Bess said.

"Not perfect, certainly," Agatha said with a sad smile and faraway eyes. "But very good, yes. My father was a difficult man, much like *your* father, perhaps." This gave Bess some insight into Agatha's wisdom and perception regarding Bess's situation. "And I was very blessed to find a husband who was quite the opposite; he was a kind and tender man." She sighed and went on. "Through the years I've had a few friends, ladies with whom I would get together regularly for tea or to play cards, and they were kind and sympathetic about the situation with my son. One of those ladies has passed on, and . . . well . . . the others have just gradually disappeared."

"Disappeared?" Bess countered, not certain what she meant.

"My lengthy stays in London were not conducive to maintaining ongoing friendships, I suppose—or at least that seems to be the excuse I was given. I believe it's more accurate that these ladies grew weary of the ongoing fact that I have a son afflicted with a terminal illness." Sounding mildly angry she added, "As if I myself might not have grown weary of the fact and might not be grateful for some concern and support from my friends."

Bess's heart swelled with compassion and sorrow for this woman who was tearfully admitting to a near stranger that she had lost her husband and her friends; the underlying message was evident—she was not only lonely, but she also felt all alone. Despite being in a house filled with servants, her social status likely made it difficult if not impossible for her to confide in those who worked for her. But Bess's position was unique, and somehow it had made Agatha comfortable enough to share her deepest feelings.

Bess took only a long moment to consider what she'd just heard. Agatha's husband had died, which had surely caused her a great deal of grief. But he had not *chosen* to leave her. However, Agatha's supposed friends had separated themselves from the discomfort of the most difficult and central point of Agatha's life. The very idea made Bess want to meet these ladies and tell them exactly what she thought about *that!* Of course, such an idea was absurd. All she could do was try and help this sweet woman deal with the grief of the present situation. And with any luck she would be able to find the right words to assuage her sorrow—if only for the moment.

"Agatha," Bess said gently, "I'm so sorry. It's been my experience that some people are very uncomfortable with death. It's almost as if people start thinking that they don't know how they would ever cope if the same thing happened to them, and by being too close to the situation, they become infected with some strange kind of fear, which makes them want to keep their distance." Agatha nodded as if that made sense to her. "Nevertheless," Bess went on, "it doesn't change the fact that no woman—or man, for that matter—should be left to face life's challenges alone, and I'm so sorry that you've been doing so. The burden upon your shoulders must feel very heavy."

Agatha nodded again more vehemently but was overtaken by a sudden rush of emotion and pressed her handkerchief over her mouth, unable to speak. Bess hoped she wasn't being too forward when she moved to sit on the edge of the chaise where she put her arms around the Lady of Astoria Abbey as if she were no different than the mother of a butcher or a blacksmith who was losing her son to death and feeling very alone in the world. Agatha wrapped her arms around Bess and wept, and Bess just held her, feeling a little teary herself. She never would have anticipated any such interaction with Lady Buxton, but if her being here could help in *this* way, then she felt even more fulfilled. She'd not even been here a day, and she already found it difficult to remember what her life had been like before she'd found herself intimately at the heart of the Buxton family.

Agatha eased away and wiped her face with her handkerchief, saying, "Oh, forgive me, my dear. I should not allow myself to be such a burden to you. Listening to me cry and complain is not any part of your occupation here."

"On the contrary," Bess said, "I learned long ago that treating someone with a serious illness always means being involved with those who care for that person. I want to be a support to you as well as to your son. I consider it a privilege that you feel comfortable enough to share your burdens with me, and of course I will keep anything that passes between us in complete confidence."

"You are so kind, my dear," Agatha said with a smile that implied she might feel a little better after having had a good cry. "I knew you would do much good here, but still I never anticipated just how much."

"I've not yet even slept one night in this house," Bess said with a little laugh that she hoped would lighten the mood.

"Still, I am amazed with all I observed today as you spoke with Hugh, and the way you helped ease his headache and helped him relax enough to go to sleep. You are truly gifted, my dear! That's why I asked for you to come and speak with me. I simply wanted to express my appreciation for your willingness to be here, and . . . to get back to the point where I started . . . to let you know that you have already given me more peace of mind and you have helped ease my guilt."

"And again, I'm wondering what on earth you would have to feel guilty about," Bess said, now more comfortable with speaking her mind and not holding back.

"I should spend more time with him," Agatha admitted. "I don't have your medical expertise, of course. But I told you that I would like you to read with him and keep him company. I'm his mother; I should be doing that. I check in on him periodically each day, and we share an honest and sincere relationship, but I have difficulty spending too much time with him. I've talked to him about it, because I don't want him to feel like my not being there is any indication of my feelings for him. I love him with all my heart and soul—which I suppose is the very reason it's so difficult to see him struggle to do even the simplest things. I'm so grateful that he's stayed alive many more years than we anticipated, although . . ." Agatha looked down and pressed a hand to her forehead. "I don't know if I can admit this out loud."

"It's up to you what you choose to tell me," Bess said. "But as I told you, I will keep our conversations in complete confidence, and . . . may I say that we all have thoughts and feelings that might sound strange or perhaps . . . inappropriate to others. It's my belief that we should allow ourselves to be human, and it's good to have a safe place to admit to our most human feelings."

Agatha looked at Bess as if to silently determine whether she could truly feel safe enough to admit to her most difficult feelings. Instinctively, Bess believed that if *she* shared something from her own heart it might help Agatha feel more comfortable. She squeezed the older woman's hand as if to remind her that she was not alone. "You surmised my situation prior to my coming here quite accurately; your insight is rather remarkable. I felt so trapped by my father's expectations of me. I love my father, Agatha. For years I have wanted nothing more than to have him express his love for me, or even some appreciation for all that I did for him. But he never has. I have always tried to give him the benefit of the doubt and attribute his behavior to the grief of losing my mother. But that was years ago. He lost his wife, but I lost my mother—and what he never realized was that I lost my father too. Physically he was there, always expecting me to do every task my mother had done and perhaps more. But he was never *there* for me, and there were many times when I cried myself to sleep, secretly wishing that *he* had died instead of my mother." Bess took in a ragged breath and chuckled uncomfortably. Her intent to share something personal had gone far deeper than she'd anticipated; the words had just seemed to come out of their own volition once she'd gotten started. "Forgive me," Bess said, "I fear I've gotten carried away and admitted too much, although . . ." she hesitated, realizing now that she'd said what she had, there was no taking it back. Therefore, she was better off to simply press forward. "I cannot deny the truth in what I just told you. I don't think that makes me a bad person; I'm only human. But I have often felt guilty for entertaining such thoughts."

"I believe such thoughts are completely understandable," Agatha said. "I'm *glad* you told me. I confess it does make it easier to admit aloud that there are times I feel so weary of living with my constant fears and concerns about Hugh, that I wonder if it would have been easier if he'd died many years ago—as doctors had initially predicted. And yet, in the light of day, I'm so grateful for every day we've had together. Still, in my weariness I often just feel . . . exhausted. I've had trouble sleeping at night because I worry about him, and then I nap too much during the day and that makes it even more difficult to sleep at night. And . . . all things together . . . I just find it difficult to sit with him for too long. I get strangely restless." She took a deep breath as if through her confession she'd forgotten to breathe at all. "As I said, I've talked to Hugh about how I find it difficult to spend much time with him, and he understands—or at least he tries. He would never judge me or be upset with me over such a thing—or *anything*. He's a kind soul. But that doesn't mean he might not be secretly thinking that he would prefer to have his mother's company more frequently." Again, she took a deep breath. "What I'm trying to say, my dear, is that your being here and keeping him company—as well as remaining aware of his medical needs—has already helped me feel less guilty. Lewis and Clive are good friends to Hugh, and they are all very comfortable with doing whatever is required to help care for him. But . . . I just don't believe they can give Hugh the . . . well . . ." She tipped her head thoughtfully. "A man in his situation needs some tender-ness . . . some . . . gentleness . . . that simply isn't present in the teasing and practicality he shares with his friends." Agatha smiled at Bess and seemed to be declaring the point at which she'd been trying to arrive. "He needs a woman's touch, my dear. And he needs more than his mother can give him.

That's what I wanted you to know, and from what I observed earlier, you are *exactly* what he needs."

"You're very kind," Bess said. "I hope I can continue to be able to help him in the best possible ways through what lies ahead."

"I have no concerns about that," Agatha said. "And you've been so very kind to me. Thank you, my dear, for everything. I'm certain you must be tired; it's been a big day for you."

"I must admit it's strange now to think that my day began at home with my father, and now I'm here; in some ways it's difficult to imagine how things were earlier today."

"I hope that means you feel comfortable here already," Agatha said.

"I do, yes. You've arranged everything very well. Thank you."

"A pleasure, my dear," Agatha said and stood, prompting Bess to do the same. She was surprised when Agatha kissed her cheek and gave her some semblance of a brief hug. Bess just received the momentary display of affection and smiled at this woman with whom she'd so quickly come to feel close. She hoped their relationship would continue to evolve in a positive way. It was evident that Agatha needed friendship, but Bess couldn't deny that she needed the same. She never would have imagined the possibility of becoming friends with the Lady of Astoria Abbey, but it seemed to be happening, and she could do nothing but count her blessings.

"I'm going to check on Hugh," Bess said, "and make certain all is well before I settle in for the night."

"If there's anything you need, don't hesitate to call on Daphne and—"

"Everything is perfectly taken care of," Bess assured Agatha, putting a hand on her arm. Agatha smiled and nodded.

"Perhaps I will see you at lunch; I always share lunch with Hugh in his room. It would be lovely if you'd join us."

"Thank you, I'd like that," Bess said, certain it would take a few days to work out a routine. She thought for a moment about the fact that her father was coming tomorrow and felt a little wave of nausea, but quickly pushed the thought away, and the nausea receded along with it.

As Bess took hold of the door handle to leave, she turned and said, "You know where to find me . . . should you ever need to talk."

"Thank you, my dear; I believe I may take you up on that offer."

Bess nodded, thinking it would be better to not get overly sentimental in that moment. Then a thought occurred to her and she laughed softly.

"I just realized that a maid brought me here and I have absolutely no idea how to find my way to my own room."

"Of course." Agatha laughed as well. "I can't tell you how lost I used to get when I first came here as a bride. Eve will be nearby, and she can help you."

Agatha knocked at a door that apparently went into an adjacent bedroom that was not her own. A middle-aged maid with graying blonde hair opened the door almost immediately, as if she'd been waiting to be called upon.

"My lady?" the maid said with an expectancy that implied she would walk through fire if the lady asked it of her.

"Bess, this is Eve, my maid of many years. She will take you where you need to go." Agatha looked more at Eve and added, "Bess is the companion for Hugh that I told you about . . . who will be helping him."

"A pleasure," Eve said, dipping quickly into a slight curtsy.

"The pleasure is mine," Bess said.

Agatha then said to Eve, "Would you guide Bess to her rooms, which are across the hall from Hugh's. She is understandably lost in this big old house."

"We've all been through *that*," Eve said with a little laugh. "I would be glad to. An evening walk will do me good."

By the way Eve said it, Bess felt as if their trek was being compared to strolling for more than a mile in the gardens. As she walked with Eve through a maze of stairs and hallways, Bess began to realize the comparison was not inaccurate. They shared polite conversation about the basic information of each other's lives, along with a few comments about the tragedy of Hugh's situation and how difficult it was for Agatha. Bess came to know that Eve had been Agatha's maid from her youth and had come to Astoria Abbey with her when Agatha had married Hugh's father. They were therefore very close, and yet Bess wondered if there was some reason why Agatha didn't feel close enough to Eve to really share her deepest emotions. Perhaps their relationship simply wasn't like that. Bess felt certain that with time she would be able to get a better feel for such things.

Bess felt relieved to turn down a hall and recognize it as being where she now lived. The paintings on the wall and a handful of elegant chairs distinguished it from other hallways.

"Thank you, Eve," Bess said. "I know where I am now."

"Have a good night, miss," Eve said.

"And you," Bess replied before the maid hurried away.

Bess went to her own room and found everything necessary for her to freshen up, which she quickly did before going across the hall to check on

Hugh. She knocked lightly at the bedroom door and heard Clive call for her to come in. She entered to see Hugh sitting at the table where they had shared tea earlier. He had a small blanket over his lap, the same one that had been there when she'd come here two days ago with her father. The very idea felt so strange; so much had changed so quickly.

Hugh and Clive were playing a game of chess, but both men smiled at her as she approached and looked at the board to see who might have the advantage. "It doesn't look good for you, Clive," she said lightly.

"You play?" Hugh asked, sounding surprised.

"A little," Bess said. "I'm not very good, but it's one of the few things I did with my father outside of work—although it happened rarely because I was very busy."

"Hence the reason for your not being very good?" Clive asked lightly. "Perhaps you need more practice."

"Perhaps I do," Bess said and sat down without waiting to be invited. She needed to make herself a comfortable part of Hugh's life and routine, and she sensed nothing in either of these men to indicate they were *not* comfortable with her being there.

Bess observed the game, occasionally teasing both Hugh and Clive about the moves they were making. Clive ended up winning and declared to Bess, "Your prediction indicates just how much practice you need."

"Fair enough," Bess said.

"And you," Clive pointed comically at Hugh, "owe me a great deal of money."

"So I do," Hugh said, although a few minutes later—after they'd continued to banter—Bess realized that the reference to money was only a joke and they never actually placed bets on their games.

"This is all very amusing," Bess said with a light sarcasm that made the men chuckle, "but I need to see how our patient is doing before I am off to bed." She looked at Clive and added, "You'll be staying with him tonight?"

"It's my turn," Clive said proudly as if he found the idea of sleeping on the sofa to be close by for Hugh's benefit as nothing short of a privilege and an honor.

"If you have any concerns in the night, just knock on my door loudly enough to wake me and I'll come straightaway."

"I confess that I'm glad for that option," Clive said more seriously. "He's scared me a few times; it will be nice to have you nearby—you and your medical expertise."

"There's a great deal I do *not* know," Bess said, "but I hope to be useful."

"No worries there," Hugh said with a warm smile.

Clive said to Hugh more lightly, "I don't want you to die on *my* watch."

"Well, I'll do my best to time my demise to your convenience," Hugh countered in the same joking manner.

Bess didn't find it at all funny, but she realized that these men had learned to joke about it as a way of coping with the inevitability of Hugh's death. And there was surely nothing wrong with that, she concluded; she needed to keep up her own good attitude and not become too somber or macabre in her interactions with Hugh and those who comprised his closest circle.

"I'll get everything prepared for His Majesty to go to bed," Clive said with his typical sarcasm as he winked at Bess and proceeded to straighten Hugh's bed, which was rumpled and disheveled.

"How are you feeling?" Bess asked Hugh.

"Truthfully, a little better than usual for this time of day. Usually I'm overcome with exhaustion by this hour, but perhaps the nap helped."

"Very good. We must put an effort into making certain you get a good nap every day."

"If that means having you perform your magic every day as you did earlier, I am in complete agreement." He said it with a smile and Bess smiled back, feeling deeply grateful that she had so quickly become comfortable with her patient—and he with her.

"I'm happy to do whatever will help make you comfortable," she said, then squatted down beside where he was sitting. "I'm going to check your ankles for swelling," she said and pushed his stockings down slightly to note that there was some swelling, but it wasn't excessive.

"Oh," she said, standing up, "I'll be right back; I forgot something."

While Bess could hear sounds of Clive in the adjoining room that indicated he was straightening the privy and preparing what Hugh would need to get ready for bed, Bess retrieved from one of the drawers of her new bureau a medical instrument that she'd taken from her father's supply. He would notice it gone and know she had taken it, but he wouldn't miss it, given that he had two others. But she needed it to *truly* be able to best evaluate Hugh's condition. When she returned to his room he noticed what she was holding and said, "Ah! The stethoscope. Every doctor in London I went to had one and made a point of telling me how much easier it made being able to hear the function of the heart and lungs."

"That's exactly right," Bess said. "My father owns a few of them for that very reason. We use them in practically every examination, but in your case, it's your heart that's causing all the problems, and your lungs that are the most affected; therefore, I can determine a great deal by listening to them regularly. So, you'd best get used to it, because we will be doing this a few times every day—perhaps more."

"I find that comforting, if you must know," Hugh said. "I've spent most of my life worried about what my heart is doing; to have you checking it regularly will help me actually *know*. Even if it's bad news, I'd rather know than wonder."

"I can understand that," Bess said as Hugh unbuttoned the top few buttons of his nightshirt, over which he was still wearing a dressing gown. It was far from the first time Bess had seen a man's chest; in fact, she'd seen far more of the human body than any respectable unmarried woman would likely ever see, simply because it was mandatory in the work she'd done while assisting her father. Under her father's guidance, she had long ago stopped being affected by such things. But as she put the ends of the stethoscope into her ear, and then put the other end of it against Hugh's bare chest, she felt an unfamiliar fluttering in her stomach, which both distracted and confused her. She forced herself to focus on listening to Hugh's heart, noting the obvious weakness and how rapid it was beating in comparison to a normal heartbeat. There was also an irregularity to its rhythm that was readily evident. She asked him to take in a deep breath as much as he could and blow it out slowly a few times while she listened to both lungs from the front and from the back. He clearly knew the routine well by the way he leaned forward without her even asking and she was able to place the stethoscope easily beneath his shirt.

Removing the stethoscope from her ears she asked, "Are you finding it difficult to breathe right now?"

"I know my breathing is more rapid and shallow than the average person," he said, "but I don't feel any discomfort or difficulty at the moment."

"That's good, then," Bess said. "Hopefully you will get a good night's sleep."

"Hopefully," he said with obvious doubt.

"Is that often not the case?" Bess asked, still standing next to him.

"I take a small dose of laudanum at bedtime, which helps. I was told months ago that any risk of addiction was not a concern since . . . well, you know."

"Since you're dying?" she asked, and he looked surprised. "Should I not speak of it so boldly?"

"On the contrary," he said. "I prefer to speak of it realistically, but my mother finds it difficult when I do so."

"I know your mother is struggling, as any mother would. But I'm *not* your mother."

"Indeed you're not," he said with a smile.

"Go on. You have a small dose of laudanum at bedtime, and . . ."

"And I sleep for four or five hours reasonably well, but once it wears off, I generally can't go back to sleep."

"Is there a reason you don't take a second dose at that time? A smaller one perhaps? I'm certain your breakfast time could be adjusted to your needs."

"I'm sure it could," he said, smiling again as if he liked her straightforwardness. She appreciated that more than he could know, since her father had most often discouraged her from speaking so boldly, which had meant she'd been continually biting her tongue since it was her instinct to speak her mind. "I haven't wanted to disturb Clive or Lewis unless there was an urgent need."

"Well, disturb them!" she said as if it were an order. "I know they are your friends, but I'm certain they're being paid well to work in your household."

"You make a fair point," Hugh said.

A moment of silence grew into more moments that became mildly awkward until Bess had an idea. "Here," she said, handing Hugh the stethoscope.

"What should I do with this?" he asked, confused.

"You've seen it used enough that I think you know what to do," she said. He still looked confused and she added, "Listen to your heart, Hugh. Perhaps you should get used to how it sounds."

He looked intrigued by the idea as he put the stethoscope into his ears and she helped guide the other end to where his heart was located. She saw his eyes widen as he said, "Incredible."

"Now," she said, knowing from experience that he could hear her talk even though the instrument was in his ears, "notice the pace of your heartbeat; it's faster than a normal heart because it's working harder, but we both need to become accustomed to what's normal for *you,* so that we can tell when it's working *too* hard. Does that make sense?"

"Yes," he said, still listening to his heart with the expression of a child fascinated by a new toy.

"If you listen closely," she said, "you'll note a slight irregularity in the way it's beating; the rhythm is not consistent. Tell me if you can hear it."

"Yes," he said after listening a long moment, "I can hear it."

"This too is something we should pay attention to. We need to get used to what sounds normal for *you,* so we can be aware of any changes."

"We?" he asked, looking up at her while he continued to listen to his own heart.

"Yes," she said, "I'm going to leave the stethoscope on your bedside table so that you can listen to your heart any time you might feel concerned, or when you just wish to do so, and then it will always be there when I need to use it. We're going to work together to make everything as easy and painless as possible."

Hugh removed the stethoscope from his ears and handed it to her. "I would like that very much," he said. "Thank you. And thank you for letting me listen; it's . . . comforting somehow."

"I'm glad," she said. "Now, is there anything I can do for you before I turn you over to Clive for the night?"

"I'm certain everything's taken care of," Hugh said, "although I find it reassuring to know that you're right across the hall."

"Well, I'm no miracle worker," Bess admitted and impulsively sat down, if only so they could speak without him having to look up at her. "I have no power over how long your heart will keep working, or what might happen. But I'm more than happy to do everything I can."

"Exactly," he said. "I'm glad you're here, Bess."

"So am I," she admitted and stifled an unexpected yawn.

"You must be exhausted," he said. "It's been a big day for you."

"That's exactly what your mother said." Bess laughed softly. "Truthfully, it feels as if I woke up on one planet, and I'm now living on another."

"*Which* planet?" he asked, leaning forward a little, his eyes lighting up in a way she'd not previously seen. "It would be my opinion that you've been living on Saturn and now you are on Venus."

Bess stated the obvious, "You have an interest in the planets."

"Planets, stars, the wide expanse of space that surrounds our earth," he said almost dreamily. "My mother believes my interest lies in my having known for years that I was going to die. She assures me that heaven is not out there in space. I don't think I'm trying to find evidence of heaven. I simply feel an undefinable fascination with what lies beyond our world. I've studied the writings of Galileo, among others who have studied the stars and planets. Ironically, no one with which I have contact shares my interest. I've wondered if I'd had the opportunity to attend university, whether I might have met people who share my fascination." He paused from his passionate declaration to catch his breath before he asked, "And what of you, Bess? Do you have any such interest?"

"I've never had the time to study anything that wasn't related to learning my father's profession," she admitted, "but I've always longed to learn new things. Perhaps we can read Galileo together and you can teach me."

"Oh, that would be lovely!" he declared. "Only if you're genuinely interested," he added more severely. "I detest having *anyone* engaging in an activity simply out of duty or obligation."

"I am genuinely intrigued," she said, "and I promise to tell you if I get bored."

"Fair enough," he said. "I will look forward to it."

Bess stood and said, "Take good care of my stethoscope, and I will see you in the morning—if everything goes well during the night. I'll leave you in Clive's care for now."

"Thank you, Bess," he said and surprised her by taking her hand before she could walk away. He squeezed it gently and she returned the gesture while they shared a smile. It was becoming more and more evident that not only was Hugh Buxton dying, but he was also lonely and very likely bored with his routine and the same old people in his life every day. Bess felt certain his mother knew this, and it surely had contributed to Bess being hired for this position.

"A pleasure," she said and meant it. Leaving the room, she couldn't help looking forward to having Hugh teach her about the stars and planets.

# CHAPTER FIVE

## UNEXPECTED

DAPHNE WAS WAITING FOR BESS and made certain she had everything she needed for the night. Accustomed to taking care of herself, Bess thanked Daphne and sent her away before she got ready for bed. Climbing into the luxuriously comfortable bed, Bess marveled at how her life had changed, and even more so at how she already felt so at home. She had expected it to take time for her to feel at ease with her charge and the people she worked with, but already she felt capable and confident in being able to do what was required of her. She wondered how the day had gone for her father—and those who had been hired to help him. But she only wondered for a few minutes before she fell into an exhausted slumber.

The following morning, Bess was grateful to have Daphne help gather the clothes she would wear that day, and to find that the maid was efficient in brushing out Bess's hair and pinning it up—all of which made it possible for her to get across the hall more quickly to check on Hugh. She found him sitting up in bed, his hair damp, and wearing a clean nightshirt. Between Hugh and Clive, she was given a report on how the night had gone; Hugh had slept well, aided by a small dose of laudanum when he'd awakened in the middle of the night. Bess noted that Hugh's hair was curlier when wet, and she also noticed how pleased he was to see her—but she couldn't deny that she was pleased to see him too. When he asked if she would share breakfast with him, she could hardly refuse. While she hadn't felt uncomfortable dining with the servants in the kitchen the previous evening, she far preferred Hugh's company.

After Bess gave Hugh the usual vital assessment, Clive helped him into a dressing gown and then to a chair next to the table. The three of them shared breakfast and pleasant conversation that was sprinkled with light banter and teasing sarcasm. Bess considered the fact that she had not once attended any kind of social event in her life. She'd shared tea and meals with the families of patients many times, and there were the few friends she'd made at church with whom she'd socialized minimally—given how little time she'd had for such frivolities. All things considered, sharing a meal and enjoyable interaction with these two men who were such good friends was nothing but gratifying for Bess. Occasionally she noticed Clive gazing at her with a warm sparkle showing in his eyes that caught her attention—even though she tried very hard not to let on that it did. She wondered if his apparent interest in her was merely some form of friendship, or if there were other underlying implications. But then she wondered the same regarding her own feelings. She liked Clive very much and had quickly become comfortable with his company. But given her own lack of experience with interactions between men and women—and the fact that she'd only known Clive so briefly—she set the matter aside and simply chose to enjoy his company. Only the passing of time would truly allow her to understand such intangible implications.

After breakfast, Clive left to see to his responsibilities regarding the household, saying that either he would return in a short while to be on hand if Hugh needed him, or Lewis would come in his place. The moment Clive was gone, Hugh told Bess where to find his books on a shelf in the sitting room, and which one he wanted her to retrieve. She quickly found the book to which he'd referred, an ominous-looking volume on the works of Galileo.

Bess returned to the table and sat down, asking, "Would you like me to read to you?"

"Yes, but . . . not from the beginning," Hugh said, and she slid the book across the table for him to thumb through the pages, quickly coming to a place that was obviously one of his favorites.

Bess began to read, pausing often for him to offer his personal insights and opinions on what they were reading. He was clearly passionate about the topic and thrilled to be able to talk about it. Bess was as genuinely interested in what she was learning as she was comfortable around Hugh. The morning passed quickly, with Hugh needing only one break where Clive helped him into the other room, and Bess took the opportunity at the same time to go to her own quarters and freshen up. Clive left again, and Hugh and Bess continued reading and talking until Agatha arrived in the late morning to visit her son. Bess noted from Hugh's genuine smile that he was pleased to see her, and she knew that for all of Agatha's confessions to feeling guilty for not spending more time with Hugh, they were close and comfortable with each other. Bess offered to leave and let them have time alone, but they both insisted she stay, promising to let her know if there was ever a time when they needed any privacy as mother and son.

Bess enjoyed observing the interaction between Agatha and Hugh, and Agatha was genuinely pleased to hear that they'd been reading Galileo and talking about one of Hugh's greatest interests. She admitted that it was a topic about which she'd never been able to feel personally interested, and she was glad that Hugh had someone with whom he could talk about such things.

"You were surely inspired to bring this angel into our home," Hugh said to his mother while he was looking at Bess. The compliment caught Bess off guard and she looked quickly away, feeling herself turn warm.

"I do believe I was," Agatha said.

"I cannot deny being here is a blessing for me," Bess admitted, now able to look at the others, "but you mustn't give me so much credit. I'm genuinely enjoying my new understanding of what's out there in space; it's certainly no sacrifice on my part to spend my time this way."

"Exactly," Hugh said, which seemed to imply that the very fact that her interest was genuine meant a great deal to him.

Bess hurried to add, "I feel rather spoiled, in truth."

"Oh, don't worry," Hugh said, his voice turning somber. "I have a reputation for making life difficult for the people around me. Don't get too comfortable."

"We will take on whatever happens in the best possible way," Bess said, trying to remain positive, even though something inside of her felt increasingly disarmed with the reality that Hugh was dying.

"And again, she proves herself an angel," Hugh said.

Bess resisted the urge to react again with embarrassment, and instead made a scoffing sound that elicited a chuckle from Hugh and his mother.

Lunch was brought to the room for the three of them, and it became evident that Clive and Lewis shared this meal with the servants in the kitchen. Hugh and his mother chatted comfortably while they ate, quite naturally including Bess in the conversation. But during a quiet lull, Bess felt the need to say, "It would seem customary that the two of you enjoy lunch together, and while I enjoy your company very much, I don't want to encroach upon the time the two of you share together."

"It's a delight to have you join us," Agatha was quick to say. "We already discussed this, my dear. And we promise to tell you if we need any time alone; otherwise, we'll just plan on having you join us for lunch. Assuming that's all right with you, Hugh."

"Me?" Hugh asked with exaggerated enthusiasm, along with a wink and a smile. "Why would it not be all right with *me?*" He leaned toward Bess and pretended to whisper what he clearly intended his mother to hear, "What she's trying to say is that I'm boring company and she's glad to have someone else to broaden our conversation."

"Perhaps it is *I* who am boring," Agatha said with the same teasing tone.

"Given that we are both likely very bored with each other," Hugh said conclusively, "it's a pleasure to have your company." Bess smiled but still felt mildly concerned about interfering with the time Agatha was able to spend with her son. Hugh seemed to read her mind—or perhaps her expression—when he added, "And yes, we promise that we will tell you if we need some time alone."

"Very well then," Bess said, "if you promise."

"Of course," Agatha said while Hugh said, "Indeed."

Bess allowed the two of them to do most of the talking during the rest of the meal. They discussed some happenings among the servants, and a few business details regarding the estate. This was a matter that had never occurred to Bess. For people like Hugh and Agatha, an enormous responsibility came with their wealth and title—there were a great many people working for them, and many more who rented tenant farms on the estate. There were overseers and servants who were loyal and efficient, but it was necessary to remain abreast of all that was going on. As Bess listened, it became evident that Hugh had never been expected to take over such duties, since it had not been anticipated that he would live into adulthood. Agatha had also expected that her husband would live a great many more years; therefore, having the responsibility of the estate fall upon her shoulders had been an immensely difficult adjustment. Hugh had been helpful and supportive in helping her figure things out, and he'd clearly had many conversations with those who were in charge of making sure that everything ran smoothly. But when Hugh died, Agatha would be left to communicate with the people who oversaw all that she alone would be responsible for. Bess listened to them talk for nearly half an hour after they'd finished their meal but remained seated at the table; she learned a great deal about the estate, things she'd never bothered to think about before. And she couldn't deny feeling a little surprised with the way they spoke so openly in front of her. Did they trust her so thoroughly after she'd been here such a short time? Adding up all that had happened—and the conversations that had been shared—in the one day she'd been here, she had every reason to believe that she'd earned their confidence and they *did* trust her. She simply had a difficult time believing how quickly her life had changed, and how smoothly she had been able to settle comfortably into the lives of these good people.

Lewis arrived, interrupting the conversation to remind Hugh that he needed to get cleaned up since the doctor was coming at two. Mention of this made Bess's stomach churn, but she was surprised to feel Agatha's hand on her arm. "It will be all right," she said. "If he chooses to be angry with you for taking an opportunity to make your own way in the world, then he has no comprehension of the most important facet of being a parent."

"What is that?" Bess asked.

"That we raise children to prepare them for adulthood, and if we love them selflessly we want nothing more than their happiness, which means allowing them to follow their own path and pursue their own dreams. It's ridiculous to think that children won't grow up and set out on their own in one way or another. I hope that even if he's angry now, eventually he will come to see this, and the two of you will be able to share a more comfortable relationship that's based in mutual respect."

"How wise you are!" Bess said. "I do hope so."

"As for today's visit," Agatha went on, "I will stay with you, and even if he doesn't acknowledge you at all, it's all right. He's simply going to have to adjust to the changes."

"Thank you," Bess said and took the opportunity to go to her bedroom and freshen up. She also wanted to mentally prepare herself to face her father, and she considered the different possibilities of what he might say to her or how he might respond to her presence.

"Are you all right, Miss?" Daphne asked, startling Bess to the realization that she wasn't alone. "You seemed so far away. I don't want to intrude, but—"

"No, it's fine," Bess said, motioning for Daphne to sit down nearby. She had no reason to believe she couldn't trust Daphne, and it wasn't as if her thoughts were related to any dark secrets. Given how closely she was meant to be working with Daphne, it surely wouldn't hurt to become more comfortable sharing conversation. "I'm certain you're aware of the situation from which I came, my reasons for coming to Lady Buxton's attention."

"If you're referring to the situation with your father, then yes," Daphne said. "When someone new comes into the household, everyone is interested to know everything they can. Word of your position spread quickly."

"And is there any particular opinion in the household about how my father might feel about me leaving behind my duties with him so that I can be here now?"

"Speaking candidly, Miss, I've only heard that most are pleased that the lady has brought in someone such as yourself to help care for her son, and word about the village is that it's been a general consensus for a good, long time that the doctor—as good a man as he's reputed to be—was not doing well by his daughter to keep her so secluded and controlled." Bess was astonished to hear what Daphne was saying, but it quickly became evident the maid had misinterpreted her stunned expression. "Forgive me, Miss, if I've spoken out of line." She sounded genuinely concerned, as if she feared Bess might ask for someone else to work with her and she'd be dismissed. "I was only repeating what—"

"I'm not upset with you, Daphne," Bess hurried to say. "I'm simply . . . astonished, I suppose. I had no idea so many people were aware of my situation." She sighed and tried to take it all in. "I am deeply grateful to be here; Lady Buxton's insight was a great blessing for me."

"And for me," Daphne said with a warm smile.

"You?"

"Oh, you are a pleasant woman to work with!" Daphne said. "This is much better than the trivial tasks I was seeing to before."

"I'm glad to hear it," Bess said; it hadn't occurred to her that Daphne being on hand to help see to her every need might be something good for the young woman.

"Are you concerned, then?" Daphne asked. "About your father coming to check on Master Hugh?"

"I confess that I am," Bess said, already feeling much more relaxed in conversing with Daphne.

"Oh, don't you worry about that!" Daphne declared. "He'd surely not speak unkindly to you in front of others."

"No," Bess said, "but he has a terribly ominous glare."

For some reason Daphne found the comment funny and started to laugh. Bess quickly joined her and felt immediately calmer with being able to find some humor in the situation. Daphne settled down and said more seriously, "If you need to, just leave the room; that's what I believe I would do. I'd say that if he makes you feel uncomfortable in any way, just leave the room. Perhaps after a few visits with you making it clear you won't be treated badly—even in silence—he will stop doing it."

"Perhaps," Bess said. "I suppose the important thing is that whether or not he figures anything out, I need to take care of myself."

"That's the spirit," Daphne said, and they laughed together again.

Bess glanced at the clock to see that it was twenty minutes before two. Of course, her father could arrive a little early or late given that the horse pulling the trap did not adhere to the clock. She distracted herself by asking Daphne questions about herself, and she learned that this young woman had spent the first twelve years of her life in an orphanage and could not remember her parents and had never been told the reasons why she had ended up in such a place, which she referred to only as dreadful. But she declared that she had been one of the lucky ones, since a kind woman had come one day and selected a handful of girls whom she had taken home with her and had taken very good care of them while she trained them in the details of being a lady's maid. This training would offer them opportunities to make a good living rather than ending up in difficult situations the remainder of their lives—which was often the case with children turned out of orphanages with no viable skills. Daphne considered herself blessed and had a positive outlook on life, and Bess genuinely liked her.

Bess was surprised when a maid appeared in her open doorway to announce that the doctor had arrived and was on his way up. Lady Buxton was with her son and asked that Bess join them.

"Thank you," Bess said, wishing she could remember the maid's name.

Bess stood up and brushed her hands down over her dark blue dress with tiny white stripes, as if that might better prepare her for this encounter. "Wish me luck," she said to Daphne.

"You'll do brilliantly!" Daphne said with an enthusiasm Bess wished she could share. "I'll be in the sitting room should you need me."

"Thank you," Bess said and hurried along, walking through the open door into Hugh's bedroom to find him in his bed, propped up with pillows. "How are you feeling?" she asked him.

"No differently than the last time you asked," Hugh said with a smile, and a slight nod toward the stethoscope on his bedside table. "It's still beating," he added lightly.

"I'm very glad to hear it," Bess said, "although if it weren't, I do believe it would be obvious to both myself and your mother."

"A detestable thought," Agatha said from where she was seated in a chair near the bed.

"Then we will do our best to not think about it for the time being," Bess said, taking a seat on the other side of the bed. But she had barely sat down when her father was escorted into the room and she stood again abruptly. A quick glance showed her that his eyes were focused on Hugh, and his expression bore no hint of disdain; but then it wouldn't because he would never reveal his own emotions in front of a patient.

Bess observed as her father did all the things she'd been doing to determine Hugh's status. He then told Hugh exactly what Bess had been telling him. As soon as it became evident she wasn't needed for this exchange, she discreetly sat back down and folded her hands in her lap.

Bess was surprised to hear Hugh say, "Bess has been taking very good care of me."

Jonas White made no comment; he just looked inside his medical bag as if he were searching for something, which Bess knew he was not.

Agatha eased the silence by adding, "Yes, she's been wonderful. You've trained her well."

Jonas put his stethoscope into his bag and looked at Agatha, then at Hugh, as he said, "You appear to be doing as well as could be expected. I will check back in three days at the same time if that suits you."

"That would be fine," Hugh said, and Bess noticed his furrowed brow as he obviously picked up on Jonas's blatant disregard for his daughter.

Bess looked down to avoid having anyone see that she was trying not to cry. She heard her father's footsteps as he left the room, then she heard Agatha crossing the room to close the door before she heard Hugh say, "Well, that was interesting. I cannot believe that he wouldn't even—"

"Please excuse me," Bess said and hurried out of the room, unprepared for the emotion that was overtaking her, and not wanting Agatha or Hugh to be present when she had no choice but to let it out.

Entering her own sitting room, she found Daphne curled up in a chair, reading a book. The maid looked up in surprise, which quickly turned to alarm when she saw Bess's expression as she closed the door and leaned against it to catch her breath. Bess's gratitude deepened for the candor she and Daphne had come to share when the maid stood and came quickly toward her, placing strong hands on her shoulders. "Are you all right, miss?"

"No, I am not," Bess said and set aside all attempts at dignity and propriety as she wrapped her arms around her new friend and wept. She recalled crying this way more than once in Mrs. Hubbard's arms, but since the death of her mother there had never been any other support or consolation wherein she'd been able to just cry out the pain that weighed on her heart.

"Come and sit down," Daphne urged, and they seated themselves close together on the sofa. Daphne wrapped her arms around Bess in a motherly gesture, whispering words of comfort and encouragement while Bess continued to cry.

"Tell me what happened," Daphne urged when Bess was able to calm down.

"He just . . . ignored me," Bess said. "He even ignored any comment that Hugh and his mother made about me."

"If I may speak candidly," Daphne said with a controlled anger in her voice, "I would consider such behavior childish and selfish—perhaps even hostile. I'd say it's high time you got away from this man who treats you in such a way. I hope that in time he will be able to see the error of his ways, but whether or not he does, you need to have the strength and courage to press forward—and I know that you do."

"Oh, you are too precious!" Bess said, wiping at her tears and attempting to appear as if everything were all right—given the likely possibility that Lady Buxton would want to speak to her soon enough.

"I can't tell you how much it means to hear someone else say such words, when I have felt them for so long, but . . ."

"But what?" Daphne encouraged.

"But I've felt perhaps . . . wicked . . . for entertaining such thoughts about my own father."

"Recognizing his weaknesses does not mean you don't love him," Daphne declared with a wisdom far beyond her years.

Bess was about to comment on Daphne's extraordinary ability to offer sound advice when a light knock at the door preceded Lady Buxton entering the sitting room without waiting for an invitation. "Are you all right, my dear?" Agatha asked.

"I think so," Bess said, amazed at how the lady of the house sat on the sofa, next to Bess on the opposite side of where Daphne was sitting—but Bess wasn't nearly as amazed as Daphne seemed to be. "I can't say I'm surprised by his behavior, but I wasn't prepared for how it would affect me. I apologize for leaving so quickly and—"

"You have nothing to apologize for," Agatha said, taking Bess's hand. "I'm grateful for his medical knowledge, and I know at heart he's a good man, but frankly I'm quite appalled that he would treat you in such a way. Nevertheless," she sighed loudly as if she were consciously settling her frustration, "whatever his attitudes in personal matters, *I* know the truth about you, my dear Bess, and I take great comfort in having you here."

"You are very kind," Bess said, offering her as much of a smile as she could come up with. "Surely more than I deserve."

"Never!" Agatha said.

"Now, I know that Hugh is waiting for you. I suggested he attempt to take a nap, but he told me he needs your help to relax because his head is hurting, as it usually is this time of day for some reason."

"Then I shall see to my patient," Bess said and stood to hurriedly leave the room, glad to have something with which to occupy herself and feel useful. Before going out the door she turned to look at the two women still sitting on the sofa, both of whom had been so kind and supportive. With deep sincerity she said, "Thank you . . . both of you . . . for everything. I am very blessed to be here."

Bess didn't hesitate long enough to allow time for either of them to feel obligated to offer any kind of response. They had both already said more than enough to help her believe she could truly make a difference here at Astoria Abbey—with or without her father's approval.

"Ah, there she is," Hugh said with a smile when she entered the room.

"Your mother said that your head is hurting. Would you like me to—"

"Whatever you did yesterday would be lovely," Hugh said. "In fact, I think we should make that a part of our daily routine."

"An excellent plan," Bess said and placed a chair next to the bed while he carefully slid down and laid across the bed sideways so that she could easily reach his neck. She noted that he didn't need any help doing so and surmised that he felt stronger today than yesterday, which was a good sign. Bess took a moment to place the covers over him and make certain he was comfortable before she sat down and reached her fingers beneath his head. As soon as she did so, Hugh let out a pleasant sigh.

Bess closed her eyes and focused on gently rubbing the tight muscles at the base of Hugh's skull. She was surprised to hear him say, "I'm sorry for the way your father treated you. I know that must feel terrible for you."

"Thank you," Bess said and forced back the temptation to start crying again. His observation as well as his kindness touched her heart. "It doesn't matter what he thinks. I'm very glad to be here."

"As I am very glad to *have* you here," Hugh said before he relaxed into silence and gradually fell asleep. Bess carefully shifted a pillow beneath his head before she made herself comfortable on the sofa with the book she and Hugh had been reading together. Much of what she attempted to read was difficult if not impossible for her to understand, but she did find herself coming up with a mental list of questions to ask Hugh the next time they talked. She found her mind wandering to the incomprehensible concept of all that existed beyond the earth on which they lived. Her own education—beyond that of learning about medicine from her father—had been very basic and minimal. Once her mother had died, there hadn't been time for lessons that went beyond the schooling she'd already had in subjects that were considered essential. Bess watched Hugh sleeping and thought of the boy who had developed a fascination with space, and planets, and stars—likely because he hadn't been able to run and play like other children. And now he'd become a man preparing for death, still fascinated with what lay beyond this world.

After reading for an hour, she became sleepy herself and lay down on the sofa to just rest her eyes for a short while. She came awake to realize she'd been asleep quite a while according to the change of the shadows on the walls. Lewis was helping Hugh into the other room, which meant that he'd come in while she'd been sleeping, and he'd clearly been here when Hugh had awakened and needed help. Bess sat up and gained her equilibrium enough to walk to her room and freshen up before she returned to find Hugh sitting at the table. He smiled to see her. His smile had already become warm and familiar, and she smiled back, grateful at how far and how quickly she'd come in feeling at ease with her place in this house and the work she was expected to do here.

As the days passed, Bess's routine became more comfortable, both for herself and for those with whom she interacted. Everyone was adjusting well to her presence in the house and the part she was playing in Hugh's care. She became accustomed to the routine Clive and Lewis shared by taking turns spending the night in Hugh's room and being on hand for him during the days. Sometimes they were both there together, and it was evident that the three of them had been close for many years. Lewis had been working as Hugh's valet from the time when Hugh had been little more than a child. Clive's father had worked for Hugh's father, which meant that Clive had grown up at Astoria Abbey. He'd started working at a young age, doing various simple tasks, and had worked his way up to becoming an under butler at the age of seventeen. But Clive and Hugh had always been friends, and it had always seemed natural for Clive to assist Hugh when necessary. Both Clive and Lewis had gone to live in London with Hugh and his mother, where they had all lived for some years, and it was during that time the head butler at Astoria Abbey had died unexpectedly. No one had been found to replace him before they'd returned from London, at which time Agatha had offered Clive the position—at least in an overseeing kind of way that would still allow him to help take care of Hugh. Clive had been thrilled with the opportunity. But any differences of class or seniority in the household were clearly irrelevant among them. When the three men engaged in conversation and laughter, Bess found it was a good time to let them enjoy each other's company while she attended to personal matters or visited with the friends she had made in the house. She enjoyed Daphne's company more every day, and she appreciated the comfortable routine they had worked out; any awkwardness between them had completely dissipated.

Once a day, Lady Buxton—who still insisted that Bess call her Agatha when they were alone—made an effort to visit privately with Bess. She wanted to hear a report on how Hugh was doing, both physically and emotionally. But she also seemed to just enjoy company and conversation, and Bess enjoyed it at least as much as the unexpected friend she had found in the Lady of Astoria Abbey.

Each day Bess checked Hugh's symptoms four times to appraise his condition, and they had developed a routine that included rubbing his swollen feet and ankles to help push the swelling upwards and distribute it more throughout his lower legs so that it would be less likely to cause him any discomfort. On some days he hardly got out of bed, and on others he sat at the table to eat his meals and sometimes play chess with Lewis or Clive. When he insisted that Bess play the game with him, she was initially reluctant but finally gave in, finding that she was very bad at it. But Hugh was apparently having a good time teaching her—and he laughed a great deal over how easily he could win when they played, declaring with feigned arrogance that winning helped him feel like more of a man.

Bess and Hugh also read together every day and shared stimulating conversation, which she felt certain was far more enjoyable for her than for him. Each afternoon, following lunch, Bess would rub the tension out of the muscles of Hugh's neck, which helped him relax enough to take a decent nap. Every third day when her father came to examine Hugh, that part of their routine was delayed by about an hour, but they were always flexible with every aspect of their regimen, depending on how Hugh might be feeling. At Agatha's suggestion, Bess had taken to remaining in her rooms with Daphne while her father was in the house. She would have preferred to consult with him regarding Hugh's health, and she would have preferred even more to have him smile at her or even hug her, to tell her that he missed her but he understood her need to move on. And most of all she longed to have him tell her that he loved her, and perhaps even that he was proud of her. But Bess quelled her wishes regarding her father, managed to avoid him completely, and settled more comfortably every day into her new way of life.

When Hugh was sleeping during the day, or was in the care of his friends, Bess took the opportunity to explore the beauty of Astoria Abbey. She got lost more than once but found it somewhat of an adventure to find her way back to a familiar place amidst the maze of stairs and hallways. Bess loved looking at the many paintings on the walls, taking in the variety of beauty exhibited in the art. She'd only heard of museums, places that were filled with such beautiful things where people could just go and look at them; she'd never had any such opportunity, but now believed that Astoria Abbey was like a home and museum merged together. All things combined, she loved the privilege of living in such a beautiful place, and even more so she loved the way that living at the Abbey had strengthened her confidence, making her feel as if the imaginary shield of light she'd carried with her throughout her life was brighter and more resilient than it had ever been. Instead of having to focus all her energy on battling negative feelings and experiences, she was now surrounded by people who contributed to that light, rather than diminishing it.

On her first Sunday at the Abbey, Bess discovered that many of those who were employed in the household went into town to attend the church service she had always attended. She found it strange to think that she might have frequently crossed paths with people who worked at the Abbey with no idea that they might one day work together. Bess was given the option of attending church with those who went, but she was also informed that either the vicar or his assistant habitually came to the Abbey following the usual service in the village in order to do a private service for Hugh and those who were close to him, since he'd not been physically able to attend church services for many years. Yet it was still something important to him. She also found it ironic to now realize that if Hugh *had* been healthy, she would have encountered him and his mother at church regularly. But surely neither of them would have ever noticed her at all under any other circumstances beyond the reasons she had been hired to help Hugh.

Bess decided to remain at the Abbey and at least explore this option. Given Hugh's recent return to the Abbey from London, the vicar greeted Hugh and Agatha with kind regard, declaring his pleasure in having them back despite the difficult circumstances. Being able to share in this private service with the people she now worked with was not only a pleasant experience for Bess but was also rejuvenating and inspiring. The following Sunday she debated whether to remain at the Abbey or go into town to worship. While a part of her missed the handful of people she'd come to know reasonably well, she also knew her father would be there, and she desperately preferred to avoid him, which made her decision easy. She quickly became comfortable with attending the private service at the Abbey, and she also found her respect deepening for Hugh and his mother as it became evident how important spiritual matters were for both of them.

A few weeks after moving to the Abbey, Bess was thrilled to receive a letter from Mrs. Hubbard. She kindly inquired about how everything was going for Bess and reassured her that all was well at the house and with her father. Mrs. Hubbard included pleasant details of the routine that had been established in the White household, and of the meals she'd been preparing— which the doctor was clearly enjoying. Bess had no doubt that Mrs. Hubbard was a far better cook than herself, and she hoped her father was appreciating the fact that Bess had surely done him a favor by hiring someone else to cook his meals. According to Mrs. Hubbard, her father was quiet but had stopped seeming upset or distressed only a few days after Bess had left. Archie was doing well at assisting the doctor, and Mrs. Hubbard enjoyed visiting with him as he cleaned instruments and stocked the medical bag. Bess felt deeply comforted to know that her father was in good hands and that all was going well in her absence; in fact, she felt remarkably relieved to know that she had been able to step away from a life that had been suffocating her, and that the world had not come to an end for Jonas White. However, she still couldn't help wishing that her father would acknowledge that fact to her. She wondered if he might have grown to appreciate all she'd done, now that he could see it was taking two people to replace her. Of course, if she avoided him he wouldn't have a chance to say anything at all. But in her heart, she felt relatively certain his pride and anger would overpower any humility or appreciation he might feel toward her, and at this point, she felt it was still best to avoid him.

Each morning, Bess shared breakfast with Hugh and either Clive or Lewis—depending on which one of them had spent the night in Hugh's room. She felt entirely comfortable with both men. It was easy to banter with them, something she'd picked up by observing the way they interacted with Hugh—and with each other. And she also had no difficulty asking them for help when she needed it, or more accurately when Hugh needed help that she couldn't give him. And they were always willing and eager to comply. While she felt equally comfortable with both men with whom she worked, Bess quickly realized she had come to enjoy Clive's company very much, and she looked forward to the times when he was on duty to be close by for whatever Hugh might need. While Hugh slept, they shared a great deal of lively conversation, and she couldn't deny that Clive had come to be a trusted friend. Lewis was a dear man and she felt no awkwardness when he was around, but he tended to be quieter than Clive, which made it more difficult to share conversation or to get to know much about him. Bess was anything but oblivious to the increasing sparkle in Clive's eyes when he looked at her, and he had taken to lightly joking about how he worshiped her as if she were royalty, and it was his pleasure to do her bidding as if he were willing to throw himself down into a mud puddle to keep her feet from getting dirty. Bess responded to his comments with the same kind of humor, and she treated him with the attitude of comfortable friendship, which she wanted to remain clearly established between them. Occasionally she felt a little flutter in her stomach or a quickening of her heart when Clive happened to brush her hand with his while they were helping Hugh, or when he'd look at her in a certain way. But Bess wasn't here to entertain any romantic notions. She needed to take care of Hugh and make certain he remained her greatest focus, and she wanted to be Clive's friend and nothing more. In all practicality, when she bothered to ponder the situation, she felt certain that Clive's attention was intended as nothing more than friendship, and her reaction to it was simply rooted in her own lack of exposure to such interactions with men who were near her age.

Bess found lunch to be her favorite meal of the day, since she had come to thoroughly enjoy spending time with Hugh and his mother. Sometimes she had tea with Hugh, sometimes with Agatha, and sometimes with Daphne—which all depended on whether Hugh was sleeping, or whether one of his friends was with him playing chess, or whatever the circumstances of the day might bring. She appreciated the flexibility of the situation, knowing that she could often choose with whom she spent her free time, depending on her mood—as long as Hugh didn't need her.

Bess always had supper in the kitchen with the servants. She enjoyed the variety that doing so added to her day, but she also felt it was important to spend time with and become better acquainted with the people with whom she shared this enormous home. She came to know more of them by name and gradually felt more comfortable among them, but she found no one there with whom she really felt the inclination to become close or share personal conversation—which made her even more grateful for Daphne's friendship, as well as Clive's. In fact, she'd come to feel almost as comfortable with Clive as she did with Daphne. He was remarkably easy to talk to, and always willing to offer up an abundance of kindness and understanding. She'd come to simply ignore the moments when she would catch a glance from him that made her wonder if his feelings for her went beyond friendship. Since he gave no other indication of any such thing, she credited the idea to her imagination.

While Bess dearly appreciated the comfortable friendships she'd formed with Clive and Daphne, she was especially grateful for that of Agatha Buxton. It felt somehow supernatural that she had come to share what she considered a deeply close relationship with the Lady of Astoria Abbey. But every day it became more evident how lonely and filled with sorrow Agatha had been for a very long time, and Bess was glad she could be here for this kind woman and be able to alleviate her loneliness somewhat. And yet Bess felt that she received far more from her relationship with Agatha than she could ever give. This woman was wise and insightful and kind, and with time, Bess began to feel her confidence growing regarding her own feelings and ways of thinking. Sometimes they talked about what Bess might do after Hugh died. They were able to speak of it matter-of-factly, even if it sometimes brought forth tender emotions, but Bess honestly didn't know what might lie ahead for her. She could only say for certain, "I will have to see how I feel when the time comes. If I *do* go back home, it will never be under the same circumstances. And unless my father softens his feelings toward me, going back is simply not an option because I won't live in a home where I'm treated with such disrespect."

"I'm so proud of you," Agatha said. "You've come a long way. And I want you to know that if you so choose, you will always have the option of staying here."

"Doing what?" Bess asked, surprised.

"There's always work to be done in a house such as this," Agatha said. "That doesn't really matter right now. I just want you to know that staying is an option. Truthfully, it's a selfish offer, because I would miss you so much if you left, but I would never want you to stay here out of some distorted sense of duty, or because you pity me; that would make me no better than your father. I want you to follow your dreams and do whatever will make you the happiest, my dear. But I don't want you to worry about whether you'll have a place to go. This can always be home for you if you choose."

"Thank you," Bess said and left it at that. She *did* feel grateful to know that she would always have a home—given the possibility that she might never again be able to live under the same roof with her father due to the rift that now existed between them. And she would miss Agatha— just as she would miss Daphne, and even the other servants. And she would miss Hugh. The difference was that Hugh would die, and missing him could never be remedied by any choice that was available to her.

Determined to just do her job and not worry about her life beyond Hugh's death, Bess focused on doing everything she could to keep him comfortable and as healthy as possible—and to keep him from getting bored. The only truly disconcerting facet of the entire arrangement was the way she found herself thinking of Hugh almost constantly. She would sometimes have trouble falling asleep due to thoughts of him, and he was usually the first thought that appeared in her mind as soon as she was fully awake in the morning. At first, she credited her preoccupation with him as falling into the category of feeling responsible for his health, along with her genuine concern for his comfort and welfare as he endured this final phase of his life. But a day came when Bess couldn't deny that her fixation had gradually transformed into something else, something deeper and more meaningful, something terrifying yet thrilling. She tried exerting all her willpower to avoid thinking of him in such a way, to avoid any acknowledgment that she felt attracted to him and wanted to be with him every possible moment. In contrast, she had come to easily conclude that despite all of Clive's attention—and how much she liked him—what she felt for Hugh made it clear that her feelings for Clive were friendship alone. She'd never been in love before, and therefore refused to believe that what she felt for Hugh could possibly be any such thing. It was surely just an excessive attachment to her patient, the very thing she'd been warned to avoid throughout her training, and she needed to keep her wits about her and not make a fool of herself. The result was a constant battle inside her head: a part of her was militant about her duties and responsibilities in simply adhering to what she'd been hired to do—even if that included the added benefits of Hugh's friendship. That militant voice in her head continually scolded the romantic, impressionable side of herself, reminding her to not be so silly, and certainly not to get caught up in any ridiculous notions. Hugh was dying, and she was his nurse, his hired companion. There were no future possibilities in such a relationship—even if there was the tiniest possibility that Hugh might share her feelings, which she knew to be absurd.

Bess kept the militant commander in her mind as much in control as she possibly could—especially when she was with Hugh. She felt certain that with time she would be able to put such silly feelings into perspective, and she just needed to do her job and do it well, each day counting her blessings regarding the comfortable and fulfilling life Lady Buxton had provided by bringing her here.

After Bess had been there a month, she was surprised to note an improvement in Hugh's symptoms. It was reported to her that her father had declared the same upon his visits. Hugh was getting better, not worse; this didn't mean that his heart wasn't still inevitably failing, but it did mean that he might live longer than expected, or if nothing else, he might be able to more fully enjoy the time he had left, experiencing less exhaustion and pain and shortness of breath. As a result, he was now getting dressed most days rather than sitting around in a nightshirt and dressing gown, and he usually preferred to spend most of his time in the sitting room, which had more natural light and—as he declared—was far less boring than his bedroom, which had become terribly tedious to him, a sentiment she could certainly understand.

Bess had become accustomed to the way Hugh often held her hand. It had started once after she'd checked the pulse in his wrist and he'd taken hold of her hand before she could move it. He'd squeezed her fingers and thanked her for being so kind to him, and then he hadn't let go while they had talked of other things, since he preferred to avoid conversation that centered around his medical issues. After that it had become common for him to take hold of her hand while they were reading or talking, and Bess had become accustomed to it, liking the way it added a tenderness to their growing friendship. And she refused to consider the possibility that it meant anything more than that. She'd held the hand of many patients, since it was a common way of silently offering connection and support. But she'd never had any patient with whom she'd spent so much time, or with whom she'd come to feel so comfortable.

Bess didn't give much thought to the way that she and Hugh were often holding hands, and that it didn't seem to matter whether anyone else was in the room. Ironically, Clive would sometimes glance at their clasped hands when Hugh wasn't paying attention, and he'd raise a comical eyebrow toward Bess, smiling with silent approval. Beyond that, no one seemed to notice at all. But a while after lunch on a cloudy afternoon when Bess and Hugh were alone in the sitting room, Bess was quick to notice when she looked up from the book she was reading aloud to see Hugh gazing at her with an affection in his eyes that was either entirely new or she'd simply been too distracted to notice before now. He squeezed her hand while she stared back, attempting to discern the meaning in his gaze. And when she did, Bess's heart fluttered, her stomach quivered, and she looked abruptly away. Again, the subtle reactions she'd felt in response to Clive's attentions were put neatly into perspective; they were utterly insignificant in contrast. The tight way Hugh held to her hand made it difficult to let go but she finally did and stood up, turning her back to him to try and gain her composure. All her own feelings came rushing forward, mowing down any militant force that might be attempting to keep her thinking rationally.

"Is something wrong?" Hugh asked, but his tone implied that he already knew *exactly* what had affected her this way.

Bess felt tempted to ignore what she had just clearly read in his expression, and the way it had affected her. She wanted to pretend that everything was simply the way it had been—and was intended to be—that they were friends, that she was there to help take care of him, to be a nurse and companion. But it only took a few moments of thought to know that ignoring what had just happened would be impossible. They spent far too much time together to ever be able to ignore and avoid any such thing; doing so would only create an excruciating awkwardness that neither of them would be able to bear.

"Perhaps you should answer that question," she said, if only to give her more time to know what to say—or perhaps to put the burden on him to acknowledge whatever he might be feeling, which had provoked him to look at her that way.

"Nothing at all is wrong, in my opinion," he said, which Bess didn't find helpful at all. More moments passed while she tried to think of what to say. "Bess," he said gently, "please sit down; talk to me. Just . . . do what you've always done. Be completely straightforward and honest with me. If we can speak honestly about the fact that I'm dying, surely we can talk about anything."

*Anything except this,* she thought. But she knew she *did* need to talk to him, and they needed to be honest and straightforward—however difficult it might be. Trying to resort to her practical nature and avoid what could be nothing but problematic, Bess finally managed a composed expression and turned to face him. He still had that almost dreamy gaze in his eyes, which didn't help keep her practicality in place at all. But she sat back down and said what she knew had to be said. Despite her own feelings, she couldn't possibly allow any kind of wrong assumptions to take place between them. "Hugh," she began, forcing herself to look at him directly if only so he would know how important this was, "it's not uncommon for a patient to become emotionally dependent or attached to the person who is caring for them. That doesn't necessarily mean that—"

"Is that what you think this is?" he asked, sounding mildly offended. "Do you think my being sheltered from the world in so many ways makes me too naive to understand my own feelings? Do you think I've never experienced attraction or affection before?"

Bess realized he was expecting her to answer his questions and she had to honestly admit, "We've never talked about it."

"And so, you assume that what I'm feeling for you must surely be based in naivete or ignorance?" he asked. "I know what you're talking about, Bess. I've spent most of my life with doctors and nurses and hired companions— more than a few of them being women who were attractive and kind. I admit to having some fanciful feelings for more than one of them. But this is not that, Bess. I've tried to convince myself that it was, mostly because I do not want to make my death any more difficult for you than it already will be, but . . . I can't hide what I'm feeling; however unexpected all of this may be, I can't pretend this doesn't exist."

"By *this,* you mean . . ." Bess hesitated, wanting him to offer further clarification, if only so she wouldn't have to wonder exactly what he meant—or perhaps, hoping that *he* would say it and she wouldn't have to.

Bess expected him to state that he was attracted to her, that he *had* come to feel emotionally dependent upon her, attached to her. But he stated with firm conviction, "By *this,* I mean that I love you, Bess. I love you in a way I never believed I would experience. I never expected to live long enough to truly know what it feels like to love someone so thoroughly and completely."

Bess became frozen; she couldn't move, couldn't speak. She just stared at him, as if doing so might help her make sense of everything he'd just admitted to—and perhaps make it possible to be able to honestly admit to her own feelings rather than just trying to avoid them. Unable to think clearly with Hugh looking at her that way, Bess rose abruptly and moved to the window, looking out at clouds so low that a heavy mistiness made it impossible to see very far. *How fitting*, she thought, wishing she could see into the future enough to know what might happen if she could muster the courage to admit to the truth of what she'd been trying to ignore for weeks now.

# CHAPTER SIX

## UNSELFISH

WHILE BESS LOOKED OUT THE window into the mist blanketing Astoria Abbey in a kind of magical quilt, she allowed herself to consider all the thoughts and feelings she had been ignoring and banishing with the edict that they were fanciful and ridiculous, and quite simply improper under the circumstances. She had lain awake many hours with thoughts of Hugh Buxton far too prominent in her mind, and any small indulgence in such thoughts had sparked flutters in her stomach and a quickening of her heart. She'd convinced herself time and time again that her feelings for him were probably the reverse effect of a patient becoming attached to a person caring for their needs. Surely her previously isolated life, combined with the amount of time they spent together, had resulted in an unhealthy preoccupation with this man whom she had been hired to watch over. Bess had worked so hard to dismiss and discredit her feelings as nonsense, but now Hugh had just admitted to feeling the same way. His declarations made it evident he had given the matter a great deal of thought, and his argument on behalf of what he felt was impossible for her to disregard. If she sincerely felt nothing for Hugh, she would have needed to come up with the courage to appropriately tell him so and hope they could continue their regular interactions without any awkwardness or tension. As it was, Bess knew that she needed to be honest with him. He had opened his heart to her; he had spoken words she had hoped to hear from the right man someday, even though a part of her had never imagined it would happen. Everything he'd said—and the way he'd looked at her as he'd said it—provoked a deep thrill in Bess. But if she was going to admit to the truth of her feelings for Hugh, she also had to admit to the harsh reality that he was dying. His life was being measured in weeks, or his heart could just stop beating at any moment without warning. Gathering the courage to tell him how she really felt seemed more difficult than anything she'd ever done; having enough courage to do so, knowing that anything they might share would be brutally temporary, seemed utterly impossible.

Bess gasped to feel Hugh's hands on her shoulders. She hadn't heard his stockinged feet on the carpet as he'd move to stand behind her. The fact that he could stand and walk that far without assistance was evidence of his recent improvement.

"I have no idea what you're thinking, Bess," he said in a hushed voice so near her ear that it sent a delightful tremor down her back, "and I have no idea what you're going to say. I could be wrong, and . . . I know you well enough to know that you won't have any trouble putting me in my place if I am, but . . . I'm guessing it might be difficult for you to figure out what you *should* say as opposed to what you *want* to say; how you really feel as opposed to how you *should* feel. I believe you've been trying to hide your true feelings from me every bit as much as I've been trying to hide mine from you. I know the situation is . . . ridiculous . . . and I have no right to ask *anything* of you—especially not your heart. Clearly there is very little—if any—future for us; even more reason for us to stop pretending, for us to be honest with each other and . . ."

He stopped when Bess turned suddenly to face him. His words were filling her with heat, making her feel as if she would melt from the inside out. But she needed to see his eyes. Only by seeing his eyes could she know for certain if such strange and remarkable words were being spoken to *her* by a man such as *him*. And only by seeing his eyes could she determine his sincerity. What she saw didn't disappoint her; in fact, it was quite the opposite.

"Bess," he whispered as if her name were a lilting note in a love song. He lifted a hand to touch her face and she leaned into his touch, considering the countless times she had touched his face—for purely practical reasons. But this was entirely different. "A part of me wants you to tell me this is nonsense and we will never speak of it again. Any other option feels entirely selfish on my part and—"

"Selfish?" she finally spoke, unable to possibly imagine any aspect of what he was saying to be selfish.

"Yes, Elizabeth," he said firmly, "selfish. No human being wants to love another without being loved in return. How can I not want you to feel the same for me that I do for you—even knowing that if you give me your heart

I will inevitably break it? If the situation were reversed, I think I would be terrified to feel anything at all. I will be leaving this world, Bess; you will be left here to pick up the pieces of whatever I leave behind."

Everything he'd been saying seemed to sink into Bess's heart all at once, and in the same moment an enormous understanding enlightened her mind. Only one thing mattered to her now, and it was easy for her to say, "I don't care, Hugh; I don't care." She wrapped her arms around him and pressed the side of her face to his chest, keenly aware of the sound of his fragile heart beating—more quickly than usual, she noticed. She loved the way he returned her embrace and held her close, even though she could feel him leaning against her for support.

"Perhaps we should sit down," she said, looking up at him.

"An excellent idea," he replied with a nervous chuckle, and she kept her arm around his waist and his arm around her shoulders as she helped him to the sofa where they sat close together. He turned toward her and took both of her hands into his. "This is crazy, Bess. I don't want to hurt you, but . . ."

When he couldn't seem to finish the sentence, she said, "It's not as if you have any control over whether or not you live or die—or *when* you will go. In all reality, any human being could have an accident or be stricken with a terminal illness with no warning. *Knowing* you're going to die simply makes it possible to be more prepared . . . to not have any regrets."

"But what if loving me is something you end up regretting when I'm gone?"

"I could never regret that, Hugh. Never!"

He smiled slightly. "Are you saying that you *do* love me?"

"Yes," she said fervidly and without hesitation.

"And you would have kept your feelings to yourself?" he asked, his brow furrowing.

"I had no idea you felt the same way," she said, marveling over how much had changed in a matter of minutes. She almost felt dizzy at the thought. "I believed you considered me a friend, and that it would never be anything more."

"And perhaps that would be wiser," he said, sadness tainting his voice.

"If that's the case, then what did you mean exactly by comparing how we *should* feel as opposed to how we really feel? Would it be better to go on pretending?"

"For you perhaps," he said, "but for me . . . I would far prefer that we are honest with each other. As I see it, admitting to the way we feel will change very little in the way we live. I can't court you, Bess . . . or ever hope to marry you. There is no future for us; there is only one day at a time. But to know that you love me . . . and for you to know I love you . . . makes all the difference to me."

"Why?" she asked, trying to understand the reasons it felt like all the difference to her, but not knowing how to she could ever explain such feelings.

Hugh looked down at her fingers while he threaded his own between them. "I never expected to fall in love, Bess. When I was a baby my parents were told I likely wouldn't live a year. But I did. And then more years. My mother has probably told you that she's considered every year a miracle."

"She has told me that, yes."

"A part of me feels the same," Hugh admitted, "but if I'm completely honest, another part of me has felt disappointed."

"I don't understand," Bess said.

"And it's difficult to explain." He looked up quickly, then averted his eyes, as if he felt some shame in his admission. "Each time another birthday . . . or a holiday would pass . . . I'd find myself thinking that I'd survived another year. But a year of what? Another year of watching cricket instead of even knowing what it's like to play the game. Another year of occasionally being able to attend a social only so I can observe other people dancing; I was never taught to dance when it was almost certain that even the exertion of slow tempo steps might result in sudden death. I feel as if I've spent my life on the outside looking in, perhaps like a hungry orphan looking through a window at a family sharing a feast." He sighed and kept his eyes turned away. "I was never expected to live long enough to care about having any kind of relationship with a woman, and when I did, my mother had no qualms about making it clear to me that expecting any kind of love to happen in my life was not realistic, and it would be entirely selfish on my part to expect any kind of emotional investment from a woman." He finally looked up at her. "And so I never expected to feel this way; I never allowed myself to even consider it. I've tried very hard *not* to fall in love with you, Bess. But I have, and I can't hide the truth from you. I just don't know what we're supposed to do about it."

Bess was able to smile at him as she tightened her hold on his hands. "We will enjoy every day we have together," she said, "and you mustn't worry about me. I'm already made better for having known you; I will surely be all the better for having loved you. If you ask me, it would have been far *more* selfish to keep your feelings from me. You, Hugh Buxton, are entirely *unselfish* for sharing your heart with me, and I will never be anything less than grateful."

Hugh's eyes practically sparkled in tune with his gentle smile as he let go of one of her hands to once again touch her face. "You are a truly remarkable woman, Bess. I can't even begin to imagine why I would be so blessed."

"It is *I* who am blessed," she said and touched his face in return, watching him close his eyes as if to more fully relish the experience.

"I wish that I had not wasted these last few years in London," he said. "I wish I could have been here . . . where I would have met you when your father came to visit . . . and all this could have come to pass so much sooner. I wish that—"

Bess put her fingers over his lips, and his eyes came open. "There are many things we could wish, my darling, but we can't change what's behind us. We must not be stuck in the past nor fearful of the future; instead we must only take on each day with hope and courage."

Hugh nodded. "How did you get to be so incredibly wise? It's as if you were born this way; it comes so naturally to you."

"I have no idea." She laughed softly. "I think you are likely biased."

"And is my mother biased, as well?" he asked. "And everyone else here who knows you? They have all commented on how very wise you are. Personally, I think it is a gift; you are very naturally perceptive and insightful . . . and compassionate. And I am greatly blessed among the men of this world to have you in my life." He sighed and smiled, tipping his head. "More often than not I've found it difficult to feel that my life is blessed—until you came. You'd not been here more than a few days before I felt so very, very grateful to be alive—a feeling as unfamiliar to me as this love I feel for you."

Bess hardly knew what to say. This was all so strange and unexpected, but at the same time, everything they were saying to each other—and all that she felt—was comfortingly familiar, as if she'd lived her entire life to be here in this time and place, and to be loved by Hugh Buxton. She couldn't think about anything beyond this moment; she couldn't even think about tomorrow. Everything beyond the present was far too precarious and frightening.

"I don't even know what to say," Bess murmured.

"You don't have to say anything," he replied. He smiled slightly, then added, "Have you ever been kissed, Bess?" His eyes revealed his intentions as he eased slightly closer.

"Never," she said. "You?"

"I kissed a woman once."

"And?" she asked if only to prolong this moment and bask in the anticipation.

"I believe the expectation was far better than the reality," he said with a little smirk.

"And now?" she asked, hearing a dreaminess in her own voice that might have been embarrassing except for the fact that she could hear it in his voice as well.

"Now . . . I'm prepared to believe it will be quite the opposite."

"Your expectations are low, then," she said, smirking at him in return.

"No, they're very high." He smiled. "I've been imagining this moment almost from the first day you came here."

"You have?" she asked, surprised, pulling away slightly so that she could better see his eyes. Had he really felt this way from the beginning?

"I really have," he said and took her face into his hands as if his patience was gone. He pressed his lips to hers with a meek, lingering kiss through which Bess was unable to draw breath. He eased back, and she opened her eyes to see his face close to hers. Their eyes mingled with a thousand questions and the seeming answer to each one while Bess exhaled slowly. He kissed her again, this time with less hesitance while the mutual innocence of their shared affection slowly merged into something more authentic and veritable, making her feel somehow more alive than she ever had. When she began to wonder if it would ever end, it did, and she immediately felt disappointed. But it was evident he did too when he kissed her once more in a way that seemed even more magical—if that were possible—while at the same time creating the sensation that they'd already grown perfectly comfortable with kissing each other, as if they were very old and had been married for decades.

Bess didn't open her eyes when Hugh finally parted his lips from hers, and she savored the way he kissed her brow, her eyelids, her brow again. "Have you told anyone?" she asked.

"What? How I feel?"

"Yes," she said, easing back to be able to look at him.

"I confess that I have," he admitted. "I hope that's all right. I never could have found the courage to talk to you about it without seeking some advice from my closest friends."

"Then Clive and Lewis both know?" she asked, trying not to feel alarmed. It wasn't that she believed she or Hugh had anything to be ashamed of; it was just all so new to her that she found it difficult to comprehend that these men with whom she worked so closely knew that Hugh was in love with her. She wondered if they suspected *her* feelings for Hugh. She had tried very hard to hide them, but she didn't necessarily believe herself to be a very good actress. Even though she couldn't deny her own feelings and knowing that Hugh felt the same left her ecstatic, she could easily see how other people might see the situation as ridiculous and could therefore express opinions that might be hurtful.

"They do," Hugh said.

"And what did they say?" she asked, almost afraid of the answer.

"Lewis said very little; as you know he's a man of few words. He simply said that I should listen to my heart . . . and then he made a terrible joke about following it even though it was weak and pathetic."

"That sounds very much like Lewis," she said, not entirely certain she appreciated the humor. "And Clive?"

"In essence, Clive said the same thing, although we actually talked about it for a long while. He said that he's happy for me, that I should have a chance to feel this way—however brief it might be. He heartily encouraged me to not keep my feelings from you; he believed that you would want to know."

"He was right about that," Bess said as she quite naturally laid her head against his shoulder. "Does anyone else know?"

"Not yet," Hugh said, and she glanced up at him. As if he'd read her mind he added, "I have no intention of trying to keep any secrets in this house, Bess—as if we could. We're never alone together for more than a moment without the doors being wide open. I don't care if people think I'm a fool, or if they feel sorry for me. I only care what *you* think. I don't want this situation to be any more difficult for you than it absolutely has to be."

"You make it sound as if it being difficult for me is inevitable."

"Is it not?"

Bess sighed and had to admit, "Perhaps, but . . . I suppose I believe the joys will far outweigh the difficulties, even if it changes nothing of our circumstances, but everything in our relationship."

He smiled and something akin to wonder showed in his eyes. "I'm so very grateful you feel the same way, Bess. I suspected; but think how foolish I would feel now if I'd misread your feelings."

"I dare say it is I who am the fool," Bess said, settling her head once more against his shoulder. "In less than an hour I've come to realize how foolish I was to believe that I could have ever concealed my feelings from you, and how tragic it would have been to try."

"Hear, hear," he said and kissed the top of her head.

"I must tell Daphne," Bess said. "She has become my friend and confidant in all things. I could never keep this from her."

"And so you should certainly tell her," he said, and she looked up at him again.

"And what of your mother?" Bess asked, unable to miss the way his brow furrowed.

"She's very perceptive. I dare say it wouldn't take her long to figure it out—if she hasn't already. But I really don't know how she'll feel about it. I think she will be concerned—especially for you. We need to tell her, but . . . I believe some time to consider exactly how to go about it would be beneficial."

"Agreed," Bess said and settled more comfortably against his shoulder, in awe of the fact that she was being held closely by Hugh Buxton. She almost felt as if she'd stepped into a fairy tale, except they could have no happily ever after—but she refused to think about that now.

They sat close together for a long while in silence, as if they both needed time to allow their minds to catch up to the enormity of the conversations they'd just shared—and the tender affection that was unlike anything Bess had ever imagined she might experience. She recounted all that had passed between them from the very first day she'd come here—every interaction and conversation, every glance and touch—and she was amazingly unsurprised that it had come to this.

When Bess felt Hugh leaning a little more heavily against her, she knew he was getting tired. "Speaking as your nurse, sir," she said lightly, "I think it's time for you to lie down and try to sleep." She glanced at the clock, noting that it was a little past the time when he took his requisite nap.

"Only if you use your magic fingers on my neck," he said, as if her doing so was truly extraordinary for him. But Bess didn't mind; in fact, she enjoyed their daily ritual, and she found fulfillment in the way it helped ease the headache that often occurred at this time of day. And it also helped him relax enough to sleep, which he apparently hadn't been able to do nearly as well before her arrival.

"Lewis?" Bess called in a voice much louder than the hushed tones in which she and Hugh had been sharing their conversation. He appeared immediately in the open doorway between the two rooms, and she wondered how much he might have overheard. But if he already knew about Hugh's feelings, and had known that Hugh had intended to talk to Bess, then surely anything he'd heard couldn't have been too much of a surprise.

She fought off any potential embarrassment over the changes taking place and simply said, "Could you help Hugh freshen up and get comfortable for his nap, and then I'll rub the tension out of his neck."

"As you wish," Lewis said with a smile, then she noticed a subtle, pleasant smirk passing between Hugh and Lewis. He *had* overheard, and yet he was clearly pleased. In fact, they both looked as pleased as Bess felt. In truth, she'd never been happier. If she didn't think about the inevitable brevity of this relationship, she felt utterly elated.

Bess went to her room to hurry and freshen up, as she always did when Hugh was doing the same. Daphne wasn't there, and Bess felt relieved. She needed and wanted to tell her friend everything, but it would take more than a few minutes and that's all the time Bess had right now.

Bess entered Hugh's bedroom to find him lying sideways on the bed—as he always did for his naps so that she could sit down and comfortably reach his neck. Lewis had removed the shoes from Hugh's feet and had tucked the bedcovers over him, and Hugh appeared to be completely relaxed. As she scooted the usual chair close to the edge of the bed, he opened his eyes and smiled up at her—a smile that seemed to repeat all the beautiful and tender words he'd said to her, all the warm expressions of his deepest feelings. Her heartbeat quickened, and her stomach fluttered as she returned his smile and sat down, impulsively giving him a quick kiss—which was upside down.

Hugh laughed softly, and she asked, "Is something funny?"

"Not at all," he said, closing his eyes again. "More . . . delightful. I dare say what's left of my life will be far more delightful if I have the privilege of sharing kisses with you every day."

"Delightful for both of us," she said and began to rub his neck and the base of his skull with her fingers in a way that had become a comfortable and ordinary practice each afternoon.

Bess could feel Hugh relax quickly. He'd become accustomed to the ritual and it was as if his head and neck immediately knew they were safe in her hands, and relaxing was their immediate response. She heard Hugh make a pleasurable humming sound, which wasn't unusual, but she was surprised to hear him say, "I love you, Elizabeth White."

"And I love you," she replied, deeply thrilled to be able to speak her feelings aloud—and to have them reciprocated. Impulsively she kissed his forehead and he made that humming sound again, as if he were the happiest man in the world. A few minutes later he was asleep, and Bess gently kissed his brow again before she carefully eased a pillow beneath his head, as she did every day. For a few minutes she just watched him sleep. It wasn't the first time she'd done so, but today everything between them had changed, and looking at him this way helped her mind catch up—if such a thing were possible. She concluded that the changes didn't make the inevitability of his death any more horrible or frightening. She'd accepted weeks ago that she *was* emotionally invested in Hugh's life—and his forthcoming death—and having him go would be devastating. Perhaps now it would be *more* devastating, but in her heart, she believed that anything good they could share in the meantime would far outweigh her grief over his passing. However, she wasn't going to think about that now. Now, he was alive and breathing and happy. And so was she. Together they would work on making every moment count—even if she didn't know exactly what that meant. But they could figure it out together, one day at a time.

While Hugh slept, Bess was hoping to speak with Daphne about all that had happened. She felt so full of life and love that it seemed she might burst if she didn't tell *someone,* and Daphne was the only person in this house she would ever trust with such a private matter—at least until Agatha was made aware of the situation. And at this point, Bess couldn't be certain that Hugh's mother would be supportive. But Bess pushed that dilemma aside for now. She suspected that eventually everyone in the house would know, but even when others were made privy to the situation, Daphne was the only person with whom she would share such intimate feelings. Bess was naturally disappointed to recall that Daphne had gone into town with a few of the other servants who needed to acquire household supplies, which would give Daphne the opportunity to purchase some personal items.

Bess took care of a few things she had to do for herself before she returned to Hugh's room to sit and read while he slept. It wasn't uncommon for her to do so, but everything had changed between them, and she found it impossible to concentrate on her reading when she far preferred just watching him sleep. She was glad that Lewis had left so she could be alone with Hugh, even if he wasn't aware of her presence. In her mind she revisited their conversation thoroughly more than once, and she asked herself with all seriousness of heart and depth of conscience if committing herself to a relationship with Hugh was the right thing—for both of them. She recalled the way he'd told her he felt selfish, believing that the situation would inevitably bring more pain and difficulty for her than for him. But Bess didn't feel that way at all. Unwilling to even think about how it might feel to lose him, she felt nothing but blessed to know that such a man loved her; it was she who felt selfish.

Bess felt impatient for Hugh to wake up. Knowing how very much he needed his sleep, she felt even *more* selfish. She wanted the pleasure of his company for every moment that it might be possible. She wanted to just share conversation with him—but at this new level at which they'd just arrived today. And when she thought of how it had felt to have him kiss her, she wanted to experience *that* again, as well. Together they had crossed a bridge and they could never go back; nothing would ever be the same between them again.

When he did come awake it only took a moment for his eyes to find her, then he smiled more widely than she'd ever seen—as if she had made him exquisitely happy.

"Hello, my darling," he said as if he'd called her that a thousand times. He reached his hand out for her and she sat on the edge of the bed, so she could hold it.

"Sweet dreams?" she asked.

"How could I ever dream anything more sweet or lovely than the very real and kind and generous woman before me?"

"You have a way with words, Hugh Buxton. How do I know you're not just flattering me?"

"Look into my eyes," he said severely, "and tell me if I'm flattering you."

Bess accepted his challenge and quickly had to say, "I have no doubt concerning your sincerity."

"Then all is well," he said and motioned for her to come closer so that he could kiss her without relinquishing his comfortable position.

Bess heard footsteps in the hall, which gave her enough warning to back away from Hugh and not appear suspicious.

"It doesn't matter," Hugh said.

"Perhaps not," she replied. "But . . . I would prefer that you have an opportunity to tell your friends that you and I have spoken about . . . the situation . . . rather than just having one of them walk in on us and . . ."

Bess stopped when Clive *did* walk in, declaring in his typical jovial way, "I suspected you might be awake by now, my friend."

"And awake I am," Hugh said.

Bess left the room while Clive helped Hugh with the usual afternoon routine. She freshened up as well and went to Hugh's sitting room where she knew the men would join her for tea. Nothing unusual was said while Bess shared little cakes and sandwiches with Hugh and Clive, which she took to mean Hugh hadn't said anything to Clive about the declarations they'd made to each other earlier. When Clive left to take the tea tray back to the kitchen, Hugh leaned across the table and quickly kissed Bess, reminding her that this fantastical feeling swelling inside of her was not born of her imagination.

When both Lewis and Clive came to the room a few minutes later, Bess excused herself, hoping that Daphne would have returned by now, and hoping that Hugh would take the opportunity to speak with his friends. She felt awkward and uncomfortable with the idea of trying to hide this strong attraction between herself and Hugh—especially among those with whom they interacted regularly throughout the course of each day. Bess was relieved to find Daphne in her own bedroom, putting some things away. Bess knocked on the open door between the maid's bedroom and the sitting room they shared.

"How did your errands go?"

"Very well," Daphne said with a smile, "although it's quite chilly outside and I'm glad to be back so I can hopefully get warm again."

"Could we sit by the fire and talk, then?" Bess asked. "There's something I need to tell you."

"Of course," Daphne said and immediately abandoned her task to follow Bess into the sitting room where a hearty fire was burning. They each scooted a comfortable chair closer to the fire and sat down. Daphne removed her shoes and lifted her stockinged feet closer to the flames; Bess was already without shoes—which was typical unless she left this little area of the house where she spent most of her time. She tucked her stockinged feet up beneath herself, loving the way that she and Daphne could be so completely at ease with each other.

Once they were settled into their chairs, Daphne turned to Bess with an expectant expression, but Bess suddenly didn't know what to say or where to begin.

"Is something wrong?" Daphne asked, furrowing her brow.

"No, quite the opposite," Bess said.

"It's *good* news, then."

"What is?"

Daphne chuckled. "You said there's something you need to tell me, but you're not saying anything. I'm glad to know it's good news. It will be even better when I know what it is."

"Forgive me," Bess said and chuckled softly herself, if only to hide her sudden nervousness. "I just feel . . . quite overcome . . . and I'm not sure where to start, so I'll just tell you the most important point." Bess took in a deep breath. "Hugh told me earlier that he loves me." Daphne gasped but Bess ignored her and hurried to add, "It came as a complete surprise to me, since I've been trying very hard to convince myself that what I felt for him surely had to be nothing more than a passing fancy."

"I can't believe what I'm hearing!" Daphne said, not sounding at all pleased, which left Bess more than a little disappointed. She had wrongly expected Daphne to be thrilled for her, but clearly, she was not. "Why have you said nothing of this to me?"

"As I told you, I've believed that my feelings were meaningless."

"And maybe they *are*," Daphne said. "Forgive me if that sounds brash, but I must be honest with you."

"And I would expect nothing less," Bess said. "However, I can assure you that I now know they are *not* meaningless. It would be more accurate to say that I was afraid to admit to what I was feeling."

"Afraid of what?" Daphne asked, sincerely trying to understand.

"Of his rejection? Of looking like a fool? I assumed that my growing affection for him was likely based in the responsibility and concern I feel for him, and the amount of time we spend together."

"And perhaps that is the case," Daphne declared firmly.

"It's *not*, Daphne!" Bess leaned more toward her and took her hand. "I can't tell you how I know, but I know. I love him; and he loves me."

Daphne still looked astonished, but she remained silent for more than a minute—as if she were attempting to fully grasp the situation. But Bess feared that the maid's silence meant she was trying to come up with some logic that might dispute Bess's feelings. When Daphne finally spoke, she did so in a gentle voice, but its gentleness reminded Bess of a parent attempting to explain to a child why their behavior might be inappropriate. "Bess, darling," she said, "if this were a normal situation, the two of you would properly court and there would be time to assess whether your feelings for each other are valid. As it is . . ." She didn't finish, but her eyes told the truth of what she didn't want to voice.

"As it is, he's dying? It's all right. You can say it." Bess wished she hadn't sounded so defensive, but she had truly believed Daphne would understand. Yet, perhaps it wasn't fair to have expected a more positive response when her friend hadn't previously had any idea whatsoever of this situation. "I know he's dying, Daphne; I know. I know that inevitably I will lose him." She heard a crack in her voice and felt a stinging of tears in her eyes, but they only helped strengthen her conviction when she added, "All the more reason to make the time we *do* have together as good as it can possibly be. And as for courting, consider the amount of time two people might spend in serious conversation over the course of courting for many months—or even years—and consider how much time Hugh and I have spent together in earnest conversation. I believe we've experienced the equivalent of a great deal of courting."

"Perhaps you have," Daphne conceded. "But what now? Where can this relationship possibly go from here? The man can't even get down the stairs of his own home without requiring more assistance than he is willing to accept. Will your time together be confined to his rooms?"

"As I see it, *where* we spend our time together is not what matters. If he loves me and he knows his love is reciprocated, he will be all the happier for it, and even with the absolute reality of knowing that he will leave me behind, I can find no reason for regret in that."

"Then perhaps you are naive," Daphne said. She didn't say it unkindly, but it still stung.

Fearing she might burst into tears, Bess stood and said in an even voice, "Perhaps I *am* naive, Daphne. But I'm willing to learn to overcome my naivete in another season of life. Right now, I feel nothing but thrilled and grateful, and I'm going to enjoy it while it lasts."

She left the room before Daphne could say anything more that might dampen her spirits. Alone in her bedroom with the doors closed, Bess had a good cry, managing to keep her tears silent so that Daphne couldn't hear her from the next room. But as she wept, her convictions only settled in more deeply. She was surprised at how nothing Daphne had said left her discouraged or afraid—quite the opposite, in truth. Maybe she *was* naive, and maybe she was making a mistake; maybe when he was gone, and she was alone and grieving, she would look back and feel some regret. But deep inside she believed she would have *more* regret if she hesitated, if she denied him or herself the opportunity to see where this love might take them in the time he had left.

Freshly determined and brimming with the elation of new love, Bess went to Hugh's room, wondering if she should give him more time to speak with Clive and Lewis. She hoped *that* conversation had gone better than the one she'd had with Daphne. She reminded herself that she didn't need Daphne's approval, but she hoped this would not dampen the friendship they'd come to share.

Bess saw that the door to Hugh's bedroom was open, and she could hear the hearty laughter of all three men, which made her smile. If they were sharing serious conversation, the door would likely be closed, and they certainly wouldn't be laughing in such a way. She stepped tentatively into the doorway, trying to gauge whether she should interrupt them. The three men were sitting around the table, where it appeared that a game of chess had been set up but never started. Clive immediately saw her there and came to his feet.

"And there she is!" he said with dramatic humor. He swept one arm in front of himself and made a low bow, which elicited more laughter from the other men, but Bess couldn't help but see the sparkle in Hugh's eyes as he gazed at her.

"What is all this?" Bess asked Clive, turning her attention to his ongoing antics as he bowed again.

Clive stood to face her and said more seriously, "I didn't believe there was a woman alive who could break into that crusty heart of his. For that, my dear, you deserve our highest accolades."

"Hear, hear," Lewis said.

"It would seem they are happy for us," Hugh said with a bright smile. Bess smiled back, wishing she could say the same about Daphne. She considered the fact that Hugh had known these men for a great many years, and she had only known Daphne for a matter of weeks. Perhaps she would be wise to give Daphne some time to get used to the idea, and not concern herself so much over the difficult conversation they'd just shared. Bess preferred to focus on her feelings for Hugh, and how grand it was just to see him look at her that way. She could see now that despite his efforts to be discreet about his love for her, it had shown in his eyes for quite some time now. She simply hadn't known what she was seeing there.

"Come sit with us," Hugh said, and Clive helped Bess with her chair before he sat back down. Hugh took Bess's hand where she'd set it on the table. Holding her hand had become common, but the unmistakable adoration she saw in his expression was not. The four of them chatted and laughed in a way that had become comfortable and familiar, but Bess was entirely unaccustomed to having Hugh stare at her, making no attempt whatsoever to hide his feelings. And she could do nothing but return his gaze, as if volumes of life and love were being expressed even in their silence. When Clive and Lewis noticed that Hugh and Bess had stopped participating in the conversation, they both teased Hugh a little bit—and Bess saw him blush, but it didn't keep him from continuing his ardent gaze. He just told his friends to play chess and mind their own business before he smiled and winked at Bess, and she wondered if she'd ever been happier.

# CHAPTER SEVEN

## CARPE DIEM

BESS WENT TO THE KITCHEN as usual to have supper with the servants, even though she didn't want to be away from Hugh for a moment. But she knew it was ridiculous to think that she could spend every waking moment with Hugh. Their routine needed to go on as it had before—especially while most of the household was unaware that anything had changed. She concluded that even a husband and wife did not typically spend all their time together, and she didn't want to become dependent on his company every minute of the day any more than she wanted to deprive his friends and his mother of their time with him. That *would* be selfish, and she would never want that.

The remainder of the evening went according to normal routine—except that after Bess had made certain all was well with Hugh before she went to bed, he took her hand and said, "I love you, Bess. You've given me something truly worth living for."

"I love you too, my darling," she said and sat on the edge of the bed. "I only wish that having something to live for could heal your heart."

"It's healed my spirit," he said and smiled as he motioned for her to come closer. "I need you to kiss me good night, woman," he muttered in a light tone that didn't mask the sincere affection in his eyes, "and I'm far too tired to do anything about it; I fear you'll have to do all the work."

"It's no sacrifice, I can assure you," Bess said and leaned over to kiss him, relishing the fact that she'd not simply imagined how lovely their earlier kisses had been. "Now," she said, keeping her face close to his, "is there anything else you need before I leave you in Lewis's care for the night?" She knew Lewis would be here any minute to give Hugh his nighttime medicine—although Hugh didn't take as much as he used to, since lately he'd been able to sleep better without any assistance. Then Lewis would make certain Hugh had everything he needed before settling himself onto the sofa for the night.

"Just another kiss will do," he said, and she kissed him again. "Perhaps one more," he chuckled, and she complied.

Bess stood up before she gave in to the temptation to just keep kissing him. "That should hold you until morning," she said. "May your dreams be sweet."

"If you're there they will be," he said and watched her leave the room.

Bess hurried to get ready for bed, feeling especially tired. Perhaps the enormity of all that had changed in her life today had been physically draining. But once she was in bed in the dark, she couldn't relax enough to fall asleep with all the thoughts that were circling around in her mind. After what felt like hours, Bess lit a lamp and looked at the clock, surprised to see that it wasn't even midnight yet. In that moment, the night before her felt long and lonely while she thought of Hugh sleeping across the hall, with Lewis there in the room in case he needed anything. It occurred to her that if both men were sleeping, neither of them would even know if she crept quietly into the room, and in that moment, she just wanted to be in the same room with Hugh.

Bess knew the way well enough to be able to get there without a candle or lantern. Both of their doors were always left open in case she was needed in the night, and with her eyes already adjusted to the dark, it was easy to settle into a comfortable chair not far from Hugh's bed, tucking her feet up beneath herself and wrapping the blanket she'd brought along more tightly around herself.

"What on earth are you doing?" Hugh asked in a whisper that made her gasp.

"I thought you'd be asleep," she whispered back, not wanting to wake Lewis.

"And so your plan was to . . . sit in the dark and listen to me sleep?" he asked lightly.

"Something like that," she said.

"Come closer." Even in the darkness she could see Hugh motion with his arm.

Bess sat on the edge of the bed, a spot with which she was very familiar. "Do you suppose Lewis is asleep?" she whispered.

"Not a chance," Hugh said more loudly. "He'd be snoring if he were."

"I was afraid you'd be on to me," Lewis said from across the room. "I was hoping to eavesdrop."

"If only you could be so lucky," Hugh said.

Bess heard Lewis sigh with feigned chagrin before he chuckled, and she could see him standing up. "I'll just . . . try out the sofa in the sitting room for a while. But I'm leaving the door open," he added like a suspicious parent, "so mind your manners."

"You know I will," Hugh said, and Lewis left the room, blankets and pillows in his arms.

"How does he know that?" Bess asked lightly.

"Because he knows I'm a gentleman," Hugh said in all seriousness.

"Well, I know that too," she said, equally serious.

"Then you know that if you come sit beside me I will not misbehave."

"I *do* know that," Bess said and scooted farther up the bed, leaning on some extra pillows that she situated against the headboard. As soon as she was comfortable, she was surprised to have Hugh shift his head into her lap, after which he let out a contented sigh and Bess impulsively began stroking his hair back off his face. It was far from the first time she'd touched his hair, but never like this. Her relationship with Hugh was opening up a whole new world of experiences that were entirely different from anything in her past. She'd never felt this way before, never imagined that just being with someone in such a quiet and benign way could be so comforting.

They remained in complete silence for many minutes, but Bess found it easier somehow for her mind to accept the changes between them when they were together, in contrast to her being alone across the hall. She didn't know how to tell him that without sounding presumptuous, so she allowed the silence to continue, surprised when he suddenly revealed his own thoughts. "I don't want to die, Bess, not now. I truly believed I'd come to terms with it. I've been expecting it for years. But now . . . I want more time with you."

Bess shouldn't have been surprised by the tears that overtook her, but she managed to keep them silent as she said, "I want that too, my darling."

"I love it when you call me that," he said. "*Why* do you call me that?"

"I love you," she said.

"I know, but . . ."

Bess thought about it for a moment. "I hadn't thought about it until now, but my mother often said that to my father. I suppose my memories must have made it the most comfortable form of endearment."

"Well, I love it," he repeated. "Don't stop."

"As you wish, my darling," she said, and he chuckled softly. A few more minutes of silence passed before he said, "May I assume that your inability to sleep was for the same reason as mine?"

"If you mean that I cannot comprehend all that's happened this day to change my life, then yes."

"That would be it," she said.

"Why didn't you ask Lewis to give you some medicine, so you could sleep and—"

"I didn't want to sleep," he said. "I only wanted to think about you, and the things you said to me today, and how gloriously it's changed my life, changed me. I can sleep any time."

"Easy for you to say," she teased. "I have a job to do."

"Well, you should definitely take a good nap when that nasty employer of yours is napping."

"That may be wise, although he's never been anything but incredibly kind."

More silence preceded Hugh asking, "So, why did you come over here to sit in *my* room in the dark?"

"I felt lonely," she admitted. "It's difficult to define, but . . . now that you know how I feel, and . . . I know how you feel . . . it just doesn't seem right for either of us to be alone at night. But it's hardly appropriate for me to be here like this . . . were it not for Lewis in the next room. I still don't hear any snoring; he must be making certain we're behaving ourselves."

"I'm sure he is," Hugh said lightly, then she could almost feel him turning more serious even before he spoke, and his voice proved it. "What happens now, Bess? I'm grateful for the possibility of being able to enrich each other's lives simply by being open about how we feel, but it . . . doesn't feel like enough—especially when life is so short."

"But what other option do we have?" she asked and saw him lean up on one elbow. She couldn't see his face, but the shadow of his form was clear against the backdrop of the windows across the room.

"Marry me," he said with enthusiasm.

"What?" she asked, not because she hadn't heard him but because she couldn't believe it.

"Marry me, Bess," he stated with firm insistence. "If we are going to make the very most of what little time we have together, then we should *not* be restricted to having to sleep across the hall from each other or continually be chaperoned. I want you close to me—as much as it's possible." He paused a long moment and asked with vulnerability in his voice, "If there's some reason you think we shouldn't get married, then—"

"It's not that at all," Bess said. "I'm not afraid of taking risks or making a mistake. My only fear is losing you and being left behind with any kind of regret; I believe my biggest regret would be *not* taking advantage of every possibility of sharing life to its fullest while we can. If that's what you want, the answer is yes."

"Is it what *you* want?" he asked.

Bess allowed her joy to come out in a little burst of delighted laughter. "I hadn't even thought of it as a possibility, but now that you've said it, I can't imagine anything ever making me happier."

Hugh laughed too, and she laughed again with him. They talked about their plans for a length of time they couldn't keep track of without a clock to look at. Hugh declared how happy it made him to simply know that he could formulate *any* kind of plans for his future, but especially such delightful plans. When Hugh began to show evidence of getting sleepy, Bess started yawning and believed that she could finally fall asleep herself. She left Hugh with a kiss and went back to her bed, indescribably happy but utterly exhausted. Knowing that tomorrow would be a big day, she was glad to quickly feel relaxed enough to sleep.

Bess awoke to sunlight, noting that the clouds and misty air of the previous day had vanished. She knew from her conversation with Hugh the night before that they needed to speak with his mother before they told anyone else of their plans. The very fact that other people already knew of their mutual feelings and his mother hadn't yet been told added to their conviction that having a conversation with her couldn't wait. Bess knew how close Agatha was to her son, and Bess also treasured the trusted friendship she had gained with Agatha, and she would never want to do anything to compromise that. A part of her felt afraid of what might happen if Agatha was against this marriage. She believed that Hugh would still follow through on making their plans come to fruition, and he had friends who were loyal enough to help him make that happen. But Bess didn't want any discord between herself and Agatha, and even more so, she didn't want anything to cause strain between Hugh and his mother when she too deserved as much happiness as possible throughout this final phase of Hugh's life.

As soon as Bess was ready for the day, she crossed the hall, glad to see the door to Hugh's bedroom open. She entered to find him sitting up in bed with a book on his lap, but he was paying no heed to it. Instead his distant gaze had a dreaminess to it that reminded her of her own feelings. Pausing to just take in his appearance—and the evidence in his expression that all she felt and believed was shared by this incredible man—she had to take a moment to catch her breath before she made him aware of her presence by simply saying, "Good morning."

Hugh turned toward her, a smile spreading over his face, accompanied by a distinct sparkle in his eyes. "Good morning," he replied, and everything in his voice—as well as his countenance—implied that just seeing her might have been the greatest experience of his life. Given the sheltered way he lived, she figured he didn't have a great deal of experience with which to compare his feelings, but she knew his love for her was real and genuine—as hers was for him—and that was all she needed.

"Good morning," Bess heard and became aware that Clive was seated on the sofa across the room, hidden behind a newspaper. He quickly folded the paper and set it aside before he stood, adding lightly, "Don't worry about me. I'm perfectly fine with feeling invisible amidst all the love and adoration in the room between the two of you." Bess felt tempted to blush over having her feelings spoken of so openly, but Clive quickly put her at ease when he took hold of both her hands and looked into her eyes. "I want you to know that nothing could make me happier. I'm more delighted for the both of you than I could ever say." He surprised Bess by kissing her cheek. "Enjoy every moment as much as you can," he whispered near her ear so that Hugh wouldn't have known he'd said anything. She nodded very slightly as Clive eased back and let go of her hands. She didn't know if she saw the tiniest glimmer of disappointment in his eyes, as if he might have hoped that something romantic might have developed between him and herself, but it came and went so quickly that it could well have been her imagination. Whether or not Clive had feelings for her was irrelevant. She loved Hugh and he loved her. And she was determined to move forward with their plans as quickly and efficiently as possible. She only wanted to be his wife, even if their marriage could very well be as brief as the passing of a storm. But she and Hugh were in the eye of every storm right now, where she could feel nothing but hope and happiness, and she could see the same mirrored in his expression.

Clive left the room, making a joke about leaving the two lovebirds alone—although he pointed out that the doors would be left open so that they'd mind their manners. Bess once again resisted the urge to blush over the implication. Instead she focused on Hugh and the hand he reached out toward her. She sat on the edge of the bed as she had done hundreds of times, but rather than setting right to work to assess his medical condition, she leaned toward him so they could exchange a kiss without him having to relinquish his comfortable position.

"Good morning," he said again, more dreamily. "I'm glad to know I didn't dream your being here during the night, and everything we talked about. I didn't, did I?"

"No." She smiled and kissed him again. "It wasn't a dream." She added more seriously, "Unless you've changed your mind and—"

"I haven't changed my mind," he said. "We need to speak with my mother straightaway . . . when she comes as usual to visit before lunch."

Bess felt decidedly nervous. "And what if she is not supportive, Hugh? What if she believes it's not a good idea?"

"I sincerely believe she will understand," Hugh assured her. "However, I also believe that even if she is not entirely in agreement, she will still be supportive; she always has been."

"I hope you're right," Bess said. "I love her dearly and I don't want my relationship with her to change in any way, although I'm willing to take that risk." She smiled at him, hoping he knew she would risk anything and everything to share whatever time they had together.

"I'm glad to hear it." He smiled back, implying that he understood, and that he too was willing to do the same. "I've been thinking of how to go about it. I want to be able to speak with her alone at first . . . to tell her myself. I believe she might be more guarded with you present."

"I understand," Bess said, even though she felt mildly disappointed over not being able to hear Agatha's initial response.

"However," Hugh added with strong emphasis, "I want you to be able to hear the conversation because I don't want to have to tell you everything that was said; therefore, I would like you to go into the sitting room, leave the door open, and stay as close to the door as you can while remaining out of view."

"Are you giving me permission to eavesdrop on your conversation?" she asked, more than a little relieved.

"Not permission," he said. "I'm begging you to do so. Even though I want her to feel at ease enough to be completely candid, I want to feel like I have your support in what I'll be telling her. I need to know you're listening. We'll come clean as soon as it's possible to do so comfortably."

"Very well," Bess said with light sarcasm, "I agree to your devious plan." He chuckled as he motioned her toward him so he could kiss her again.

"Now, down to business," she said and picked up the stethoscope from the bedside table so she could listen to his heart and lungs. She checked his feet and lower legs for swelling and asked all the usual questions about how he'd slept, how he was feeling, his level of pain, and his ability to breathe.

"Overall, I'd say you're doing rather well," she said, returning the stethoscope to its now-permanent resting place whenever it was not in use—on the bedside table within Hugh's reach.

"Perhaps the love you give me is healing my broken heart," he said with no humor at all. "Or at the very least, giving it the strength to keep living long enough to make some good memories for you, and to let me leave this world happier than I'd ever imagined possible."

"That is my hope," she said and kissed him still again. She was tempted to keep kissing him, but they heard footsteps in the hall and Bess stood up just before Clive brought in the breakfast tray and set it on the table, where he set out the dishes for three as usual.

Clive then came to the edge of the bed to help Hugh get up, as was their usual routine. "Do you need time in the privy before we eat?" Clive asked.

"No, thank you," Hugh said. "I'm fine; just hungry."

"I like to hear that," Clive said as he helped Hugh get to the table. "A good appetite will help you keep up your strength."

"We can hope," Hugh said as he sat down and smiled up at Bess just as she set a cup of tea in front of him. She sat down herself to hold a warm cup of tea in her hands, taking an occasional careful sip as it cooled just enough to be able to drink it. While she shared breakfast with Hugh and Clive, the former could hardly take his eyes off her—which made her feel more loved and adored than she'd ever believed possible—and the latter couldn't keep himself from teasing them both about the lovesickness in the air. But Bess didn't mind. She knew Clive genuinely cared about both herself and Hugh, and his humor helped ease the continual tension of Hugh's gaze that kept her riveted to observing his every move and gesture.

After they'd finished eating, Clive took the tray back to the kitchen, leaving Hugh and Bess alone to revisit the conversation they'd shared during the night and—as Hugh said more than once—to be absolutely certain it was the course they both wanted to take, and that their plans for carrying out a speedy wedding had merit. Hugh told her he didn't feel nervous about speaking with his mother; their relationship was solid, and even if she might be surprised, he knew she would be reasonable because she always had been. Bess wished she could share his confidence and told him so.

"There's no reason for you to be concerned," he said firmly, taking her hand across the table. "You have told me yourself how close you and my mother have become. Why would you believe she'd be anything less than happy for us?"

Bess momentarily considered whether she should put a voice to her thoughts, but immediately knew they were committed to being completely honest with each other, and they could never go forward with such an unusual situation by behaving otherwise. "Do I have to say it out loud?" she asked.

"Yes," he insisted. When she hesitated, he guessed, "Because I'm dying? You think she'll stand in the way of our getting married because we all know it's so temporary?"

Bess hated hearing that part of the situation put into words, even though she knew it was true and the very reality was never far from her mind. "That's part of it," she said.

"And what's the other part?" he asked. Again, she hesitated, and he leaned toward her, saying in an imperative whisper, "Bess, you must talk to me. Tell me what's troubling you, now . . . while we're alone . . . before she comes to see me."

"Isn't it obvious?" she countered, certain he must know to what she was referring, even though it had never been voiced between them.

"Forgive me, darling, but no, I see nothing obvious that should be of any concern."

Bess sighed, realizing that she *did* have to say it out loud. "Hugh," she began with a soft voice, looking directly into his eyes, "I am a servant in this household. I was hired to help care for you. And you—you're Hugh Buxton of Astoria Abbey."

"Do you think any of that matters to me?" he asked, sounding mildly offended.

"No," she replied quickly and firmly, "but will it matter to your mother?"

"No," he responded in the same tone, "it will not. She's never cared a whit about such things. And if you're going to ask about how *other* people might view this choice we're making, none of that matters *at all!*"

Bess took in his words with a deep, soothing breath. "I suspected you felt that way," she said, unable to keep her voice from quivering, "but I'm glad to hear you say it and to know that you mean it. I don't know what repercussions I might be left with after you're gone, and I really don't care—as long as I know that you made this decision for the same reasons that *I* am making this decision."

"And what is that?" he asked as if it were a challenge.

"One reason only, Hugh. I love you. I don't care what anyone else says or thinks. I may be called an impulsive fool, and when I'm left alone people may criticize my decision and tell me I deserve my fate. I'm all right with that. I just need to know that you're all right with marrying a simple woman with nothing."

"I'm marrying *you,*" he said with gentle conviction. "I'm marrying the woman I love; nothing else matters." Bess smiled at him, feeling better now after having cleared that up. She was surprised to hear him say, "I'm not worried about my mother's response, but are you worried about your father's?"

Bess had mostly chosen to push away any thoughts of her father who had blatantly and consistently ignored and disregarded her ever since she'd first come here. As for informing him of this enormous change about to take place in her life, she had to admit, "I would wish for his blessing and acceptance; I would wish that he might want to be present when we're married, to give me away even if there's no aisle to walk down." They both laughed softly, then together they became more somber as she went on and tears stung her eyes. "But I fear he'll only use my decision to marry you as more evidence of what he considers my foolishness in leaving what he believes was the perfect life for me. I know he's a good man, Hugh, but it's as if he has selective blindness regarding me, and I don't know why. But living here in your home has taught me that I don't need his validation in my life to be happy; it seems he's simply not capable of giving me the love and respect I deserve." She took a deep breath and blinked back her tears. "So, we will inform him of our decision next time he comes to check on you, and if he chooses to remain uninvolved, that is up to him. The day I came here, I stopped living my life to please my father."

"I love you, Elizabeth," Hugh said with admiration glowing in his eyes. "And I'm proud of you for having the courage to break free from that life, and the insight to understand how much it was hurting you. It's one of many reasons I love you. I only wish . . ."

"What?" she asked when he stopped.

"I think there are some wishes that shouldn't be spoken," he added with obvious sadness.

"Perhaps," she said, "but say it anyway."

"I wish that we could have years together, that we could have a family and grow old together." Tears came with his confession, but Bess reached across the table and wiped her fingers over his cheeks.

"I wish for that too," she whispered, "but we will simply have to cram as much joy and happiness as we possibly can into each day while we do our best to ignore that we have no idea how many days or weeks we might have."

"With any luck and God's blessings, I pray we will have months."

"Amen," she said and kissed him. Even with the prospect of so little time together, Bess had never imagined feeling such happiness.

Clive returned to help Hugh get cleaned up and dressed for the day. He wanted to be wearing regular clothes when he shared this important conversation with his mother—instead of being in his most common attire of a nightshirt and dressing gown. While Clive was assisting Hugh, Bess went to her own room to freshen up and give herself a chance to rethink all that was happening. She was relieved but not surprised to conclude that she didn't feel even the tiniest iota of hesitation about moving forward. She knew in the deepest part of her soul that this was the right course for her life. She couldn't see life beyond Hugh's death; but the life she was meant to live until then was explicitly clear before her and she was prepared to commit herself fully to him in every way.

Bess was relieved to note in her interaction with Daphne that nothing appeared to be any different between them. It was as if the awkward conversation they'd shared concerning Bess's intentions had never happened. While Bess would have preferred to be able to talk about the situation with Daphne, and share her overwhelming emotions with a friend, she was at least glad that Daphne was implying by her complete absence of any negative attitude that she would not disrespect Bess's decisions—even if she didn't agree with them. While Daphne put away some freshly laundered clothing, they chatted about all the things they had chatted about every day before Bess had confessed her feelings for Hugh.

When Bess knew it was nearly the time that Agatha usually arrived to visit with Hugh, she crossed the hall to find him sitting on the sofa near the window of his bedroom, looking out, his expression distant and thoughtful. Before he realized she was there, she allowed herself a long moment to just observe him. His damp hair and neatly trimmed beard—combined with the billowy white shirt and brocade waistcoat he wore—quite simply took her breath away. Recalling the moment when she'd seen him dressed much the same way when she'd come here with her father not so many weeks ago, she found it impossible to comprehend the threshold upon which she stood, about to welcome this fine man as an integral part of her life. She knew in her heart that even when he was physically gone from this world, the impression of all they were sharing would be forever left upon her life; she would never be the same.

"Don't you look fine!" she said and crossed the room, unable to bear the distance from him another moment.

"I'm hoping that if I'm actually dressed like a gentleman I'll feel more confident."

"Is it working?" she asked and sat down beside him, taking his hand.

"Maybe," was all he said before he kissed her. As if he'd read her mind, he looked into her eyes and said, "You mustn't worry. Even if it takes her some time to get used to the idea, she'll come around. She loves us both; she'll want us to be happy."

"She loves *you*," Bess corrected. "She's very fond of me, but—"

"She loves you, as well," Hugh said. "She's told me as much."

The very notion took Bess off guard, but she quickly removed her hand from Hugh's grasp when they heard footsteps in the hall and knew that Agatha was approaching. Bess suddenly didn't want to be in the room even for the usual greetings, which would require her to excuse herself and she couldn't think of what reasons she might give for leaving Hugh and his mother alone without drawing attention to an awkwardness she didn't want to create. Offering no explanation to Hugh, she stood and rushed into the sitting room through the open door and leaned against the wall—out of sight—to catch her breath from her hasty retreat.

Bess could clearly hear Agatha exchanging the usual greetings with her son, followed by the obvious question, "Where is Bess?"

Bess wondered if Hugh would get right to the point or engage in idle conversation first. Given that she was doomed to this clandestine eavesdropping until he told his mother their news, she hoped he would not delay the inevitable. She was relieved to hear him say, "She's in the sitting room. I wanted to speak with you about something and we both thought it best that she not be in the room, which might create a distraction. But she's not far away."

Bess appreciated the way he subtly implied that she might be able to overhear the conversation, since her own sense of honesty—and that of Hugh—would demand that Agatha be told Bess had indeed been close enough to hear everything.

"You've certainly piqued my curiosity," Agatha said, sounding mildly concerned.

"There's something I need to tell you, Mother, and it may come as somewhat of a shock to you, so I ask you to be patient and hear me out."

"Very well," she said in a voice of forced patience, the words being both preceded and followed by a loud sigh. Bess eased into a chair and tried to make herself comfortable while she listened, but every muscle in her body felt tense.

"I'm dying," Hugh said in a tone that implied it was a grand and dreadful announcement that had never been spoken before. He then chuckled, and Agatha made a scoffing sound, disgusted by his macabre humor, but then she chuckled as well, and Bess couldn't help but smile, even though she shook her head with the same feeling of mild disgust that she surely shared with Agatha. She was glad Hugh could laugh about the awful truth, but still it was difficult to consider the reality.

"And . . . ?" Agatha drawled. "You're dying, and . . . ?"

"And I've fallen hopelessly in love with Bess," he added firmly, with no apology or explanation. Bess heard Agatha gasp and Hugh hurried on, as if to fully explain before his mother could offer any opinion. "By some miracle she loves me too, and before you get all practical and tell me the obvious, this is not some fanciful notion that has arisen from the fact that I'm very dependent upon her for my care and we spend many hours together every day. This is love, Mother, real love. I've already mulled it over a thousand times and compared it to anything and everything I've ever felt before, and she has done the same. To state the other obvious point, I *am* dying. We all know that. It's a ludicrous time of life to fall in love . . . when you know that you're dying. I held back from sharing my feelings with Bess, because I don't want to hurt her in any way. But I talked it through extensively with Clive and Lewis; you know how I trust them both implicitly. They both agreed that I should live what is left of my life to its fullest; Clive especially encouraged me to be honest with Bess and allow her the option to declare her own feelings and choose her own path. I believe you would agree with that principle. Still, I hesitated. Again, I didn't want to bring the complication into her life of becoming involved with a man who is dying. But as I observed her closely, I realized she felt something for me and I couldn't keep myself from telling her the truth any longer. We love each other very much, Mother, and we don't have much time. We both want to make the most of this in every possible way."

"What exactly are you trying to tell me, Hugh?" Agatha asked, and Bess felt disheartened to hear evidence that she was upset.

"We are going to be married, Mother," Hugh said, and Agatha gasped again, more loudly. "And I don't need to say that we intend to do so as quickly as it can possibly be arranged."

Bess held on to the warm conviction she heard in Hugh's voice while an excruciating stretch of silence preceded Agatha's saying, "You are both setting yourself up for inevitable heartbreak."

"No, *you* set this up, Mother," Hugh said, a comment that completely surprised Bess. He'd never shared any such thoughts with her. "What did you think would happen by bringing a beautiful, kind woman into my life and having her in my presence nearly every waking minute? I believe you *wanted* this to happen, and that you're not nearly as distressed as you're letting on."

Again, there was more silence, a loud sigh from Agatha, and still more silence except for a slight rustling that could only be the sound of her skirts as she adjusted the way she was sitting. "Am I so easy to read?" she finally said, again surprising Bess. This was not how she had expected the conversation to go.

"For me, perhaps," Hugh said. "So, it's true? When you hired Bess . . . you hoped that something like this might evolve?"

"I hired Bess for all the reasons I have already explained to you. If there had been an ugly old man who had been available with the same skills, I would have hired *him*. And I've told you many times how right I felt about her, that I believed she needed to get out of her situation as much as we needed her. I had my mind made up before she came here that day with her father. It was *after* I'd offered her the job that the thought occurred to me . . . well . . . how sad it was that you'd never been in love, that you'd never experienced what that feels like. And how could I not notice how well the two of you took to each other? I suppose it would have been ridiculous for any of us to believe that the two of you wouldn't become emotionally attached, but no one could have predicted—especially not me—whether that attachment would become romantic. However, I did not expect *this.*"

"*This?*" he echoed.

"Marriage? You want to marry her? I don't have to tell you that she could be a widow in weeks, perhaps days."

"No, Mother, you don't have to tell either of us that."

More silence ensued, and Bess closed her eyes, clearly able to imagine how Agatha might hang her head in such a moment, a gesture that was common for her when she was attempting to hide her emotions. Hugh had told

Bess that he'd come to recognize his mother's occasional need to gather her composure and maintain her dignity, and he'd become accustomed to allowing her the time to do so. Bess had seen the same in her own conversations with Agatha. But in that moment, Bess felt as if her entire life was hanging in the balance. If Agatha was supportive of their decision, everything would come together smoothly; if she was against it, their plans to be married would be difficult. Bess knew that Hugh would proceed either way, but they both loved and respected Agatha a great deal, and they both desperately wanted her blessing in this decision.

When Agatha spoke again, there was a quiver in her voice that made it evident she'd not been successful at trying to swallow the emotion this conversation was evoking for her. "Forgive me, Hugh, but . . . it's just so . . . sad . . . that you would fall in love *now.*"

"Which is sadder, Mother? That I would die never having known love? Or that I would die, having experienced love for even a short time?" He sighed, and Bess could hear Agatha sniffle, which meant she was crying. "Don't be sad for me, Mother," he added. "It's Bess who will be left here to face the unconscionable consequences of the way I've taken her so completely into my heart. She's far too young and precious to be dealing with matters of death and love being tangled together."

"Then why do you suppose she wants to actually go through with a marriage . . . as opposed to just . . ."

"Just what? Courting?" Bess felt certain he couldn't help his sarcasm *or* his cynicism in response to such a question. "Should I escort her to a ball? Take her for long walks in the garden? Perhaps we could go riding or—"

"Your point is taken," Agatha said, sounding frustrated, but Bess knew her frustration was not directed toward Hugh; she was surely almost as frustrated with his circumstances as Hugh was—which made Bess worry about how Agatha would manage when he was gone. Bess couldn't begin to fathom how she would cope herself. But Agatha had spent years watching over him, making his health and comfort her purpose for living. What would she do? What would either of them do? Bess couldn't think about that now. She had to take hold of every good moment and make the most of it.

As if she and Hugh were of one mind, she heard him say, "I have a new motto, Mother, and I intend to live by it. *Carpe diem.*"

"Seize the day," Agatha said, stating the meaning of the Latin phrase.

"With everything I have in me," Hugh added with fervor, only to be followed by a thoughtful quiet that Bess found unnerving.

The silence was broken by Hugh saying to his mother, "You and Bess have become very close. Perhaps this could be a blessing for both of you. If I marry her she will become your daughter." Bess felt deeply soothed by his comment, although she couldn't be certain how Agatha felt about such a prospect. Trying very hard not to get emotional, she listened closely as Hugh went on. "But as far as her reasons for wanting to marry me, I think you need to ask *her.*"

Agatha sighed. "Do you think it has anything to do with—I hate to even say it—the money, with security?" Bess was surprised by the question since it had never even crossed her mind. She expected nothing in that regard, and simply assumed that she would find work for herself once she became a widow.

Hugh's voice was firm when he said, "I believe you know Bess well enough to know the answer to that, Mother."

"Yes, you're right. I wouldn't want her to have unrealistic expectations."

"Therefore, it's a blessing to know her motivations have nothing to do with that," Hugh said while Bess's mind was swirling with so many thoughts she could hardly think clearly at all. She felt suddenly frustrated with her separation from the conversation, and perhaps a little guilty for remaining concealed. At the very moment she was wondering how to appropriately make herself known, Hugh said to Agatha, "Just . . . ask her."

Bess hurried to stand up and move into the open doorway, trying to ignore the pounding of her heart as she said, "Ask me what?"

They both turned to see her standing in the open doorway. Hugh smiled and reached his hand toward her, which she interpreted as approval of her interruption. She focused on the ardent love in his gaze as she stepped forward to take his hand and sit close beside him.

"We were talking about you," he said proudly. "Hopefully you over-heard all of it, so you don't have to wonder what we were saying."

Bess felt deeply relieved to have him remove the burden of her having to explain that she'd been listening to the entire conversation. "I confess that I *did* hear everything you've been saying." She glanced at Agatha who looked mildly alarmed. Bess quickly added, "We thought it would be better for the two of you to speak candidly, but . . ."

He rescued her again by saying, "But I *asked* her to remain where she could overhear so I wouldn't have to try and repeat everything we said."

"I see," Agatha said, seeming to accept the explanation; her expression showed only concern and a deep thoughtfulness; the alarm had completely vanished. Bess took that to mean she wasn't upset over their eavesdropping.

Bess found the courage to look directly at Agatha and say, "I believe there's something you want to ask me."

Agatha sighed, and Bess noted the way she was wringing the handkerchief she had likely been using to dry her tears. "I don't need to tell you that Hugh has informed me he wants to marry you—very soon for obvious reasons. I believe I understand his reasons for such a decision, but I would like to understand yours."

Bess glanced at Hugh who nodded his approval for her to be candid. She turned to look again at her potential mother-in-law and said, "May I be frank?"

"Of course," Agatha said. "Have we not always been so?"

"Yes, but this is surely different, more sensitive."

"Say whatever you feel the need to say, my dear," Agatha said and seemed to mean it.

Bess took a deep breath and just said it. "I don't want to spend whatever time he has left in a room across the hall, rushing in and out to check on him and see if he's still breathing while one of his friends might be in the room but sound asleep on the sofa and oblivious. I want to sleep in the same bed and be able to hold him close. I want to sleep with my hand resting lightly on his neck to be able to feel his pulse. I want to hear him breathing. And when he finally goes, I want to be holding him in my arms. I love your son, my lady. I know he's dying, and I dread facing life without him, but I want to make the very most of what time he has left—together. I have no expectations beyond that time. I don't know whether I'll stay or go; I have no idea what I'll do. But it really doesn't matter, does it? Right now, I simply want to be his wife so that it's not inappropriate for me to be here with him night and day. Does that make sense to you? Because it's the only truly plausible explanation I can give."

"Yes, my dear," Agatha said with a quiver in her voice, "it makes perfect sense to me, and I confess that—all things considered—I'm very happy for the both of you."

Bess drew in a breath so sharp that it made her realize she'd barely been breathing. She heard Hugh let out a long sigh and suspected he felt much the same. The way he tightened his hold on her hand was added evidence that he did.

"Then why are you trying not to cry?" Hugh asked, and his mother immediately dabbed at her eyes with her handkerchief, making it evident that her efforts to hold back her tears were not working.

"I think you know very well why," Agatha said, quickly wiping away the tears that rolled down her cheeks. "I want you to be happier; I want to think of the two of you sharing a long and happy life together." She looked directly at her son and added, "We're losing you, Hugh. You and I have always been committed to being honest about the situation and our feelings, and it's not the first time I've declared the right to cry over my son being cheated out of being able to enjoy a normal, healthy life. You know that sometimes I just . . . need to cry."

"As we all do, Mother," Hugh said, glancing toward Bess just as she too wiped a hand across her cheeks. But she quickly offered him a warm and sincere smile, hoping to mirror back the love in his eyes that was as evident as ever. "The thing is," he said and lifted Bess's hand to his lips to kiss it, "my life has been far from conventional, and you know I've struggled with a great deal of anger at times over that fact. But right now . . . I feel more grateful than I ever have . . . for the life I *have* been able to live, that I've lived until now so that I *could* experience what I feel for Bess and the joy she's brought to me." He smiled at Bess and then at his mother. "Being confined to my rooms will look a great deal brighter with Bess here—not as someone hired to take care of me, but as my wife." He sighed and tightened his hold on Bess's hand. "Truthfully, Mother, I've never wanted to admit this aloud, but to never experience love and marriage has been my greatest disappointment over the prospect of knowing I would die young."

Bess was surprised to hear Agatha laugh softly, even though she continued to wipe away tears, but they seemed to be tears of happiness rather than grief. "In that case I can only say I am nothing but happy for the both of you." She looked directly at Bess and smiled through her ongoing tears. "I can't deny some concern for you, my dear, but I suppose we will take that on together when the time comes, and I hope it doesn't sound selfish to say that perhaps I'm glad to think I won't be facing my grief of losing Hugh all on my own."

"That's not selfish at all," Bess said. "I certainly feel the same."

Agatha laughed again and declared with nothing but enthusiasm, "It would seem we have a wedding to plan, and we'd do well to get to it."

Hugh laughed as well, and Bess turned to look at him, noting the pure joy in his expression as he echoed, "Yes, we'd do well to get to it."

# CHAPTER EIGHT

## THE DECLARATION

AGATHA STOOD UP LONG ENOUGH to ring for a maid before she returned to her seat and initiated conversation regarding the best way to go about arranging a wedding very quickly due to extenuating circumstances, which she felt certain others would understand and over which they would surely be supportive and helpful—especially those from whom they specifically needed assistance. When the maid arrived, Agatha asked that she tell Clive to send for the vicar and the family solicitor. When the maid left to see to her assigned task, Agatha said to Hugh and Bess, "Clearly we need to take care of the legal and religious aspects of this first and foremost. Everything else is provisionary upon working out the marriage itself. Would you not agree?"

Bess recognized in Agatha's question an effort to make certain that the potential bride and groom were given the opportunity to offer their input. "Yes, of course," Hugh said, and Bess felt giddy inside to consider herself being the potential bride. She really was going to marry Hugh Buxton. Having his mother's approval meant that nothing would impede their plans; Bess felt certain that Agatha would personally confront Parliament if she had to, in order to make this happen for the sake of her son's happiness.

In spite of Agatha's declaration that being able to legally carry out a marriage was the only thing that *really* mattered, she went on talking with great enthusiasm about plans for a wedding cake to be made by the cook who was reputed to have great skill in not only making delicious meals and desserts, but also in creating beautiful works of art in her craft. And in fact, she enjoyed such opportunities and would surely be thrilled to oversee not only the making of the perfect cake but also a fine meal for everyone involved in the wedding party, which they all agreed would be a very small gathering.

Hugh's isolation had kept him from having anything more than minimal association with people beyond those he saw regularly within the household. His mother had a very few acquaintances she wanted to invite, but Bess became so caught up in listening to Agatha's excitement over the upcoming event that she felt completely unprepared to be asked, "And who will you be inviting, my dear? Surely you have some friends and acquaintances whom you would want to attend."

"Perhaps," was all Bess could say as her mind went to her father. As of yet, they'd not mentioned him, but they were all aware of the present strain between Jonas White and his daughter. She was wondering how to bring up her concerns when Agatha's perception saved her from having to find the words.

"You must be thinking of your father," Agatha said with compassion. Bess could only nod, suddenly overcome with the urge to cry. She was getting married and she wasn't certain her father would even care. "Surely despite your differences, he would want to attend your wedding . . . to do what is customary and give the bride away."

Bess looked down, attempting futilely to blink back her tears. "That would be my hope," she said, hearing her own voice tremble, which gave away her present sorrow. Hugh put his arm around her shoulders and Agatha moved closer, taking hold of Bess's hand. "But I fear this will only make him angrier. If he's upset with me for leaving him, would he not be more upset over my making such a decision as this?"

Agatha was quick to say, "If his pride keeps him from attending his own daughter's wedding, he is hurting himself more than anyone."

"And yet his absence can't help but be hurtful for you," Hugh said and pressed a kiss into her hair as she leaned against his shoulder.

Bess wiped her tears away with the handkerchief she'd pulled out of her pocket, aware of the way Agatha was taking in the evidence of affection between Bess and Hugh. They were discussing wedding plans, but it was the first time Agatha had seen her son hold a woman close to offer comfort. When Agatha abruptly looked away as if to force herself to stop staring, she cleared her throat and said with kind vehemence, "All you can do is ask him to be there, my dear. If he gets upset . . . if he chooses not to be involved . . . we will have a glorious celebration despite his absence."

"Thank you," Bess said, squeezing Agatha's hand and settling her head a little lower onto Hugh's shoulder as he tightened his arm around her. "I don't believe I've ever felt so loved and cared for . . . at least not since my mother died."

"Then it's high time you did," Agatha said before she immediately lightened the mood with more talk of wedding plans, asking their opinions on every matter. Even though they all agreed it should be simple, and they didn't have much time for preparations, Agatha insisted that it still be memorable. Hugh agreed, declaring it would be the highlight of his life— a comment that seemed to hold equal amounts of joy and sadness. And for Bess, who would find a way to go forward in her life without Hugh, it could very well be the same. She couldn't imagine ever loving any man the way she loved Hugh, and therefore the possibility of ever marrying again seemed impossible. She didn't need a fancy or elaborate wedding; she only wanted to marry Hugh as soon as possible. But she couldn't deny Agatha's wisdom in declaring that the occasion should still be properly celebrated. And when Agatha insisted that they would go into town together the following day to choose a proper wedding gown and order flowers, Bess had to admit that such things hadn't even occurred to her, but she could well imagine that in the future when she looked back on her marriage to Hugh, she would want to remember herself wearing something that made her feel like a bride, and carrying a bouquet as any bride should do.

Their conversation continued over lunch, then according to an established routine, Lewis arrived to help Hugh with the usual private matters before helping him get comfortable so that Bess could massage his neck and the back of his head to help him relax and get the necessary rest to sustain him through the evening.

While Hugh was sleeping, Bess went to her bedroom, surprised to find Daphne there, reading a book, apparently waiting for Bess. Her doing so wasn't at all unusual, but following their conversation regarding Bess's feelings for Hugh and her subsequent plans for the future, Bess wasn't certain where she stood with Daphne.

"Hello," Bess said.

"Do you need anything?" Daphne asked in her role as a dutiful maid.

"No, thank you," Bess said, noting that Daphne remained seated, which implied that perhaps she wanted to talk.

Bess sat down and waited a long moment before Daphne said, "There's word about the house that Clive was asked to send for the vicar and the solicitor. And there's speculation over the possible reasons, since it's evident most of the staff have no idea of your . . . relationship . . . with Hugh. Might I assume that the two of you have now spoken to Lady Buxton . . . about your plans?"

"We have," Bess said.

"May I ask how she reacted?" Daphne's tone and expression perhaps implied that the attitude of the lady of the house might very well affect her own attitude. Bess would have far preferred that Daphne might express support and encouragement of her own volition, but if Agatha's position regarding the marriage encouraged Daphne to be more accepting, Bess could live with that and even be grateful for it. Daphne was an integral part of her daily life; she did not want any tension between them, especially while planning and carrying out a wedding.

"You certainly may," Bess said. "She was surprised initially but very understanding. Once she was reassured of our motives, she became rather enthusiastic. I think she sees that Hugh is likely happier than he's ever been."

Daphne sighed rather loudly but was quick to say, "Forgive me for my lack of support when we spoke. I suppose I was taken off guard and . . . I cannot deny that I'm concerned for you. This will bring inevitable heartbreak into your life."

"Lady Buxton said something very similar. But, Daphne . . . I see this as . . . well, perhaps an act of faith. When two people marry, they vow to care for each other in sickness and in health, no matter what may come into their lives. Who in this world gets married with a guarantee that their spouse won't become ill or meet with harm and the marriage will be cut unimaginably short? In our case, we know that Hugh's death is inevitable, and our time together will be brief, but that doesn't mean there aren't a great many people out there who have lost spouses to untimely and tragic deaths. And they go on. I will find a way to go on. I am grateful for your friendship, and it would mean a great deal to me if I felt I had your support—even if we are not in agreement."

"I want you to be happy," Daphne said. "If this will make you happy . . . if you're certain it's what you want . . . then you have my full support."

"Oh, thank you," Bess said with an exuberance that made it evident to Daphne as well as herself how heavily the disagreement between them had been weighing on her.

* * * * *

Bess was surprised to be informed that the vicar had arrived, and even though Hugh was asleep, Lady Buxton was requesting that Bess join her in speaking with the clergyman about the situation and their request for his assistance. Given his weekly visits to the Abbey every Sunday, he had become their friend as well as their clergyman. The conversation went well and both Bess and Agatha were pleased with his support and apparent pleasure over the intended union between Hugh and Bess. He believed that with the extenuating circumstances—especially given the fact that certain marriage laws had been modified in England the previous year—they would have no trouble arranging a somewhat hasty marriage. However, he agreed that a solicitor would be more qualified to answer those questions and see that everything was in order legally.

Once Hugh was awake and Lewis had helped him freshen up, Agatha joined him and Bess for tea, and Lewis made a graceful exit with a declaration that he had some personal things to attend to. Bess suspected he simply knew they would be discussing wedding plans and he either preferred not to be directly involved, or he felt it would be more appropriate for him to give them their privacy. Agatha took the lead in repeating to Hugh everything they had discussed with the vicar, and he was clearly pleased. Bess noted an increased sparkle in his eyes when he looked at her, as if having crossed these barriers that brought them closer to marriage gave him added anticipation and hope, and perhaps peace. At least that's how Bess felt; she could only assume Hugh felt the same.

They were barely finished with tea when a maid came to tell Lady Buxton that her solicitor had arrived. Agatha asked the maid to bring him to Hugh's sitting room, since she wanted him to be included in this conversation. By the time the solicitor was escorted into the room, Hugh was sitting comfortably on one of the sofas, holding Bess's hand. Bess noted how at ease Agatha was as she greeted Mr. Newberry; they had obviously known each other a great many years, and Agatha's trust and reliance upon him was evident even before she formally introduced him to Bess, explaining that Mr. Newberry had worked closely with Hugh's father for more than a decade prior to his death, assisting him in making certain that all things regarding the estate and any other matter were all managed legally and in a manner that was completely proper regarding the law *and* society. The solicitor was very average in appearance—average build, average brown hair, and average features. Nevertheless, he seemed to have an excessive amount of energy for a middle-aged man, and it seemed difficult for him to sit still for long, as if he were accustomed to remaining busy. Still, he sat down in a disciplined manner, crossed one knee over the other, and listened attentively while Agatha briefly explained the situation and asked Hugh to fill in personal details of his reasons for needing to be married as soon as possible. Bess's heart swelled with hope and joy to hear him speak of his convictions about the marriage, and his love for her, with such fervency. Mr. Newberry was visibly moved by Hugh's plea for him to do everything he could to legally arrange all that was necessary for the marriage to take place quickly, and the solicitor felt confident that with his understanding of the current marriage laws—and a connection he had with someone in the legal profession who had some authority—that he could arrange everything for the following week. He promised to work diligently to make it happen and to keep them informed before he was quickly off to devote his seemingly unlimited energy on their behalf.

After the solicitor left, Agatha took charge of leaving Hugh in Lewis's care while she and Bess went to speak with the housekeeper and the cook about wedding plans. The servant women were both clearly surprised with the announcement that there would be a wedding, making it evident that the closer personal servants who had been told about the relationship between Hugh and Bess had not shared the secret with anyone else. But they were both pleased and enthusiastic over the impending union and seemed excited to be involved with planning and preparation; in fact, they were nothing less than enthused, as if having a diversion from their usual work, and an excuse for a celebration in the household, was a gift and a privilege for them. They wrote down lists of what needed to be done and agreed to inform the remainder of the staff about what was taking place, and to assign tasks accordingly so that the work would be fairly distributed—which pleased Agatha, since she made it clear that she wanted members of the staff who had known Hugh throughout his life, and whom he'd relied upon for his care, to be present for the marriage ceremony. They had decided that the wedding would take place in the music room, which not only had a lovely piano that would be used to provide the appropriate accompaniment, but it was also large enough to seat the number of people who would be invited. They would then move to the formal dining room for a luncheon; it was not only large enough to accommodate such a meal, but it was also very near the music room and Hugh would not have to walk far. They had already determined that Clive and Lewis would help Hugh get down to the main floor the morning of the wedding, with enough time to relax on a parlor sofa in order to recover sufficiently from whatever exertion might be required—although Lewis had declared that Hugh just had to lose his pride enough to allow his friends to carry him down the stairs, and they would manage nicely.

With everything arranged as much as possible for the time being, Bess left to go about her normal evening routine, and she walked slowly up the stairs to Hugh's room, allowing herself time to contemplate the whirlwind of the day. She almost couldn't recall how nervous she'd felt about informing Agatha of their intentions, but Agatha had quickly accepted the proposed marriage once she'd been assured that they truly loved each other and were being realistic about their expectations for the future. Beyond that, she had taken the lead on setting all the necessary arrangements into motion, seeing to matters that Bess wouldn't have even thought about. But then, she'd never been married before. And in fact, she'd only attended two weddings in her life, and they were not people with whom she'd been close; therefore, she'd only been at the outer perimeter of the celebrations. She was grateful for Agatha's insight about making the event proper and memorable, but in her heart, she only wanted to be married to Hugh, and even waiting the week or so that Mr. Newberry had said it might take to be certain all was legal and valid seemed far too long. In her mind she separated her concerns about the possible length of Hugh's life from her natural anticipation to be his wife. She offered a silent prayer that his heart would hold out until the wedding and as far beyond that as possible, then she pushed away any thoughts regarding his health and focused on visualizing how her wedding day might be regarding all the plans that had been discussed. Recalling that she and Agatha would be going into town tomorrow to purchase a wedding gown and order flowers, a little quiver of excitement erupted within her—a sensation that increased when she stepped quietly into the open doorway of Hugh's sitting room to see him relaxed in the corner of a sofa, reading. Given that he'd not heard her approach, she took a long moment to just watch him and try to fully comprehend how dramatically he had changed her life, most especially the miraculous fact that he loved her as much as she'd grown to love him. Then she realized that it was simply incomprehensible. Perhaps when the wedding itself had taken place and she had been able to witness and participate in the actual event and all the associated celebrations, her mind might be able to accept that this was real.

As if Hugh sensed her presence, he glanced up from his book to see her there and immediately smiled. His eyes sparkled in a way that had become familiar since he had confessed his love for her, and Bess found it a little easier to comprehend that he was the greatest and most incredible thing that had ever happened to her, and for whatever amount of time they might be allowed to share, she would be nothing less than grateful to God for bringing them together and making it possible for the deep impression of his character to be forever imprinted upon her heart and soul.

"How long have you been standing there?" he asked, reaching out a hand toward her as he set the book aside.

"Not long enough to believe that this is all really happening," she said, stepping toward him to take his hand. Sitting close beside him she added, "But long enough to be amazed all over again to realize that you love me the way you do."

"Oh, I *do* love you, my dear, sweet Bess!" he declared quietly and kissed her brow. "How did your planning go?"

"Very well," she said and told him everything that had been discussed, which was mostly to let him know that all they had talked about earlier with his mother had now been communicated to the cook and housekeeper, and their plans were officially underway. She told him about the menu suggestions they had discussed, and a few particulars regarding specific details. He seemed pleased and comfortable with their plans, even though he admitted that it would be nice if the groom could get down the stairs of his own home without so much assistance.

"You need to save your strength to stand beside the bride and declare your vows," she said. "No one but Lewis or Clive will be privy to that part of the day, and I believe they are more than happy to help you—which means you should be gracious and allow them to do so."

Hugh sighed loudly. "Very well," he said. "Your point is taken." He then touched her face and added, "All I want is to marry you, Bess. I'm more than willing to set aside my pride to make that happen."

"Then it seems we are all set," she declared with triumph and couldn't help laughing over the sheer delight consuming her. Hugh laughed as if her delight were contagious, then he kissed her in a way that subtly betrayed his anticipation of their becoming husband and wife. Their marriage would be far from conventional, but wonderful nevertheless, and Bess completely shared his anticipation.

* * * * *

The following day, Bess thoroughly enjoyed her excursion into town with Agatha, and she was glad to have Daphne along, as well. Agatha had suggested that the maid accompany them; given the fact that she would be helping Bess get dressed for the wedding, it seemed appropriate that she be involved in choosing Bess's attire. Lady Buxton was clearly well-known and respected by the dressmaker who was more than willing to sew whatever they ordered with the speed required to have it completed in time. The fact that Bess chose a simple style and fabric that was not difficult to work with made the hurried completion of the gown more feasible, and Lady Buxton was more than eager to pay the dressmaker a generous bonus for her willingness to put in extra time on their behalf.

They also ordered satin slippers and a veil, as well as a variety of flowers from the local hothouse where beautiful blooms grew vibrantly all year round. Not only was a bouquet ordered for the bride, but Agatha also ordered several coordinated floral arrangements to be a part of the decor in the music room where the ceremony would take place.

They were so efficient in their errands that they returned to the Abbey in time for Bess to help Hugh relax for his nap according to their normal routine, then she shared a late lunch with Agatha and Daphne, who were both almost as enthusiastic about the upcoming wedding as Bess was. The only reason Bess found to be nervous was the fact that her father had not yet been informed of the upcoming nuptials. Since she'd avoided him completely during his visits to the Abbey after that first time in which he'd completely snubbed her, she had no idea how to go about talking to him regarding this enormous decision. She discussed it with Hugh and Agatha, not at all surprised that they shared her concerns, since they were both aware of the situation.

"Well, I'll talk to him," Hugh volunteered. "A man shouldn't get married without properly discussing it with the bride's father. Under the circumstances I don't need—or even expect—his approval or blessing. But I believe it should be me who informs him of our plans."

"Perhaps you're right," Bess said, "but I still need to face him and not cower away in hiding, not regarding this. Therefore, I think we need to tell him together."

"Very well," Hugh agreed. "Is he not coming tomorrow?"

"He is," Agatha stated. "And I will certainly leave this up to the two of you; but I believe I would also like to be present for this conversation. I do not wish to intrude or to make the situation more difficult, so please be honest with me about this."

"Truthfully," Bess said, "I was hoping you *would* be there. He has a great deal of respect for you, my lady, and while I have little doubt about the disdain he feels toward me, I do not wish to hear him speak it, and I don't believe he would say anything disrespectful to me in your presence."

"If he does, *I* shall not hesitate to put him in his place," Hugh said, "father of the bride or not. For all that I may be an invalid, I'll not have *anyone* treat the woman I love with anything less than the respect she deserves."

Bess smiled at him, then at Agatha, more grateful than she could say for their support of her strange situation, and for the sincere and unconditional love they gave her.

The following day after lunch, Bess paced and wrung her hands incessantly in anticipation of her father's visit.

"Do sit down," Hugh said from where he was leaning back against pillows stacked against the headboard of his bed. "I feel exhausted just watching you."

"So sorry," she said and forced herself to be seated.

"There's no need to apologize, darling. Just . . . talk to me instead of wearing out the carpet."

"I don't believe there's anything to be said that we haven't already talked about far too much. I just . . . want to have this over with."

Hugh asked with sincerity, "Do you really believe he will be so against it that he would not attend his own daughter's wedding for the sake of . . . what? His wounded pride? Some bizarre belief that he's been abandoned or cheated or betrayed?"

"I don't know, Hugh. How can I know what he's thinking or feeling when he won't talk to me?"

"You've avoided him for many weeks," Hugh said. "Perhaps he's had a change of heart by now."

"He certainly could have asked to see me on any of his frequent visits," she pointed out.

"Yes, he could have, but just because he didn't doesn't mean he hasn't softened his stance, at least to some degree."

"We can hope," she said, finding it difficult to resist the urge to start pacing again. "But I fear nothing will have changed; I fear that he *won't* be willing to come to my wedding, for reasons I may never understand."

"And that must be his decision," Hugh said. "As we've already discussed, we will speak to him appropriately and respectfully, and how he responds is up to him and has nothing to do with you."

Bess sighed and suppressed the temptation to continue discussing what had already been discussed. She knew everything Hugh was saying to be true; she simply couldn't help her own anticipation of disappointment and sorrow when she firmly believed her father would not bend.

Bess was glad to have Hugh change the subject of the conversation. She did her best to focus on the new joy that had come into her life by way of the love she shared with Hugh and the anticipation of their being married. Overall, she tried very hard not to even think about her father, trying to convince herself that his opinion didn't matter, and whether or not he chose to be involved in her marriage ceremony didn't matter; she would be happy and thrilled on her wedding day—with or without her father's presence, or his approval. But she couldn't deny the piece of her heart that felt broken at the thought of her own father finding any possible reason to disapprove of the situation and therefore refuse to be involved. Hugh encouraged her to be more hopeful and to believe that her father might be happy for her, or at least tolerant, but Bess's deepest instincts told her that Jonas White's stubbornness would override all else.

When a maid announced the doctor's arrival, Bess went to the sitting room, leaving the door open, not because she felt any need to eavesdrop during Hugh's usual medical examination, but because she knew that Agatha planned for Hugh and her father to come to this room after they were finished so they could all sit and talk in a setting more appropriate and comfortable than the bedroom. Hugh had been firm on wanting to be dressed for this conversation, and to be anywhere but his bed, if only to feel some dignity and self-respect when asking for the doctor's blessing in his desire to marry Bess. She was glad when Agatha slipped quietly into the room and sat nearby. They exchanged a smile but didn't speak, which was likely due to having nothing new to say regarding the situation.

Bess could hear only bits and pieces of the conversation that took place between the two men in the other room, which was purely medical in nature. She did hear her father declare with a positive ring in his voice that—all things considered—Hugh was doing better in many respects, perhaps miraculously so. Bess already knew that, and she wished her father would discuss Hugh's condition with her on his visits, since she *had* been hired to oversee his care and she would continue to do so, even as his wife.

Bess's ears perked up when she heard her father say a little more loudly, "And to what might you attribute the improvement of your health, young man?"

"I have a theory on that," Hugh said, "which I would actually like to discuss with you in more detail, but I'd prefer that we move to the sitting room, if you wouldn't mind helping me just a bit."

"Of course," Jonas said, and Bess's heart pounded to realize she was about to see her father face-to-face for the first time in many weeks—and the ensuing conversation could likely be a disaster. She forced herself to look up when the two men entered the room, Hugh leaning only slightly against the support Jonas offered by holding to Hugh's upper arm. Jonas stopped walking when he saw Bess sitting there, which forced Hugh to do the same. Tense glances were exchanged all around, creating an awkward silence that felt as if a heavy fog had descended very suddenly over the room.

As she was so skilled at doing, Agatha relieved the silence by speaking. "Dr. White," she said in greeting as if nothing at all was wrong, "how good to see you. And how is my son faring today?"

"Very well, my lady," Jonas said, resuming his steps as he helped Hugh toward a chair—until Hugh motioned toward the sofa where Bess was sitting, letting the doctor know silently that he would be sitting next to her. Jonas looked confused but helped Hugh get seated before he stood up straight and focused his attention on Lady Buxton. "Was there something else you wished to discuss with me?" he asked, ignoring Bess completely.

"There is certainly something that needs to be discussed," Agatha said to him with the kind authority she wore so comfortably. "But it is Hugh who wishes to speak with you. Please," she motioned with her hand toward a chair that was directly facing Hugh and Bess, "sit down. Make yourself comfortable. You should know by now that you are a welcome guest in our home."

"Thank you, my lady," Jonas said and was seated. Bess saw her father barely dart his eyes toward her, a glance that seemed to skeptically question her reasons for being present for whatever serious conversation was about to take place. *If he had any idea of what he was about to learn,* she thought, *he would likely have trouble breathing.* She prayed silently that a miracle might occur, and that her father would be receptive to their plans, while at the same time she felt utterly bereft of faith, knowing her father's character so well—at least as far as it applied to her.

Jonas gazed directly at Hugh as if doing so would prevent him from having to look at Bess. The expectancy in his expression was evident, but Bess felt certain he likely believed this conversation had something to do with Hugh's medical care; he surely couldn't comprehend anything else.

"I respect and admire your medical expertise very much, Dr. White," Hugh began, "and I want you to know that I'm very grateful for the care you've given me and for your kindness toward me in such a challenging situation. However," Hugh cleared his throat, and Jonas looked mildly alarmed, as if he feared his services might be terminated, "what I need to discuss with you has nothing to do with my health—except perhaps in the regard that I believe it's the reason my symptoms have improved of late." Before saying anything else, Hugh took Bess's hand. The movement caught Jonas's attention before his eyes widened and he looked again at Hugh—aghast—still ignoring Bess. Hugh didn't give Jonas a chance to speak; he simply said, "I've fallen very much in love with your precious daughter, sir, and I intend to marry her. It's my hope that you will give us your blessing. Clearly we need to get married as soon as humanly possible; arrangements are being made as we speak."

Hugh paused only for a long moment, long enough to allow Jonas the opportunity to jump in, but not long enough to impede his momentum. "You know as well as anyone that our situation is far from normal; otherwise, I would have been more formal in approaching you, and in courting Bess more properly. Such an option is not available for me. Because we have spent a great deal of time together—always chaperoned, of course—I believe we have come to know each other far better than most couples who have courted for many months. We understand the situation has much heartache mingled with the joy we feel, but we have discussed every facet of this extensively, and we still feel strongly that it is right for both of us to move forward and make the most of the time we have together. Again, I would hope that you will give us your blessing. It would not only mean the world to Bess to have you there for the wedding, to give her away and be a part of our celebration, but it would also mean a great deal to me."

"And to me," Agatha interjected, and Jonas turned abruptly toward the sound of her voice, as if the shock of Hugh's announcement had prevented him from recalling that she was in the room. His eyes seemed to say that he couldn't believe she would approve of such a ludicrous idea, but he was too polite to say so. Bess felt her heart sinking; without Jonas speaking a word, she already knew that her worst fears regarding her father would come to pass. He would indeed refuse to be a part of her wedding—or her life. In that moment, she believed he would likely use this as an excuse to cut her off completely, although for the life of her she couldn't imagine what his reasoning might be. But she knew him well enough to know that he likely didn't need a reason—at least not a reason that would make sense to anyone else. He was hurt and angry and felt abandoned, and he'd surely found a way to justify within his own thinking that all of this was Bess's fault. And now she was binding herself to the family who had stolen her away from him, which in his mind was just cause for his fury.

Silence stretched on into an almost eerie stillness as it became evident Jonas White was expected to offer a response to Hugh's declaration, and Jonas seemed to be measuring his words very carefully. Bess could well imagine that he was far too proper to allow himself to lose his temper in front of Lady Buxton *or* her son, but there was likely a great deal of angry words he would like to speak to her if the two of them were alone. That, among many other reasons, made her unspeakably grateful to *not* be alone with him, and to have the love and support of Hugh and his mother.

While Bess was waiting with a dry mouth and sweating palms for her father to speak, she was startled when he stood abruptly, saying with a voice of barely concealed anger, "I mean no disrespect, my lady." He nodded toward Agatha. "Nor to you." He nodded at Hugh. "But I cannot condone this marriage nor offer my blessing. I hope this will not negatively impact our professional relationship."

*Professional relationship?* Bess wanted to scream. Was that his greatest concern? Before she could even wonder how Hugh might respond to what his potential father-in-law had just said, she stood as well, unable to remain silent another moment. "Will you not even acknowledge me?" she said to her father. "You will speak to Hugh? To Lady Buxton? But you will hardly even glance my way? I'm your daughter, and I'm getting married. Can you not find the tiniest grain of happiness for me? Can you not be even a little bit supportive of the choice I've made?"

Jonas finally *did* look at her, his eyes burning with a fury he was fighting to conceal without much success. He stated with the same suppressed rage, "You chose this family above me the day you came here, and—"

"Is that how you see it?" Bess asked, astonished. "I'm a grown woman, Father. Choosing to take a path independent from yours was not choosing anyone or anything *above* you. Is it not normal for children to grow up and make their own way? Please tell me what I've done to earn such disdain!"

As if he'd heard nothing she'd said, Jonas countered in a voice that was barely polite, "And now you've clearly chosen to make yourself a part of this family permanently, for reasons I cannot begin to understand."

Managing to remain composed, Bess retorted, "Does a woman have to choose between her father and the family into which she marries? Never in my life have I known of a woman having to make such a choice. Is that truly how you see what's happening here?"

"And what will you do when he's gone?" Jonas asked Bess, ignoring her words, his voice now rising in pitch as if he'd begun to forget they weren't the only ones in the room. "Be alone and filled with regret like me?"

Bess let out a noise of astonishment, marveling that every emotional matter always came back to his own pain; she wondered how he could be so thoroughly self-absorbed. But she resisted the urge to point that out and focused her effort on remaining calm.

"No," Bess insisted firmly but with kindness, "not like you, Father. I will have no regret because I will always know in my heart that I made the most of every day Hugh and I had together, and I will not be bitter or spend my life feeling cheated and miserable, and I will certainly not be laying blame on anyone or anything else. I will miss him more than I can possibly imagine, but I will find a way to be happy and have joy in my life." She glanced at Hugh and felt strengthened by the love and admiration in his eyes. "I believe that's the only way Hugh will be able to go in peace, knowing that despite the utter tragedy of our separation, I will be all right." She turned back to stare at her father, hoping he could see the heat in her eyes that she could feel there. Had he heard the accusations she had implied in her declaration? She knew beyond any doubt that he had chosen his attitudes following his wife's death. Of course, he'd been entitled to grieve as any person would. But the position into which he had put Bess, and the way he had treated her—which had only worsened over the years—had been selfish and inappropriate, and Bess simply wouldn't stand for it any further. She'd forgiven him, but she didn't trust him to treat her the way she deserved to be treated. And if that meant he chose not to attend her wedding, or to be even a little bit happy for her, then so be it. In that moment, her desire to have him there was greatly overshadowed by the reality that if he came and was even the slightest bit cynical or negative, she would prefer his absence. She didn't want anyone or anything—especially not her father—to mar the beauty of this precious experience she would share with Hugh.

Given her sudden but firm change of heart, she took a deep breath and stated, "So, now you've been informed of our intentions, but let me make it perfectly clear that you are *not* invited to the wedding, nor will you be welcome there. If Hugh and his mother choose to keep you on as his physician, that's up to them, but I will continue to keep myself hidden during your visits. I would prefer no father at all over one who treats me with such disdain."

Bess hurried out of the room before she lost all control and began shouting at him. She hoped that neither Hugh nor his mother had lowered their opinion of her, given what they'd just heard her say to her father, but she couldn't deny that she felt some degree of relief in having said it. And surprisingly, she felt an even deeper relief to know that he *wouldn't* be at the wedding, and that she no longer ever had to concern herself with trying to please him in any way. She *had* found a new family, one that loved and accepted her as she was, without expecting her to solve every problem and take full responsibility for every facet of their lives. Agatha and Hugh had made her feel loved and respected; something she had never felt from her father. And now it was over, and she pushed away any temptation to feel sorrow; she'd experienced far too much sorrow already over her father's difficult attitudes. She had far too little of life left to share with Hugh; she would not waste a moment of it by wallowing in any regret regarding her father.

Bess slumped into a chair in her sitting room, glad to know that Daphne had gone into town and she could be there alone. A part of her wanted to cry like a baby, but recounting all the tears she'd cried over her father's disregard and disappointment in her, she felt all dried up and beyond caring enough to cry. She wondered what conversation might have ensued after she left the room, and even though she knew that both Hugh and his mother would likely be very understanding of how she'd reacted and the things she'd said, she still wondered if one or both of them might feel some disappointment in her. Then again, perhaps she was just in the habit of believing she would disappoint the people she loved. She hoped that her father *would* continue to be Hugh's doctor, even though the very idea of him treating his son-in-law while ignoring the fact of his relationship with his own daughter seemed ludicrous. Still, she knew Jonas White was a very good doctor, and any other doctor they could find would have to travel much farther to get to Astoria Abbey. The entire situation just felt so strange and impossible to comprehend, and she felt as if a swarm of bees was flying around in her head.

Bess gasped when she heard Hugh say, "So, here you are."

"And what are you doing here?" she asked, turning more toward him.

"What you're really wondering is how could I have been brazen enough to venture all the way across the hall to find you. If you'd gone down to the kitchen in search of some cake or biscuits I would have been out of luck."

"You shouldn't overexert yourself," she scolded gently.

"I'm fine," he said and sat down across from her. "Although, I suspect that you are *not* fine."

"Finer than I expected to be," she said, and he raised one eyebrow in question. She settled for the simplest explanation she could think of. "If he's going to carry such an attitude about me and my life, I don't want him at my wedding, and I don't want him in my life. I'm done trying to please a man who will never be pleased with any choice I make that contradicts his narrow ideas of how I should be devoted to making *his* life more comfortable. I will never again compromise my own sense of self simply to make him—or anyone else—less uncomfortable."

"I think that is one of the most amazing things I've ever heard anyone say," Hugh said, surprising Bess. "It's no wonder I love you so dearly."

Needing clarification—if not validation—she had to ask, "You're not embarrassed or disgusted by the way I just spoke to my father?"

"Quite the contrary," he said.

Bess sighed and took in the enormity of what he was saying. "You are so very good to me, my dear Hugh."

"If that's the case, it's the easiest thing I've ever done."

"So," Bess said on the wave of a sigh, "I don't know if I dare ask what was said after I left."

"Very little," Hugh said. "I told him that his daughter was the most remarkable woman I'd ever met, and I hoped that eventually he would be able to see that. He made no comment. My mother rescued our silent impasse by stating that she would like him to continue being my physician, to which I agreed, although she made it clear she wouldn't keep him in our employ if any further difficulties arise regarding the situation. I believe he nodded but didn't say anything. He began to excuse himself, but my mother interrupted him, declaring there was something she needed to say. You know how good she is at doing such things."

"Dare I ask?" Bess turned to look at him sideways, wondering what Lady Agatha had said.

"Oh, you would have been proud of her, as she is of you—clearly," Hugh said with a smile that implied he shared the same pride. "She told him that the opinions and behaviors of his personal life were none of her affair but given the fact that his daughter was marrying her son, she felt inclined to offer just one opinion of her own before he left."

"And what was that?" Bess asked when Hugh seemed to be pausing for dramatic effect.

"She told him he should be ashamed of himself, and then she got up and left the room."

Bess took in her breath and held it, wishing she'd stayed close enough to eavesdrop. "And?" she finally asked.

"That's it. He too left the room without bothering to even look at me; I'm sure you know how that feels. I wonder how he'll continue to be my physician if he won't look at me, but I suspect that the next time he comes he will simply behave as if nothing is any different." Hugh sighed and added more lightly, "Given the fact that everyone had left the room, I set out on the extreme adventure of crossing the hall with the hopes of finding you."

"Do you still want to marry me?" She sighed.

"That is the silliest question I've ever heard," he stated. "But I'm going to answer it anyway, just so you don't have to wonder. Your father's attitude toward you or me regarding this situation has absolutely nothing to do with all that you and I have come to share. My only regret is the same as it's always been—that the length of time we have together will be far too brief. But I love you more now than I did an hour ago; and I respect you more, as well. I think we should change the subject and talk about the wedding cake, or something, because we're getting married in not so many days, and there's only one thing that matters to me other than actually making you my wife, and that's the wedding cake."

"I'm certain the wedding cake will be scrumptious," Bess said with a little laugh. "I'm told it will be decorated with doves and flowers made from a magical mixture of sugar and egg whites—I think. And the cake itself will be carrot, with nuts and spices—just the way you like it. I know how much you love it when carrot cake is served with tea."

"Yes, I do love carrot cake," he said as if it were an important business matter.

"That's why I requested it," she declared with a smile.

"Then everything will be perfect," Hugh said, and Bess couldn't agree more.

# CHAPTER NINE

## LOOKING UP

THROUGHOUT THE FOLLOWING DAYS, EVERYTHING came together for the wedding surprisingly well. There were a few minor problems that required sorting out, but Agatha was quick to do so in a way that made it evident she had done well in learning to oversee every matter of the estate in her husband's absence—and the fact that she had never expected her son to live to adulthood, or to be healthy enough to participate very much in all that needed to managed. When Mr. Newberry let them know he had been able to conquer all the legal hurdles and everything was in order, an actual date was set and everyone they wanted to invite to the wedding was informed. No invitation was extended to Bess's father, even though he came to check on Hugh according to their usual schedule, and just as Hugh had predicted, he behaved as if nothing at all had changed between them. Beyond Hugh telling Bess that much, and that the doctor had declared him to be doing as well as could be expected, the topic of Jonas White didn't come up again.

Bess was as pleased as everyone else involved to see daily evidence that Hugh was doing very well, and his symptoms were as nominal as they possibly could be considering his condition. Agatha declared more than once that Bess had given him great incentive to live, and surely his enthusiasm and lack of discouragement were contributing to his improved condition. However, they all agreed he should not take feeling better as a sign that he should exert himself any more than he normally did. None of them wanted his condition to suddenly worsen because of overdoing it in any way. Therefore, wedding plans took place all around him while he was kept informed of every little detail, which Bess noticed always made him smile with the same excitement and anticipation that she felt. Each night she spent alone across the hall from Hugh's bedroom, she counted the decreasing number of nights until they would no longer have to be separated in such a way.

The morning before the wedding, Bess awoke feeling happier and more content than she ever had. Nothing but peace and sweet anticipation filled her spirit. While she prepared herself for the day, Daphne assisted her as usual and they visited comfortably about how Bess was feeling, and Daphne herself seemed genuinely happy for Bess; she too was pleasantly caught up in anticipation of tomorrow's celebration here at Astoria Abbey.

When Bess stepped out of her room to cross the hall and see Hugh, she was surprised to find Clive waiting for her.

"Is everything all right?" she asked, noting the door to Hugh's bedroom was closed. Her heart quickened suddenly over the thought that his health might have taken a sudden turn for the worse. She knew that such a moment was inevitable; she only hoped that for now he could feel well enough to enjoy his own wedding, and they might have some good weeks together at the very least.

"Yes, of course," Clive said with immediate reassurance, as if he understood the depth of concern in her question. "Lewis is helping him get dressed. I just wanted a moment to talk to you alone."

"Very well," she said, relieved regarding Hugh but wondering what Clive might consider so important. She was surprised but not uncomfortable with the way he took hold of her shoulders and looked into her eyes. They'd become very good friends, united in caring for Hugh. And she'd been touched by his absolute support of her and Hugh being together and proceeding with their marriage. "What is it?" she asked when he hesitated.

"I just want to tell you how very happy I am for you, Bess. I've come to treasure our friendship very much, and it's given me a great deal of joy to see how you have brightened Hugh's life."

"Thank you," she said. "That means a great deal . . . especially coming from you. I too have come to treasure our friendship."

"I suppose I simply need to clarify something that's probably obvious, but I didn't ever want you to have to wonder."

"Of course," she said, encouraging him to go on.

"None of us can deny that there is a dark cloud lurking behind all the happiness you've given Hugh—and that he has given you. All of us who care for the both of you hope that we will be blessed with a miracle and he may yet live a long time, but of course that is in God's hands alone."

"Yes," Bess agreed, hoping he might move past his reference of the *dark cloud* to something more cheerful.

"The thing is, I want you to know—to really know—how very happy I am about this marriage, and I want both you and Hugh to enjoy every minute. If there's *anything* I can do, ever, to make things easier for either of you, I want you to tell me. I'm here for you. And I'll be here for you when it's finally time for him to go. You'll never be alone in any of this. I suppose that's what I really wanted to say."

"Thank you, Clive," she said and impulsively hugged him. He returned her embrace with a certain fervor that gave her an undefinable strength; she knew that he *would* be there for her, and for Hugh. Even though she vehemently avoided even thinking about what life might be like for her after Hugh's death, she couldn't deny being grateful for the reassurance that she wouldn't be alone. Returning to her father's home would never be an option, but the idea of remaining at the Abbey was becoming more comfortable to her, given that she would officially be a part of the family. Even though they had never specifically discussed it after the engagement, Bess assumed Agatha would be all right with her staying, especially if Bess found a way to earn her keep. Bess felt certain Agatha shared her reluctance to think about what life might be like in Hugh's absence.

Bess drew away from their friendly embrace and smiled at Clive. "I should see how Hugh is doing. Was there anything else or—"

"No," he smiled back, "that's all. Thank you. By all means . . . see to the patient. Lewis is on duty to assist at the moment. I'll see you later."

"Of course," Bess said and watched him walk away, recalling fondly how kind he'd been to her the first day she'd come here with her father, and when he'd arrived at her home with the carriage to accompany her to the Abbey that first day when she'd been so nervous. Now they'd settled into a comfortable friendship, and they'd been able to work together caring for Hugh almost as if they could read each other's minds regarding his needs. Bess silently thanked God for giving her good friends in this house, as well as a mother figure and a husband—almost. She felt so incredibly blessed.

Bess found Hugh in good spirits, and his symptoms very mild, which filled them with hope that he would be in the best possible health, considering the circumstances, for his wedding day. He was determined to rest up and take the day even more slowly than usual so that he could save his strength for being transported down the stairs by his friends and standing with Bess to exchange vows.

"I can eat and visit with guests sitting down," he told her, "but I want to be able to stand up like a real man when I marry you."

"You are no less or more of a man whether sitting or standing," she reassured him. "If you don't feel up to standing, then I will sit as well. Either way it's going to be a beautiful wedding. I keep being assured of that by everyone in the house who is involved in the preparations, and I've hardly had to do a thing."

"It's your job to take care of *me,*" Hugh said with a sly grin. "And you do your job very well."

"Even better when I'm your wife, I hope."

"I've no doubt of that," he said and kissed her.

The routine of the day went as usual despite the anticipation that seemed to fill the entire Abbey to the rafters. While Hugh was napping in the afternoon, Bess's gown and all that went with it was delivered. Daphne helped her try everything on and they both agreed that Bess looked lovely without appearing too ostentatious or extravagant. The gown was made of ivory-colored lace, woven into an intricate floral pattern, with satin of the same color beneath it. The style of the gown was simple, as was the modest veil of the same ivory color; it hung from a beaded hair comb past Bess's waist. Bess wanted to feel like a bride—as she did when examining her reflection in the mirror. But it wasn't her personality to wear anything too extravagant—especially considering the lack of formality of her wedding taking place right here at the Abbey, quietly and without any pomp or frivolities. She felt confident that everything was going to be perfect!

Bess slept surprisingly well that night, and the following morning was far too busy to have time to hardly think about the enormity of all that was taking place. Bess saw Hugh for a few minutes, mostly to fulfill her need to check his physical symptoms and make certain all was well—and it was. Beyond that, Clive and Lewis only allowed her to give him a quick kiss before they insisted she leave and go get herself ready while they helped Hugh do the same at a leisurely pace that would not tire him out.

Bess returned to her own room to find Agatha there with Daphne. Her mother-in-law-to-be was beaming with a joy that seemed to literally add light to her countenance. She humbly asked if it would be all right for her to be there while Bess was getting ready; since she didn't have a daughter, she'd never had such an opportunity. Bess was more than happy for Agatha's presence and her help.

The next time Bess saw Hugh, he was standing in the music room near the vicar, in front of their guests who were seated in chairs that had been arranged into neat rows. The chairs all had pink satin ribbon tied around them, which matched the pink and white floral arrangements that had been added to the decor of the room, the same flowers that comprised the bouquet Bess carried as she walked toward Hugh. He looked so handsome—and so happy—that she could hardly breathe as she closed the distance between them, barely aware of anything but the smile on Hugh's face. They both laughed softly when he took her hand and she handed her bouquet to Agatha for safekeeping.

"You look so beautiful," Hugh whispered near her ear before the vicar had a chance to begin.

"So do you," she replied and looked into his eyes as if she might see there the entire purpose of her life.

Hugh had no difficulty standing to face her as they exchanged their vows. Bess noted that there was nothing in his appearance that would lead anyone to believe anything was wrong at all. She could hear the normal, subtle strain of his breathing—but they were both well accustomed to that, and he'd learned how to breathe as deeply as possible to try and keep his lungs strong. Today, in this moment, he was stronger than she'd ever seen him, and she felt as much joy over the fact that her presence in his life might have contributed to his improvement as she did over her own happiness in becoming his wife.

When the ceremony was complete, and they kissed to seal their vows, Bess laughed and tried to comprehend that she was now Mrs. Hugh Buxton. They sat together on a lovely small sofa that had been conveniently placed for them to greet their guests and receive well-wishes while Hugh remained seated. Many people she'd known from church and the village had come, and she felt thrilled to see them here and to take in their genuine joy on her behalf. She loved introducing Hugh to them personally, and she loved the way that both Hugh and the guests kept referring to her as Mrs. Buxton. The happiness Bess could see in Hugh's countenance added to her own, and the sincere wishes of all who had come to share this occasion with them only boosted her spirits further. She thought of her father's absence for only a moment before she pushed it away, grateful to not have him present when he likely would have exuded some degree of cynicism or disdain that would have only dampened the happiness she felt.

After all their guests had been given the opportunity to personally greet the bride and groom, everyone moved into the nearby dining room where they enjoyed a beautiful meal that had been prepared and served lovingly by the staff. Bess knew that everyone in the house working to make the celebration possible would later be enjoying food from the same meal, and plenty of wedding cake had been made for them to enjoy as well.

Following the meal, the cake was cut and served before the bride and groom made a graceful exit after thanking everyone for their love and support. Lewis and Clive helped Hugh back to his rooms where he couldn't deny he was understandably exhausted. This had been anticipated and they all quickly went through the established routine of helping him relax enough to take a nap. He even agreed to take a small amount of the medicine that would help him sleep more deeply, so that he would be rested enough to spend time with his wife in the evening.

Once Hugh was asleep, Bess went to her room where Daphne was waiting to help her out of the veil and wedding gown. Bess touched them lovingly after they'd been draped over the back of a chair to be put away carefully later. For a moment she wondered how it might feel one day—likely not so far into the future—to look at what she'd worn on her wedding day, and to be a widow with nothing but her memories and a few tangible mementos to hold on to. She allowed the thought to linger in her mind only long enough to know that she was strong enough to face that season of her life, and as prepared as she possibly could be to do so. For now, she was finally married to Hugh and for as long as they were blessed enough to have him remain in this mortal state, she would find joy in simply being his wife.

Wearing one of her most comfortable dresses and thick stockings on her feet, Bess crossed the hall to the bedroom she would now be sharing with Hugh. She quietly closed the doors to the hall and the sitting room, deeply thrilled over the simple fact that they no longer needed to be chaperoned, and they could be alone together without the doors remaining open. She carefully eased onto the bed beside Hugh, where he was lying sideways on it as he always did for his naps so that she could rub his neck to help him fall asleep. Easing beneath the covers, she cautiously settled her head onto the same pillow and relaxed, glad that she'd not disturbed his sleep. For a few minutes she just watched him, thinking of how much she liked the view of Hugh Buxton from this close proximity. Tears filled her eyes because of her joy mingled with the potential sorrow of the future, but she let them come and kissed his brow without interrupting his sleep.

She finally closed her eyes and was able to relax more fully, conscious of his breathing mingled with her own.

Bess's next awareness was a familiar sensation on her lips, although she'd never before been awakened by Hugh's kiss.

"Hello, sweet wife," he said when she opened her eyes to see him looking at her. "What a remarkable surprise to wake up and find you here."

"And where else would I be?" she asked, stretching the sleep out of her arms.

"Reading a book, perhaps?" he said. "Or—"

"It's my wedding day, silly. And I'm not letting the groom out of my sight for more than a minute."

"How delightful!" he declared and kissed her in a way he never had before. They were married now. Most of the way they lived their lives wouldn't change—much could *not* be changed—but between them, everything was different.

"Be careful now," she said when his kiss became more passionate. "I don't want your heart giving out on you during an intimate moment." She kept her voice light as she added, "Not only would it be terribly awkward when I try to explain it to the staff, but it would also not be conducive to your leaving me with only good memories."

Hugh chuckled and kissed her again. "I promise to be careful. We already talked about this."

"I know, but—"

"I have my nurse right here with me to make certain I'm all right."

"Yes, you do," she said and wrapped him completely in her arms, relishing the way he fully returned her embrace. The evidence of his physical weakness in no way diminished the evidence of his love for her. The life they would share together might be ridiculously brief, but she felt confident they could find more joy together in a month than many people might find in a lifetime.

\* \* \* \* \*

It took a few days for Bess and Hugh and those who assisted them daily to adjust to the changes in their routine. Daphne and Lewis worked together to move Bess's things into the ample wardrobe and drawer space in Hugh's room, and the newly married couple shared some frank conversations with Clive and Lewis about the shifting of certain responsibilities in Hugh's care now that Hugh had a wife who could assist him with some of the personal things that previously would not have been appropriate. Their routine with Agatha and the rest of the household didn't change, and for all that Bess knew, no one else would even take notice of things being different beyond the fact that Bess now shared a room with her husband.

Winter settled in fully with a series of lovely snowstorms. Bess and Hugh both enjoyed sitting close together beneath a warm blanket while they watched the snow fall and talked about the mysteries of the universe and the beauties and wonders of the world, and the stars and planets far beyond it.

Hugh's physical symptoms remained minimal, and he continued to feel reasonably well all the way through Christmas and into the new year. Bess's father continued his visits every few days, always giving an assessment that was exactly what Bess already knew—even though it was only repeated to her through Hugh. She was careful to avoid seeing her father, and he never asked about her at all.

January became bitterly cold, and the storms were comprised of more wind than snow. It was one of those times when the entire household was glad to be well stocked with every supply they needed so no one had to go into town. The only exception was one of the stable hands who bundled himself up sufficiently to ride quickly into town and leave a message with the doctor to assure him that he need not brave the terrible weather to check on Hugh; until the series of storms cleared, he could assume that all was well unless they sent for him. Bess felt some relief to not have to even think about hiding from him, and she wondered why this hadn't become their normal routine previously. Even when Hugh's symptoms inevitably worsened, she couldn't think of a single thing her father could do for him that she couldn't do—except for providing the medicine Hugh needed to help him sleep. When Hugh's breathing became more difficult, he would need more of that medicine to ease the pain and help him relax. Bess dreaded the onset of that stage, already knowing she would likely find it more difficult to see him suffer than it would be to let him go. But the timing was out of their control; she only hoped he wouldn't suffer too long when the end was finally drawing near, and that she could prove to be as strong as she hoped when she had no choice but to face life without him.

Hugh truly became the center of her life. She devoted herself to his every comfort, but she also enjoyed his company almost every waking moment, nearly as much as she enjoyed just being able to sleep in the same bed with him and know that he was close beside her. She loved falling asleep with the sound of his voice being the last thing she heard and waking up every morning to fresh evidence of his love and adoration.

Clive and Lewis were still around a great deal, going in and out to help with certain tasks and to spend some time with Hugh. They all agreed that Hugh's marriage hadn't diminished the friendship he shared with these men, and they all teased each other about how they couldn't let Hugh and Bess become agitated with each other by being together constantly. Bess was so thoroughly comfortable with Hugh that she doubted any agitation could be possible. But she respected the fact that she wasn't the only person who cared for Hugh, and his friends as well as his mother needed to share time with him, especially when they all knew how precious each day could be.

Winter eased into spring with only a slight worsening of Hugh's symptoms. Bess's father had resumed his regular visits, and Bess couldn't deny being grateful for that when Hugh began to find it more difficult to breathe than he had in months, and the swelling in his feet and lower legs increased. Even while lying in bed, exerting no energy at all, he often found it difficult to take in the breath he needed, and he was starting to cough occasionally in a way that frightened Bess. All his symptoms were normal and even expected, but she knew it could likely mean their time was running out. They'd already been blessed with more time than either of them had hoped for, but they also knew that the miracle of his symptoms having improved was not likely to repeat itself. A year earlier, more than one doctor in London had told him he had only weeks to live. He was still alive, and Bess had heard him admit more than once that he needed to be grateful for the extra time he'd been given, rather than giving in to the temptation of being angry over being cheated out of the life he wanted to live.

Bess's favorite time of day was late at night when she and Hugh snuggled close together in the dark, wrapped in each other's arms, relaxed enough to fall asleep but neither of them wanting to. Eventually they always did of course, but not before they talked about everything they could possibly think they might one day hope they had talked about when being together was no longer possible.

"You know," she said one night following a quiet lull while he gently stroked her hair where it fell over her shoulder, "I was thinking today about the first day I came here, and your mother came down to meet me personally and bring me up to your room. I was so in awe of the beauty of the house: the art on the walls, the exquisite detail of the carpets, the bannisters;

everything—especially the ceilings. The ceilings are like a work of art all on their own, with their patterns and the gold-leafing. I've many times since then just wandered the house looking at them, wondering how many years ago they were designed and created, and by whom. They're truly beautiful."

"I'm ashamed to say that I've hardly noticed," Hugh said. "I suppose growing up surrounded by such things made them easy to take for granted. And now I can hardly just go wandering about the house to admire its beauty." He sighed. "In fact, if I think about it realistically, I suppose that was never an option. My entire life has been about being escorted or carried from one place or another just to make certain I got there without falling over dead."

"Then how could you possibly even think about looking up?"

"Perhaps that's true," he said sadly, "and now it's simply not possible. The house is the size of Australia, I think; or at least it feels that big when I think of being able to traverse it."

Bess laughed softly at the comparison, then said more seriously, "No need for regret. I'll just tell you about it."

"Australia?" he asked, making her laugh again.

"No, silly. The house."

"I would like that very much," he said with tenderness.

"But I was trying to make a point," she added.

"Oh, were you? Then, by all means . . ."

"That first day . . . when your mother met me downstairs . . . and I commented on the beauty of the ceiling, she said something I'll never forget. She said, 'I think we are often so preoccupied with what's going on around us, that we don't take the time to look up.' I don't know why her words have stuck with me," Bess went on, "but they have. I believe she was right, and I believe she meant it in a very deep way. Perhaps she's had her own experiences with learning to look up. I mean . . . if we were outside we could look up into the night sky and see the stars; they're always there whether we're looking at them or not. Even when it's cloudy, the stars and the moon and the sun are always still there. I suppose that looking up could mean looking toward heaven, seeking God in our lives, seeking the answers to our prayers, seeking the hope and peace that He offers." Bess felt Hugh turn his head more toward her on the pillow they shared, as if doing so implied a more intent interest in what she was saying. She simply went on to finish expressing her idea. "I've thought about it many times as we have been here together in the dark at night, or even in the mornings when sunlight is filling the room and we can actually see the ceiling."

"Now, *this* ceiling I am very familiar with," Hugh said lightly, but there was a hint of solemnity in his voice that Bess had come to know well; he was thoughtfully taking in her analogy, and as always, he held a deep respect for anything and everything that was meaningful to her.

"And is it not beautiful?" she asked.

"I confess that it is," he admitted, "although I have truthfully never thought about it in that way. And I suppose that every ceiling in the house is at least as beautiful, the bedrooms likely being where the least amount of effort was put into making the ceilings attractive."

"That's likely true," Bess said. "And I think that what I really want to say is . . . even here in the dark . . . when I'm with you . . . looking up seems significant, important. Perhaps the very fact that we can't see anything at all makes it possible to imagine anything. We can't see the stars from here, but we know what a starlit sky looks like, and we can imagine the stars above us, twinkling over the roof of the house. And . . ."

"What?" he pressed when she hesitated.

Bess sniffled, and he turned even more toward her as soon as she'd let on that she was crying. "Forgive me," she said. "I didn't intend to get emotional; I was only trying to share something I've thought about and . . ."

"You never have to apologize to me for your tears, Bess," he said. "Have I not made that repeatedly clear?"

"Yes, you have," she said, wiping the sleeve of her nightgown over her face.

"So, go on," he encouraged. "Tell me the rest of what you want to say."

"I've simply . . . wondered many times what I might feel like when you're gone, and I'm alone, and how it might feel to look up into the darkness, or to look up at the stars, or the beautiful ceilings, and . . . this might sound strange, but . . . I believe that looking up will give me comfort, because in a way that I could never explain . . . I believe you will be there . . . that your spirit will live on, that you will somehow be able to watch over me, and that . . . when I look up and think of you, perhaps you'll be looking down and thinking of me."

"That's a beautiful thought," he said. "I like it very much. I know in my heart that somehow my spirit *will* live on, and it seems impossible to me that I wouldn't continue to love you and be aware of you—even if we can't begin to imagine how such things work; I suppose that's why we call it faith."

"Yes, I would think so."

"As long as we're discussing such a thing, there's something I want to say . . . that I've wanted to make clear to you, but perhaps I haven't wanted to bring it up, or I haven't known exactly how to put it. However, you and I have always been committed to complete honesty with each other, and we've also been very straightforward—right from the start—about discussing my death openly, and not holding back."

"Yes," she drawled, knowing he was right but not necessarily wanting to talk about his death any more than they already had.

"We both know it's getting closer, my love," he said, pressing a hand to her face. "I'm grateful for every moment we've had together, and I have no regrets beyond the very fact that I'm leaving you behind to face the grief and loneliness of being without me. If it were the other way around, I can't even imagine how I would cope. But I believe you are stronger than I am in that regard; I truly believe you'll be all right. And that's just it. I *need* you to be all right. I need to know that you will go forward, that you will make a good life for yourself, that you will *never* hold back out of some bizarre sense of guilt or duty toward me."

"What are you saying?" she asked, confused but also wary.

"You're so young, Bess. You have the potential of living for many decades. I feel a deep sadness to think of us not being able to share all those years, but you know because we've talked about it that I've made peace with dying; I'm all right, and I will *be* all right. And you need to find a way to be the same. Take some time to grieve if you must; cry if you must and get it over with. And then move on and find the path that is right for you. I don't want you to feel *any* sense of guilt or duty towards me," he repeated, as if that point was especially important. "And even more so, I don't want you to be lonely. Love will find you again, Bess, and you have to—"

"I can't even think about that now!" she insisted, feeling almost angry. "I can't imagine *ever* loving any man the way I love you and—"

"You can't imagine it now." He chuckled. "I don't really *want* you to try and imagine it now, but . . . it will happen. You're intelligent and beautiful and loving; you have so much to give, and you deserve a full and complete life; you deserve to be completely and utterly happy. I am only a very brief season in your life. So, treasure the memories as I will, but don't hold back. When you find love again, take hold of it and find joy. Look up now and then and think of me, but don't look up so much that you miss what might be right in front of you—and all around you. That's what I needed to say."

Bess couldn't speak. The reality that his death *was* drawing near suddenly felt real and overwhelming; the possibility of ever moving beyond it felt impossible in that moment. To avoid bursting into uncontrollable sobbing, she eased her head onto his shoulder and relaxed, holding him as close as she possibly could, and allowing the silence around them to conclude their conversation. In the deepest places of her heart she had no regrets, and she wouldn't trade away a moment of what they'd shared. She'd gone into this relationship with full knowledge of how it would end, and they'd had more time together than she might have realistically hoped for. She felt blessed and loved and grateful. But she also felt terrified of losing him and of the adjustment that would follow. However, the strain of his breathing and the irregular beating of his heart let her know that his life was now being measured in days. She squeezed her eyes closed tightly and allowed her senses to take in every bit of evidence that he was still alive and in her arms. She refused to cry now; she would have all the time and solitude in the world to cry after he was gone.

\* \* \* \* \*

Two days later while Bess was sitting next to Hugh's bed, holding his hand, she realized that he hadn't been out of bed for several days except for his necessary and very difficult treks to the nearby privy. He'd not been able to eat without assistance for almost as many days, simply because his arms were too weak to feed himself—not that he had much appetite. He was sleeping more and more, partly due to the natural exhaustion of his heart having to work so hard, and partly because of his asking for small doses of medicine more frequently since the increased difficulty of his breathing had become more painful. Bess also knew from her medical training that when death was coming, the body often began to slip into what her father had called the dying slumber. The previous day Jonas White had visited in his capacity as Hugh's physician and had—in essence—told Lady Buxton that there was nothing more he could do beyond leaving an ample supply of the medicine Hugh needed to ease the pain; it was time for nature to take its course, and his being present would not assist Hugh in any way. Agatha had told Bess that she believed Jonas was implying that Bess was capable of caring for Hugh now without any other assistance. Bess thought that might be partly true; she also believed that her father knew Bess wouldn't want to leave her husband's side, and he simply didn't want to be in the same room with her. Since she agreed with that, she felt relieved to know he wouldn't be coming back. His services regarding Hugh had come to an end.

Hugh had times every day when he was lucid, and they were able to talk. She selfishly kept much of that time between the two of them, but she was not so insensitive as to not recognize that his friends and his mother also needed time with him when he was awake. They each took turns helping him eat and drink what little he would, and while Hugh was in the care of others, she often took the opportunity to be alone in the room that used to be hers and cry just enough to release the building pressure of knowing that it was nearly time to let her husband go.

Bess was continually grateful for the support of those around her. Since she rarely left the rooms she shared with Hugh, she had no interaction with most of the staff, but she still felt the evidence of their support in the meals that came from the kitchen—along with everything else they could possibly need or want to make this process more comfortable. Occasionally a note was left for her on the tray, along with tea or a meal, a simple written expression of love and kindness from the cook or housekeeper or one of the maids. Bess treasured them all and tucked them away in a drawer, knowing she would always cherish them.

Bess had more direct support from her interaction with those who were also close to Hugh. She cared for and respected Lewis, but he was a quiet sort and the two of them had never become personally close. Still, she knew that Hugh loved him dearly and had relied heavily upon him for years, and she often took the opportunity to let Lewis know how much she appreciated his help and his kindness.

Bess felt much closer to Clive, and while Agatha or Lewis were sitting with Hugh, she and Clive often sat together in the sitting room or in the hallway, holding hands and discussing the enormity of all that was happening. She was able to be completely candid with him, and he with her, and ironically, she felt more comfortable crying in Clive's presence than she did with Hugh. They both agreed that she didn't want Hugh to see her sorrow; she only wanted to be able to smile for him and talk with him about all the happiness they shared.

Daphne was also supportive, mostly in the way she seemed to predict anything Bess might need, and she was most often nearby, silently remaining on hand to do anything any time of the day or night that might help Bess get through this. The two of them didn't talk much, but then there was little to say that hadn't already been said many times.

Agatha and Bess became naturally closer as Hugh's time to leave this world drew nearer. They both loved him, and they both had—as Agatha had said—the tenderness of a woman's heart in losing such a dear and precious part of their lives. Agatha often told Bess how grateful she was to not be facing this alone, but Bess felt certain that her need for Agatha—and her gratitude for this woman's kindness and acceptance—far exceeded anything she could ever give to her husband's mother.

On a bleak afternoon in March when dark skies and heavy rain made the house feel colder and more dismal, Bess sat as she most often did close to Hugh's bedside, holding his hand in hers while he drifted in and out of sleep. She wanted to be there whenever there might be any brief amount of time that he became alert enough to share even a few words with her. She often tried to read to distract herself, but mostly failed to concentrate on anything besides the raspy sound of his breathing, and her frequent preoccupation with listening to his heart through the stethoscope. Even though listening to his heart only gave her more evidence that it was failing, the very fact that she could still hear it beating offered her some abstract comfort, and so she kept the stethoscope at hand and used it frequently.

Bess was utterly startled to hear footsteps in the hall that were obviously a man's, and not at all familiar. Clive and Lewis were the only men who came to this part of the house, and they always used a light step so as not to disturb Hugh if he was resting. She looked up curiously at the very moment when this man appeared in the open doorway to Hugh's bedroom, as if he'd known exactly where to find Hugh. No servant had escorted him here, and Bess wondered who on earth this man could be. It took only a second to determine the probability that he was related by blood, because he looked so much like Hugh it was eerie. His hair was a shade darker and a tad wavier; he was clean-shaven, which showed that his features were similar to Hugh's but far from identical. Still, if Bess had not known that Hugh had no siblings, she would have assumed this man to be his brother. The likelihood of their being cousins struck her as the most obvious possibility only a moment before this man greeted Hugh with the jubilant word, "Cousin!"

Hugh's eyes came open and he turned to focus on this man as he approached the bed, wearing a smile that bore no indication he'd come to visit someone who was dying. Bess didn't know if this meant they weren't terribly close, or if this man was simply disciplined enough to not bring any grief to Hugh's bedside.

"Graham?" Hugh said, reaching out a feeble hand. "Is that you? Or am I hallucinating?" Hugh turned to glance at Bess and said with more animation than she'd seen in days, "Am I hallucinating, darling, or is there a very odd-looking man in the room? Besides me, I mean?"

"If you mean that he looks a great deal like you," Bess said, going along with his humor, "then he is very odd looking, indeed. And very real, it would seem."

Hugh turned to look again at his cousin, and Graham waited for no invitation before he sat on the bed, took hold of Hugh's hand, and leaned over him saying with mock severity, "You look dreadful, old boy. Since we've always been told we look so much alike, is this what I'm to expect when *I've* got one foot in the grave?"

Bess bristled at the tactlessness of the question, but Hugh smiled, and she told herself that she simply needed to become familiar with their relationship and their way of communicating. She'd never even heard of this Graham, and certainly hadn't expected any visits from relatives; in fact, she couldn't recall relatives ever being spoken of at all.

As if Graham might have just noticed he wasn't alone with his cousin, he looked up at Bess, his eyes expressing curiosity while she distinctly saw some level of disdain in his countenance. A moment ago, she'd believed she might like this man; now she felt quite the opposite, a feeling that expanded when he said, "So this is the nurse-turned-wife your mother wrote to me about. How very convenient."

"Convenient perhaps," Hugh said immediately, smiling weakly toward Bess, "but only in the sense that God's hand was surely present in bringing us together. She is the light of my life and the greatest thing that's ever happened to me." Hugh turned to look at Graham and added with a hint of severity that made it clear he expected to be taken seriously. "I realize much has changed since you were last here, but I assume you still trust my judgment. I may be dying but I haven't lost my mind. I'm certain you'll treat my wife with the respect she deserves."

"Of course," Graham said firmly to Hugh but with the subtlest glance toward Bess that perhaps intimated he might just be making such a promise to appease his cousin, while he had no respect for Bess whatsoever. But it only took her a long moment to assess that Hugh was obviously glad to see this cousin of his, and it didn't matter what Graham thought of her. It was Hugh's love and respect that mattered, and she certainly had that. She also knew it would be polite and appropriate for her to make a graceful exit and allow the two men some time alone.

"I'm certain the two of you have much to talk about," Bess said, coming to her feet. She leaned over to kiss Hugh's brow and looked him in the eye as she added, "Don't overdo, my love. If I come back to find you dead I shall be very angry."

He smiled to indicate that he appreciated her use of humor in regard to his impending death; she didn't necessarily like doing so, but she'd come to realize he far preferred it, and so she had followed his lead and taken to treating it all very lightly, all the while feeling inside as if the probability that he could leave her at any moment threatened to rip her heart quite literally in half. "I promise not to overdo," he said firmly to her. "I have no control over when my heart will stop beating."

"Just do your best," she added, as if they were discussing some sporting competition.

"Of course," he said, and she kissed his lips, looking into his eyes for a long moment as she'd become accustomed to doing, afraid that each time she did so might be the last, and she needed to fully absorb his gaze into her memory at every possible opportunity.

# CHAPTER TEN

## THE COUSIN

ON HER WAY TOWARD THE sitting room door, Bess said to the newly arrived cousin, "I'll just be in here should you need me." She didn't want to but felt the need to add, "He tires very quickly and has difficulty staying awake; if there's something specific you feel the need to talk about, I suggest you come quickly to the point."

Graham tossed her a glance that seemed to say he understood, but Bess also read in his eyes that he somehow resented this power she had over Hugh's care—or perhaps his life, what little was left of it. Bess tried not to assume messages that hadn't been spoken and give this man the benefit of the doubt. They had barely met, and she knew nothing about him. Hugh was obviously glad to see him, but Bess felt a prickly discomfort regarding Graham. They'd not been properly introduced so she didn't even know his surname, but it was likely the same as her own if they were cousins— unless the relationship was through Hugh's mother, in which case they would have different surnames. But she really didn't care.

Bess went into the sitting room and left the door open, as was customary when she knew she might be needed. She resisted the urge to sit close to the door as she'd done when Hugh had given her permission to eavesdrop on his conversation with his mother. She had no such permission now, and out of respect for Hugh she allowed him his privacy. She made herself comfortable on a sofa some distance from the door where she could neither see nor hear the men while they spoke in normal tones. But Graham only had to call for her and she would be able to hear him immediately.

Attempting to distract herself from the same old fears and concerns that were deepening every day—combined with the appearance of this new mysterious man—Bess picked up a book she'd left in that very spot, but she found it as difficult to focus on reading now as she had when she'd been attempting to read earlier while Hugh had been receiving a visit from his mother.

Bess settled for trying to be content with her most common pastime of late: staring out the window while she wondered if she was as strong as she hoped herself to be. And she prayed silently, as she did dozens of times every day, that Hugh would be able to leave this world without suffering. She didn't want him to die while struggling to breathe; she didn't want him to be in pain. And she didn't want her final memories of him to be of such an experience. But even while she prayed and was overcome with seemingly endless pondering of what it might be like when it finally happened, she knew that only God had control over such things, and sometimes human suffering was simply a part of life and death. She'd seen death enough to know this to be true. Still, she couldn't help wanting to believe that Hugh might be blessed in that regard, and his suffering would be minimal.

"There you are," Graham said and startled Bess so much that she gasped and then felt embarrassed for doing so.

"Forgive me," she said. "I'm afraid my mind was very far away."

"He told me he needed to rest, and we could talk more later." Graham moved to a chair across the room from her and sat down, which she found agitating. She had no desire to engage in any kind of conversation that might require him staying long enough to be seated. "It seems you were right; he does tire very quickly."

"You sound surprised," Bess noted. "Perhaps you thought I might be making it up."

"Or perhaps," he said, sounding slightly humbler, "I was futilely hoping that he was not nearly as bad off as my aunt's recent letters had indicated."

Bess couldn't help sounding mildly terse as she said, "Now you have seen for yourself that he is not doing well at all."

"Yes, I certainly have," he admitted, then a painful silence settled between them.

Bess cleared her throat, determined to get through whatever conversation might be necessary so that he could leave. "You must forgive me, sir," she hurried to say, "I've been here for many months and not once has Hugh or Agatha even mentioned you—or any other relatives for that matter. I'm not certain why, but Agatha isn't here right now, and Hugh is not presently capable of lengthy explanations. Your visit has come as a complete surprise, and given the fact that my husband is dying, I cannot deny that I'm not feeling very sociable."

"All perfectly reasonable," he said, and she wondered why she felt surprised, why she had perhaps expected him to argue with her—even though she couldn't think of what he could possibly say to oppose such an admission. "I've been on the continent, the south of France to be precise. Winter in England has become long and dreary to me, so I take advantage of my home there. Agatha has sent letters to keep me apprised of all that's happened. I can't tell you why they've not informed you of my existence; perhaps they are ashamed of me." He laughed softly, but Bess caught something serious in his eyes, and she wondered what kind of man he might be to believe that Hugh and Agatha might be ashamed of him—even if Agatha considered him worthy of regular communication.

Graham cleared his throat as if he felt uncomfortable over what he'd just said—or perhaps the fact that Bess had not laughed too. She felt no humor in the comment, but then she'd found it difficult to feel humor over anything of late. He crossed his legs the other way and said, "I confess I was surprised to hear that Hugh was marrying the woman his mother had hired to care for him. That must have stirred up the household."

"To my knowledge, everyone was quite pleased, unless they're all talking behind my back. If that's the case they're very good about it."

"Agatha is certainly pleased, and Hugh is *obviously* pleased."

"How can you know that? You only visited with him for less than five minutes."

"Oh, it's evident," he said with a gaze that Bess took to mean that Graham was not at *all* pleased, and she wondered why. She was surprised to hear him go on in a different vein, "And as for your not hearing about any other relatives, it's because there aren't any. My father is Agatha's brother, or rather was. He passed away a few years back; my mother passed the previous year. Every other relative died too long ago for me to remember well. And that only leaves me. And my aunt and cousin, both of whom you know very well. Agatha has always been very kind to me, and she makes a point of keeping me abreast of the happenings here, which I assume is her attempt to help me remember that I have *some* measure of a family. I could say that Hugh and I have been close, but that's a debatable issue. We've seen each other once or twice a year throughout the course of our lives, and we've never had any discomfort or awkwardness in our interactions, but I confess it's difficult to get close to someone you rarely see, and each time you do, you're told by the adults in your life that it will likely be the last time." Graham sighed, and Bess swallowed hard to force down any temptation to get emotional. "You see, in this family—what little there is of it—there has been a continual expectation that Hugh would die at any time. Each year he remained alive was called a surprise and a miracle. And each time I've been able to see him, I've expected it to surely be the last. So, I suppose when Agatha wrote and implored me to come and see him, I was somewhat dubious about the seriousness of her plea. But now I've seen for myself that she was right. He really *is* dying this time; his heart is finally giving out."

"Yes," Bess said, looking out the window with the hope that doing so would help keep her hovering grief from showing itself, "he really is dying."

Bess heard Graham sigh loudly and glanced toward him long enough to see that he was rubbing his eyes with a thumb and forefinger. She wondered if the gesture was some attempt to conceal the threat of tears, but she turned back to the window to allow him his privacy over that possibility. After a length of taut silence that almost allowed Bess to forget he was there, Graham cleared his throat and said, "Since that is the case, I'm afraid you won't be seeing the back of me for some time." Bess finally looked at him, wondering what he meant. "I intend to stay until it's over, to be here for the funeral, and to help Agatha with whatever she might need. I promise to stay out of the way. I just . . . need to be here; Agatha requested it, and I would do almost anything for her."

"So, your staying is for Agatha's benefit?"

"You ask me that as if you think I would not want to be here for my cousin in his final hours." Graham's tone was mildly haughty, and Bess again felt prickly toward him. "I sincerely care for both Agatha and Hugh. I don't believe I owe you any further explanation."

"Forgive me," she said, even though she wasn't certain she meant it. "I'm rather . . . on edge these days."

"As would be expected," Graham said with a kindness that almost made her angrier. For reasons she couldn't explain, she didn't *want* to like him. But trying to figure him out was far from a priority for her, given the present circumstances. She was relieved when he stood to leave the room, until he looked directly at her and asked, "Why did you marry him?"

"Why?" she echoed, wishing it hadn't sounded so thoroughly sharp. But he didn't seem at all affected by her unfavorable response.

"Agatha gave me practically no explanation," he said as if they were discussing the dinner menu. "I've just . . . wondered . . . why two people would get married when it would be so inevitably brief."

Bess stated vehemently, with tears in her eyes that refused to be held back any longer, "I can't speak for Hugh's motives, but I married him because I love him. There's no other reason."

"Forgive me if I've been presumptuous or caused you distress," he said, and Bess turned abruptly back to the view out the window, if only to hide her increasing surge of tears. She was glad to hear his footsteps leave the room, and only when she was certain of being alone did she allow herself to really cry. She did her best to indulge her grief when she was alone, trying always to show a brave face to her husband, to not burden him with her sorrow. But she *was* grieving, and she knew that tears were inevitable, and she needed to give herself the time and permission to cry when it was necessary, or she would surely explode. She didn't at all like the complication of having this cousin show up, knowing that he wasn't leaving anytime soon. But he'd promised to stay out of her way; she took that to mean he would respect her place as Hugh's wife, and her overseeing his care. Perhaps Agatha could help her better understand the best way to appropriately include Graham without allowing him to interfere with what precious little time the rest of Hugh's loved ones had to spend with him—when he was awake less and less.

Suddenly feeling exhausted and needing to be close to Hugh, Bess returned to the bedroom to find him sleeping, the sound of his breathing strained and raspy in a way that had become alarmingly normal. She slipped off her shoes and eased between the covers, moving carefully close to him, wanting to be as near as possible without waking him. He shifted slightly in his sleep to ease his arm around her in a way that seemed to have become completely natural for him, given that he didn't awaken. Bess settled her head against his shoulder and closed her eyes, focusing on the physical evidence that he was alive, wondering what it might be like when she was here in this bed alone and no such evidence existed. She kept telling herself that she couldn't think about such things, that she needed to do her best to enjoy these final moments with him—however long they might last—and deal with the reality of his death when it happened. But her spirit seemed instinctively desperate to be prepared for the dramatic changes about to take place, now that they were getting too close to ignore. Months ago, when they'd been embarking on their marriage and his health had been better, Bess had found it easier to not think of anything but living each day to its fullest. But the end was drawing near, and she felt the need to allow herself to consider how she was going to cope. She felt relaxed but couldn't sleep; her mind wandered through the details of the funeral they had planned together, and how it might feel to make regular visits to his grave, even though she knew in her heart that his spirit was likely to linger in far more cheerful places than a cemetery. She wondered if she would feel inclined to continue sleeping in this room they had shared for months, or whether she would go back to the room she'd used before. She'd talked it through with him and they concluded that she couldn't make that decision until he was gone; only then would she know which was easier for her.

Bess finally slept and came awake to an immediate awareness that time had passed, due to the changed shadows on the wall. But she was more keenly aware of the increased difficulty of Hugh's breathing. She sat up to see him struggling to pull air into his lungs, his expression mildly pan-icked, his hand tightly holding to her arm as if doing so might somehow help him. She sensed that he wanted to speak but couldn't, when he could barely breathe.

"Relax," she whispered gently, close to his face, even though she felt anything but relaxed herself. "I know it's difficult, my darling, but try to relax." She felt him attempting to do so; the tightness of his grip lessened, and she saw his head sink back onto the pillow a bit more. But he still looked afraid as he put a great deal of effort into trying to take slow, even breaths, the way they had practiced hundreds of times. Despite his inability to do so, he tried very hard to pull as much air into his lungs as he possibly could, and then blow it out until he could no longer do so. Even though his breathing was swift and shallow, Bess had taught him that he needed to try to take in as much air as he let out, because doing otherwise would cause other problems.

Bess looked deeply into his eyes, wondering more and more as she did if this would be the end, if this would be the moment she had to allow him to let go and slip away. She'd long ago told him—more than once—that whenever he felt ready to go, whenever the pain and effort to live became too much, he needed to go and not try and stay for her benefit. He knew that; they'd agreed to it. Bess knew she was as prepared as anyone could possibly be for such an incomprehensible event, and yet she felt entirely unprepared. Still, she didn't allow such feelings to show in her expression. All the love she felt for him was mirrored in her eyes, and she kept her gaze firmly connected to his, glad to note that he *was* relaxing more, and his breathing was becoming slightly easier—but only slightly. "I love you," he managed to whisper between his strained breaths.

"Oh, I love you too, my darling," she said and kissed his brow before she again locked her gaze with his.

While minutes passed, and he continued to struggle, Bess began to feel certain this was the end, especially when the strain didn't pass, and she could almost literally feel his exhaustion in simply attempting to breathe enough to ease the pain in his chest, which he surely felt from the effort. Part of Bess wished that someone would come to check on them, to see if help was needed. They had missed the usual tea time, although it was likely someone had peeked in to see if they wanted tea, and seeing that they'd been asleep, had left them undisturbed. Despite her wish that someone might check on them, Bess was overwhelmingly relieved that no one came. Everyone else involved in his care knew she was with him, and she would be certain he had what he needed. While she silently prayed to know what to do, it occurred to her that the medicine available for him would help him relax and ease his pain. She overcame her fear that giving it to him would relax him so much that it would be the end; the most important thing was doing anything possible to ease his suffering. She finally moved away to get the medicine and urged him to take some, which he barely managed between his excruciating efforts to breathe and the unmerciful battle being waged between Hugh and his own body.

It seemed forever before Bess could see evidence of the medicine taking effect, and she felt indescribable relief to see Hugh drift off to sleep, however unnatural it seemed as manifested by the ongoing strain in his breathing—though not as intense. For many more minutes she just watched him sleeping, touching his face and hair, and whispering to him of the depth of her love, and her gratitude for the happiness he had brought into her life. She kissed his brow, his cheeks, his closed eyelids, and finally his lips, before she settled her head again on his shoulder, overcome with her own exhaustion, as if she had personally been striving to help him breathe and it had completely worn her out.

Bess didn't realize she'd fallen asleep until she awoke to find the room dusky; it was still light enough to see, but the evidence of night coming on blanketed every detail of her surroundings. It only took her a few seconds to consider how long she might have been asleep, and how surprised she felt at being able to sleep so deeply. Then it only took another sharp and painful moment to become aware of the strangeness of the situation—more accurately, the absolute silence in the room. She'd become thoroughly accustomed to the raspiness of Hugh's breathing, which let her know by its absence that he was gone, even before she gingerly reached out to touch his face, not surprised but still horrified to find it cold.

Bess felt frozen herself beyond the unheeded weeping that overcame her. She didn't have the strength to sob audibly; she just held Hugh in her arms and wept a continual flow of quiet tears, knowing that the moment she'd dreaded for many months had come to pass as she'd known it would, and nothing would ever be the same. She couldn't deny some relief on Hugh's behalf, knowing that he was free of pain and suffering, and even the lifelong anticipation of always having death at the forefront of his life. For herself, there was also a strange sense of relief; she already missed him more than she could grasp and understand within the limited capacity of her mortal mind, but she no longer had to dread this moment; she no longer had to spend her days wondering how and when it would happen. But most of all, she just missed him already and couldn't imagine how she would get through her days without being able to talk to him about every little thing. Recalling how much he'd been sleeping for many days now, and how he'd struggled to breathe when he *had* been awake, she reminded herself that having him alive didn't necessarily mean he had been living enough to truly share a life with her.

Bess was startled but also relieved when someone *did* come to check on them. It was Clive who appeared and lit a lamp in the darkening room. Before he could ask any questions, he knew immediately from what he saw that Hugh was gone. He looked both panicked and horrified as he said with a quaver in his voice, "I need to get help. I will only be a few minutes. I promise."

Bess nodded and held more tightly to Hugh's body, even though she hated the coldness of what had not so long ago been warm and real. If nothing else, spending this time close to his body made it inescapably clear to her that he was indeed gone. This was no longer Hugh; it was a cold and empty shell, a physical body that had no longer been able to function enough to live, and it was no longer needed. She reminded herself that his spirit lived on elsewhere; she didn't understand exactly where or how that was possible, but she absolutely believed it to be true, and perhaps more importantly she knew that Hugh had firmly believed it. She wanted to think that his spirit was still nearby, that he would continue to be close to her when she needed him. But she could feel nothing, and she had to settle for believing that Hugh was in God's hands now, and his life was going on in a heavenly realm beyond human imagination. He was free, and she felt enough relief and happiness on his behalf to soothe her own grief.

Within what felt like no time at all after Clive had left, he returned with Lewis, Daphne, and Agatha. He must have sent Daphne to get Agatha while he'd gone for Lewis, and they all must have literally run through the long hallways of the house to have gotten here so quickly. Bess saw the hint of tears in Clive's eyes, while Lewis's expression remained stoic but nevertheless betrayed his sorrow. Agatha sank down on the bed on the other side of Hugh, sobbing without restraint as the moment she'd dreaded from Hugh's infancy had finally come to pass. Bess wanted to allow Agatha time alone with the body, but she felt incapable of moving, of letting go. She felt indescribably grateful for the way that Clive and Daphne seemed to sense the need for her to do so. Daphne spoke quietly near her ear that she needed to go into the other room and give Hugh's mother some time. She tenderly explained to Bess that remaining there under the circumstances would only become more difficult. Bess knew she was right but still found it difficult to let go of her husband and move away. She only looked up with what she could guess was a silent pleading, which Clive and Daphne both seemed to understand as they shared a glance that held silent meaning just before they worked together to carefully ease her arms from around Hugh, and then to move her away from him. She was surprised to hear her own crying become more audible as the physical separation began to feel real, but Clive lifted her into his arms and carried her out of the room and across the hall to the bedroom that had once been hers. He laid her carefully on the bed, and Daphne covered her with a blanket, reassuring Clive that she would stay with Bess, while Clive said something about the need to make arrangements. *Arrangements?* Bess silently echoed. She knew what that meant. She and Hugh had thoroughly discussed and planned every arrangement, but now it was actually happening. The undertaker would be sent for so that he could appropriately care for the body, and funeral preparations would quickly be underway. Bess groaned to think of facing a funeral, but Daphne seemed to read her mind when she whispered tenderly, "You don't need to concern yourself with anything right now except your own sorrow, dearest. Cry all you need to; that's your right, surely. I'll take care of everything. You need not see anyone or even show your face outside this room for a few days if you prefer. Right now, just rest. I'll be right here if you need anything."

"Thank you," Bess managed to say and immediately became swallowed again by her grief, which was far more tangible and unavoidably painful than she ever could have imagined. Still, each moment she wept for the loss of her husband, she was conscious of a quiet warmth in her heart that reminded her she would not have traded away a moment with him to avoid what she was feeling now. He had awakened her to life, real life. And even in sharing his death she instinctively knew she had become a better and stronger person; she was becoming the woman she needed to be, perhaps the woman God wanted her to be—a woman whose encounters with life and death, with love and sorrow, would strengthen her for whatever might lie ahead.

* * * * *

The next few days went by in a blur for Bess. She mostly slept and cried, losing all sense of day and night, since she insisted that the draperies remain closed; but Daphne kept a lamp continually burning low in the room in case Bess needed to get up. She managed to eat only a little bit here and there at Daphne's insistence, to keep up her strength and not make herself sick. Bess couldn't deny Daphne's logic, but her lack of appetite was overwhelming. However, she noted that when she went too long without eating, an equally overwhelming nausea consumed her, which was even more uncomfortable. Therefore, she heeded Daphne's instructions to eat when food was brought to her room.

Agatha came once to visit with her, although they had little to say to each other and ended up mostly just crying together before Agatha went back to her own rooms, likely to just try and get from one hour to the next, much as Bess was doing.

When the day of the funeral arrived, Bess had no choice but to get out of bed and make herself presentable, and fight to maintain a composure she could hold onto in public. The hot bath Daphne had prepared felt good; Bess had completely neglected her personal hygiene since Hugh had left her.

Once bathed and dressed in the layers of underclothing that would go beneath her dress, Bess sat down in front of her mirror so that Daphne could wind up Bess's damp hair and pin it neatly into place. Daphne then helped Bess into the black dress that had ironically been ordered many weeks ago with the knowledge that she would soon become a widow, and Hugh had insisted that she must look ravishing at his funeral; he had also told her that she should consider it a celebration of his freedom from suffering, and his going on to a better place—and therefore in spite of her needing to wear black for the sake of social protocol, he wanted her to wear something that made her look and feel beautiful. Bess looked at her reflection in the long mirror as Daphne fastened the many buttons down the back of the new dress; it was indeed beautiful, but Bess saw nothing in her face but a gaunt shadow. She was glad for the fashionable little hat that Daphne pinned carefully into Bess's hair, and the little veil that came forward over Bess's face. She still didn't feel beautiful, but she did feel properly dressed to appear in public as the widow of Hugh Buxton, a man adored and revered by all who had truly known him. But no one had known him as closely or deeply as she had, and for that she felt deeply gratified and immensely grateful.

The funeral was an appropriately lovely service, followed by an equally appropriate burial in the cemetery next to the church. She was taken aback slightly to see Graham present, when she'd not seen him at all since the day she'd met him—the day Hugh had died. She'd been told that he'd been assisting Agatha with arrangements, both for the funeral and regarding business matters of the estate, and some legal business that needed to be updated now that Hugh was gone. Bess had no mind or concern for such things; they had nothing to do with her. However, she couldn't deny being grateful to know that someone was able and willing to help Agatha with things for which Bess had no understanding.

At the funeral, Bess remained next to Agatha, often holding her hand or her arm, while Graham remained on the opposite side of his aunt, doing the same. Yet Bess and Graham exchanged no words. She found his resemblance to Hugh more than a little unnerving, and her interaction with him had been such a mixture of both positive and negative that she really didn't know what to think of him. Agatha trusted him and that was all she needed to know.

Bess was vaguely aware of most of the staff attending the service, although they remained at some distance from the family. She knew such separation was normal and appropriate according to social protocol, but she still found it preposterous. Clive and Lewis were like brothers to Hugh; it seemed ridiculous that they couldn't sit with the family. And the same with Daphne. But as with everything that wasn't directly related to her own grief, thoughts went quickly in and out of her head and she could only think of how much she missed her precious husband. Somewhere deep inside, she had the firm belief that she would get beyond feeling this way and be able to go on living, but right now, she could only think of getting from one moment to the next, of putting one foot in front of the other—which often took all the inner strength she could muster.

Bess managed to keep her composure throughout the services and remain engaged in what was taking place, but she mostly longed for it to be over, so she could get out of this dress and go back to bed. When she was finally able to do just that, she cried herself to sleep, trying to be convinced that it was now time to do what she had known she would need to do ever since the moment she had admitted her love for Hugh: she needed to face life as his widow, and she needed to do as she'd promised him over and over. She needed to have courage, she needed to find joy and a reason to go on living and have a happy life. But she felt neither inclined nor motivated to do anything but wallow in her loneliness and sorrow. Thankfully, Daphne helped make certain she took care of herself, and was always nearby during the moments when Bess felt like talking about her grief. Daphne just kept telling her to give the matter some time, that the number of days—or even weeks—that a person needed in order to feel ready to face life was a completely individual matter. Still, Bess knew that wallowing too long could not be good for anyone.

Bess saw Agatha at least once a day, and it was no surprise that Hugh's mother too was struggling a great deal, even though she admitted to feeling a tad guilty for having some relief that it was over.

"There's no need to feel guilty," Bess assured her. "You've spent most of Hugh's life in anticipation of losing him; it must have been so emotionally exhausting. To no longer have to dread his death would naturally bring some relief." Bess sniffled and wiped her eyes with her handkerchief, amazed that the source of her tears hadn't dried up long ago. "I confess to feeling a tiny bit of relief myself; he's no longer suffering, and we no longer have to wonder when and how it will happen. But then . . . I've only had him as a part of my life for a few months. He's been the center of your life since the day he was born."

"Yes," Agatha said, "but the role you played in his life was enormous, my dear. And I'm so grateful you were there for him . . . and that you're here for me now."

"Where else would I go?" Bess asked, then hurried to add, "I mean . . . eventually I'll move on and find work and—"

"Why?" Agatha demanded. "This is your home; you are loved and needed here."

Bess didn't want to feel like a burden to Agatha or anyone else, but the look on her mother-in-law's face made it evident that becoming a part of this family certainly had made her future more complicated. They both agreed not to concern themselves about that for now, but they pledged to each other that they would do their best to try and regain some normalcy and a sense of routine. Still, Bess couldn't help thinking that she had come here as a hired employee, and now that Hugh was gone, she should surely find a way to earn her keep. Despite her comfortable relationship with Agatha, she still felt far more like she fit in with the servants, and that being among them was right and expected. But she was grateful for Agatha's insistence that they needed time to grieve before making any big decisions, because Bess felt incapable of anything beyond barely getting through the days.

Graham's name frequently came up in her regular conversations with Agatha. She told Bess how grateful she was to have him here, how helpful he had been, what a good man he was. And Bess just listened, not certain if she had misjudged Graham to some degree, or whether Agatha had the kind of relationship with her nephew that allowed her to see only the good in him, blinded to his tendency to be arrogant and impertinent regarding certain matters. But as with everything else that didn't concern her directly, Bess pushed Graham out of her mind, and she was glad that their paths never crossed.

A week beyond Hugh's death, Bess forced herself to get out of bed in the morning, and she washed and dressed before she shared breakfast with Daphne in their sitting room. She'd continued to sleep in her old room, finding it difficult to go into the room she'd shared with Hugh, perhaps because of the memories, or perhaps because he had died there. Either way, she was comfortable and grateful for Daphne's help as well as her friendship.

Bess and Agatha decided they should continue sharing lunch, just as they had done when Hugh was alive. Bess went to Agatha's sitting room each day shortly before lunch would be brought there, and they both found it was good to have this time together, to openly share their feelings of grief, and even their tears when they needed to.

Bess resumed her habit of sharing supper in the kitchen with the staff, who were all kind and compassionate over her loss, although she quickly made it clear that she preferred them to enjoy their meals along with normal conversation and interaction, rather than focusing on Hugh's death. She did plenty of that when she was alone.

Nighttime was the most difficult, when she had to try and sleep alone, and Hugh's absence was so keenly felt. She often found herself absently reaching for him and feeling surprised to find the other side of the bed empty and cold.

Clive came to visit her every day, declaring with earnest candor that he'd come to feel a certain responsibility for her, and he wanted to be certain she was all right. She felt touched by his admission, and deeply grateful for his friendship. It was evident that he also missed Hugh very much, and they were able to talk openly about their memories and the emptiness Hugh's death had left in their lives. They'd taken to comfortably holding hands while they sat together on the sofa in her sitting room, and it had become a habit for him to kiss her brow or her cheek when he was arriving or departing. Bess found nothing in his gestures that made her uncomfortable or ill at ease, even though there were moments when she wondered if Clive felt something for her that she simply didn't feel for him. But he knew she was grieving and showed complete respect for her need to do so. Bess didn't know if one day her feelings toward Clive might change, given the fact that he was obviously a good man and they'd always been comfortable in each other's company. She felt it more likely that they would always just remain as friends. Anything else felt impossible right now, but she could never forget how Hugh had repeatedly implored her to find love again, and to not be alone. She couldn't imagine ever feeling anything for any man that might compare to how she'd felt for Hugh, and perhaps such an expectation was simply unrealistic. She believed it more likely that Hugh had been the love of her life, and perhaps one day she would find a man with whom she could live a comfortable life of caring and mutual respect. Anything more than that felt impossible. But perhaps that would be all right with Clive someday; there was no way of knowing until she was able to move beyond Hugh's death, and that would take time—a great deal of it.

Bess was surprised one day at lunch to hear Agatha tell her that Graham had left earlier that morning to return to his home, which was a few hours' travel from Astoria Abbey. Bess's first thought was relief that she'd not had to see him before he left; she could only think of how his appearance unnerved her, perhaps simply because of his resemblance to Hugh, and perhaps because the most prominent thing she recalled from their one conversation was how uncomfortable she'd felt in his presence. She felt nothing but relief to know that he was gone, and she wouldn't have to worry about coming upon him somewhere in the house. Bess's next thought was the realization that Graham had an estate—not dissimilar to Astoria Abbey, according to Agatha—somewhere in England, as well as his house in the south of France where he chose to spend certain months to avoid the cold dreariness of England's winter. Bess listened to Agatha once again express appreciation and praise for Graham, but she had no comment at all to offer in return. Her thoughts were completely preoccupied with Hugh.

As more days passed, and despite all of Bess's concerted efforts to adhere to a rigorous routine, she just couldn't get past feeling exhausted and wanting to cling to her bed. She regressed to eating breakfast in her nightclothes and dressing gown, and always ended up back in bed after sharing lunch with Agatha. It was about three weeks after Hugh's death that she found herself looking up at the ceiling after waking up from a nap, thinking about how she and Hugh had talked about looking up, and its metaphorical significance. With tears leaking from the corners of her eyes into her hair, Bess reminded herself that she needed to keep looking up, to look heavenward for divine assistance and perspective, and to remember that Hugh was surely in some way looking down at her, and she needed to hold fast to the memories of all the good they had shared and not get so bogged down in the difficulties of the present. *Easier said than done,* she thought, wishing she felt any motivation at all to get out of bed, knowing that Daphne would soon be bringing tea. In the minutes left before Daphne's arrival, Bess considered many facts and facets of how life had become for her in the present, then she forced herself to get up and look presentable before Daphne arrived.

Feeling somewhat better after enjoying some warm, savory tea and a variety of little sandwiches and biscuits, which felt especially satisfying, Bess felt inclined to go and speak with Agatha—even though they rarely interacted during this time of the day. Agatha could be resting for all Bess knew, or perhaps she might not even be in her rooms—or even in the house. Bess was certainly not in the habit of keeping track of the Lady of Astoria Abbey.

Bess found Agatha in her sitting room, just finishing her own tea, looking thoughtful while she cradled a dainty teacup in her hands.

"Oh, hello, my dear," she said, looking up to see Bess standing in the open doorway. "What a nice surprise! Do come and sit down."

"Thank you," Bess said and sat on the same sofa with Agatha.

"What might I do for you?" Agatha asked, setting her nearly empty teacup aside.

"There's something I need to tell you. It's a rather delicate matter, but . . . I'll come straight to the point."

"Of course," Agatha said, looking concerned.

Bess just said it. "I'm pregnant."

Agatha's eyes widened, and her mouth formed a perfect circle although no sound came out. Bess waited for the news to settle in, wondering what her mother-in-law's reaction might be. She didn't want to express any of her own feelings until Agatha had been given a fair chance to state what she felt over the news.

"Are . . . you certain?" Agatha asked.

Bess laughed softly, but not because anything was funny; it was more an attempt to cover her nervousness before she cleared her throat and answered a question she had predicted might come up. "My lady, you hired me because you know I'm well-versed in medical matters. I assure you that I'm keenly aware of the symptoms of pregnancy, and that I have already cautiously considered all my own symptoms. I would not have come to you with such a declaration if I were not absolutely certain."

"Good heavens!" Agatha muttered on the wake of a sharp gasp, at the same time putting a hand over her heart. For a minute or more she seemed to be finding it difficult to breathe evenly. Bess put a hand on her mother-in-law's arm and waited patiently for her to consider all the possible implications of how this would dramatically change both of their lives.

As if she'd finally been able to piece her thoughts together enough to speak, Agatha looked directly at Bess and said, "Forgive me if I'm being brash, but . . . I wouldn't have thought it was possible."

Bess looked down, perhaps fearing she might blush over such a comment. This too was something she'd suspected that Agatha—and others—might wonder about, and she felt prepared to explain—at least to a point; it was a personal matter, which she intended to keep to herself. She cleared her throat and looked up again, saying simply, "Of course we were both keenly aware of Hugh's limitations, and I can assure you that we were very careful not to ever put his health at risk. But we were husband and wife, and I don't believe anyone needs any further explanation than that."

"Of course," Agatha said immediately and took hold of Bess's hand. "It's just that . . ." Before she could finish her thought, tears trickled down her face.

"What is it?" Bess asked, alarmed.

Agatha used her free hand to wipe her tears with a lace handkerchief. "It's just that . . . I secretly wished many times that it was possible for him to leave a child behind, but I'd convinced myself that it simply wasn't.

Clearly, I underestimated the situation. I . . . I . . ." She looked again at Bess with awe in her eyes, as if she were viewing the parting of the Red Sea. "Oh, my dear! Through all the years of knowing I would lose him, I never imagined . . . never dared hope . . . for such a miracle."

This prompted tears to trickle down *Bess's* face, which she promptly wiped away with her own handkerchief. It *was* a miracle! And her gratitude for having this tangible part of Hugh still with her was beyond her ability to express. But her plans for the future—however vague they may have been—had to be completely reevaluated and reconsidered. Hugh's child was now at the center of her life as her most important priority, and it always would be.

# CHAPTER ELEVEN

## LEFT BEHIND

"BESS, MY DEAR," AGATHA SAID with deep fervor, "I hope now that you will realize you truly are a part of this family and that you need to stay. I don't want you to believe in any way that you must work in order to earn your right to live here; you've only mentioned such a thing a time or two, but I know you well enough to know that for some reason you feel inclined to believe that such measures are necessary."

Bess couldn't deny the truth in what Agatha was saying, and she was reminded of the insight and perception of this kind woman. "I confess it's difficult *not* to feel that such measures are necessary. I came here as a hired employee; I belong with the staff and—"

"You are Hugh's wife," she said as if Hugh were still alive. "You have become a part of the family. Your stubbornness will never change that fact. He would loathe the very idea of your believing you need to work to remain in our home and be provided for."

"We never talked about money, Agatha, not at all. He never brought it up, and so I didn't either. I always just assumed he agreed with my belief that I would leave here after his death and find work elsewhere."

"You *assumed?*" Agatha countered. "For all that you knew Hugh better in many ways than anyone, you cannot assume what he would believe regarding such things. He *should* have talked to you about the financial situation, because it's important. Perhaps he was simply so accustomed to such things being out of his control that he didn't give it much thought. But I can assure you, my dear—because we *did* talk about money—that he assumed you would always be cared for with the money that was meant to take care of him."

"I didn't marry him for any such reason!" Bess insisted, almost embarrassed with how defensive she sounded.

"He knew that, or he never would have wanted to marry you; and *I* knew that the first time we discussed the two of you getting married. This is not about money, my dear. Your father taught you a strong work ethic and to not expect something for nothing. For all his faults, he raised you well regarding such things. But let me assure you, Bess, you are *family*, and with or without Hugh's child growing inside of you, the security entitled to any member of this family is rightfully yours. I admire the way you continue to treat the staff as your equals; it's one of the things Hugh loved about you, and you should never change such precious facets of your character. But you must come to see yourself as Hugh's wife! The briefness of your marriage does not negate that you were in fact married, and you are his legal widow. I will hear no more about it. You will stay here where you and your child will be loved and cared for, and you will *not* be working to earn your keep." Agatha took a deep breath and blew it out slowly. "Forgive me for becoming so heated. I suppose I just . . ." She sniffled and got teary, but that wasn't at all unusual for either of them since Hugh's death. "I love you so dearly, Bess. I don't want you to stay because you feel sorry for a silly old woman, but I can't deny that I don't know what I'd do without you. And now to know that Hugh left a child behind. How could I bear not being a part of that child's life? So, make me a very happy, silly old woman and . . . stay." Agatha sighed and added, "We are blessed with great abundance, Bess, and you shall be cared for in every way. I'll hear no more about it."

Bess could find no argument for any point Agatha had made, so she simply said, "Very well. I confess that I don't *want* to leave; I just—"

"Ah!" Agatha put up a finger to stop her and Bess said no more about it. She realized then that it was up to her to become accustomed to this new reality. The circumstances were as Agatha had described; it was up to Bess to truly learn to accept herself as a part of the family, even though that didn't mean she couldn't keep interacting socially with the staff as much as she chose. Being pregnant with Hugh's child certainly strengthened Agatha's case. Bess couldn't go elsewhere and try to find work in this condition, and once the baby was born, Agatha would want to be involved in the child's life, an idea that gave Bess great joy. How could she *ever* leave here and take Hugh's child with her? In truth, the thought of being able to remain here at the Abbey indefinitely gave Bess a great deal of peace. She couldn't think of any other place she might want to live out the rest of her life—here, where

Hugh's spirit would surely abide, here where the memories of him were so much easier to keep close, here where she felt completely at home and able to be herself without criticism or ridicule. Astoria Abbey *did* feel like home, more than her previous home had ever felt since her mother's death. She *wanted* to stay and was glad that Agatha not only agreed but was also adamant.

"What about your father?" Agatha asked, and Bess wondered if she had some supernatural ability to pick up on the fact that Bess had just been silently comparing her life now to the one she had lived with her father.

"What *about* my father?" Bess countered, not wanting to even think about him, let alone *talk* about him.

"There are a number of things to be considered," Agatha said. "And I believe we've come past the shock of Hugh's death enough to be able to talk about such things. Given the news you just gave me, your life is going to be much different than you perhaps expected from this point forward. I know at one time you talked of possibly returning to your father's home after—"

"I'm never going back there," Bess stated, not at all angry, but certainly firm in her decision. Her father's repeated slights toward her, and his overt disdain regarding her decisions, had firmly cemented what she had already felt and perhaps tried to ignore for years. She was done thinking she could try and change him; she would find her own way and her own life. And Agatha knew that.

"I never expected you to," Agatha said. "I'm just wondering if . . . well . . . he's the only doctor in the village, Bess, and you're going to need medical care to bring a child into the world and—"

The notion took Bess off guard; it had simply not occurred to her. But she was quick to say, "I will not have him involved in any way! Even *if* my father and I were on good terms, I'm not certain I would want him to deliver my baby. It's just so . . . personal and intimate."

"I can certainly understand that," Agatha said. "So, we need to discuss other options. There is a very good doctor who lives not so far away. It would be a little more of an inconvenience for him to come here for regular visits to monitor your health, and to send for him when it's time. But of course, he would be more than fairly compensated. I know him; he's a good man. He had his fair share of involvement in Hugh's care at one time when I was determined to get every opinion available."

"I suppose that *is* a possibility," Bess said, "although I'm not certain I like the idea of someone having to travel such a distance to care for me. If anything went wrong, it could be frightening to think of help being so far away, and . . . I know the life of a doctor. If he must travel farther to take care of me, it could very well take him away from being there for other patients who need him."

"You make a fair point," Agatha said. "But what else can we possibly do? I want to know that you are being looked after properly, and that you'll have the help you need to deliver safely when the time comes." She was silently thoughtful a moment, which allowed Bess time to search her own mind for possible solutions that would allow her to completely avoid her father in every way. "Perhaps," Agatha finally said, "we should go to London and stay there until after the baby is born and you are both able to travel. The best of medical care is available there and given all my past efforts to give Hugh the best possible care, I have come to know a great many excellent doctors there."

"Is such a thing possible?" Bess asked, even while knowing that Agatha and Hugh had lived in London a great deal.

"Of course it is," Agatha said. "We have a house there, which is always staffed whether we're there or not. It's ready any time we need it. Well, actually it's Graham's house, but he rarely uses it, and if he chooses to be there at the same time, there is more than ample room for all of us. He's made it repeatedly clear that it is continually at our disposal when we choose to stay in London."

"I see," Bess said, marveling that one family—or one man—could own so many homes and travel between them whenever he chose, always knowing that he had a place waiting for him, and a staff to see to his every need. The wealth of the family Bess had married into was something she'd hardly given a thought to beyond her gratitude for simply having her own needs met without causing any strain on the family. It was Hugh's love, and only Hugh's love, that had brought her into the family. But right now, the most prominent concern was the well-being of Hugh's child.

"That's certainly an option to consider," Bess said, although she didn't necessarily feel fond of the idea of leaving the Abbey. It wasn't that she wouldn't love to see London and spend some time there; she'd heard many stories of the great city and would love to see it for herself. But in her heart, she wanted to have her baby here, surrounded by a staff that already knew her, and in surroundings that had come to represent home to her in every way. She also didn't feel fond of the idea of traveling so far, especially when she was already feeling the fatigue and occasional nausea associated with pregnancy, and she suspected the symptoms would worsen.

"I suppose I need to think about it," Bess said.

Once again seeming to perceive feelings Bess had not even hinted at, Agatha said, "I can understand why you would want to remain here during your confinement; I just don't know exactly how we would manage that and be certain you get the care you need."

An idea popped into Bess's mind so abruptly that she could almost believe it had been whispered in her ear by some power beyond herself. For a moment she had the fanciful idea that Hugh was there beside her, guiding her to the answers she was seeking. Whether or not it could be true, or it was simply her imagination, didn't really matter. She liked the idea and clung to it as she said to Agatha, "It's just occurred to me that there is a competent midwife who lives in the village. She's quite well respected by my father; they are colleagues of a sort, I suppose. There were a few times when a woman was in labor and my father was overwhelmed with the needs of other patients when he expressed his gratitude to me that the village had a midwife who was well-trained and very skilled so that she could care for the delivery of babies when he couldn't be in two places at once. It's my understanding that she was trained by her mother, who delivered hundreds of babies during her lifetime, as did her mother before her. I think I should like to meet with her and see if the possibility of relying on her feels comfortable to me. If not, then perhaps going to London is the best option."

"An excellent plan, my dear," Agatha said. "Perhaps you can have Clive send for her to come and visit at her next convenience, and if it's all right with you, I'd like to be present when you speak with her."

"Of course," Bess said, wondering why Agatha would sound hesitant to make such a suggestion.

"I never want to be intrusive, my dear, and I want you to promise to tell me if I ever become that way. I won't be offended. However, if the father of this baby were still alive, he would want to be at your side throughout the process of making such decisions and seeing that you're cared for. I want very much to try and do for you what he would do if he were here, and I also want to be involved in my grandchild's life—beginning now."

"Of course," Bess said and took Agatha's hand. "You are not being intrusive at all. I dearly appreciate your help and support, and yes, I promise to tell you if there's ever a problem."

Agatha sighed and smiled. "That's settled then. We'll decide after we speak to the midwife. I assume it's all right for the rest of the household to know. It will be difficult to keep your pregnancy a secret when we're sending for a midwife—not to mention that your daily habits will surely be affected by your symptoms."

"There's no need for secrecy," Bess said. "I just wanted to tell you first."

Agatha sighed again. "I'm so happy about this, my dear. I do believe I feel better than I've felt since we lost him. We have something good to focus on, something to hope for, and a tangible reminder that he was such an enormous part of our lives."

"I couldn't have said it better myself," Bess said, and they shared a long, firm embrace.

Agatha surprised Bess by saying, "I love you, my dear. I hope you know that."

Even though it had been implied many times, the words had never been spoken between them. But Bess felt warmed by Agatha's declaration, recalling how desperately she'd wanted to hear those words from her father, and how much she'd missed having a mother with whom to share her life—a mother who had readily admitted her love for Bess every day.

"I do know it," Bess said, looking fondly at Agatha. "And I love you! You've become so dear to me that I can't imagine how I ever lived before I came here . . . before you became the best friend I've ever had. You've very much helped compensate for the lack of a mother in my life, Agatha, and I'm inexpressibly grateful."

"And you, my dear, have very much made up for my not having a daughter." An expression of deep sadness passed briefly over Agatha's countenance.

"What is it?" Bess asked, tightening her hold on Agatha's hand.

"I've never told you this; it's not something I've talked about much. Hardly anyone knew except for Hugh—and his father, of course. I don't think it's even been brought up since my husband passed, but . . . Hugh was our firstborn. At the time of his birth we anticipated having a large family; it's what we both wanted. I had many ensuing pregnancies, but none of them ever came to fruition."

"Oh, Agatha!" Bess said, overcome with sorrow and compassion on her behalf, and unable to even think about the possibility that the baby inside her might not be born healthy and alive.

"I had four that miscarried . . . that I lost within the first few months of pregnancy. And there were two that went full term but were born already dead."

The grief of Agatha's countenance combined with Bess's own sense of horror over hearing of such an experience prompted her to once again embrace her mother-in-law, whispering as she did so, "I'm so very sorry you had to go through that. I can't even imagine!"

Agatha eased back and offered Bess a sincere smile. "But I'm certain that everything will be just fine with this baby. We are not going to even think of any other possibility. It's a miracle that Hugh will live on through this child, and I know we both believe in miracles."

"Indeed we do," Bess said, grateful for Agatha's optimism, and for her trust in confiding such a difficult part of her past. She'd wondered why Hugh had been an only child, and now she knew. She hoped and prayed that this baby *would* be healthy and strong, for her own sake as well as Agatha's. Perhaps this grandchild might help compensate for the lack of children in Agatha's life.

* * * * *

Many weeks passed while Bess continued to feel as though she were barely functioning—but at least she *was* functioning. Each day she gave herself credit for simply having the strength and will to get out of bed, make herself presentable, and to interact with the people with whom she now shared her life. Every person who lived and worked at Astoria Abbey was kind to her, and she relished her interaction with them and the way many of them helped contribute to her feeling safe and cared for. But there were only three people at the Abbey with whom she felt comfortable enough to truly be herself. She made a point each day of sharing conversation with each of these people, certain that being able to talk freely about the grief of losing Hugh was often the only thing that kept her from losing her mind, surrounded continually as she was by the emptiness created by his absence.

Each morning Bess shared breakfast with Daphne in the sitting room and they often talked long after they finished eating. Soon afterward, Bess would go to Agatha's rooms, where Eve, her devoted maid, had become accustomed to the daily visits and always helped Bess feel comfortable before she left them to share private conversation until lunch was brought from the kitchen for the two women to share. Sometimes Agatha was up and dressed and lounging in her sitting room. At other times the Lady of Astoria Abbey was curled up in bed, lost in consuming grief. Wherever Bess found her mother-in-law, or whatever state she might be in, Bess just remained close by, sometimes in silence, sometimes in the same old routine of needing to share the same feelings over and over, perhaps until those feelings could find a peaceful place to settle within each of their hearts.

After lunch with Agatha, Bess had made a habit of returning to her own room to lie down and try to take a nap. Pregnancy had made her perpetually tired, and even if she couldn't fall asleep, she'd found it necessary to at least try and rest, so she could get through the evening.

Bess generally shared tea with Clive at the usual time when the entire household seemed to pause to enjoy the late-afternoon respite of hot tea, accompanied by tasty sandwiches and biscuits and pleasant conversation. Clive's kindness and support became invaluable to Bess, and she often told him—as she did Daphne and Agatha—that she didn't know how she would ever get through this adjustment in her life without him.

Everyone who knew and worked with Lewis was surprised when he made the announcement that he was leaving Astoria Abbey. He now revealed that he had known for quite some time through letters from his distant home that his mother had been developing health challenges as she was aging, and now that Hugh was gone, and he no longer felt the personal obligation of being there for him, he felt drawn to returning to his mother's home to help care for her. Bess felt some sadness to see him go; he was one of her strong connections to Hugh and her memories of him. But she'd never felt close to him the way she had with Clive, and truthfully once he'd left the Abbey she hardly noticed his absence; he'd rarely shown his face since Hugh's death anyway. In her heart she wished him well and hoped that his life from this point forward would bring good things to him.

Bess continued to share supper in the kitchen with the members of the staff who ate at the same time, and she always went to bed early, grateful for the almost unnatural exhaustion of pregnancy combined with grief that usually lulled her to sleep quickly. She hated being alone in the bed and far preferred the oblivion of sleep when she didn't have to think about Hugh's absence, almost against her own will.

Occasionally Bess felt compelled to go into Hugh's room, the room she had shared with him following their marriage and up to the day of his death. But she never stayed there for long. It was as if she simply needed reassurance that what they'd shared had been real, but more than a few minutes there was too much to bear.

Following Hugh's death, the vicar naturally stopped coming to the Abbey to perform a separate church service. The first time Bess went into town for church surrounded by the people she'd come to think of as her new family, she felt decidedly nervous about the possibility of seeing her father. But she caught only a brief sight of him out of the corner of her eye for a moment; it seemed he was even more intent on avoiding her than she was on avoiding him. Bess enjoyed seeing her old friends there, and it quickly became evident that the entire village was aware of her marriage to Hugh and that she was now officially a part of Lady Buxton's family. People almost seemed in awe of such a change in her life, as if she'd somehow become royalty. Bess only felt grateful to be able to share her life with people who genuinely loved her and made her feel safe and cared for.

Following Bess's initial conversation with Agatha about her pregnancy, the local midwife they'd talked about had been easily found and brought to the Abbey to assess Bess's health. Bess liked the midwife and felt comfortable with her, and she was deeply grateful for the option of having someone besides her father oversee her health throughout this pregnancy, and to help bring this baby into the world. The midwife came once a week, even though Bess felt certain that such frequent visits were not necessary. But Agatha insisted that Bess's medical care was of the utmost importance, and even though nothing was stated about the matter, Bess believed the midwife very much needed the extra income that Agatha was providing for her. Bess barely had to hint to Agatha that she didn't want to be any kind of financial burden, and her mother-in-law repeated almost word-for-word the kind lecture she'd given the last time they'd talked about money; she insisted that it was a privilege to care for Bess, and that she personally had enough money to care for all their needs for the remainder of their lives and more. Bess couldn't comprehend such wealth, but she didn't think about it beyond being grateful to not have to work to provide for herself, pregnant as she was and feeling poorly more often than not.

The day when Bess felt the baby moving inside her, she felt startled at how many months had passed since Hugh's death. Bess could no longer hide her pregnancy beneath the gathered skirts of dresses that had fit her previously. A day came when a new wardrobe became necessary, and it seemed that as soon as Bess began wearing dresses that were made to accommodate pregnancy, the baby had a sudden spurt of growth and Bess marveled at the growing child within her. She developed a habit of gently rubbing her rounded belly, and often singing quietly to the baby—usually when she was alone, but sometimes when she was with Agatha, who declared that Bess's gentle lullabies had a soothing effect.

When Bess's pregnancy reached a point where its strain began to make it difficult to go about her normal daily routine, Bess was surprised to realize that she'd come to feel more at peace over Hugh's death. She still missed him immensely, but perhaps she'd gotten used to his absence, and she certainly couldn't deny that she had much to be grateful for. Conversations with Agatha and Clive let her know they were both feeling the same, and Bess noticed that Agatha was doing much better overall, and she was even beginning to show a vibrancy Bess had never seen before. Given the fact that Bess had gotten to know Agatha when she had been drained and exhausted from years of caring for her terminally ill son, it made sense that Agatha would gradually be able to find herself again, and subsequently find more peace over Hugh's passing.

When Bess had to accept that she was far too pregnant to get up and down the stairs without assistance, she resigned herself to remaining in her rooms, and Agatha came there to share lunch. Bess hated not being able to attend church, but Agatha and Daphne always returned to sit with her and share their thoughts and impressions of the vicar's sermon. And Bess was pleased when the vicar came to visit her, to let her know that he was praying for her and the baby, as he knew that many in the congregation were also doing. After the vicar left, Bess thought about her father for the first time in many weeks. She wondered after the vicar's mention of people praying for her and the baby, whether her father ever thought of her with any kind wishes or prayers on her behalf; she wondered if he wanted her to be happy, or if he still felt upset with her for abandoning him—as he would have seen it—and if that meant he would never let go of his anger toward her. In her brief communication with the people who worked for him, they'd said that he never mentioned her at all. Perhaps Jonas White was more comfortable behaving as if Bess were as dead to him as his wife. And it was something Bess simply had to accept. Given the facts, she was glad to note that she had made more peace over accepting the loss of her father in her life, just as she was finding peace over losing Hugh—the difference was that Hugh had not chosen to leave her, and for that she only loved and respected him more. In fact, she had come to realize that even though she was learning to miss him less, she only grew to love him more—and she knew she would always love him. But as he'd pointed out to her many times, life was going on without him, and she had to try and keep up or she had no hope of ever finding any real happiness without her beloved deceased husband.

The evidence of life going on without Hugh hit Bess like the winds of a brutal storm when labor began, and she was hurled into an experience more frightening and painful than she'd ever imagined possible. Despite feeling confident in the care of a midwife who was as kind as she was competent, Bess still couldn't fathom how she would ever get through this ordeal. She hadn't missed Hugh this much since those first few weeks following his death, but she was endlessly grateful to have Agatha at her side throughout the seemingly endless hours of grueling labor. Daphne was also nearby, assisting the midwife in any way that was needed. Bess was glad to be surrounded by these women, grateful for their continual encouragement; but as the labor only worsened, she felt as if her body might split in half and she would surely die. There were many moments when she secretly wished that she *would* die, and then she would be freed from this unfathomable misery, as well as every other hardship of this world. And most especially, she would be with Hugh. As the pain worsened, her desire to leave this world became stronger, until an unexplainable warmth enveloped her, and even though she knew it was impossible, for a moment she almost believed that she could hear Hugh telling her that everything would be all right. Bess could have never described why or how she suddenly felt more at peace, and more confident in her ability to see this experience through to the end, but she did. If there was ever a time she needed Hugh, it would be during the birth of their child, and she chose to believe that he *was* there with her.

Following a moment when Bess believed the pain couldn't possibly get any worse, the ordeal was suddenly over. She heard the midwife chuckle softly, while at the same time she was keenly aware of Agatha holding her breath just as tightly as she was holding Bess's hand. Then a baby's cry filled the room with a sound that seemed to light every dark corner and eradicate every shadow.

"You have a beautiful baby girl," the midwife said, chuckling again, "and she appears to be perfectly healthy!"

"Oh!" Agatha muttered on the wake of a joyful sob. Bess considered all the babies Agatha had lost, and the hope she'd placed in this child being able to carry on a part of her son, and she could well imagine what this meant to Agatha. But she wondered if anyone else could ever fully comprehend what it meant to *her;* she had loved Hugh with all her heart and soul, and now they had a daughter, a child who would always be a part of her life. Hugh would live on through this tiny girl, and Bess's gratitude overflowed into uncontrollable tears as the baby was wrapped tightly in a little blanket and laid in Bess's arms. Even though the baby had not yet been bathed, it was obvious that her hair was a dark, golden color, and it was definitely curly.

"Like her father," Agatha said, setting a hand gently on the baby's head, voicing Bess's thought exactly.

"She looks like him," Bess managed to say through her tears. Fully taking in this opportunity to finally meet her child face-to-face, Bess recalled how many times she'd heard women declare that all the pain and horror of childbirth was more than worth it once the baby arrived. She'd helped women through childbirth herself and had personally wondered how they could feel that way, despite witnessing the joyful moments of mothers and babies greeting one another. But now Bess understood completely. Even though she was still throbbing with intense pain, she knew she would do it all again—and worse—just to have this beautiful, precious child in her life.

"What will you call her?" the midwife asked while she was obviously still busy overseeing the remainder of the necessary process of birth.

"Yes, what *will* you call her?" Agatha repeated. "With all our happy anticipation of this moment, we've never talked about possible names."

Keeping her focus completely on the baby, as if she feared her daughter's existence was too good to be true and she didn't want to look away, Bess spoke with the tenderness she recalled feeling when she and Hugh had discussed the topic of naming a baby. "We talked about it," Bess said. "We didn't know whether or not it would happen; some people try for many months or even years to have a baby. But Hugh insisted that on the chance it *did* happen, he wanted some say in choosing a name. And so we did. And now that I've met her, I do believe the name fits her perfectly."

"What?" Agatha pressed insistently.

"Well," Bess said, finally turning to look at the grandmother of her child, "it was Hugh's idea . . . a name he not only liked very much, but he considered it to be somewhat of a combination of my name and yours, of Agatha and Bess." Turning back to look at the baby, Bess declared lovingly, "Agnes. Her name is Agnes."

"Oh, it's perfect!" Daphne declared, and Bess could hear Agatha sniffling softly.

Bess just gazed at her new little daughter, feeling closer to heaven somehow by doing so. She whispered too softly for anyone else to hear, "Thank you, Hugh . . . for loving me . . . for giving me this beautiful child. Thank you."

\* \* \* \* \*

Bess recovered from childbirth, surrounded by a generous outpouring of added care and assistance from many of the servants as well as Agatha's willingness to do almost any little thing that might help Bess or the baby. Bess enjoyed observing Agatha's adoration for little Agnes; it practically glowed in her countenance whenever she'd hold the baby or talk to her in a gentle, lilting voice. Agatha looked happier than Bess had ever seen her; the gift of this daughter that Hugh had left behind was doing much to heal his mother's broken heart. And Bess couldn't deny that Agnes's presence was helping to heal her own broken heart. The infant was not only beautiful—with a strong resemblance to her father—she was also a calm and undemanding baby, as if she were there at the center of life at the Abbey only to spread joy and love. Many of the maids in the household, and even the cook and the housekeeper, took advantage of Bess's invitation to come and see the baby whenever they could as long as it didn't interfere with Bess's need to rest, and Daphne did well at making certain that Bess remained undisturbed during such times. But it seemed every woman in the house had immediately grown to love Agnes and wanted to just look at her for a few minutes every day, or perhaps hold her if they could. Bess and Agatha simply agreed that observing the joy Agnes generated was heartwarming, and they enjoyed observing how this tiny little girl was strengthening the bonds among many who lived and worked here at the Abbey. It was also heartwarming to see how many of the women in the household had made gifts for the baby, most of them things they had been sewing by hand for many weeks in anticipation of the birth. There were beautiful little quilts and blankets, and lovely gowns and bonnets for Agnes to wear.

Bess was pleased to receive visits from Mrs. Hubbard, as well as some other ladies she knew from church who wanted to meet the baby and offer their well wishes. They were thrilled for Bess, and all declared Agnes to be one of the most beautiful babies they'd ever seen. And they too came bearing gifts that were handmade and filled with countless hours of love that had gone into their humble creation.

Bess quickly regained her strength under the guidance of the midwife who continued visiting regularly for the first few weeks. She helped Bess get out of bed and move around enough to not let her body grow weak from spending too much time being inactive. This wise woman had a special instinct about the proper balance between rest and activity, so that Bess could heal well and quickly. Bess trusted her completely, and the results were positive as Bess felt a little stronger every day, and more and more able to care for Agnes on her own. Agatha suggested that they hire a nanny, but Bess didn't feel it was at all necessary. Since she had no official occupation within the house, she believed she could certainly take care of her own baby. And Daphne—who was very good with caring for Agnes—eagerly volunteered to be on hand to watch over the baby whenever Bess needed or wanted to be elsewhere. Agatha finally relented to *not* hire a nanny, and a routine was quickly established regarding the care of little Agnes. Agatha was understandably drawn to her granddaughter and wanted to spend time with her every day, but she was sensitive about not interfering, and she had a definite respect toward allowing Bess plenty of time alone with her daughter.

The only man who showed an interest in Agnes was Clive, but Bess found it endearing if not downright adorable how he had a distinct fascination with the baby. Even though he rarely held Agnes, as if he were afraid he might break her, he loved talking to her in funny voices, and he often spoke to her as if she were an adult, telling her about her father.

Hugh's cousin Graham came to visit when Agnes was a few weeks old, and he too showed a strange fascination with the baby. It was as if her very existence was a miracle to those who had known Hugh well. They often commented on the baby's resemblance to her father, as if the physical evidence might be the only thing that helped make it possible to comprehend that Hugh had indeed left behind this remarkable gift. For some reason, Graham commented on the resemblance more frequently and with more awe than anyone else. Bess felt a strange kind of fascination herself as she observed his interaction with the baby. She didn't at all mind allowing Hugh's cousin time with Agnes; the baby seemed to him—as she did to others—a tangible comfort that eased the grief of having lost Hugh. And unlike Clive, Graham wasn't at all afraid of holding the baby. He asked for guidance the first couple of times he picked her up, and then he became very comfortable holding her in the crook of his arm while he just sat on the sofa of Bess's sitting room, gazing at Agnes's little face as if he could have done so forever. Bess secretly appreciated the opportunity to gaze at Graham while he remained oblivious, due to his attention to the baby. She was still adjusting to his striking resemblance to Hugh, and sometimes she had to sternly remind herself that this was *not* Hugh. She'd grown less uncomfortable with Graham, although he said very little, which denied her the opportunity to get to know him better. But he was always gracious about her allowing him time with the baby, and he always inquired politely about her well-being as he came and went.

Graham stayed for about a week and then was off again to one of his homes; Bess couldn't keep track. But she couldn't deny feeling indescribably lonely when she knew he was no longer at the Abbey. The very notion seemed ridiculous. It wasn't as if he spent large amounts of time with her and the baby, and he'd hardly said a word to her when he did, so it certainly wasn't his company or companionship she missed. She didn't wish to analyze her strange feelings with Agatha or Daphne, simply because she didn't want anyone to know that she even gave Graham a second thought. Bess felt certain it was nothing more than Graham's strong physical resemblance to Hugh that made her miss him. She couldn't comprehend any other possible reason.

Agnes grew and changed every day, and before long she was smiling and cooing at anyone who took the time to talk to her. Weeks slipped into months, and life for Bess began to feel as if it had always been this way, as if Agnes had always been at the center of everything at the Abbey. And the memory of caring for Hugh and then being married to him began to feel more and more like a dream. She could feel her grief easing more into a peacefulness that surrounded her tender memories of their time together. She was able to talk with Clive and Agatha about her memories without any of them experiencing the immense sorrow they'd felt in the past; instead it became easier to talk about the good times and the profound influence Hugh had left on all their lives.

Clive continued to spend time with Bess and Agnes every day, and their comfortable friendship deepened—even though Bess suspected that Clive might have stronger feelings for her, which he was trying very hard to keep concealed, likely out of respect for Hugh, allowing her all the time she needed to get beyond Hugh's death. But Bess hoped she was wrong, mostly because she knew in her heart she did not—and could never—feel anything for Clive beyond what she already felt. She cared very much for him as a friend, but any romantic notion simply did not exist, and she couldn't force herself to feel something that was completely absent. Therefore, she hoped that Clive would never bring up the matter of his feelings for her; she felt certain that once he did and she had no choice but to tell him the truth regarding her own feelings, nothing would ever be the same between them.

Agnes learned to laugh and did so a great deal, which made everyone else laugh—as if the baby created a kind of ripple effect with her innocent laughter, filling the house with an unexplainable joy. When the baby learned to roll over, all the maids were talking about it as if it were the greatest event in history. And when Agnes began to move herself across the carpet like a chubby little worm, wiggling and using her elbows to ease forward, the

Abbey was filled with delight. Agnes quickly graduated to crawling on her hands and knees, a skill that offered the baby an ability to move with remarkable speed—and to get into many things not intended for babies. Bess's bedroom and sitting room were efficiently modified so that nothing within Agnes's reach could do her harm or make a mess, and the nursery, which hadn't been used since Hugh's childhood, was thoroughly cleaned and made completely suitable for a crawling baby. Some of Hugh's old toys that were still in good condition had been cleaned, and Agatha loved to see her granddaughter play with them. They all now spent most of their daytime hours in the nursery, except when Agnes was napping. There were comfortable sofas where the adults could sit and visit, and there was also a table and chairs that were perfect for having tea or even a meal so that Bess could be with her baby in an environment that was safe and comfortable.

It was Agatha's idea to turn Hugh's old bedroom into a room for Agnes, since she would soon need her own room instead of sleeping in the crib that had been added to Bess's room. Agatha felt like it would be a proper tribute to Hugh, and it would be a good way to change the decor so as not to allow the room to become some kind of shrine. Bess liked Agatha's idea and they both agreed that Hugh would be pleased to see his room become the space where his daughter would grow from a baby to a child to a woman.

Bess and Agatha both shed some tears while observing the changes taking place as old furnishings were moved out, wallpaper and drapes were changed, and new furnishings were moved in. There was sadness combined with joy in seeing the alteration of the room taking place, which seemed somehow representative of the need to move beyond Hugh's death. He'd been gone more than a year, and they had adjusted as well as anyone could who had lost someone so close and dear, but Bess noted that—given how briefly Hugh had been a part of her life—the time they'd spent together was feeling more and more like a dream.

Bess was surprised to note that Graham's visits were increasing, and he was staying longer. Agatha didn't seem surprised, but she was certainly pleased. It was evident they'd always been close, and Agatha clearly found joy in having her nephew around—perhaps especially given the absence of her son. Bess noted that when Agatha was around, Graham spoke more than a few necessary words. Bess rarely participated in their conversations; she just sat and observed while the two of them talked of times gone by and of their mutual adoration for little Agnes. Through listening to them converse, Bess learned that Graham's father was a brother to Agatha—although she believed she might have learned that when she first met him, but she'd for-gotten. Graham and Hugh had always shared a certain closeness as cousins, even though they'd not seen each other as much as they'd liked. But apparently once Graham had completed his schooling somewhere abroad, he had lived in the same home in London with Hugh and Agatha, and he'd been as involved in Hugh's care as Clive and Lewis had been. Bess was glad that Agatha had Graham in her life, and for the way her nephew brightened her countenance. For each other, they were the last remaining relatives, a point they deeply appreciated and never took for granted.

With Graham spending more and more time at the Abbey, Bess found herself growing more comfortable in his presence, although he still said practically nothing to her directly. But that didn't keep him from wanting to spend time with Agnes—always with Bess's permission and with overt respect for her place as the child's mother. Bess was glad to know that Agnes would grow up with Graham in her life; every child needed a positive male influence. And Bess told Graham so. He seemed pleased but didn't comment, which was typical of him. Occasionally Bess recalled the way Graham had interacted with Hugh during the very brief time she had observed them together when Hugh was on the brink of death. But she'd observed enough to know there was far more to Graham than he was allowing her to see, and she wondered why he might be so reserved in her presence. She also wondered why the time he was not staying at the Abbey began to feel more and more wrong. But since her curiosity and associated emotions didn't make sense, she mostly just tried to push any analytical thoughts regarding Graham out of her mind.

A day never passed in which Bess didn't thank God for how very blessed she was. Despite losing Hugh, she'd been given a good life with a beautiful daughter, surrounded by people who loved and cared for them both. All things considered, she felt content and at ease, and looked forward to her future, raising Agnes in her father's home where the child had brought a great deal of joy to people who had experienced so much sorrow through being a part of Hugh's life of poor health and the continual anticipation of his death. Agnes's very existence and the daily evidence of her perfect health were never taken for granted—neither by Bess nor by anyone else who had grown to love her—family and servants alike. There was every reason for Bess to believe that her future was neatly in place, and she relished the peace and joy she had come to feel with that knowledge.

# CHAPTER TWELVE

## THE UNWANTED SUITORS

THE DAY WHEN AGNES TOOK her first steps was like a national holiday at the Abbey. Bess told Agatha she wouldn't be surprised to find that the stable hands had secretly arranged for a display of fireworks to fill the sky after the sun went down.

On Agnes's first birthday, there *was* a display of fireworks—which Bess had not known would happen. It turned out that Agatha had acted upon Bess's previous comment and had asked the stable hands to arrange it, mostly as somewhat of a joke regarding how much the entire household had come to somehow mark time according to Agnes's milestones. During the party that had preceded the fireworks, Bess had mostly sat and observed the way Agnes was passed around among the people who loved her, and how everything she did was met with great praise and excitement: her unsteady walking, her interest in the new toys that had been given to her as birthday gifts, and her preference for playing with the paper and boxes in which the gifts had been given. Agatha sat close to Bess so that they could both enjoy observing how Agnes was the center of attention, and how much joy she brought to everyone present.

"She'll be spoiled terribly," Bess said to Agatha.

"Yes, isn't it wonderful!" Agatha replied with a little laugh. She added more seriously, "But remember, darling, surrounding a child with love and even providing them with luxuries does not a spoiled child make."

"I don't understand."

"No matter how rich or poor a child may be; no matter how few or many people they have in their lives who love and care for them—it is the love and discipline with which they are guided that makes their character. In my view, being spoiled means being raised with an attitude of arrogance or entitlement, as opposed to understanding humility and equality and knowing that they need to have respect for all people and gratitude for all things. Agnes may never be *spoiled* unless she is raised to be so. And I know that her mother would never allow that."

"You're right," Bess said. "I wouldn't. But I greatly appreciate the insight. I shall need the experience and wisdom of Agnes's grandmother to help guide me in such things."

Agatha squeezed Bess's hand and smiled at her, and Bess felt increasingly grateful to have been able to be a part of bringing a grandchild into Agatha's life. In that moment she felt entirely content.

They were distracted by a sudden giggling from Agnes that was especially loud. They turned to see that Graham—who had come home specifically to be there for the baby's birthday—was down on the floor, pretending to be a bear or a tiger; it was difficult to tell which exactly. Each time he teasingly growled at Agnes she laughed so hard that everyone in the room couldn't help laughing in response. Bess allowed the laughter to fill her spirit, not only her own laughter, but that of those around her. Mrs. Hubbard and Archie Wilson had come to the party, as well as a few other people Bess knew from church and in the village. And every person who worked here at the Abbey was gathered in the enormous parlor. And they all loved Agnes, and by doing so implied a love and respect for her deceased father. Bess concluded that it was a lovely way for her daughter to grow up. She allowed herself only a fleeting, momentary thought that her own father should have been there, that Agnes had a grandfather who had never bothered to come and meet her—or even to greet Bess at church and have a look at the baby Bess always had with her when she attended. But Bess quickly dismissed the thought, knowing in her heart there was nothing she could do to change this. If she believed that reaching out to him might be accepted with anything besides disdain and anger, she would have done so a long time ago. She needed to let go of the hope that he would ever be a part of their lives, and to accept that the situation was *his* choice, not hers—even if he would never see it that way.

That night after she had put Agnes to bed, Bess lay in her own bed in the darkness, knowing that with the doors to both rooms left open she could easily hear the baby if and when she awoke. It felt strange to recall how she'd once done the same for Hugh's sake, sleeping with the knowledge that she could easily hear any evidence of being needed in the night.

Bess silently counted the months between Hugh's death and Agnes's birth, and now a year had passed since the birth. She felt content and at peace. But she also felt lonely. She missed Hugh, and she had also completely come to terms with the fact that he was never coming back, and that he'd made it clear he wanted her to be happy—and he didn't want her to be alone. At the time she hadn't been able to comprehend ever wanting to seek out any kind of romantic relationship with *anyone* but Hugh. But she was beginning to grasp the wisdom of what he'd been saying, that she was still so young, that she had a whole lifetime ahead of her, and that she shouldn't be alone.

Practically speaking, if she began attending socials with the possibility of meeting and being courted by some man who yet remained without face or name, she couldn't comprehend the likely outcome of marrying a man who would take her and Agnes away from Astoria Abbey. How could she take Agnes away from Agatha and everyone else who loved her? How could she ever leave this beautiful home she'd come to love so dearly? And how could she ever feel as comfortable with any man as she'd felt with Hugh? It all felt impossible! Perhaps this loneliness was something she needed to come to terms with. Agatha had come to terms with the absence of her husband and son; surely Bess could find strength in her mother-in-law's example. And what made Bess think that *any* man would want to take on the raising of another man's child? She could never commit herself to a man who didn't love Agnes as much as he loved her.

Bess distracted herself with another avenue of thought as she fondly recalled the delightful birthday celebration she'd enjoyed earlier. She recounted the hearty amount of laughter and joy that had filled the space around her—or rather around Agnes, who was already proving to be highly sociable, thriving on the company of anyone who offered her smiles and attention. Bess recalled Graham on his hands and knees on the carpet playing with Agnes, making an utter fool of himself, and something in her stomach quivered. She immediately put a hand there as if she could make the sensation go away—or at least make sense of it. Bess had become accustomed to Graham coming and going, and she had never paid any mind to how long he stayed or how long he was absent between his visits—except for an awareness of him seeming to enjoy Agnes's company so much that he was spending much more time here than he had in the past. She'd become accustomed to his company, and she'd even gotten used to how much he looked like Hugh—although the resemblance had ceased to remind her of Hugh; she'd come to see Graham as simply being Graham, with his own appearance and personality and character traits. She'd even gotten over her initial negative impressions of him and had come to realize that he was a fine man—Agatha's adoration for him stood as a second witness on that count; she was far too sharp and discerning to sing such praises for a man if she had any notion that he was not a person of integrity and good character.

Still, despite all that, Bess didn't necessarily feel like she knew Graham very well. He spent a fair amount of time wanting to play with Agnes in the nursery, and his countenance always lit up when he saw the baby. The baby had quickly come to do the same whenever Graham came into the room, knowing that this man represented great fun with the way he would get down on the floor with Agnes and play as if he too were a child. Bess had certainly grown to appreciate and enjoy his obvious love for Agnes, but that didn't explain the sudden quivering in her stomach as she thought of him, nor the way that sensation spread throughout the whole of her limbs, all the way to her fingers and toes, as if electricity had radiated through her entire being. They barely shared any conversation that didn't directly relate to Agnes. Beyond her observations of his character over the course of their interaction since Hugh's death, she hardly knew him at all—although everything she had observed had certainly left a positive impression.

Disarmed and uncomfortable over such an experience now in the middle of the night, Bess fluffed her pillows and rolled over, pushing thoughts of Graham out of her head, along with anything else that might keep her from relaxing. She needed her sleep and was glad to awaken to sunlight filling the room and the realization that she'd slept long and deep. The activities of the previous day had been exhausting. Hearing the happy noises her daughter made, Bess hurried to freshen up and put on a dressing gown before she entered the sitting room to find Daphne playing with Agnes.

"Good morning," Daphne said with a quick smile toward Bess. "She's only been awake a few minutes. I was already awake, so I got her up and changed her nappy, so you could rest."

"Thank you," Bess said and sat on the floor with Agnes, taking hold of her to enjoy what little of a hug the wiggly child would endure before she squirmed away to play with her new toys, some of which were spread out upon the carpet.

The day proceeded as normal, except that every time Bess thought of Graham, she was assaulted—quite against her will—by a repetition of the tingling she'd experienced the previous night. She wondered why she was thinking of him at all, and almost felt angry with herself for doing so.

Bess was glad to be given a pleasant distraction from the turmoil over her strange inability to avoid thinking of Graham. Clive approached her just as she was leaving the nursery to put Agnes down for her afternoon nap. Even though Daphne was standing nearby, Clive didn't seem at all uncomfortable saying, "I wonder if we could talk, Bess . . . alone." Having been friends for so long, Bess could have logically assumed that his purpose for wanting to share a serious conversation had nothing to do with the deeper feelings she suspected he'd been harboring for a very long time. But his countenance betrayed it was precisely those feelings that he wanted to discuss, and Bess felt decidedly nervous. Her gratitude for being given a distraction immediately fled. A part of her had feared the coming of this day, but perhaps it would be best to get it over with, and she could only hope that once Clive knew where she stood, he would let go of any fanciful ideas regarding the two of them.

While Bess was trying to find an excuse to get out of this—or at least postpone it—Daphne volunteered cheerfully, "Oh, I'll put the little miss down for her nap and listen for her. Take as long as you need."

"Thank you," Bess said to Daphne, certain her mild sarcasm was missed by both Daphne and Clive.

"Shall we, then?" Clive asked, offering his arm.

Bess looked at it and knew she needed at least a little time to prepare herself. "I need to freshen up and just take care of something quickly. I'll meet you in the library in . . . shall we say twenty minutes?"

"I'll be there," Clive said, smiling with a sparkle of hope that she dreaded eliminating. But she was not the kind of woman who would ever pretend to feel something she didn't, simply to avoid hurting someone else's feelings. Doing such a thing would be completely disrespectful to herself and the other person—in this case, Clive—and she cared about him too much to ever allow such a thing to happen between them.

Bess took advantage of her few minutes alone to prepare herself in body and spirit to face a conversation that would inevitably be difficult. She left her room only after a silent prayer and taking in a deep breath of courage, which she slowly let out as she began her trek to the library. Before going in, she paused to take in another of those deep breaths, then entered to find Clive sitting comfortably in one of the two overstuffed chairs facing the fireplace. He stood when he saw her and smiled in lieu of any verbal greeting. Once she was seated, he sat back down and Bess noted that thus far nothing seemed out of the ordinary according to their habit of countless friendly conversations in the past—except that she just *knew* what he was thinking and feeling, and as much as she had dreaded having to discuss it at all, now that she was here, she wanted to have it over with and let the consequences be what they may. She didn't want this tension between them any longer, and if he was so immature as to allow her rejection to mar their friendship, then that would have to be his choice. She utterly hated the possibility of losing him as a friend, but she would not be engaged in any friendship that carried with it tension or unrealistic expectations.

When Clive didn't speak, Bess realized her mind was swirling with conclusions based only on her assumptions, and they needed to talk to know where they stood. Signs of his nervousness—however subtle—increased the evidence that he intended to have a conversation unlike anything they'd ever shared before. Hoping to hurry the matter along, Bess finally said, "You clearly have something on your mind, Clive, and you're the one who asked to speak to me."

"Forgive me," he said and chuckled tensely. "I confess there is something I must say that is difficult, and I ask for your patience."

"Of course," Bess said, even though she didn't feel patient at all.

More than a minute of silence passed while the ticking of the clock sounded deafening to Bess, but she focused on her breathing and prayed for the right words to come to her mind.

"We've been friends right from the start," Clive began, stating the obvious.

"Yes," Bess agreed.

"We shared the heartbreak of losing Hugh . . . of all that led up to that event, and everything that followed," Clive went on. "You must know how much I care for you, Bess." He blew out a loud, harsh breath that seemed to announce that something difficult was about to come out of his mouth, and she wasn't at all surprised to hear him say, "But you must know that my feelings for you are so much more than anything I've expressed in the friendship we share."

Bess stole a quick glance at Clive, if only to be assured of his sincerity, but she couldn't look at him long enough to be assured of anything except her own nervousness, so she looked down at her hands, clasped in her lap, brutally aware of how her palms were sweating and her heart was beating too fast. She waited for him to go on, knowing she couldn't even hope for the power of speech until she knew he'd said all he intended to say.

"I felt drawn to you from the very beginning, Bess," he said, "but it quickly became evident that you shared something very special with Hugh, and I never would have intruded upon that. I was sincerely happy for both of you, and—as you know—I was nothing but supportive in the two of you marrying and making the most of the time you had together. The fact that Agnes is now a part of our lives because of your marriage to Hugh is a miracle that blesses all of us."

"I cannot disagree with that," Bess said, if only to prove to herself that she could still speak, given how nervous she felt.

"I knew that it would be selfish and unfair of me to not allow you sufficient time to move beyond Hugh's death; therefore, I've kept my feelings to myself—out of respect for him *and* for you. However, he's been gone more than a year and a half, Bess, and . . . I can't remain silent any longer." He drew in a deep ragged breath and let it out, accompanied by the firm declaration, "I love you, Bess." This made her look up at him. Even though she'd expected him to voice his feelings for her, she was completely caught off guard to hear him put it so boldly. She'd expected perhaps some admission of affection or attraction. But love? Did he *really* love her? Or did he just think that he did? She certainly could not judge *his* feelings; she could only be firm in declaring her own. But having declarations of *love* mixed into this situation did not make it any easier.

"Bess." He spoke her name with quiet reverence as he leaned over the side of his chair so that he could reach her hand, which he took and held with a certain possessiveness that had never been present before in the friendly encounters they'd shared. This too made the situation even more difficult for Bess. "I know Hugh told you that you needed to find love again, that you needed to be happy. He didn't want you to pine your life away alone. I know because he told me. Now that he's been gone as long as he has, I'm asking you to consider allowing me to ease your loneliness, to share your life with *me*. We would never have to leave the Abbey; you could always be here where Agnes has her grandmother and we're surrounded by so many people who are like family to you and your daughter. In a word, Bess, will you—"

"Please stop," Bess said, realizing that to allow him to go on any further would only be unkind. What she had to say would hurt him, but she had to be honest. She had to! Better to hurt him once now and have it over with, instead of leaving any room for him to hope for something that could never be. She found the courage to lift her eyes and look directly at him, wanting him to see her convictions regarding what she was about to say. "I confess that I have wondered if you felt something deeper for me than the friendship you've displayed. And because I've wondered, I've given the matter a great deal of thought, and I've not taken the situation lightly. I care very much for you, Clive; you have been a dear friend in so many ways, and I never could have gotten through losing Hugh without you. However," she said and noticed the fear that came into his eyes, but she didn't let it deter her. "I must be completely honest with you, just as I've worked very hard to be completely honest with myself. Truthfully, Clive, I've *wanted* to feel the kind of affection and attraction for you that could help me move forward with my life . . . move beyond my life with Hugh. And I've tried. But that's just it; a person shouldn't have to *try* to feel such things. As much as I care for you, my dear friend, my affection is not—nor could it ever be—anything more than friendship alone." She let out a long, slow breath and willed her heart to slow down now that she'd gotten the worst of the truth out into the open. "I have dreaded this conversation, Clive, which I think has made me hope that whatever I might have sensed about your feelings may have simply been my imagination. But I will not show any disrespect toward you or myself by pretending to feel something I simply don't feel. Such love is not something that can happen simply because we might want it; such feelings are beyond our control. What we do with our feelings is a matter of taking charge of our own free will, and such choices determine our character; at least that's how I see it." She sighed and gave his hand a little squeeze. "Forgive me, Clive, but I just don't love you, and I cannot be anything less than honest with you."

Bess hated the silence that followed, while she couldn't make herself look away from his gaze. He seemed to be trying to silently convince her that she was wrong, while she did her best to convince *him* that she knew her own mind and her own heart and would not be swayed. She felt a deep compassion for him over the heartache he was surely contending with right now, and she had no doubt it would take time to come to terms with it; she only hoped that when all was said and done, their friendship would not suffer from this.

"Do you not think," he asked, tightening his hold on her hand as if that might aid his cause, "that you could grow to love me? Do you not think that despite any feelings—or lack of them—we could make a good marriage? That our friendship might compensate for anything else? I could make you happy, Bess; I know I could. I love you. I love Agnes. This is our home; I truly believe we belong here together."

Bess felt choked up by his plea, knowing it was coming from a place of deep heartbreak for him, and it took all her willpower to not give in to his reasoning for the sake of easing his discomfort in that moment. To give him hope when there was none would be nothing short of cruel. "Clive," she said, measuring her words carefully before she spoke them, "I do not doubt that you would do everything in your power to take care of me and Agnes, and to make us happy, but . . . what I shared with Hugh was . . . deep and remarkable. I don't think I could ever be happy in a marriage where I didn't feel the same, or at least something close to it. Maybe I won't ever find that kind of love again; maybe I will. Either way, I know I'll be all right. I'm truly sorry for any hurt this is causing for you, but I must honor my own heart, Clive. I must! You surely know me well enough to know this to be true about me."

Clive removed his hand from hers abruptly, a gesture that hinted at anger. Something sparked in his eyes that also implied anger, but Bess knew well enough that any human being feeling hurt and confused might be quickly prone to try and protect those feelings with anger. And if he chose to be angry with her, that was simply beyond her control.

While still gazing at her, Clive said earnestly, "I can't believe what I'm hearing, Bess. I know you care for me. I know you do!"

"Yes, I do!" Bess countered. "But not in the way you're implying. I believe I've always made it very clear how much I appreciate our friendship, but given the love I've felt for Hugh all along, I know that I have never done or said anything to allow you to believe I had any other such feelings for you. Whatever your assumptions regarding *my* feelings, you must hear me now when I tell you what I know to be true."

"So," Clive sounded mildly angry, but Bess ignored that, determined to remain completely calm herself, "you're saying that you won't marry me—not now, not ever."

Bess cleared her throat and swallowed hard, so she could speak with all the conviction she felt. "That's what I'm saying, yes."

"Well, I don't believe that," Clive said so firmly that Bess was taken aback. "I think with the passing of time you'll come to see what I see; that we *can* make each other happy, and that our being together is best for all of us. I think you're fooling yourself into believing you could ever love *any* man the way you loved Hugh. And I'm all right with that. I'm not trying to compete with him, Bess. I just want to take care of you and your daughter, and if you can't see and feel the sincere love in my intentions now, I believe that eventually you will."

Bess couldn't even respond to that. In her heart she just knew it wasn't true, but he obviously wasn't going to be convinced. Right now, she could only hope that with time he would come to accept the reality, perhaps when he could get past his own hurt feelings and look at the situation more real-istically. She was startled when he stood abruptly, but glad when he said, "I hope this doesn't change the friendship we've shared. I'd prefer to just pre-tend this conversation never occurred, so we can go on as we have before." As he said it, Bess knew he was hoping that as they spent more time together as friends she would eventually come to realize that she *should* marry him, and in her heart, she knew it would never be. But for now, what he was proposing suited her just fine.

"Of course," she said, and he hurried from the room, as if he couldn't get out of there fast enough. He left behind him a cloud of his roiling emotions: confusion, heartache, embarrassment, disappointment. She couldn't blame him for feeling all those things and likely much more that she couldn't begin to understand. But given her years of inadvertently taking the blame for her father's unhappiness and being made to believe that she was expected to somehow fix it, she refused to take responsibility for any of Clive's emotions. She felt compassion for him, she would pray for him, but beyond that, she needed to let it all go. When sitting there in the library did nothing to help her shake off that cloud he'd left behind, she went outside for a brisk walk, allowing the fresh air to cleanse away the discomfort of what had just taken place—even though the winter air was cold. She didn't doubt there would be some awkwardness with Clive when she saw him again, but she hoped it would fade quickly, and they could resume their friendship. Unable to endure the cold air for long, she went back inside and resumed her walk down the quiet, rarely used hallways of the Abbey.

As she walked, Bess became more preoccupied with memories of Hugh. Talking with Clive about her feelings for him in such a context had brought the love they'd shared closer to the surface than it had been in a long time. She found a comfortable chair where she sat and cried over Hugh's absence for the first time in many weeks. She suspected that moments of missing him would always be a part of her life, but contrary to what Clive had said, she believed it was possible to find such love again. Whether or not she did remained to be seen, but she knew for certain that she could never be content married to Clive, and Hugh would never want her to make such a decision only for the sake of someone else's happiness. The very idea was completely contradictory to all she had risen above when she'd left her father's home and the strength she'd gained since then in learning that it was not her responsi-bility to make other people happy at the expense of her own happiness and dignity; rather, it was up to her to strive to be a good person and therefore do good to others, to make others happy because *she* was happy. And she *was* happy. Lonely perhaps, but still happy.

Bess returned to the nursery in time to have tea with Daphne, where they watched Agnes playing contentedly, refreshed by a long afternoon nap. Bess wondered briefly if she should talk about what had happened between her and Clive earlier, and she conceded that she needed Daphne's clear thinking to help her make certain she was doing the right thing. Daphne wasn't surprised by Clive's declaration of love; apparently, she too had seen the signs for a long time. But she adamantly agreed with Bess regarding the fact that Bess should not settle for a lifetime of marriage simply for the sake of not being alone, and Clive would simply have to come to terms with that. Daphne felt confident that he would, even if it took him some time.

After they'd finished enjoying their tea, Clive appeared in the nursery, behaving as if nothing at all had changed as he mostly played with Agnes for a short while before leaving, explaining that he had work to do.

"Well, at least he's not pouting or behaving strangely," Bess said to Daphne once she was certain Clive had gone a safe distance from the nursery and she would not be overheard.

"Indeed," Daphne said, "and I hope it will be the same when I'm not around."

Bess didn't comment; she just hoped for the same.

The following morning Bess was pleased to note that—given a night to sleep on it—she felt at peace over her responses to Clive. She only hoped that with time he would come to feel the same, and she prayed he wouldn't hopelessly expect her feelings to somehow change. But she chose to put the matter completely out of her mind as she greeted Agnes at the first indication her daughter was awake. The baby was always extraordinarily happy first thing in the morning—especially after she'd had a bottle of milk—and her happiness rubbed off on Bess as she bathed the baby and dressed her for the day. Daphne brought breakfast to the nursery, where Agnes sat on her mother's lap, enjoying little bits and pieces of Bess's breakfast and the opportunity to explore new foods with different flavors and textures. Once Agnes was satisfied, she quickly toddled off to explore the toys in the room, always finding her favorites first, which were the dolls and a vast variety of plush animals she loved to carry around.

It wasn't a surprise when Graham showed up, wanting to play with Agnes. He exchanged the usual brief but polite greetings with the ladies before he made himself comfortable on the floor near where Agnes was lining up all the dolls and animals and babbling in a language that no one could understand, but which made everyone laugh. Bess enjoyed watching Graham's playful interaction with Agnes, wondering why that fluttering sensation had returned. Caught up in trying to analyze it, Bess was surprised—and perhaps a little nervous—when Daphne stood and announced that she had some personal matters to attend to, but she wouldn't be terribly long.

In Daphne's absence, Bess was startled by how the fluttering in her stomach increased, along with a sweatiness in her palms, which she attempted to wipe away by pressing her hands over her skirt. Her mind drifted far away from what was happening in the nursery, even though her thoughts were—quite against her will—focused on Graham. She was startled to hear him speak, then embarrassed when she realized that she'd not actually heard what he'd said.

"Forgive me," she had no choice but to admit, "I'm afraid my mind was wandering, and I wasn't listening."

Bess noted the casual way he was comfortably lying on his side, his elbow on the floor, which supported the way his head was leaning in his hand while Agnes crawled over him repeatedly, back and forth, quite enthralled with her discovery that she could do so. "I asked," Graham smirked at her slightly and said, "why it is that you seem somehow . . . nervous or . . . different . . . when you and I are alone. Have I done something to offend you? To make you uncomfortable?"

"No, of course not!" she insisted, perhaps a little too vehemently. "You've always been perfectly gracious."

"Then, what is it?" he asked. "And don't try to tell me it's my imagination; I'm no fool, Bess, and neither are you. Just be honest with me. I can take it."

"I really don't know what to say," she admitted honestly, although she found it impossible to look at him directly. She gasped when he sat down close beside her; she'd barely realized that he'd stood up and crossed the room.

"Look at me," he said, his voice barely above a whisper. "Look at me . . . talk to me." She found it increasingly difficult to speak, or even to breathe, given how close he was sitting; she had no doubt that he was keenly aware of the sound of her breathing, harsh and shallow as it was. "I have no idea what you're thinking, Bess," he said in a hushed voice so near her ear that it sent a delightful tremor down her back, "and I have no idea what you're going to say. I could be wrong, and . . . despite how infrequently you and I have shared any serious conversation, I know you well enough to know that you won't have any trouble putting me in my place if I *am* wrong, but . . . I'm guessing it might be difficult for you to figure out what you *should* say as opposed to what you want to say, how you really feel as opposed to how you *should* feel. I believe you've been trying to hide your true feelings from me every bit as much as I've been trying to hide mine from you."

The present clashed with a memory inside Bess's mind and she gasped—far too loudly to be ignored—as she turned to look at Graham, freshly startled by his resemblance to Hugh as much as by what he'd just said.

"What?" he asked, seeming as stunned as she felt.

"How is that possible?"

"How is *what* possible?" he asked, making no effort to put any distance between them, even though he was sitting closer to her than he ever had, and far too close to ever believe that his intention was anything but to share an intimate conversation.

"What you just said . . ." Bess murmured, "it's so much like what Hugh said to me—almost verbatim—when he . . ." She looked away, feeling herself blush, which resulted in embarrassment, which made her blush even more.

"Perhaps," Graham said, apparently unaffected by her response, or at least gentlemanly enough to not draw attention to it, "he's the angel sitting on my shoulder, prompting me on what to say because he's becoming frustrated by the way we continue to avoid talking about the obvious."

Bess looked at him again, freshly startled. "The obvious?" she echoed, both hoping and fearing he would admit to sharing the same kind of attraction toward her that she'd been feeling toward him—however much she'd been trying to deny and suppress it. This was not what she wanted! Was it?

"I can't pretend any longer, Bess," he said, his voice turning mildly husky while he took her hand into his. Bess looked at their joined hands, realizing he'd never once held her hand, and yet it felt so comfortable and familiar. She looked back to his unwavering gaze while a quiver erupted somewhere deep inside herself and reverberated outward to every finger and toe. "I know I could never replace Hugh in your life, or in your heart," he said and took a deep, ragged breath, which indicated this was taking a great amount of courage, "and I would never be foolish enough to believe that you could ever love me the way you loved him; he was surely a far better man than I could ever be, but . . . I know you feel something for me, Bess; I've sensed it for a long time, and . . . we need to talk about it. As I said, I can't pretend any longer; I can't be in the same room with you day after day and leave our feelings for each other unspoken." He took a deep breath as if to declare that he'd said what he felt the need to say. Bess could only stare at him, perhaps hoping to see evidence of his sincerity, or to find something inside herself that might convince her that admitting to her own feelings was the right course to take—or perhaps that it wasn't. When she said nothing at all, Graham chuckled uncomfortably and murmured, "Please say something, Bess. I've just spilled my heart to you, and I think you know I'm not the kind of man to do such a thing easily; in fact, I never have before in the whole of my life, and—"

"I . . . appreciate your candor, Graham. You're right. We need to talk about our feelings, but . . . I . . . need some time . . . to think . . . to take everything in." What Graham *didn't* know was that it had only been yesterday afternoon when Clive had declared *his* romantic feelings for her. And while what she felt for Graham was entirely different, she was suddenly overwhelmed with the weight of having to deal with and sort out the amorous confessions of *two* men in less than a day's time. Noting that he looked concerned, perhaps even afraid, she gently squeezed his hand and added, "May we talk later? This evening, perhaps? After Agnes has gone to bed? I simply need . . . some time."

"Of course," he said. "Will you meet me in the west parlor?" he asked.

"I'll be there," she said, adding fervidly, "I promise." He nodded as if her promise helped appease his obvious concerns. Bess impulsively stood up and eased her hand from his. "Would you . . . watch over Agnes until Daphne or Agatha arrive? One or the other of them should be here soon, I should think."

"Yes, of course," he said without hesitation, which she found admirable; most men would be put out by such a request—especially those of his social class.

"Thank you," she said and hurried from the room, almost fearing she would burst into tears, and she certainly didn't want to do so in front of Graham.

Bess hurried to her room where she locked both the doors before curling up on the bed, her arms wrapped tightly around a pillow. She felt like sobbing, but the tears that came were quieter, spilling endlessly from her eyes as her mind escorted her through a lengthy series of memories she'd shared with Hugh. Once she'd allowed herself to cry over her sorrow of losing him, of missing him, she was left with her most prominent thought:

his repeated admonition for her to find love again, to live a full life, to not be held back out of an unwarranted sense of duty or obligation to him. But she wondered if he'd had any idea that she and Graham might eventually be drawn together. A part of her felt certain that he couldn't possibly have known, but she had to admit that Hugh had been uncannily perceptive. If he hadn't considered the possibility then, perhaps he *was* aware of the situation now—from wherever he might be—and perhaps he *was* nudging Graham along. The very idea felt unfathomably strange, even somewhat crazy. But still she found some comfort in it, and she chose to take hold of that comfort and allow it to soothe her troubled emotions.

A part of Bess wanted to completely reject the appearance of two poten-tial suitors in her life. She was a widow who still loved her husband more than she could comprehend, and she knew a part of her always would. But she was also lonely, a fact she couldn't deny. If nothing else, Clive's declara-tions of love had made her realize what she did *not* want in her life, and what she could not accept. The contrast between what she *didn't* feel for Clive with what she *did* feel for Graham helped her come to a place of being able to finally admit to herself that Graham had been right when he'd said that he'd sensed she had feelings for him. She certainly did. And if she pushed away any thoughts of how she'd hurt Clive—and how his becoming aware of her caring for another man might impact him—she felt decidedly com-fortable with Graham's confession. Given how she'd been trying to ignore and push away her thoughts and feelings for Graham, being able to admit to them felt like breathing in fresh air after being confined to a hot and stuffy room. Once she'd finally taken her mind through all that had happened and all that she felt, she even felt at peace over Hugh's place in her life, and she knew as surely as she knew the sun would rise and set that Hugh would be pleased to have her at least consider her feelings for Graham and see if it might be possible for them to share a future together.

Bess fell asleep while memories of Hugh mingled with a distinct hope-fulness regarding Graham. She felt mildly nervous over the prospect of their appointment this evening when they would continue their conversa-tion, but much less nervous than she'd felt earlier. If sharing a future with him was meant to be, then surely their talking about what they both felt would make that readily evident.

Bess awakened at the sound of Agnes having done the same. She hurried to the baby's room and picked up her daughter just before Daphne entered the room through a different door and smiled to observe the tender moment. "I put her down after we shared lunch with her grandmother," Daphne reported.

"Thank you," Bess said and hurried to add some explanation of her disappearance. "I was terribly tired for some reason." Mention of lunch reminded her that she'd missed eating while she'd been crying and stewing over the present circumstances. Recalling that she would see Graham later—alone—with the sole purpose of talking through their feelings, that same fluttering erupted inside of her. But instead of causing her any distress, she felt rather delighted.

Daphne stated the obvious when Bess's stomach growled loudly enough for both of them to hear. "You missed lunch; you must be hungry."

"Tea will be served soon," Bess said as she changed Agnes's nappy. "I can wait that long."

The remainder of the day went far more quickly than Bess had expected. Caring for Agnes always kept Bess very busy, and before she knew it she was putting the baby down for the night. Once Agnes was settled, Bess asked Daphne to listen for her, explaining that she felt restless and needed to wander the house before she went to bed herself. It wasn't an uncommon request, and Daphne gave no sign of being suspicious, but Bess felt as if she were sneaking off to do something secretive and improper as she hurried away—even though she knew there was nothing improper about it. After freshening up and checking her appearance in the mirror with far more attentiveness than usual, Bess made her way to the west parlor, forcing herself to go slowly. She didn't want to arrive out of breath. Just the thought of being in the same room with Graham made her breathless as it was. She could only hope and pray that her instincts were leading her in the right direction, and that this was indeed the path that Hugh would have her follow.

# CHAPTER THIRTEEN

## THE INHERITANCE

BESS ARRIVED AT THE WEST parlor to find the door open and Graham leaning back on one of the sofas with his booted ankles stacked on the table in front of him. He came abruptly to his feet when he saw her, and she fought to quell the acute response of her every sense in response to just seeing him.

"I confess that I feared you might not come," he admitted, making no attempt to conceal a distinct vulnerability in his voice.

"I told you I would be here," she said, not feeling the need to add that she was a woman who kept her word. She hoped he knew that about her. Despite very little personal conversation between them, she felt sure he had been observing her behavior for many months, just as she'd been observing his. They'd shared countless meals, and countless hours playing with Agnes. They'd attended church together, and she'd observed more keenly than she wanted to admit how he interacted with the servants and the people in the village, as well as with Agatha and Bess's daughter. The first day she'd met him she'd been put off by his being abrupt and terse with her. But she'd seen no sign of such behavior since, and she knew now he'd been upset by how bad off Hugh had been; in fact, he'd died that very day. Graham was a good man, and she knew it. And she believed that he knew she was a woman who strived to live up to a high standard of integrity and kindness, or he wouldn't have even considered confiding in her as he'd done earlier. Now they were here alone; she'd asked for some time to think and he'd graciously honored her request. It was only right that she be forthright and honest with him, just as she hoped he would continue to be with her.

Bess turned to close the door, not wanting anyone to overhear anything they said. Graham motioned for her to be seated on the sofa next to him. She sat down, leaving a proper distance between them, which made it easier to turn toward him and see his face as they spoke. He sat back down but remained at the edge of his seat, as if he were nervous, even though his expression appeared calm.

Since Bess had been the one to end their conversation earlier, the ensuing silence made her realize it was up to her to speak first. She cleared her throat softly as if to somehow declare that she intended to speak. Wondering where to begin, she decided that just getting straight to the point would be best. "You were right," she said.

"About what?" he asked when she was slow to clarify what she meant exactly.

Bess took a deep breath. "I do have feelings for you, Graham; I've been trying to make sense of them for quite some time now, wondering if . . . what I feel is right . . . or real."

He let out a lengthy sigh that indicated deep relief at her admission. "And what conclusion have you come to?" he asked.

"That perhaps what you said earlier is true; perhaps Hugh *is* nudging us along. That sounds like him. I'd like to believe that such a thing is possible." She laughed softly and looked down for only a moment before meeting his gaze directly. She needed to see his eyes while they spoke of such tender and important matters. "In some ways I feel like I don't know you at all, and in others I feel as if I know you so well."

"And I could say the same."

"Therefore," she added, her tone more pragmatic, "I suggest that we . . . try to get to know each other better. It stands to reason that we should acknowledge the truth of our feelings, rather than trying to ignore them. We need . . . some time . . . to discern whether what we share has substance, to know if we are compatible enough to . . . consider sharing a future."

"That all sounds very practical and reasonable," he said, "and I can't dispute that you're right, but . . ."

"But?" she countered, and he took her hand.

"While we're taking some time to figure out all the practical reasons of whether our relationship is valid enough to withstand the test of time, I . . ."

"Yes?" she asked when he hesitated far too long.

"I think we should also consider . . . this," he said and leaned across the distance between them to kiss her before she'd even had the chance to anticipate such a moment. His kiss was brief, and meek, and gentle. But it awakened something inside her that she'd often believed had died along with Hugh. He looked into her eyes as if to gauge her response, and before she could give any indication of her desire for him to kiss her again, he did. She felt his hand at the back of her head, holding it gently in place as if he didn't want her to move away and bring this experience to a halt too soon. When he separated his lips from hers and again looked into her eyes, Bess felt almost as if she were in a sort of trance. She'd not felt anything like this since Hugh had died, and for all that she'd held a tiny portion of inner hope, she'd sincerely believed that she would never experience any such thing again. She could only gaze into Graham's eyes, searching for sincerity and feeling deeply relieved to find it.

"Bess," he said in a dreamy voice without moving away or relinquishing his hold on her, "may I ask you something . . . sensitive? I don't want to offend you, or . . . dampen the mood, but . . . I have to know."

"It's all right," she said despite feeling some nervousness over what kind of question might require such a preamble.

"Bess," he repeated, and she loved the way he said her name, "I know I bear a strong resemblance to Hugh; it's been that way since we were children. Everyone we encountered commented on it. But . . . what I need to know is . . . when you look at me, do you see *me,* or do you see my resemblance to *him?*"

Bess was determined to answer honestly but it took a long moment and more than one deep breath to be able to do so. "Both, perhaps. And truthfully . . . I admit that's been one of the biggest reasons I've questioned my feelings for you. How could I not wonder if my attraction was simply because you reminded me of him? But Graham . . . I've come beyond that. I don't see him in you, at least not anymore. I only see you; I hope you can believe me."

He smiled slightly, but it was a genuine smile of relief. "I do *now,"* he said. "Your sincerity is exquisitely evident; I don't think you could lie even if you wanted to." His smile broadened. "It's one of the things I love about you."

Bess shifted slightly at his mention of the word *love.* She tightened her gaze, wondering if it were possible for her to detect his honesty as easily as he'd just claimed he could detect hers. She was surprised to note that she could. "You really mean that," she said.

"Mean what?" he asked, sincerely baffled.

"You love me?"

"Oh, I do!" he murmured and kissed her again before he added, "I've spent years attending tedious socials and accepting countless dinner invitations where eligible young ladies would be there—always with the hope that some matchmaking might occur. And never once have I felt the tiniest inkling of what I've heard described by the people I know who have been happily married for many years; those are the opinions I've paid attention to. And then I met you, and little by little I've come to understand what such people were talking about. I've never felt anything like this before, Bess. You've changed me, and I doubt that I could ever find the words to explain my feelings."

While Bess allowed herself to take in all he was saying, she felt nothing but truth in his declarations, which prompted her to want to share candidly all *she* had been feeling, but she was suddenly so overcome that she erupted to her feet and crossed the room, where she stood facing a painting of a lovely landscape, even though she barely glanced at it before her mind drifted to a barrage of memories and the strange reality of what was taking place in the present. She was startled but not surprised to feel Graham's hands on her shoulders.

"Forgive me," he said, "if I said anything to make you feel—"

"No, it's not that," she reassured him. "I'm grateful for your candor . . . and your sincerity." She drew the courage to turn and face him, knowing that as she did so she was facing her feelings for him with no means to conceal them any further. "I'm inexplicably glad to know it's not just me, Graham, that I'm not in this alone." He smiled, and his eyes showed relief as he gently touched her face and rubbed a thumb over her cheek. "I think I'm just . . . overwhelmed."

"Why?" he murmured. "Please tell me why."

Bess liked the way he wanted to understand her more deeply, and she found it far easier than she might have expected to delve into some of her most tender thoughts and be willing to share them. "When I realized that I loved Hugh, I never dreamed that he would love me in return. And once we admitted the truth to each other, everything moved so quickly that I hardly had time to consider the depth of my own surprise at such love coming into my life." Pausing to consider what she'd just said, Bess added with some apology, "I mustn't talk about Hugh so much. I'm certain you don't want to hear every detail of my relationship with my deceased—"

"On the contrary," he said. "I loved him too, and I'm so grateful for all the happiness you brought into his life, and that he didn't die alone—or lonely. I want you to talk about him as much as you need to—or wish to.

He will always be a part of our lives; he brought us together. Please . . . don't ever apologize for talking about Hugh."

Bess was a little stunned to realize how much that meant to her, and what it indicated about Graham's character. "Thank you," she said, knowing the words were sorely insufficient to express the depth of her gratitude. But she could expound another time. Instead, she attempted to finish her thought. "I suppose I'm trying to say that . . . I'm quite overcome to realize that I would find such love not only once, but twice, right here at Astoria Abbey."

Graham laughed softly. "The Abbey is a magical place, I believe; at least it's always felt that way to me. I far prefer being here than anywhere else in the world."

Bess took the inference to heart and seized the opportunity to ask something she considered of utmost importance when considering any decision pertaining to her future—and that of her daughter and the people who were a part of their lives. "Does that mean you would be willing to stay here? Here where Agnes has her grandmother . . . and so many others who love her?"

"I would never presume to remove you *or* Agnes from this place that is so obviously your home, in every sense of the word."

Bess breathed in her relief and allowed it to fill her completely—body and spirit. She felt so deeply and perfectly hopeful and content in that moment that she had to admit, "This all just feels too good to be true."

"I was thinking the same thing," he said, but before she could respond he kissed her, as if doing so might prevent anything being said that might give them the tiniest cause to believe that this *was* too good to be true. During Graham's kiss, he wrapped her completely in his arms, holding her with a strength that seemed to express the depth of his love for her. Bess took hold of his shoulders if only to keep herself upright, considering the strange headiness consuming her.

When their kiss ended, he looked into her eyes, his face still very close to hers. "Are you all right?" he asked. "You look . . . bewildered."

"I've just . . . never experienced anything like this before," she admitted.

"But surely you—"

Bess interrupted him so that she could hurry and make her explanation and get it over with. "He could never hold me like this," Bess murmured with an unexpected quaver in her voice. "Forgive me . . . for making a comparison to Hugh, but . . . it just occurred to me that . . . he could never hold me like this. Believe me, he wanted to, but he was too weak; he didn't have the strength."

A long moment of silence implied he was considering what she'd said, while he tightened his embrace as if to reassure her of his strength. He finally said, "We just talked about this, Bess. But if you need me to remind you I will. You never have to apologize for talking about Hugh—as much as you need to or want to. He was your husband; what you shared with him may have been brief but I have the deepest respect for it. He was the best man I ever knew; if he loved you and trusted you, then I have no doubt that what the two of you shared was special." He sighed in a way that seemed to wordlessly express how much he missed his cousin. "And you are welcome to make comparisons if you need to." He looked more directly into Bess's eyes. "As long as you know that I may be physically stronger than he was and blessed to be of good health. But I always felt inferior to him, always wanted to be more like him." He pressed a gentle hand over her hair. "Perhaps with how well you knew him, you could help me learn how to do that."

"Perhaps," she said in a tone that lightened the mood, "but right now I think I'd just like to enjoy . . ." She moved her hands down his arms and back up again, implying a silent reference to what she'd said about his physical strength. He smiled at her and picked up on the hint as he tightened his embrace impossibly further and kissed her again.

*  *  *  *  *

Bess could hardly remember how she'd finally managed to say good night to Graham and make her way to her room and get ready for bed. Snug beneath the covers, she still felt blanketed in the warmth of Graham's love, wondering why she would be so blessed as to find such love twice in a lifetime. Rather than questioning it too long, she simply thanked God and vowed to never take such a blessing for granted.

The following morning, Bess awoke feeling rested and realized she'd not heard Agnes, whose noises from the next room usually awakened her. She stretched and rolled over, enjoying the way the sun plunged through the large windows and sprayed out over the room. Recalling her time with Graham the previous evening, she closed her eyes and felt a smile overtake her face while a warm tingling consumed her completely. She only enjoyed her respite for a few minutes before she heard Agnes and hurried to get the baby out of her crib. She'd barely done so when Daphne came rushing into the room, more distraught and upset than Bess had ever seen her.

"Oh, you must go down to the office at once! You must hurry! Lady Agatha is ill and not to be disturbed. You must come!"

"The office?" Bess echoed, barely knowing where the room was; she'd likely only been there once or twice.

"Where the lady manages all the business of the estate, and—"

"I know what the room is used for," Bess said impatiently as Daphne took Agnes from her almost abruptly. "Why on earth do I need to go there at this hour when—"

"They've come to blows," Daphne said, her voice indicating that she was in shock. "They've actually come to blows, and I was sent to get you. That's all I know."

"*Who* has come to blows?" Bess demanded, suddenly feeling nauseous.

"Just . . . hurry!" Daphne insisted, waving Bess toward the door.

Bess did as she was told, tying her dressing gown tightly around her even as she practically ran in bare feet down the stairs and to the office, only making a wrong turn once. Her heart was pounding as much from dread as from her hurried trek by the time she arrived at the office door to find a handful of servants hovering near the open doorway, while she could hear arguing from inside the room—and both voices involved were keenly familiar.

"Get back to work!" Bess ordered the servants, surprised at her own ability to sound so authoritative. "This is not some kind of entertainment. I will take care of it."

The servants scurried away, and Bess channeled all her anger into courage as she stepped through the open doorway, despite having absolutely no idea what might be going on. Even though she'd clearly heard Clive and Graham arguing—although their words had been indiscernible—she was still astonished to see both men with blood on their faces, engaged in a shouting match, the likes of which she had never witnessed.

"What on *earth* is going on?" she demanded, feeling very much like the mother of two little boys who had been caught misbehaving very badly.

Both men turned toward her in a surprised response to seeing her there. They both looked embarrassed, but not enough to hide the fact that they were both *extremely* angry.

Bess blurted out the first thought that came to mind. "Please don't tell me this has something to do with *me.*"

"Don't flatter yourself," Clive snapped in a voice she'd never heard before. She could give him the benefit of the doubt of being angry—even if she had no idea regarding the reasons. But she could feel a personal insult in the words he'd just said, and she wasn't sure what to make of it.

Bess watched both men visibly will themselves to composure. Clive pushed his hands through his hair to straighten it at the same time Graham tugged on his waistcoat and retrieved his handkerchief from his pocket, which he dabbed beneath his nose to absorb the blood there.

"Well?" she growled, feeling even more like a mother figure, which she credited to the obvious fact that they were behaving like children.

Graham said in a surprisingly even voice, which indicated his anger was not at all directed toward her, "I would be happy to discuss the matter with you . . . alone."

"So that you can fill her with your lies?" Clive snarled at Graham, whose face tightened, and his cheek twitched, as if it was taking all his willpower to not respond to Clive's taunting.

Graham kept his eyes focused on Bess and she saw the same sincerity there that she'd seen the previous evening, but given how upset Clive was—and how long she had known and trusted him—she found herself questioning Graham's sincerity; perhaps he was a very good actor. "Don't believe everything you're told, Bess," Graham said. "Please . . . listen to your instincts and gather *all* the information before you come to any conclusions."

Bess took in what sounded like perfectly sound advice, but she still felt horribly baffled and confused—not to mention utterly torn when it was evident that these two men were at such odds as to actually strike each other, and she was so thoroughly fond of them both.

Graham left the room quickly, and Bess wondered if that was meant to be an admission that he knew his behavior had been out of line, or if he was simply angry and wanted to cool down before he attempted to explain. While she felt generally baffled over how to get to the bottom of this, she did feel inclined to at least take Graham's advice: she needed to gather all the information before she came to any conclusions; she needed to hear both sides of the story. But then what? Was she meant to play judge and jury over whatever they'd been arguing about? The very idea made her feel resentful, but she wasn't certain what to do about it.

In Graham's absence, Clive just stood where he was, having now retrieved his own handkerchief, which he had pressed against his bleeding lip. Unnerved by the silence, Bess said, "I assume you're going to explain what has spurred such childish behavior between two grown men."

"If you're willing to really listen and not just assume that everything you may have come to believe is true."

"You've always told me I'm a perceptive woman," Bess said, instinctively closing the door as she wondered if any of the servants might have sneaked back, hoping to overhear some delicious gossip. "I believe I have the ability to know the truth when I hear it."

"Then you must know that Graham Astor's declarations of love to you are purely based in selfish motives."

Bess was taken aback by the statement, but she found herself mentally stuck on one shocking realization. *Graham Astor?* Good heavens! Bess had known the man for over a year and a half and had never known his surname. How was that possible? She quickly recounted the way that people at church and in the village—and even in the household—simply called him *m'lord,* or often just *sir.* Astor? As in—Astoria Abbey?

Clive cleared his throat impatiently, as if to remind Bess that he was there, and he'd said something that warranted a response. She focused on the *other* shocking aspects of his statement, forced to ask herself if her instincts were so badly out of tune that she would sincerely believe Graham had been nothing but truthful with her, when it might have been otherwise. If anyone else were telling her this, she would have been likely to dismiss the possibility completely. But this was Clive! He'd been her trusted friend ever since she'd come to the Abbey. She couldn't just immediately discount what he was saying for the sake of defending the fact that she'd fallen hopelessly in love with Graham. Perhaps it *was* too good to be true. The very idea made her feel even more ill, but she composed herself, gathered her dignity, and forced herself to take this on with sound reason and practicality.

"And how do you know what Graham's declarations to me have been?" she asked; since their conversations about their feelings for each other had taken place only the day before, she couldn't imagine how *anyone* in the house might know.

"Because he *told* me," Clive said as if he resented it. "So, you could never love *me,* but you can love someone like *him?*"

"I will not apologize for my feelings, Clive," Bess declared. "I've never been anything but completely honest with you. But what exactly do you mean by *someone like him?*"

"Born into privilege, well accustomed to getting whatever he sets out to get. I've known him almost as long as I've known Hugh, and perhaps *you* should consider the possibility that you don't know him as well as you think you do."

Bess hated the way Clive's words pricked her—painfully. But still she managed to keep her dignity intact. "Perhaps I should," she said, but she added what she considered a fair point, "And perhaps the same could be said of you. I never imagined you as the kind of man to engage in a childish argument that actually resorted to violence."

"And yet you were not here to see how he provoked me," Clive said and stepped toward her. His tone turned to pleading—desperate pleading. "Bess, you must believe me when I tell you that Graham may very well feel some affection for you, but his greatest motive in his declarations of love has far more to do with your inheritance."

"*What* inheritance?" Bess countered, astonished and upset enough to not be able to hide it.

"You're the widow of Hugh Buxton, Bess. Surely you must know that—"

"I think you should stop now," Bess said, mostly because she felt suddenly very ignorant and naive. Hugh's wealth had never played the tiniest part in their relationship, or her being drawn to him. She'd been grateful to have Agatha want her to remain here, especially when she had realized a baby was coming. And she was grateful now that she and Agnes had a home and people who loved and cared for them. Any kind of inheritance had never even crossed her mind. But if *that* was the true source of the argument between Graham and Hugh, then she needed a great deal more information before she could come to any conclusions on where she stood on *anything* related to the heated altercation she'd just stepped into.

"Fine!" Clive said in a brittle tone that was so unlike him. "We can talk about this when we're both a little calmer."

He left the room before she had any opportunity to comment, but she felt certain he was right. The Clive she'd just seen was unfamiliar to her, but she could give him the benefit of the doubt, based on all the evidence she had of the man she'd come to know over the course of their entire relationship. She didn't understand his reasons for being angry, nor did she understand Graham's side of the story. She *did* need more information—and a great deal of it, apparently. Standing in the office alone, she felt ridiculously naive and gullible. She'd never heard of any inheritance, and she'd not even known Graham's surname—a man with whom she'd shared affection and bold disclosures of love. She wanted to just go back upstairs and crawl into bed and never get out again. But there was obviously a very big problem going on within the walls of the Abbey, and for some reason it had fallen upon her to solve it. She sighed and squeezed her eyes closed as the full weight of what she might be facing seemed to literally come down upon her shoulders. It was going to be a long day. She only prayed that by the time it ended, all of this would be cleared up, and that she would learn that this was not nearly as serious as it currently appeared to be.

\* \* \* \* \*

Bess returned to her rooms to find Daphne filled with concern and curiosity. Bess gave her the simplest explanation possible before she got cleaned up and dressed and forced herself to eat some of the breakfast that had been brought to her room. She felt little appetite but instinctively knew she needed her strength—both physically and emotionally. It was more her emotional strength that she needed to draw on, but becoming nauseous or light-headed because she'd not eaten properly would not serve her well as she devoted her day to gathering information and trying to get to the bottom of what had *really* started the argument between Clive and Graham, and what exactly it had to do with her.

Grateful to be able to leave Agnes contentedly in Daphne's care, Bess went to speak with Agatha. Despite having been told earlier that Agatha wasn't feeling well and had asked not to be disturbed, she hoped that the urgency of the matter might give her enough privilege to be able to see her anyway. Bess knew her mother-in-law would be honest and forthright, and that she also knew both men very well. Surely this woman who was as much her friend as the grandmother of her child would be able to help solve this problem quickly and easily. But Bess was disappointed beyond words to be strictly informed by Agatha's maid that the Lady had not slept at all the previous night and had gone back to bed right after eating breakfast, asking not to be disturbed for as long as she was able to sleep.

Bess walked slowly back to her own rooms, mentally trying to make sense of this unexpected and confusing dilemma. Everything she knew personally about these two men as individuals was nothing but positive. She had no reason to believe that either of them was deceptive in any way or lacking in integrity. So, what reason could there possibly be for the two of them to be at such intense odds against each other? Her mind frantically searched for any plausible explanation, but she kept coming up empty. She continued going back to the possibility that it had something to do with her. Clive had declared his love for her—which she had rejected; however appropriate and forthright she might have been, she could understand why he might be upset. And in the brief time since, Graham had also come forward with declarations of his own love for Bess; the difference being that Bess shared Graham's affection, and she also shared his hope that they could build a future together. Now Clive himself had told her that Graham had told *him* about their mutual affection. Bess wondered if this *was* about her, except each time she seriously considered that possibility, she vividly remembered Clive snarling, *Don't flatter yourself.* What did *that* mean, exactly? It certainly hadn't been very kind. Was she flattering herself to believe that two fine men could really care for her as much as they'd claimed? Was Clive right in saying that Graham was not everything she believed him to be? Her instincts told her that Graham was a good man, but she knew Clive to be a good man, as well. Oh, how she longed to speak with Agatha—soon, before her head exploded!

Bess was startled to approach her bedroom and find Clive sitting in the hall, waiting for her. He stood up when he saw her, and she couldn't help noticing some slight bruising near the cut on his lip and on one cheek. The very idea of Graham doing this to him infuriated her, but then, Graham himself had been bleeding from his nose. She wondered what had started this ridiculous argument, and who had struck the first blow. And she wondered—for all their apparent integrity—if she could trust either of them to tell her the whole truth over their obviously childish behavior.

"May we talk?" he asked, and she wanted to reply that she would rather scrub every floor in the Abbey than talk to him right now, as confused and upset as she felt.

Trying to perhaps be able to avoid any serious conversation, she stated what she believed to be obvious, "I'm not certain I have enough information to be able to talk about any of this right now." She could hear in her own voice the evidence of how frustrated she felt, but she wondered if he had any idea how she felt tempted to hit him herself. And Graham too, for that matter.

"And how do you suppose you will obtain information if you don't talk to me?" he asked, also sounding upset—although she sensed he was far more upset than he was allowing himself to let on. And she wondered why. What could *possibly* have upset him this much?

"You make a fair point," Bess said, but she still didn't want to talk to him.

Bess was trying to think of a way to ask if they could talk *later*, when he motioned toward her sitting room door and said, "Please, Bess; you've been my closest friend since we lost Hugh. Surely you can do me the kindness of hearing me out."

Bess couldn't argue with that. She took a deep breath and willed herself to set all anger aside and simply hear what he had to say. She nodded and led the way into the sitting room, noting how he closed both doors as if he didn't want to be overheard; she couldn't recall ever being alone with him in any room with the doors closed. It wasn't as if she felt like they needed any kind of a chaperone. It was simply odd, given the pattern of their relationship. Although, recalling his recent declarations of love for her, she realized their relationship was not what it used to be, and she did feel a little wary as she sat down, remaining on the edge of her seat. Reminding herself that she and Clive *had* been friends—even long before Hugh's death—she took another deep breath, certain she had nothing to be concerned about. And perhaps he *could* shed some light on this problem that would help her understand what was going on.

"I'll get right to the point," Clive said as he sat down, also remaining at the edge of his seat.

"I would appreciate that," Bess replied.

"I don't wish to speak ill of Graham," he began, which induced a prickly sensation that rushed over her back, "which is why I've said nothing to you about him before now. He's family and he certainly has every right to come here and visit, and I never saw anything about his presence here that caused me concern. But I absolutely did not expect him to come up with this preposterous ruse about being in love with you." That prickly sensation increased but Bess kept her expression resolute and just listened as Clive went on. "When I happened upon him in the office, rifling around in the contents of desk drawers—where he simply had no right to be—we naturally started arguing when he couldn't give me a good reason for being there, doing what he was doing."

"May I ask *your* reason for being there?" Bess felt proud of the confidence in her voice that completely belied her absolute *lack* of confidence at the moment.

"Bess," he said as if he were completely surprised that she didn't already know the answer to that question, leaving her to feel even more ignorant and naive. Oh, how she longed to go back to when Hugh was alive so that he could explain such things to her and not leave her so unprepared over such matters. "I've helped Agatha with estate matters for years. Surely you haven't forgotten that despite the personal help I gave Hugh—because we had become friends—it's my job to see that this household runs smoothly."

"Of course," Bess said, too ashamed to admit that she *had* forgotten. She knew he had work that kept him busy, but since Hugh's death she'd barely given any thought to the fact that he was officially the head butler at Astoria Abbey, and that he worked closely with Agatha and the housekeeper to keep everything in line.

"As I was saying," Clive went on, "Graham became angry over my questioning his being there, and he tried to convince me that he had every right to his aunt's business matters—which he does not. And when he told me that he intended to marry you . . . that you were in love with him . . . as if that somehow justified his being there . . . searching for who knows what without Lady Buxton's approval, I was incensed. When I told him that I knew you would never be foolish enough to fall for him . . . that you would surely see through his ulterior motives . . . he hit me; I hit him back. I admit it was childish, but Bess, I am sincerely concerned about what he's doing and why. And to realize that you've somehow become caught in the middle of his scheming, I felt terrified on your behalf. The last thing I want is for you to get hurt. Please, Bess, I implore you to take to heart what I said earlier. I truly believe this has everything to do with the inheritance, and little or nothing to do with matters of the heart."

Again, Bess desperately wished she'd been able to speak with Agatha before this conversation had taken place. *What inheritance?* She knew nothing of any inheritance. Had Hugh and Agatha simply assumed that she knew something she was supposed to know when she'd married Hugh? Had they each assumed that the other had told her some piece of vital information? Information so vital that Clive and Graham would be driven to strike each other while arguing over the matter?

An awkward silence surrounded them while Bess took far too long to think about everything he'd said and how she might respond. Clive reached for her hand, but she withdrew, not wanting him to even touch her right now. She had no reason not to believe he was telling her the truth, but given his recent declarations of love—a love she did not share—she didn't want him to think that under duress she might have changed her mind. Truthfully, she was far more preoccupied by the possibility that Graham's motives might not be as she believed. The very idea made her want to throw up. She'd fallen hopelessly in love with him, and the memory of being in his arms made her want to melt into the floor. But what if it *had* all been a ruse? Was she so gullible?

"Bess," Clive broke the silence, "please say something."

Bess took another moment to find an emotional foundation she could stand on—even if it was temporary and very shaky. "As I said before: I need more information. Right now, I'm just confused and . . . upset. I appreciate hearing your side of the story. However . . . I'm tired and I have a headache." *That* was certainly true. "I would like to continue this conversation later . . . when my head is clearer."

"Of course," Clive said kindly.

Even though Bess felt the need to rest, and she intended to ask Daphne to get something from the cook to help ease the growing pain in her head, what she really needed was time to think, and time to speak with Agatha— and with Graham. She needed to hear his side of the story, and she needed to find a way to remove any prejudices inside of her that were a result of her feelings for him.

Clive left the room surprisingly fast, as if he wanted to get away before she could ask him any possible questions. Given how much she wanted to be alone, she was glad for his hasty retreat. Bess found Daphne in the nursery with Agnes, and Bess played with her daughter for a few minutes while Daphne went down to the kitchen to retrieve a dose of the cook's special remedy for headaches. The woman was gifted in her culinary talents, but she also had a keen interest in growing herbs and mixing them to alleviate many ailments according to her avid apothecary studies. Every person in the household had come to rely on these remedies, because they usually worked. Bess knew that her father held a certain respect for such remedies and even relied on them himself. Everyone in the household had always considered it a pity that there hadn't been any such remedy to aid Hugh's broken heart, or to at least help alleviate his symptoms. But his health challenges had been extreme. However, when it came to an average headache or a typical upset stomach, the cook always had just the thing. And Bess was glad when Daphne returned from the kitchen quickly. Bess kissed Agnes and left her in Daphne's care. Within minutes she had taken the herbal concoction and crawled into her bed—even though it had already been made and she was making a mess of it again. But she felt so overwhelmed—and even afraid— that she didn't care. Once she had mentally admitted to the fear she'd been feeling ever since she'd been summoned to the office, tears burst out of her and she pressed her face into her pillow to keep them silent. How could it be possible for these two men—both of whom were so dear to her—to be at such odds? And how could she be so naive and gullible as to have no idea what the problem might be? And more than anything, she felt terrified that the wondrous feelings Graham had awakened in her might have been elicited by nothing more than a ruse for his selfish gain. Could she really be *that* stupid? Was he truly such a remarkable actor? Sorting the matter out as much as she could with what little information she had, Bess believed that with Agatha's help she would be able to get to the bottom of whatever this had to do with the inheritance, which she had to assume was meant to be hers by right of being Hugh's widow. Right now, it was more the probability of her broken heart that provoked her tears to go on and on, which only made her head hurt worse. If Graham turned out to be the kind of scoundrel that Clive believed him to be, then Bess could do nothing but end their relationship immediately—but that didn't mean she would stop loving him. The very idea made her feel as if her chest would burst wide open from the pain growing there. A part of her couldn't imagine Graham being anything less than sincere; but on the other hand, she couldn't imagine Clive doing or saying anything lacking integrity or perfect concern for her well-being.

Bess finally managed to stop crying and was relieved to note that the remedy seemed to be working, since the pain in her head had lessened. She was finally able to relax and fall asleep, waking up to note from a glance at the clock that she'd missed lunch. As she sat up and stretched the sleep from her arms, she saw a tray with a couple of covered dishes on the table near the window. Daphne must have sneaked in and left something for her to eat. The very thought made Bess's stomach rumble, and she was quick to sit at the table and enjoy the fruit, cheese, and buttered bread that had been left for her. But her enjoyment plummeted when she found a note on the tray and unfolded it to read: *We need to talk. I'll be waiting in the west parlor. Graham.*

Bess suddenly lost her appetite. She *did* need to speak with Graham, but given all that Clive had said, she now wondered if she could trust him. Perhaps even worse, Bess wondered if she could trust herself. Was she wise enough, discerning enough, to be able to see through her own love for him to know if he was purposely deceiving her in some way?

Knowing that putting this off would only make things worse, Bess hurried to peek in on Agnes who was napping, and she spoke for a moment with Daphne who assured her that watching over the baby while Bess dealt with other things would not be a problem. Bess then hurried to Agatha's room, sometimes actually running because of the urgency of her need to be able to speak with her mother-in-law about this inheritance business before she had to face Graham. But Eve met Bess at the door of Agatha's room, informing her that the lady was feeling ill—hence her having been so extremely fatigued.

"I'm certain it's nothing serious," Agatha's loyal maid said reassuringly. "She insisted I not send for the doctor unless her symptoms worsen. She tells me she just feels achy and tired, with a bit of a sore throat. But she is once again sleeping, and I don't believe we should disturb her."

"No, of course not," Bess said, unable to disagree with Eve, but certain that if Agatha had any idea about what was going on she would *want* to be disturbed. Still, how could Bess explain that to Eve without sounding foolish?

Bess worked her way through the house toward the west parlor, now having to force herself to not walk slowly on purpose. With all her soul, she dreaded facing Graham; the irony was that she'd awakened this morning wanting nothing more than to just see him, and now it almost made her sick.

Arriving at the open door of the west parlor, Bess paused to take a deep breath and steel herself to be strong. And she uttered a quick, silent prayer for wisdom and discernment. Her hesitation about entering the room was thwarted when she realized Graham was pacing, and he couldn't help but see her when he passed the doorway.

"Bess," he said and stopped pacing, gazing at her with overt fear in his countenance. But was it fear of being exposed in some terrible misdeed? Or fear of her believing that he was guilty when he'd done nothing wrong? Bess had no idea, which likely made her every bit as afraid as he was.

Bess summoned her courage more firmly and entered the room, closing the door behind her. The servants were all surely aware that a drama of some kind was taking place in the house, but she had no desire for them to be privy to the details—especially when she herself had no idea what was going on.

# CHAPTER FOURTEEN

## THE LADY OF THE ABBEY

"Bess," Graham said again, sounding desperate, "we need to talk."

"Yes, we certainly do," she said and forced herself to sit down, mostly because she felt a little shaky.

Graham moved a chair so that it was facing her directly. When he sat on it and leaned his forearms on his thighs, she wasn't certain she liked how near he was. Given her concerns about her own ability to discern his motives, his closeness felt unnerving.

Bess had expected him to jump into an explanation of his earlier actions, and was taken completely off guard when he said, "Ask me anything you want, anything you need to know, and I will answer you honestly. I swear to you that I'll tell you the truth. I hope you can believe me."

*I'm trying to,* she wanted to say, but couldn't bring herself to put a voice to the words.

"Very well," she muttered instead, if only to give herself a few more seconds to come up with at least one suitable question. The love she felt for him rushed up in response to just looking into his eyes, and she had to fight to push such sentimentality aside; it had no place in her need to discern the truth. She cleared her throat to give herself a few *more* seconds, which also helped choke back any temptation to get emotional. Recalling all that Clive had told her earlier, she began with what seemed a logical inquiry. "Why were you in the office this morning? Why go there at all?"

"*Why?*" he echoed with such incredulity that she already felt her discomfort growing. "I spend time there every day, Bess. I've *always* worked with Agatha in running the estate. Did you believe that I would leave her to bear the burden of such responsibilities without my assistance?"

Bess swallowed hard, alarmed over the realization that she already had a direct contradiction between Clive's version of the situation, and Graham's, and she completely doubted her own ability to discern which one was telling her the truth. But she would never know if she didn't move the conversation forward. "So," she continued, "you were there when Clive came in this morning, and—"

"Is that what he told you?" Graham asked, even more incredulous. "Bess, I arrived there to find him rummaging through drawers—which always remain locked, I might add; how he came to know the whereabouts of the key I cannot begin to imagine. He had no business being there, and he had no plausible explanation to offer. His duties in this house have nothing to do with anything kept in that room. He has his own office elsewhere."

Bess couldn't even speak. Now the stories of each of these men were growing further and further apart. One of them was lying to her, and given the depth and severity of the lies, she had to believe that whatever might be kept in those desk drawers was of great importance—and beyond her ability to believe, it had something to do with her. Unnerved by how close Graham was sitting, she stood up and crossed the room, pretending to look out the window. But the effort proved pointless when he stood and followed her, standing just as close to her as he'd been when they were sitting.

"Bess, listen to me," he implored more quietly, "I love you." His words startled her to a different—and perhaps the most difficult—realization. She loved him too; but she also loved her father. She'd learned the hard way that love alone could not create happiness in any relationship when respect and integrity were absent. "I want you to be happy, Bess," he went on. "I have no motive here beyond serving your best interests—and those of the Abbey. I realize that our admission of the way we feel about each other is new . . . and we yet have much to learn about each other, but . . . we have still spent so much time together. You know me, Bess; in your heart you know me. Surely you must know that you can trust me."

Bess swallowed carefully and forced herself to voice her most prominent thought. "I want to believe that's true, Graham; I want it more than anything. But I also know Clive; we've been friends for so long . . . before Hugh and I were even married."

Graham let out a frustrated sigh. From his expression alone, she read his understanding of her confusion and the obvious quandary for her. But she had no idea if he was telling her the truth, which forced her to fully acknowledge that she had no idea if Clive had told her the truth. Whatever the truth might be, one of these men had betrayed her. Even if she didn't understand the reasons, she could almost literally feel her heart cracking to consider herself to be so gullible, so taken advantage of for *any* reason.

The strained silence was broken when Graham said, "I know he's been a good friend to you, Bess. I admit that I do not understand his motives, but you must believe me when I tell you that something is not right . . . something is not what it appears to be, and we must—"

Without even considering her words, Bess jumped in to defend Clive. "If what you're telling me is true . . . that *you* found *him* there, and he wasn't supposed to be, then—"

"*If?*" Graham retorted. "Are you saying you really don't believe me? Do you really think I would lie to you for the sake of—"

"Right now, I don't know what to believe," Bess said, sounding more upset than she wanted to let on. "I know Clive. I'm certain there is a reasonable explanation for his being there. He would simply never be motivated by anything untoward."

"Oh, Bess!" Graham countered. "Your naivete and gullibility are precious, truly. But you cannot get by in this world by only choosing to see the good in everyone you know. It's a commendable trait, certainly, but you cannot allow it to cloud your judgment when it comes to the absolute reality that not everyone is who they might seem to be; some people are very good actors, and very keen on deceiving those around them."

Bess couldn't believe what she was hearing. "Are you trying to say that he is *acting? Deceiving?* Do you mean to imply that all his kindness toward Hugh—and toward me—have been false? That he is only driven by some malicious ulterior motive?"

Graham sighed and looked at the floor, as if he were trying very hard to remain calm and reasonable—but it was taking a great deal of effort. "Bess," he said in a gentle tone, looking up at her, "I am not in a position to judge his intentions. I've known him for many years, and I believe his affinity with Hugh was genuine. Beyond that, I can only tell you what I've perceived from my own observations, my own interactions with him in more recent months. He's changed, Bess. I can't explain exactly how or why, but I can tell you that I do *not* trust him, nor should you. I greatly fear that if you *do* trust him—to the point that you would defend him at all costs—you will only set yourself up for heartache and disappointment."

"Well, I think you've lost your mind," Bess retorted, amazed at the anger that came out in her own voice. "I know him!"

"You *think* you know him!" Graham countered just as hotly, and she realized they were arguing. "You know a part of him that he's allowed you to see, and he's very good at concealing what he does *not* want you to see."

"Or perhaps *you* are choosing to see something in him that is simply not there because . . . because . . ." she stammered then blurted, "you're jealous."

"Jealous?" he echoed, astonished. "What on earth would I have to be jealous about? There is absolutely nothing about him or his life over which I should feel any jealousy. I cannot even begin to imagine what would make you think—"

"Because he's in love with me," she impulsively uttered and immediately wished she hadn't. Graham's eyes widened in astonishment and he was amazingly silent. She took advantage of his silence to add, "If you believe there is absolutely no reason for you to feel any jealousy, then you cannot possibly think there is any reason for *me* to have any concerns regarding my relationship with him."

"Relationship?" he repeated. "What kind of *relationship*? Is there something I should know about?"

"No!" she insisted.

"*No* because you don't want me to know? Or *no* because there isn't a *relationship*? Please, Bess, don't tell me that you have any kind of . . . involvement . . . with *that man.*"

"Just . . . *no,*" she declared, not wanting to talk about Clive with him *at all* when he was so determined to believe that her dear friend was involved in a malicious scheme. "*That man,*" she mimicked Graham's tone, "helped care for Hugh every day for most of his life, and he did so lovingly and selflessly. *That man* has been there for me for as long as I've known him, helping me through every difficulty—large and small."

Graham inhaled and exhaled slowly, again seeming to fight for an ability to remain calm. "I don't doubt that what you're saying is true, Bess. I'm not trying to say he's a bad person, or that his care for Hugh wasn't genuine. That doesn't mean he isn't capable of—"

"I don't want to hear it!" Bess said, putting up a hand.

"So, you *are* in love with him," Graham said as if he resented the very possibility.

"I did *not* say that," Bess insisted hotly.

"But he is in love with *you?*" Graham asked. "You *did* say *that!*"

Bess quieted her voice and tried to be calm as well as truthful. "I can't deny that he's admitted to such feelings; there's no crime in that."

Seconds of silence passed, as if Graham were trying to choose his words carefully. "No, it's certainly no crime for a man to be in love. I'm not nearly as concerned about his feelings as I am about yours. You didn't *say* that you're in love with him, but are you? Do you have feelings for him?"

"I don't see how that's any business of yours," Bess countered without even considering how foolish the statement sounded.

Apparently agreeing with the foolishness of her words, Graham took her shoulders into his hands and put his face close to hers, reminding her by the gesture alone of the affection they'd shared. "Don't you?" he asked in a voice that was low and husky. "Then your memory is very poor, my darling. Let me make something perfectly clear, so you'll know exactly where I stand. The selfish part of me wants to be the man to whom you give your heart, Bess. Me and only me. I would not have crossed the boundaries with you that I have crossed if I felt any other way. I'm not the kind of man to flirt with or tease a woman just for fun. My affection is an offering of my heart, Bess, and I believed when I gave it to you that you were the kind of woman who would not take such an offering lightly. If I were completely selfless I would want above all else for you to be happy, and if you love another man—a man who would treat you well and make you happy—then I would strive to do the honorable thing and bow out graciously. But you have led me to believe that you share my affection, and you've given me no indications that you have romantic feelings for Clive or any other man, so don't toss such insinuations around now because we disagree over his character. Please . . . just . . . set aside for a moment what started this argument and tell me the truth. Do you have feelings for him?"

Bess drew in a quivering breath, unsettled by his nearness as much as the bold clarifications of his affection for her. It took a long moment for her thoughts to sort themselves out enough to do as he'd asked and just answer a simple question, with all other biases set aside. "He's a dear friend," she stated with full sincerity. "He has been for as long as I've known him. As I told you, he admitted to being in love with me. But I do not have any such feelings for him; I never have, and I never will."

The relief Bess saw in Graham's eyes made her heart quicken. No matter how much they might disagree about Clive's character and possible motives, she knew in that moment he loved her as much as she loved him.

She could find some peace in knowing that at least his admission of his love for her was true. But that didn't solve the problem at hand.

"May I say," Graham muttered, his voice lowering almost to a whisper and perhaps growing even more husky, "how very glad I am to hear that?"

Bess wasn't prepared to have him kiss her, but she had no difficulty enjoying it—which surprised her, given that they'd been arguing not a minute ago. She took hold of his upper arms when he kissed her again, almost fearing she might lose her balance as she became thoroughly lost in the experience. He tightened his hands around her shoulders and she unwillingly relaxed into the strength of his grasp until it almost felt as if she might fall if he let go.

"Bess," he whispered close to her lips, "I know you're probably wondering if I'm telling you the truth; you're probably wondering if *I* am the one pretending to be something I'm not." She couldn't deny that, but she didn't want to admit to it outright, so she said nothing before he pressed on. "I need you to trust me, Bess. And before you say that you don't know me well enough to trust me, please bear in mind that Agatha trusts me; Hugh trusted me. Hugh is gone but you are welcome to speak to Agatha about this issue if you feel the need to do so." Bess didn't want to tell him how desperately she'd been trying to do just that all day. Right now, she wanted to just burst into her mother-in-law's room and insist on having a conversation, no matter how ill Agatha felt. "I have nothing to hide from her," Graham added, and Bess continued holding to him as tightly as he held to her while she listened to what he had to say. His kiss had calmed her anger and reminded her that she had become invested in this relationship with Graham, and she needed to at least give him the benefit of the doubt and hear what he had to say. "If Clive is a man of high character as you believe him to be, then let's simply give him the opportunity to prove that it's true. If he has feelings for you but is a good and decent man, he will want you to be happy, even if it means accepting that you don't share his affection. Would you not agree?"

Bess only had to think about it for a moment, but it took her a few moments more to answer, distracted as she was by Graham's nearness. "Yes, I agree," she said and meant it, sincerely believing that Clive genuinely cared for her enough to want her happiness above all else.

"Then . . . I believe a simple conversation between the two of you will help clear all of this up," Graham said. "Just . . . trust me . . . and . . . if I'm wrong, I will apologize to him *and* you."

"You really mean that?" she asked.

"I really do," he said with undeniable sincerity.

Bess forced herself to step away from him, needing to put some distance between them to think more clearly. She readily admitted, "I spoke to him earlier, and . . . well . . . his story contradicts yours; that's all I'm going to say." She looked directly at Graham and was surprised at the sincerity of her plea to him when she was so filled with doubt over whether she could even trust him. "I don't know who to believe, Graham. I don't know how to resolve this when I don't even know what's really going on. You're asking me to trust you, and . . . I want to, but . . ." She tried to think of the words to finish but simply couldn't.

"Bess," he said, not sounding at all defensive over being told that she didn't know if she could trust him, "I really believe all of this is mostly a matter of poor communication. So . . . do whatever you need to do to figure out the truth. I'm more than happy to help you if you want me to, or I will keep my distance if that's what you prefer."

Graham seemed every bit as sincere as he ever had; she only had to wonder if she was discerning enough to see deception when it was right in front of her. But his reasoning made sense. One of these men was lying to her, and was hiding a selfish motive, and she would never be able to figure it out until she understood the situation.

"Thank you," she said, knowing she needed to speak with Agatha no matter how difficult doing so might be. "I need . . . some time. I'll see you in the morning."

Bess hurried out of the room before he could say anything more that might only confuse her further. He'd been very convincing, but she needed distance from the effect he had on her, and she needed her mother-in-law's sound wisdom. She was prepared to face Eve and insist on ignoring Agatha's request to not be disturbed, but she arrived at Agatha's bedroom door to find it slightly ajar, and Eve was nowhere in sight.

Bess knocked lightly on the open door and peered around it to see Agatha leaning against a stack of pillows, looking a little tired but not unlike her usual self otherwise.

"Oh, hello," Agatha said, smiling. "Eve told me you wanted to speak with me; I was hoping you'd come back. I apologize for not being available earlier."

"No need to apologize," Bess said, closing the door behind her to ensure their privacy. "How are you feeling?"

"Better than earlier, given some rest and a few concoctions from the kitchen." She laughed softly. "It's just a little cold; I'll be well enough in a day or two, I'm certain." Agatha motioned toward a chair. "Come and sit down, my dear—but don't get too close. I wouldn't want you catching anything."

Bess moved the chair a little closer to the bed and sat down, grateful beyond words for the way Agatha could so quickly put her at ease. Already she felt more confident about being able to solve this problem. With Agatha on her side, almost anything felt possible. While Bess was feeling a great deal of doubt about her own ability to be wise and discerning, she had complete confidence in Agatha's ability to be both—objectively and fairly. The Lady of Astoria Abbey was simply that kind of woman, and Bess knew it from a great deal of experience.

Before Bess could think of where to begin, Agatha said, "I heard there was a scuffle earlier . . . in the office, I believe. The servants love to gossip, which is usually how I know what's going on in my own house, but evidently no one seems to know much of anything except that Graham and Clive were fighting. Is that true?" Her astonishment validated Bess's own amazement over these two men lowering themselves to such behavior.

"It *is* true," Bess said, "and as you might have guessed, that is *exactly* what I need to speak with you about. I fear I am caught in the middle of their disagreement, but I am filled with doubt and confusion."

"Then we must talk it through," Agatha said, putting Bess immediately at ease and feeling some hope that this problem could be solved without any unnecessary drama.

Bess told Agatha everything she knew, right from the moment she'd been summoned to the office, including every detail of her conversations with both Clive and Graham—including those that had taken place prior to today. Agatha didn't seem at all surprised that both men had declared feelings of love for Bess. Had she been so observant? Had she seen evidence that Bess had missed? Clearly, yes, which was not at all surprising once Bess took a moment to think about it. Agatha also didn't seem surprised to hear Bess admit that she could never love Clive enough to marry him, but her feelings for Graham were something completely different altogether. The conversation regarding the issue at hand was put on hold as Bess and Agatha spoke earnestly of the tender feelings associated with Bess moving on with her life now that Hugh had been gone more than a year and a half. Agatha was completely supportive and encouraging of Bess finding love again, but Bess found no indication in anything Agatha said of whether she believed Graham to be a good choice as a potential husband. It was as if Agatha refused to sway Bess in any way regarding such a life-altering decision. Bess appreciated the theory, even though a part of her wanted Agatha to be able to just tell her whether Graham was as trustworthy as he seemed, and whether she had any reason to be suspicious of Clive's motives.

As the conversation went back to the altercation between these two men, and their dramatically different versions of what had happened, again Bess hoped for profound wisdom to spew forth from this woman she so greatly admired and looked to for guidance. She was deeply surprised—even astounded—to hear Agatha say, "My dear Bess, I believe you are so much wiser than you believe you are. And I think that if you take the time to just be still and listen to your deepest instincts, you will know the truth, and you will know exactly what you should do with your life." She sighed and smiled at Bess, with a sparkle in her eyes that seemed to say she felt nothing but pride in Bess, and that she felt no concern over the present situation whatsoever.

Before Bess could ask any one of the questions still rumbling around in her head, Agatha added, "Now, while you keep in mind what I just said—and you always remember that I truly mean it—a wise person needs proper information before they can manage any given problem. So, I'm going to tell you what *I* know—which is something I had believed Hugh would have told you, but apparently, he did not. I believe you mentioned as much to me at one time, but at that moment I didn't consider the matter relevant. But of course, you have a right to know the truth. And then I have no doubt that you will be able to put everything straight in no time."

Bess leaned forward in her chair expectantly, her heart quickening as she wondered what Agatha might tell her. She'd never imagined that there might be some great secret regarding Astoria Abbey—and apparently whatever it was had never been meant to be a secret—but Bess felt a little afraid to hear what Agatha intended to tell her. After Agatha had clearly explained the situation—which was not complicated at all, but more than a little surprising—Bess was amazed at how completely calm and peaceful she felt. Agatha offered a couple of suggestions about how Bess might handle the situation now that she knew the truth, but she added firmly that she was confident Bess would know what was best and would have the courage to act upon her instincts to do what was right—no matter how difficult. Agatha also told Bess where to find the legal paperwork to verify everything she'd been told so that she would have legal proof in hand, instead of having to rely on differing opinions and misunderstandings. Ironically, these highly important papers were *not* in any of the drawers of the desk—the desk which both Clive and Graham had accused the other of rummaging through. If these documents were the true source of the problem, then Bess felt absolute confidence in being able to get to the truth.

"Thank you," Bess said to Agatha with an earnestness that brought tears to her eyes. "You are so very dear to me. I will be forever grateful for the way you brought me here and gave me a new life—a life more blessed than I ever could have imagined."

"Oh, my dear," Agatha replied, "bringing you here is absolutely the best thing I have ever done—except perhaps giving birth to Hugh. You and your precious daughter have filled my life with a happiness I never thought possible."

Bess promised to come back the following day and report the outcome of the situation. She hurried to the office, glad to find no one there. She closed the door and locked it, not wanting to be interrupted or discovered by anyone for any reason. Even though Agatha had told her there was a small safe in the wall hidden behind a mirror, Bess was still surprised to remove the mirror and find it there. Dust on the mirror's frame indicated it had not been disturbed for a very long time, and it wasn't something the maids would likely pay much attention to. Bess found her heart pounding as she reached into her pocket for the key Agatha had given her. Apparently, there were two copies of the key, and since Hugh's death only Agatha had known their whereabouts; neither of them had ever been kept in the office. The key turned so easily in the lock that Bess felt momentarily breathless. Agatha had assured her that everything she needed to know was on the papers that were kept here, and she would never again have to question the situation or anyone else's opinions or beliefs.

Bess removed the small stack of papers that were the only contents of the safe. She sat down in the chair behind the desk and took a moment to catch her breath before she determined that she was holding two separate sets of the exact same documents. It was clearly stated on the first page that there were three sets, and Bess wondered where the third might be. The two in front of her were meant to be in Agatha's possession, and Hugh's— for as long as he remained alive. Agatha had explained that since Bess was Hugh's widow, this copy of documents now legally belonged to her—only for the sake of protecting the future security of herself and her child.

As Bess relaxed and slowly read the carefully scribed pages, it took her a little time to become accustomed to the formality of the text and the legal jargon, but she soon found it easier to understand, and there was absolutely no question as to what she was reading and what it meant. After rereading a specific section to be certain she understood it correctly, she couldn't hold back a little laugh. She assumed that many women would find the situation disappointing, but to her it was a great relief. And given the obvious confusion that had been taking place among certain people here at the Abbey, she couldn't help but find it even a little bit amusing.

After taking more than sufficient time to be assured that everything Agatha had told her was true, Bess returned one copy of the documents to the safe, which she locked securely before returning the mirror to its proper place to keep the safe hidden. She used her handkerchief to dust the frame of the mirror if only to remove any evidence that the frame had been handled. With the safe key tucked deeply into her pocket beneath the dusty handkerchief, Bess discreetly left the office, knowing exactly what she needed to do and how to go about it. She walked upstairs to check on Agnes and freshen up, feeling badly about how little time she'd spent with her daughter since this problem had erupted early this morning. But she knew Agnes was in good hands, and Daphne was completely compassionate about allowing Bess all the time she needed to deal with the matter. Bess looked forward to having all this behind her and being able to make up some time with her daughter.

Reviewing everything she now knew, Bess concluded that she'd learned a great deal since all of this had blown up. *Gather all available information before getting upset or jumping to conclusions.* It was a lesson she would never forget, and she hoped that—if nothing else—this experience had made her wiser *and* more discerning. She might end up spending the rest of her life a widow and alone, but at least she would be able to be at peace with herself, knowing that she was a woman who had always strived to remain compassionate to others despite their shortcomings, and that she'd never compromised her own integrity or dignity. These were traits she had learned from Agatha—among many other things—and she felt deeply comforted to think of her close personal association with the Lady of Astoria Abbey, and to know that the Abbey would always be her home—no matter how the present situation turned out.

\* \* \* \* \*

Bess was surprisingly calm as she sat on a little sofa in the office and waited for Clive. She'd sent a maid to go and find him with the message that she needed to speak with him immediately. Supper was long since over, and Agnes had been put to bed. The office was well lit with lamps and candles scattered about the room. Bess looked around and noted that it was actually a very beautiful room, with shelves of books and lovely brocade furnishings and drapes. The large desk that was the central focus of the room was so elegantly crafted that it could be called a work of art. Bess doubted that Hugh had spent much time in this room—especially in his adulthood, and likely not much if ever in any official capacity—but it was easy for Bess to imagine Agatha here, meeting with the overseers of the estate and managing all matters of business in lieu of her husband, following his death. Even though Bess had never known Hugh's father, she'd heard many stories about him and she could easily imagine *him* in this room, seated behind the desk with an air of kind authority; he'd likely spent countless hours of his life here. And now Bess found the room surprisingly comfortable, as if she'd been meant to be here. She'd felt at ease here at the Abbey from the first day she'd come here, and once she'd married Hugh she'd never had any trouble feeling like a part of the family and accepting the Abbey as her home. It had *always* felt right. But this was different, deeper somehow, perhaps more intrinsic. The idea didn't make any practical sense considering the legalities regarding Astoria Abbey, but Bess felt that way nevertheless, and it helped her feel more at ease and fully prepared to do what needed to be done.

Bess's mind went to Hugh. She closed her eyes and felt herself smile, certain he would be pleased with the confidence she had gained just today, and with her intentions regarding the problem. She knew that in spite of how much he had loved and trusted these two men who were now at such odds with each other, he would want nothing less than for her to insist on the absolute truth, and to never tolerate any kind of behavior from those around her that might in any way compromise the dignity and respect she deserved—not only as the widow of Hugh Buxton, but simply as a woman of good character and integrity.

The sound of footsteps approaching brought Bess abruptly back to the present, and a rush of nervousness overshadowed the calm she'd been feeling. But she took in a deep breath and drew back her shoulders, determined to remain unruffled and appropriately assertive.

"Bess," Clive said as if she might be a damsel in distress and he'd come to rescue her. He closed the door and leaned against it for a long moment, slightly breathless as if he'd been running to get there quickly.

"Come in," Bess said and stood. "Make yourself comfortable; we have much to talk about."

"We do indeed," he said, sitting on the same sofa. But Bess stood up and crossed the room to open the door he'd just closed.

"Why do we need the—" Clive began to ask but she interrupted him.

"There will be no secrets in this house—not anymore," she stated and sat down in a chair that faced the sofa.

He looked a little taken aback but otherwise unaffected. Bess carefully put the necessary facade in place and reminded herself that one of these two men whom she had trusted and come to depend on had willfully deceived her; she could surely be a little deceptive herself—if only for a few minutes—to properly gauge the situation. It was a plan Agatha had agreed with, which helped Bess hold on to her confidence.

"We both know there has been an unseemly amount of uproar and confusion of late," Bess began, "which has prompted me to do a great deal of thinking on a number of things in my life. Even though there are some things that need to be cleared up regarding whatever might be going on between you and Graham, I hope you'll indulge me by going back to the last serious conversation we had—before all of this happened. You opened your heart and shared your deepest feelings with me; I know that can't have been easy. And perhaps I was too hasty in my response." Clive's eyes brightened with a hope that provoked guilt in Bess, knowing that her position hadn't changed, but to get to the truth, she had to allow him to believe it might have.

"Oh, Bess!" he said as if she might save him from drowning. "Dare I believe that you might be willing, after all, to share your life with me?"

Bess searched for a response that would be as truthful as possible. "And if I were?"

"Oh, Bess!" he repeated, and went down on one knee in front of her, taking both of her hands into his. "We could be so happy together. You, and me, and Agnes. And we'll have more children, and they'll grow up here at the Abbey, and—"

"About that," Bess interrupted, "given all that's happened recently, I've wondered if . . . perhaps it might be better if . . . well, perhaps I should at least consider the possibility of . . . leaving the Abbey; of starting over somewhere else."

Clive looked astonished and disoriented, but after he'd had a moment to take in what Bess had said, he chuckled and declared, "If that's what you want . . . of course. Anything for you, Bess. I'll do whatever it takes to make you happy."

Bess rehearsed her plan and reminded herself of the necessity to step a little further into deception; it was the only way to know the truth. "Such gallantry is so very admirable, Clive, especially when you know that I'm not certain I could ever come to love you the way I loved Hugh. And if we leave the Abbey, we'll have to find a way to support ourselves. But I can work; I have my medical expertise, and you have a great deal of experience in running a household. I'm certain the Lady would write letters on our behalf to help us find gainful employment and—"

"What on earth do you mean?" Clive asked with an almost brusque agitation in his voice. That, combined with his alarmed expression, made Bess's heart sink. The truth was plainly evident now, even before he added, "Why would there ever be any need for either of us to ever work again, Bess, when you are the widow of Hugh Buxton? Whether we stay at the Abbey or not, you must surely be the wealthiest woman in the county—short of Lady Buxton herself."

Bess pulled her hands from his grasp and stood up to put some distance between them. Clive rose to his feet as well, seeming confused by her reaction. "Is that what you think?" she asked, keeping her back turned to him. It was easier to say such things when she didn't have to look at him. "Is that what you've thought all along? That my marrying Hugh would make me a wealthy woman upon his death?"

"It's obvious, isn't it?" Clive countered, as if his assumption was completely benign. But the comment suddenly spurred Bess to a level of anger she'd rarely felt in her life.

Bess turned to face Clive, glad to now be able to shed any attempt at deception, and grateful for the ability to keep her voice steady and reasonably calm. "Did you have that thought in mind when you encouraged both me and Hugh to go forward with getting married?" Bess's chest tightened at the brief glimmer of guilt she saw in his eyes before he managed to mask it with false innocence. He *was* a good actor, very good indeed. And the thought made her sick. "You knew Hugh was dying, and therefore with the close friendship you and I had come to share, I'm certain you must have felt confident that if you just bided your time and remained patient, you could marry Hugh's widow and inherit everything he left to me."

"That's ludicrous, Bess," Clive said with a bite to his words that actually made her afraid of what kind of husband he might have made. If she *had* fallen in love with him, if she *had* married him, how might he have treated her when he no longer had to pretend?

"Is it?" she retorted. "If you truly love me, Clive, if it's me you love, and not the potential inheritance, then you should not be concerned about leaving all of this behind." She motioned with her arms to indicate their surroundings. "You just said yourself that you would do whatever it takes to make me happy. May I assume then that I if I choose to leave the Abbey with its wealth and bounty behind, you would be willing to work just as any man would to provide for his wife and children? That's not too much to ask, is it?"

"Bess," he said her name on the wave of a tense chuckle, "what you're saying doesn't even make sense when it simply isn't relevant. The money is yours by right of—"

"There is no money," Bess declared and loved the sound of it as she said it. She'd not given even a second's thought to Hugh's possible wealth when she'd married him. She'd never assumed that being his wife—and subsequently his widow—would change her monetary status in this world in the slightest. She had assumed until Agatha had convinced her to stay that she would leave here after Hugh's death and find work elsewhere. But all this time Clive's thinking had been in a completely different vein. While he had been putting a great deal of effort into schemes and plans that were solely for his financial gain, he'd been completely oblivious to the facts—facts that Bess now knew beyond any doubt.

"What on earth are you talking about?" Clive asked, beginning to sound angry. She found it alarming but somehow not surprising to see how quickly his facade of love and friendship was melting away. A part of her just wanted to melt right here and now into a puddle on the carpet; she wanted to sob with all the grief assaulting her as she considered the friendship she'd found in him, the way she'd confided in him, the depth to which Hugh had loved and trusted him. But she couldn't think about that now. Right now, she had to be strong. She had to remember who she was and what really mattered. She was not the overworked and intimidated young woman who had seen to her father's every whim without any appreciation or respect. She was Elizabeth Buxton, and she would live her life honoring the remarkable man she'd had the privilege to know and love. And if he were here now, he would be disgusted—just as she was.

"I'm telling you," Bess said, proud of herself for the strength and con-fidence she heard in her own voice, even though she was trembling inside, "that there is no inheritance. Hugh stood to inherit nothing; therefore, as his widow, the same is true for me."

"That's impossible!" Clive argued, as if doing so might make the situation what he wanted it to be.

"It's not only possible, it's absolutely true. Astoria Abbey never belonged to Lady Buxton, or even her husband when he was alive. Her older brother inherited this estate, along with other property elsewhere. Their father made certain in his will that the Abbey was designated as a home for Hugh's father and his family indefinitely, and there is an annual allowance that is sufficient to care for the Abbey and its residents. But that's all. Hugh was never an heir to anything monetary, Clive. Funny he never told you, as close as the two of you were. But he never told me, either. Knowing him as I did, I believe it just didn't matter to him, and he assumed it wouldn't matter to the people who really loved him. But apparently in your case he was wrong; we were all wrong."

"I don't believe it!" Clive insisted. "Surely you've been deceived by that malicious blackguard who—"

"Lady Buxton herself explained everything to me, and I have seen the legal documents with my own eyes."

Clive was surprisingly silent, but Bess could see him seething, almost as if smoke were pouring out of his nostrils and heat was radiating off his entire body. Thankfully unaffected by his demeanor, Bess said matter-of-factly, "I assume this means your affection for me has vanished. Under the circumstances, I believe it's safe to say that your interest in me is considerably less keen than it was prior to this conversation."

"You deceived me!" Clive hissed in a way that made Bess wonder who this man standing before her had become. Where was her friend? Hugh's friend?

"How ironic that you could make yourself believe yourself deceived, when you have been so cleverly scheming your deceptions in this house for such a long time." She took a deep breath, knowing there was only one more thing she needed to say. "You need to leave this house immediately. Two of your fellow employees are waiting in the hall to escort you to your room only long enough to pack your things, and they will see you into the carriage that is waiting in the drive. You'll be given a month's wages, which should give you ample time to find employment elsewhere. Don't ever come back; you will never be welcome here in any capacity. And if by chance you ever try to deceive yourself into thinking that you've somehow been wronged, I just want you to try and imagine what it would be like if you were facing Hugh right now." Bess shook her head. "I thank God he didn't live to see this."

Bess saw the tiniest glimmer of regret in Clive's eyes, but it quickly disappeared. She hurried toward the open doorway and called, "I'm quite finished. Please get him out of here."

The two servants she had been referring to—who had been standing in the hallway all along—entered the room and took hold of Clive's arms. He shrugged them away and marched out with the other men following him. Bess stood frozen for a long moment, wondering when the enormity of all that had just happened would hit her. For now, she was grateful for the blanket of shock that shielded her from her own sorrow—and even horror—for how thoroughly Clive had deceived her. She found a bit of comfort in knowing he'd deceived Agatha as well, along with everyone else who lived at the Abbey. Still, it was despicably horrible, and it would take time for her to fully comprehend all that had happened.

Bess looked up when she heard footsteps slowly entering the room. Seeing Graham reminded her that he too had been in the hall, listening to her conversation with Clive. She'd asked to see him earlier after she'd spoken with Agatha and had examined the legal documents. She'd said nothing to him except that she wanted him and two of their trusted servants to be nearby while she spoke to Clive, if only to act as witnesses to whatever might be said. Graham had surely had no idea what to expect. And now that she was facing him, she felt so much regret over the way she had doubted him. But in light of her doubts having fled, the love she felt for him flooded her so completely that she found it easier to believe her sorrow and disappointment could be easily eradicated by such love.

"Forgive me," she said, "for doubting you."

"There's nothing to forgive, Bess," he said and clearly meant it. "How could you have known?"

Instead of trying to analyze that question with all the complicated emotions associated with it, Bess sighed deeply and tried to push away any thought of her ugly confrontation with Clive. "So," she said in a light tone that she hoped would brighten her own mood, "*you're* the legal heir of Astoria Abbey, and *you* have the third copy of the documents I found in the safe."

"I confess that is all true," he said, somewhat sheepishly. "When my grandfather made certain that each of his four sons would have a home of their own, I don't think he counted on only one of them either living long enough to have a son or having a son who would live. I've often wondered why a man like me who had always tried to be a good person, but who hadn't necessarily done anything profoundly good, would end up with so much worldly wealth. But it doesn't really matter, I suppose; it's just the way things turned out. The thing is," his tone of voice shifted, and he stepped closer to Bess, taking her hands into his, "I've spent my adult life surrounded by shallow, simple-minded women, the kind of women who are easily prone to falling in love with ridiculously huge houses and enormous amounts of money. I can't tell you how refreshing it's been to be loved by a person of the female persuasion who loves me just for me. I might say she's a little simple-minded, but not shallow and—"

"I beg your pardon!" Bess said with a little laugh; she could tell he was teasing, but she didn't understand the point until he laughed as well and explained.

"But I do believe that as Agnes grows up she will be every bit as intelligent and wise as her mother—and with any luck she will *still* love me."

"I do believe she will . . . love you, that is," Bess said. "But she's not the only person of female persuasion around here who will always love you."

"Well," he drawled then chuckled, "Agatha *has* to love me; I'm her nephew, her only blood relative."

"That's true," Bess said in the same teasing manner, "which would perhaps require her to love you, but not necessarily *like* you. I'm absolutely certain that she likes you very much . . . and loves you; and she also trusts you." More seriously she added, "I hope you'll be glad to know that I agree with her on all counts."

"I'm very glad to hear it," Graham said, his eyes showing how deeply warmed he was by such a declaration, "because now that we have all that nasty business straightened out, I feel very much inclined to take Aunt Agatha's advice on a particular matter."

"And what is that?" Bess asked.

"She told me not long ago that she'd grown weary of her position . . . of overseeing the household and the estate . . . even though she's had to do very little in a technical sense. She said that she just wants to enjoy being a grandmother and turn her title over to someone else, and she made it clear that if I had any sense whatsoever, I would heed her advice and follow my heart and see that it was all taken care of."

"I don't understand," Bess said; while she had some idea of what Agatha was implying, not all of what he was saying made sense.

"I'm asking you, Elizabeth Buxton, to marry me . . . to become the Lady of Astoria Abbey." Bess gasped softly, and he added, "No one belongs here more than you do, and I've become convinced that it's time to make alternate permanent arrangements for the other properties I own. I want to stay *here* with *you*. Forever."

Bess found herself unable to speak. Tears tingled in her eyes as she lifted her lips to his and he eagerly responded to her kiss. He chuckled softly before he said, "Does that mean yes?"

"Yes, it means yes," Bess said with perfect confidence and complete trust in this man she had come to love so dearly. "Yes, Graham, yes. Now kiss me again," she implored—and he did.

# EPILOGUE

Bess leaned back on her hands, her legs stretched out in front of her. She lifted her closed eyes toward the sun, loving the warmth she felt on her face as much as she loved the sensation of the cool grass on which she sat. She listened to the sounds of many different birds singing from nearby trees, taking in every part of the moment with great pleasure. Her quiet respite was interrupted by the high-pitched squeal of Agnes—immediately followed by a streak of giggling—as she ran past Bess.

"Save me, Mama!" Agnes cried and giggled, running past Bess in the other direction now. "Save me!"

"I'm far too comfortable to save you," Bess said without moving. "I'm afraid you're on your own, precious."

The sound of Agnes's continued giggling made Bess smile, but she couldn't help laughing when it became intermixed with Graham's growling noises as he chased Agnes around the garden, pretending as he always did to not be able to catch her—at least long enough to make the game exciting. When he finally *did* catch her, the giggling increased, intermingled with Graham's hearty laughter. He let the child go, saying, "You've worn me out, little lady. Go pick some flowers for your mother and then it's nearly time to join Grandmother for tea."

Bess kept her face lifted toward the sun while she listened to Agnes's laughter become more distant. The child knew well where to find the section of the garden where it was acceptable to pick a variety of flowers to be taken into the house.

"And what are *you* doing, little lady?" Graham asked, sitting beside Bess.

Bess laughed over the fact that he would call her the same thing he'd called Agnes—especially under the present circumstances. She looked down at her enormously rounded belly just as she felt the baby kick from inside her and laughed. "I am anything but little," she declared and rubbed her belly in response to the kicking.

"I've seen you this way before, you know," he said, and she turned to look at him. "I think that's when I really began falling in love with you."

Bess looked more earnestly at him, wondering how he could have been attracted to a woman swollen with pregnancy. She felt every bit as bloated and unattractive now as she had when she'd been pregnant with Agnes. "You're serious," she said, unable to help sounding astonished.

"Quite serious," he said, lying on his side with his elbow on the ground and his head resting in his hand. She wanted to comment on how she'd started to fall in love with him when he used to lie that way on the floor of the nursery while baby Agnes would crawl endlessly back and forth over him. "I remember thinking that you were like some work of art that could be in a museum, a perfect representation of everything that was perfectly beautiful, a tribute to femininity in every way. So strong, so confident, so courageous."

Bess made a quiet scoffing sound, unable to imagine such a perspective when she felt so awkward and uncomfortable; but given his earnest sincerity she didn't want to protest—and somewhere deep inside she couldn't help but feel warmed by the sincerity of such a compliment. But Graham Astor was like that; he could say the most remarkable things during an ordinary conversation and take Bess's breath away.

Instead of trying to figure out how to respond to such lovely words, Bess looked up at the nearby Abbey, declaring fondly, "You know, the view of the Abbey is beautiful from almost anywhere, but I think the very best view is from this exact spot. It's just so . . . lovely."

"Yes, it is," he said, and she turned toward him to see that he was still looking at *her*. "The view is truly lovely."

Bess reached up a hand to touch his face, relieved when he sat up so that he could kiss her. "Oh, that was nice," Bess said and kissed him again.

"Well, don't let yourself enjoy it too much because—"

"Mama, Papa!" Agnes shouted as she ran toward them. "I found some flowers! It's time for tea with Grandmother!"

"Yes, that's what I was about to warn you of," Graham said with a chuckle and jumped to his feet before he carefully helped Bess stand. Once she was steady enough to begin her slow trek back to the house, Graham picked up Agnes who was holding tightly to her bouquet of flowers.

"Papa?" she asked inquisitively.

"Yes, my darling?" Graham said to her.

"Do you think that my Papa Angel is watching out for our new baby until it comes to live with us?"

Bess saw Graham glance briefly toward her, showing by his expression that he was as touched and surprised by the comment as she was. But Agnes was often saying things that surprised them; she was deeply insightful for a child so young, and she spoke of her Papa Angel as if he were as much a part of her life as everyone else with whom she interacted within the walls of Astoria Abbey.

"I can't say for certain," Graham said to Agnes, "but I think it could well be true, and it's a very nice thought."

"Is it one of those thoughts that means you have faith in something?" Agnes asked. "Because you can't know for sure, but it feels right?"

"I couldn't have said it better myself," Bess said, and Graham put his free arm around her shoulders as they continued slowly toward the Abbey for tea.

"Nor could I," Graham said, sounding as perfectly content as Bess felt.

## ABOUT THE AUTHOR

Anita Stansfield has more than fifty published books and is the recipient of many awards, including two Lifetime Achievement Awards. Her books go far beyond being enjoyable, memorable stories. Anita resonates particularly well with a broad range of devoted readers because of her sensitive and insightful examination of contemporary issues that are faced by many of those readers, even when her venue is a historical romance. Readers come away from her compelling stories equipped with new ideas about how to enrich their own lives, regardless of their circumstances.

Anita was born and raised in Provo, Utah. She is the mother of five and has a growing number of grandchildren. She also writes for the general trade market under the name Elizabeth D. Michaels.

For more information and a complete list of her publications, go to anitastansfield.blogspot.com or anitastansfield.com, where you can sign up to receive email updates. You can also follow her on Facebook and Twitter.